Praise for the novels of Emilie Richards

"Infinitely readable and emotionally deep. In *A Family of Strangers*, Emilie seamlessly mixes intrigue, romance and emotional drama as she puts family ties to the test with a protagonist you won't soon forget... A page-turner to the end!"
—Diane Chamberlain, *New York Times* bestselling author of *Big Lies in a Small Town*

"*A Family of Strangers* is an absolutely riveting, thrilling read. I could not put it down. The suspense starts with the first line and does not let up until the last sentence. Emilie Richards writes electrifying family drama. There are deep emotions and startling secrets on every page. This one will keep you up all night."
—Jayne Ann Krentz, *New York Times* bestselling author

"Richards deftly shifts from women's fiction into domestic suspense, but she doesn't sacrifice the emotional acuity that her fans expect... Readers of relationship-focused domestic-suspense authors such as Lisa Jewell will enjoy Richards' pivot into the genre."
—*Booklist* on *A Family of Strangers*

"I emerged at the last page as a better and more thoughtful person."
—Catherine Anderson, *New York Times* bestselling author, on *When We Were Sisters*

"Emilie Richards is at the top of her game in this richly rewarding tale of love and family and the ties that bind us all. *One Mountain Away* is everything I want in a novel and more. A must-buy!"
—Barbara Bretton, *New York Times* bestselling author

"Richards creates a heart-wrenching atmosphere that slowly builds to the final pages, and continues to echo after the book is finished."
—*Publishers Weekly* on *One Mountain Away*

"Emotional, suspenseful drama."
—*Library Journal* on *No River Too Wide*

EMILIE RICHARDS

THE

HOUSE

GUESTS

mira

mira™

Recycling programs
for this product may
not exist in your area.

ISBN-13: 978-0-7783-3186-5

The House Guests

Mira
22 Adelaide St. West, 40th Floor
Toronto, Ontario M5H 4E3, Canada
BookClubbish.com

Printed in U.S.A.

To Michael, first and always. Thank you for all our amazing years together.

THE

HOUSE

GUESTS

1

AMBER BLAIR HAD SPENT MOST OF HER THIRTY- four years trying not to think about luck. Her daddy had told her there were only two kinds. Either you came into the world with the luck of the early bird or the early worm. The kind he'd been born with was obvious. Nothing that had gone wrong in all his years had to do with simply hanging around the edges of life, waiting for something good to fall in his lap. It was all about luck.

Her mother, tight-lipped and seething, had rarely voiced opinions. As a receptionist at the Halfway to Paradise motel, she had been too busy checking people in, and giving out room keys—and probably a little extra—to worry about luck.

Like most people, Amber had acquired something from both parents. She had inherited her father's early worm luck, oddly coupled with her mother's work ethic. Against tremendous odds she had scrambled to support herself and her son on her feet in restaurants, instead of on her back in cheap motels. Her mother had been remote and disinterested, but years of watching her determination to survive had helped.

"Haven't seen you for a while." The manager at the cash register of Things From the Springs greeted Amber with a wide smile. She was middle-aged and overweight, refreshingly unaware that spandex and sequins weren't good choices for minimizing either. Her plastic nameplate read Ida, but Amber had never told Ida her own name, a habit she'd developed after leaving home at sixteen. Still, Ida never forgot a face.

"It has been a while," Amber said.

"You feeling better?"

Amber wasn't surprised that Ida remembered the day two months before when she had fainted facedown in the women's clothing aisle, strawberry blond hair spread wide on a table stacked with shorts and T-shirts. The manager had insisted Amber go right to the hospital. Amber had thanked her, then headed to work instead. Three days later, though, she had seen a doctor after Will, her son, gazed at her in horror and announced that her green eyes were rimmed by an ominous yellow.

Of course, the news hadn't been good. Hepatitis A had arrived with a flourish, and she had been so dehydrated that, despite all her protests, she'd been hospitalized for a day, a bill that had nearly sunk them.

Health insurance was a luxury she had never indulged in.

"Yes. Definitely better," she said now. She didn't add that she still tired easily or that she was struggling to regain the weight she'd lost. Jaundice, the colorful bonus, was finally gone, and she was back at work.

"You were caught up in that hepatitis thing, weren't you? The one at that restaurant…" The manager snapped her fingers. "Electric something?"

"Dine Eclectic."

"You closed for a while, right?"

Because two of the kitchen staff had also been infected,

Dine Eclectic, the much promoted addition to restaurants in Tarpon Springs, Florida, had closed until health inspectors had given permission to reopen. Amber had been forbidden to go back to work until the jaundice and other symptoms disappeared. During most of the weeks of illness, she had been far too sick to work even if she'd wanted to. She certainly had *needed* to, because from an armchair in the apartment she shared with sixteen-year-old Will, she'd watched the savings she had so carefully hoarded dwindle to nothing.

"We've been open again for a while now," she said. "We've passed all the inspections. The problem was an infected line cook. Luckily hepatitis A is almost never fatal."

"I imagine the publicity wasn't good for business."

More customers arrived, and Amber headed for the rear of the store and the men's section.

Things From the Springs was smaller than many thrift stores she'd frequented. They were loosely affiliated with a local children's charity, and volunteers did much of the sorting and pricing.

She liked visiting Things because she could be in and out in less than an hour, often with vintage clothing she could cut and use for crafts to sell in her Etsy shop. An example was tucked securely in her purse today, a zipper pouch created from a brocade jacket and embroidered with the name of her landlord's wife. It had turned out so well she posted a photo on her shop's page, hoping to get orders for more.

The pouch bulged with money, mostly tips she had carefully collected to pay one of the two months of back rent she owed. Even after she'd showed her suspicious landlord a letter from the health department, he had begun eviction proceedings. She had managed to stave him off, promising to pay the first month today and the second in two weeks. She hoped the additional gift for his wife might make him feel better about his decision.

Her son had been more than patient during her months of unemployment. Will was a straight A student at the local high school and held down a part-time job stocking shelves at a local grocery store. He had taken on additional hours during her illness and brought home expired or damaged food that was destined for salvage stores or landfills. He had treated his quest like a treasure hunt and never wished out loud that his life was more like the easier ones of the other teens in his advanced placement classes.

Will wasn't perfect. He was sometimes messy, sometimes oblivious, often determined his way was best, but they'd been a team, just the two of them, from the very beginning of his life. And Amber knew her son would do anything for her, just as she had done everything for him. Much more than Will knew.

Today if she had early bird luck, she was going to buy him a surprise. Things From the Springs had a special rack dedicated to sports teams, and there was always a good selection. She was hoping to find one with the pirate flag of Will's favorite professional football team, the Tampa Bay Buccaneers. For the first time, her tips from the night before had been nearly as large as pre-hepatitis days, and she was hopeful she might be digging her way out of trouble. She would be happy just to pay rent on time, put a full tank of gas in the car and buy fresh food at the grocery store now and then.

Fifteen minutes later she was on her way back to the front of the now-empty store, a paper-thin but appropriately logoed T-shirt clutched under her arm. The size and price were right, and while Will wouldn't get much wear before it fell apart, he would be delighted.

She was starting to feel lucky. Her landlord had begrudgingly given her a little time to settle their account. After everything she still had her job, and restaurant traffic showed signs of improving. Today she had just enough extra to buy the shirt.

"You found something," Ida said. "I saw you heading to the back."

"It's for my son." Amber laid the shirt on the long counter. "He's a Bucs fan."

"These have been going fast. Apparently, he's not alone." She rang up the amount as Amber reached down to unzip her purse.

Only the purse wasn't zipped.

She spread it wide and peered inside. Without ceremony and with more than a touch of panic, she dumped the contents on the counter. Keys fell out. A pack of tissues. Her tiny coin purse, which held the extra money she hadn't put into the zip purse destined for the landlord and his wife. Nothing else.

"Run into a problem?"

Amber gazed at the concerned woman's face. "I had a zipper pouch in here, dark green silk, a name embroidered across it."

Ida read her expression correctly. "Did you open your purse here in the store? Could the pouch have fallen out?"

Amber knew she'd had the zipper pouch when she left her apartment. She'd so carefully slipped it inside the purse. Surely she'd zipped it closed. She always did. She had lived in cities with pickpockets. But by now panic had obliterated all memories of the past hour.

"I had it when I left my house."

"We'll look together." As Amber scraped her belongings back into her purse, the manager walked to the door, turned the lock and flipped the Closed sign. "That will buy us some time. We'll find it."

Half an hour later, though, they were still empty-handed. They'd looked under tables, sorted through all the shirts in

the back, followed Amber's route through the store four separate times peering at the ground.

"I'm so sorry," Ida said. "But I have to unlock the front
door. The high school lets out about now. They'll start banging on the glass. I just know you're going to find it somewhere.
Your house or car maybe?"

Amber knew she wasn't. The truth was a tight knot in her
stomach, all too familiar. She'd been slapped down again. The
landlord wouldn't believe her, and who could blame him? He
probably didn't need the money right away, but he would be
furious she'd lied to him.

She and Will would see that eviction notice after all.

"Thank you for helping me look." Amber cleared her
throat. "I don't think I'll buy the shirt."

"Why don't I just let you have it?"

"No." Amber took a breath and softened her tone. "But
thank you."

She followed the manager to the front door as she unlocked
it. "You'll let me know when you find it?" Ida asked.

Amber managed the tiniest of smiles. But in her mind she
saw the early worm being swallowed, inch by wiggling inch.
And somewhere, after the meal, a fat, happy robin was looking for more just like it.

2

SAVANNAH WESTMORE HATED TARPON SPRINGS.
She hated the cloying, inescapable heat; the tourist shops devoted to sponge diving; and most of all Coastal Winds, the public high school where she'd been parked by her stepmother, Cassie Costas, to finish her education without friends or allies.

Until now she'd spent every one of her fifteen years in Manhattan, where stores were filled with colorful designer merchandise, and she could stroll and shop Fifth Avenue with a wide circle of friends. She had attended Pfeiffer Grant Academy, an elite private school, studied creative movement at the School of American Ballet and Shotokan karate with an internationally acclaimed black belt.

Karate was something she had done with her father. It had been his idea to take classes together, just the two of them. Mark Westmore had steadily progressed with his daughter, learning kata, kicks and punches, and practicing together until he injured his back on his sailboat and was banned from returning.

After his death Cassie had urged Savannah to keep attending classes because she thought karate would be an outlet for her grief and anger. She'd even volunteered to go with her, although martial arts had never interested her in the past. Savannah had seen straight through the offer. Cassie wanted her forgiveness. She wanted the world to think she was struggling through her own grief to help the girl she treated like a real daughter.

But Savannah knew the truth. Cassie was responsible for her father's death.

Now one of the two girls standing next to her at the edge of the parking lot pulled out cigarettes, selected one and slid it between her lips. Savannah watched her dig in her purse for a lighter, long green fingernails scraping against the sides. Witchy hands went perfectly with the girl's purple fauxhawk, neck tattoo of a phoenix and perpetual scowl.

The other girl tossed a waterfall of black hair over one shoulder and began to buff her nails against a white T-shirt tied at the waist. She inclined her head toward a store across the parking lot. "There's a bunch of cool stuff in there. I found a denim jacket at the beginning of the summer, ripped in all the right places."

As far as Savannah could tell, it would always be too hot in this excuse for a town to wear any kind of jacket. Every morning she pulled her long brown hair into a knot on the top of her head to keep her neck from melting. Instead of the uniform she'd worn at the academy, she wore shorts or capris, shirts that barely covered her navel, skirts that just skimmed past her underwear.

But even though she'd always yearned to toss her school uniform aside, her new freedom meant nothing. She would never fit in. The girls here had some kind of secret code, and nothing she wore, did or said made the grade. She was reasonably pretty, with large hazel eyes and no feature overwhelming any other. She wasn't short or tall, fat or skinny. Once someone had told her she was 1960s small-town cheerleader material. It wasn't a compliment.

Minh, the girl buffing her nails, had told Savannah she was trying too hard. Minh's family had come from Vietnam when she was still in elementary school, and after they moved to Tarpon Springs, she'd just watched and waited until she figured out what to do and who to do it with.

From what Savannah could tell, Minh hadn't exactly grasped the rules. The girls she hung around with were, for the most part, losers. Helia, the purple-haired outcast, who was now taking deep drags on her cigarette, was the prime example. At least Minh was smart enough not to draw attention to herself. Helia reminded Savannah of a pit bull. Stocky build and a suspicious squint made more sinister by thick black eyeliner. Of course pit bulls could be loyal and funny, but Savannah was pretty sure Helia was neither.

The kind of girls Savannah had been friends with at Pfeiffer Grant and in Battery Park City, where she had lived in a spacious high-rise, weren't available to her in Tarpon Springs, so she'd been forced to settle. All the popular girls seemed to have been born on the same day in the same hospital to mothers who'd known each other since childhood. They weren't interested in strangers, especially one with a New York accent. She knew they talked about her behind her back, giggling at anything she did. Cassie, sensing her unhappiness, had told her to give the adjustment time, to be friendly but not too, to concentrate on schoolwork and look for clubs to join where she would be welcome. Cassie had gone to school in Tarpon Springs herself. She was sure Savannah would make friends.

Cassie had also been sure that moving here would help her stepdaughter heal. How many bad guesses could one person make?

"So, are we going to go inside or what?" Helia blew a

smoke ring, something she was obviously proud of because she almost smiled.

"We can cut across the lot," Minh said. "They have a pile of cool hats in the corner by the door. We could each buy one and wear it to school tomorrow."

Savannah was pretty sure wearing a weird hat would sink her with everybody except the small group of girls who hung around Minh and Helia. Or maybe it would be even worse, like that awful scene in *Legally Blonde* when Reese Witherspoon showed up at a law school costume party dressed as a pink bunny to find nobody else had gotten the costume memo.

They crossed the small parking lot that separated them from the row of shops. Helia cut between cars, banging against the side mirror of a lackluster sedan and purposely shoving it farther out of position, like it had wounded her on purpose. "My brother and I used to let air out of tires in parking lots," she said.

"Why would you do that?" Minh asked.

"Something to do. It's easy. You just take the cap off the valve, like this." She demonstrated. "Then you poke something sharp, like a screwdriver inside." She didn't demonstrate the last. In fact she put the cap back on and straightened. "No point now, I guess."

Savannah was more sure than ever that Helia was trouble. She steered her way to the aisle that ran along the edge and continued in the same direction. Three steps later her toe caught something, and she stumbled. When she looked down, she saw what had tripped her.

"Hey, look." She bent over and picked up a purse, a small one, waving it in the air for the other girls to see. Minh joined her and eventually so did Helia. The purse was shiny and green, some kind of heavy woven fabric with a gold tassel at the end of a long zipper and the name Jeannie embroidered in the same color gold with three-dimensional red roses on either side.

"So?" Helia said. "Open it."

Savannah unzipped the pouch and stared. "Wow, that's a lot of money."

Helia peered inside, then poked a finger among the bills. "Looks like a lot of ones to me."

Savannah took out the wad and started counting. There were a lot of ones, but plenty of fives, and farther in there were tens and twenties and a couple of fifties. "I think there's like eight hundred dollars here."

Minh gave a low whistle. "That is a lot of money. I wonder who lost it?"

"What do we do with it?" Savannah looked at the others. "I mean, how do we figure out who it belongs to?"

"Like we could," Helia said. "There are three dozen cars in this lot right now. Who knows how many came and went in the last few hours."

"Maybe we ought to put an ad in the newspaper." Minh took the empty pouch and fingered the fabric. "We know it belongs to somebody named Jeannie. I'd keep it if that was my name."

"Nobody's named Jeannie anymore. Do you know any Jeannies? And nobody reads the newspaper." Helia frowned, at least Savannah thought she was frowning. It was hard to tell.

"I guess we ought to take it to a police station," Minh said. "There's probably one somewhere near here, right? Isn't that what we're supposed to do?"

"What, so some dumb cop can pocket the money and toss the purse?" Helia was screeching now. "I don't think so!"

Holding this much money in plain view made Savannah uneasy. She had Manhattan street smarts and knew better than to wave money around. She took the purse back from Minh and stuffed the cash inside. "You have a better idea?"

"You two dumbasses can't see what's right in front of you?" Helia demanded. "This is *our* money now. Some woman with a stupid name dropped it and doesn't even know she did. She doesn't know it's here or she doesn't know it's gone or maybe she just doesn't care."

"Well, if we use your logic, it's actually *my* money," Savannah said. "I found it."

"But *we* know about it…" Helia was practically drooling now. "Do you know what we could do with this much money? We could have the best party ever."

Minh brightened. "We could invite everybody we know."

"My brother might buy us beer." Helia glared at Savannah. "Unless that doesn't suit Your Highness."

Until that moment Savannah had thought Helia was kidding. "You're serious? You think we ought to spend the money on a party?"

"I think it would up our game, that's for sure. People would talk about it for the rest of the year."

"We'd have to find a place." Minh shook her head before anybody could ask. "Not at my house. No way my parents would let me have a party with a bunch of girls they don't know."

Helia was on a roll. "Nobody's parents will be there! Besides who said anything about girls? You think this is going to be a PG party? Silly paper hats and a DVD of *Frozen*? We need a place where parents are either out of the house or too drunk to notice."

Savannah tried to imagine a family like that. She hated her own life, but that might be worse. She swung her backpack over her shoulder, zipped the pouch and stuffed it deep inside before she slipped the pack back on. "How about your house?" she asked Helia. "Would your parents look the other way?"

"No." Helia didn't say more.

Savannah chewed her lip. "My stepmother's going to be gone this weekend."

"What about your dad?" Minh asked.

"He died. That's why we're living in this hellhole." Savannah managed a shrug, as if it didn't matter.

"Tarpon Springs isn't so bad," Minh said. "Give it a chance. I'm sorry about your dad."

"I never even had one, so get over yourself." Helia dropped what was left of her cigarette and ground it out with the black high tops she always wore. "Having just one parent might make it easier to have the party."

"It doesn't seem to work for you."

"I don't have parents period, okay? There are like six creepy kids in my house and foster parents too creepy to be sorted for Slytherin. Does that bother you?"

Savannah hadn't run into foster kids at the academy. There had been a few scholarship students, who had been carefully screened and for the most part fit in okay. Now she wondered if they'd felt the way she did at Winds.

"I don't know why it would bother me," she said. "My stepmother Cassie's like Voldemort in a dress." She hoped her own Harry Potter reference would lighten the tension.

"Are you supposed to stay with somebody while she's gone?" Minh asked.

"Some loser named Dorian is spending the night. She's related to my stepmother. She's coming home from Florida State for the weekend."

Helia waved her cigarette in Savannah's face. "Can you get rid of her?"

For a moment Savannah thought Helia meant "get rid of"

as in dump Dorian's body in the Anclote River. Apparently Helia had read her thoughts. "I mean make sure she's not hanging around! For God's sake!" She followed with a stream of profanity.

Savannah waited until she'd finished. "I haven't met her, but she has a boyfriend in town. If I promised I wouldn't tell anybody she was with him instead of me, she'd leave me alone in the house."

"What if she shows up, you know, to check on you?" Minh asked.

"I'll check in by text. I'll figure something out."

Minh turned to Helia. "You said you have a brother? Like a foster brother?"

"A real one. He's not old enough to be my guardian, but he comes to see me all the time. He'll do whatever I ask him to."

Somehow that made Savannah feel better about Helia's life. She had always wanted a brother.

"Are we going to do this or not?" Helia asked.

Savannah was thinking. "My house isn't that big, so we have to keep the party small. I don't want word to get back to Cassie. Just invite the people who are most important."

Helia was already planning. "We can buy food, lots and lots of it, beer, maybe get a deejay. I know a guy who would set up his sound system."

Savannah didn't know how much money all that would take, but she was pretty sure there was enough in the pouch now burning a hole in her backpack.

Minh was shaking her head. "I just wonder. You know... This money belongs to somebody. I mean, it could matter to her, you know? A lot."

"You planning to knock on every door in Pinellas County and see if it belongs to a Jeannie?" Helia asked.

"Maybe we ought to wait and like, you know, see if somebody reports it missing. Look on the internet, maybe. Call the police and ask about it without telling them who we are."

Savannah thought out loud. "If we wait, we won't have a place for the party."

Helia's squinty eyes were narrowing even more. "For all we know, it's drug money or something, which is why it's all cash, and nobody's going to visit the police over that." She made her voice into a whine. *"Hello, Officer. I lost the money I made selling smack on my street corner. Can you help?"*

Savannah doubted that drug money would be stashed in a pretty little zipper purse with a woman's name on it. "Maybe we still ought to look a little." Even as she said it, she knew the idea was ridiculous.

"You going to do it or not?" Helia asked. "There are a lot of guys who would like to come to a party like this."

"We can't have a lot," Savannah said again.

"Then how about just the best?"

Savannah wondered what she was getting herself into. Of course Cassie thought she was a loser anyway. This was exactly the kind of thing she had expected from her stepdaughter since the day Savannah had been expelled from Pfeiffer Grant for injuring another student. Part of the reason Cassie had dragged Savannah to Tarpon Springs was because she thought her stepdaughter needed a fresh start in a place where nobody knew her checkered past.

For a moment picturing the horrified look on Cassie's face if she found out about the party gave Savannah pleasure. Why not? Telling the truth and doing the right thing hadn't got her anywhere.

"Let's do it," she said. "I'm in. But you have to help plan and clean up. I'm not doing this by myself."

"We'll help," Helia said. "We'll do it all."

"Minh?" Savannah asked.

Minh still looked troubled. "I guess it's okay. I can tell my parents I'm spending the night with a girl they approve of."

Without even discussing their next move, they turned and walked away from the parked cars and the shops beyond. In a moment they were deep into plans for the weekend.

3

FROM THE MOMENT SHE'D BECOME A MOTHER,
Amber had been careful not to collect too many possessions.
She had known that without notice, she might need to pile
everything she and Will owned into their car and head quickly
for the open road. Today a new reality had become obvious.
Not everything they had acquired in Florida would fit in their
car now. Not by a long shot.

Will was the culprit. Teenage boys were magnets, and everything they touched came along for the ride. Where once
she could pack his belongings in a small rolling suitcase and
have room for linens, too, now jeans and hoodies took up all
the room. And shoes? These days her son's shoes and boots
rated their own carry-on. His school backpack and extra books
took up a wide space on the back seat floor. Then there was
sports paraphernalia. The beloved baseball glove, a basketball
he had won as most valuable player when they lived in Ocala.
The list went on. How could she demand he discard any of
it? Will's life had been unusual from day one. He deserved

some of the ordinary things other kids took for granted. Like a roof over his head.

For the first time that morning Will sat down, his long legs spread out straight in front of him, his broad shoulders sagging just a little. "There's a lot of stuff left," he said. The apartment had two small bedrooms, and she had turned over the largest to him, claiming the smaller for herself, along with the tiny coat closet by the front door. She was afraid his bedroom closet held more of his treasures.

Even in the midst of moving again, she took time to admire her son. No one would automatically assume he was hers. She was five-eight, with her mother's red-gold hair and her father's green eyes. Like Amber, Will was slender, but at five-eleven, he was still growing taller. He had wide shoulders and narrow hips, but he would add muscle and bulk once the frightening amount of food he inhaled added pounds instead of inches.

Will was dark-haired, brown-eyed and at sixteen, still somehow unformed, but she knew what he would look like in another year because he was the spitting image of his father. And at seventeen, his father had turned heads. Most notably hers.

"We can leave some of it here," she said. "I checked online. Legally Mr. Blevin has to store our boxes for ten days, fifteen if he doesn't give me written notice before we leave."

"It wasn't such a good place to live anyway. The hot water heater kept shutting off. He should have fixed it. And the roaches kept coming back."

Will was trying to make her feel better. They had camped when they first arrived in Tarpon Springs. Tonight he would remember this apartment fondly when they were sleeping in two small tents pitched side by side. And this time there was very little hope they could leave until the end of the school year.

In the past, if she suffered a reversal like this one, Amber would have moved on to another town. The timing was perfect to leave Tarpon Springs, the way they had left so many other places. They could start over again, some town with cheaper rent, good schools and restaurants with job openings. But even though Dine Eclectic might not recover from the hepatitis scare, and her own job was shaky, Will was happily settled in school. He was taking advanced placement classes and the guidance counselor had called to encourage Amber to find extracurricular activities Will could pursue to make him more appealing to the best universities.

With his after-school job, her son barely had time to do homework, and the fees and gear for sports teams and computer camps were out of reach. But she had been convinced that this time, they had to put down roots until Will was ready to leave home. He had support here, professionals rooting for him and willing to help him move forward. No matter how much staying in one place scared her, Tarpon Springs was a stepping-stone to the life she so badly wanted for him.

Now she tried to put a good face on things. "We'll find another apartment, I promise. In the meantime figure out what you need most, and that's what we'll take in the car." Amber looked at her watch. "I promised Mr. Blevin we'd be out by three, so we'll need to get to our site and set up camp before I head into work. I have to stay late tonight to close. You'll be okay?"

"I have a lot of homework. I'll try to finish before it's too dark."

She had managed to reserve a site at the same rustic campground where they had stayed before. It was harder than it would have been in the summer because snowbirds were already arriving in fancy RVs to enjoy the Florida winter. The few available tent sites were relegated to the farthest edge of the grounds, a hike from the small lake and the showers, but she and Will would be surrounded by other campers and safe. Best of all she could afford the fee.

"You can always go to the clubhouse to do homework," she reminded him. The clubhouse was just a screened pavilion, but there were tables, electricity and wireless.

Somebody knocked, and Amber started toward the door. "That's probably Mr. Blevin. Let's be nice."

Will made a rude noise in response.

Amber tried to put a good face on things. "He's a scared old man convinced everybody is trying to cheat him. You keep packing while he's here."

Will went into the bedroom and closed the door behind him.

She tried not to picture the old man tripping over the loose plank on the stoop or standing in the doorway when the rusting screen door finally parted company with its hinges. Until she'd got sick, she'd paid her rent on time, and she and Will had taken on chores around the property he should have done himself. After losing the zipper pouch, she'd promised Mr. Blevin she would bring him every cent she earned that night and all others until he was paid with interest. But by then he'd been apoplectic. She supposed she couldn't blame him.

The door was a three-second trip since the apartment was cramped. She peered through the peephole she'd installed herself, but the man standing on the doorstep wasn't Blevin. He was much younger and definitely easier on the eyes. She debated first, but she opened it a crack and peeked out. "Yes?"

The man, who was somewhere around her own age, handed her a card. "I'm Travis Elliott and I freelance for the *Tarpon Times*. Do you have time to talk?"

Amber turned the card around and around before she opened the door wider. The *Tarpon Times* was a weekly paper specializing in human-interest stories and local gatherings. She used it to wrap garbage before she put it in the can.

She handed back the card. "Talk about what?"

Travis Elliott was probably a shade taller than Will, with sandy brown hair and eyes many shades darker. The hair was long enough to show a definite wave, and he pushed a strand behind his ears before he spoke.

"I know your neighbor…" He inclined his head to Amber's left. "Nancy tells me you're being evicted because you lost your rent money last week. And that you were one of those caught up in the hepatitis A problem at Dine Eclectic and couldn't work for weeks."

The day she lost the pouch, Nancy had caught Amber searching in the bushes around the old house. Amber had told her why, hoping that Nancy, who tended a small garden and everybody's business, might have come across it.

"Yes, well…" Amber shrugged.

"And the landlord, a John Blevin, didn't believe you?"

"I don't know what he believed. Look, I—"

"You don't want to talk about it. I can see why. This must be pretty traumatic." He smiled sympathetically. "For you and your son."

Amber studied him. He was definitely easy to look at. In her eyes that neither recommended nor doomed him. His profession was a different matter.

"I don't want to talk about it," she said. "I'm trying to pack and get out of here before Mr. Blevin shows up to harass me some more."

"He's harassing you?"

"As much as anybody might who thinks he's been cheated."

"Nancy said the money was in a pouch you made yourself. Do you make many?"

Amber tried not scowl. She didn't want the paper to say that she'd been angry and uncooperative. "I have an Etsy store. And I'd made that one for Mr. Blevin's wife. I even took a photo to put on my shop page."

"Is that how you get orders?"

"One way."

"Can you really make money like that?"

Her sigh took a while to complete. "As far as Etsy goes, I don't have time to do much. So yes, I make some money, but not enough to pay my back rent. Now I've got to finish packing." She started to close the door, but he put his hand against it and looked so sad, she grunted. "What?"

"The thing is, that pouch is still out there somewhere, right? Maybe nobody found it, but maybe somebody did and wants to return it."

"I reported it to the police."

"Did you give them the photo you took?"

"Why?"

"Because I'd like the *Times* to do a story. A photo of you and then one of the pouch. Maybe somebody has it and would like to return it. And I'd like to talk about what happened afterward."

"No way."

"Is that too intrusive? I thought it might be helpful."

"I have a son at Winds. Wouldn't a story about how destitute we are bring him lots of new friends? He could embellish the gossip with stories of the campground where we'll be living tonight."

"Campground?" He folded his arms over a tropical shirt sporting palm trees and beach chairs.

"I'm really busy," she said.

"Could I do the story with no names and just a photo of the pouch? If you have one?"

She nearly closed the door in his face, but something stopped her. Without her name, without her photo, with nothing about Will in the story, what would be the harm? Was there really a chance someone would step forward? Because she still had to pay Blevin the back rent. She had other bills to pay, too, including the hospital and doctors. She needed that money.

"I won't take much of your time," he promised.

Finally, she nodded. "How good are you at carrying boxes? We can talk while I pack our car."

"I'm surprisingly strong and totally willing. Except…" He frowned. "You're moving to a campground?"

"It's better than sleeping in our car. And don't look like that. Do you know how many people are one paycheck away from being out on the streets? I work hard. I pick up extra shifts whenever I can. At night, I sew for my Etsy shop, and on top of that my son gives me most of the money he makes from his job after school."

"And you still couldn't make it."

"No, because our line cook never learned to wash his hands properly, and he contaminated food I either ate or served. So that's the origin of another deluxe vacation at Sunny Acres Estates."

"Look, I'd be more than happy to pay for a motel tonight while you figure out a better place to go. No strings. This whole thing is—" he shook his head "—not fair."

He had planned to say something more colorful and profane. She almost smiled. "That's very kind, but we'll be fine. We always are. We camped there when we first got to town. It will feel like home."

"The story?"

She considered. "Five minutes. That's all I've got. Come in and meet Will and then grab a box to carry to the car."

"You'll give me the photo?"

"I'll tell you how to get to my Etsy page. It's the green

pouch that says Jeannie. While you're there, shop." She didn't know why she added the next part. "Your wife or girlfriend would probably like one of my pouches. Great for cash."

"I don't have either, but I'll file that away for the future."

She nodded. "No names in the article, and no identifying information."

"Can I say that your landlord was unforgiving and intolerant?"

This time she did smile. "If you didn't, it would be fake news."

4

ON SUNDAY MORNING SAVANNAH WAS AFRAID SHE was going to die, but not fast enough. She lifted her head from her pillow, and the room spun. For a moment she imagined herself on a carousel, like the one in Central Park. As a little girl she had loved going round and round on her favorite white horse, her father on a black one, while Cassie took their photos from the ground.

Spinning wasn't fun now. She barely made it to the en suite bathroom before she lost the contents of her stomach.

The party.

She plopped down on the edge of the bathtub and tried to remember if the party had really happened last night, or if she was caught in some kind of horrible time warp. Light was coming in through the glass block window—but was it sun or the security lights in the back of the house? She was still wearing last night's jeans and T-shirt. Would she open the door into the hall to find the party was still in full swing, hordes and hordes of kids who hadn't been invited swirling through her alcohol-fogged brain, turning over furniture, throwing a beach ball at Cassie's beloved houseplants like they were bowling pins?

Would she see the disgusted deejay packing up because kids kept slamming into him? Would she glimpse Minh or Helia disappearing after everything got completely out of hand?

She was almost certain all of that had happened, but was it still happening? From the edge of her tub, the house seemed quiet.

Minutes later she got to her feet again, weaving but erect. She flushed the toilet and bent her head over the sink, splashing cold water on her face and washing her hands over and over again. She had to brush her teeth, but her stomach didn't agree.

In the bedroom all seemed fine. She ventured into the sitting room beyond it, that extra perk that Cassie had claimed made this a second master suite. The sitting room looked okay. She dropped to the sofa, dreading the moment when she had to explore farther. She'd had the foresight to lock the suite door when the party began, and she thought she'd remembered to lock Cassie's.

Things hadn't gone badly at first. Minh had arrived with a stack of pizza boxes and grocery bags of chips. Helia and her brother had arrived with multiple six-packs of cheap beer, soft drinks and bottles of vodka and rum. A dozen girls with a handful of guys had shown up about the time they were supposed to. The deejay, a high school senior, had arrived and set up his equipment in a corner. Things were noisy and chaotic, but under control.

Then the party crashers arrived.

Savannah's head was clearer now, and she was almost sure she remembered dozens of crashers. After a while it had seemed like hundreds. She had expected the police, but the house was near the end of a block, and either the neighbors had ignored the commotion or been absent for the evening. Things had gotten wild, but Savannah was pretty sure that at first, she'd tried to control it. Then Helia had handed her a drink and told her to shut up and chill. Kids she'd never seen before kept saying "great party," like it was some sort of password. A guy with zits and dandruff had danced with her and tried to kiss her.

She had no idea when things had finally broken up. Was there another party somewhere and people had left to check it out? Had that happened right after the beer and liquor ran out, along with the food?

At some point Savannah had stumbled back to her bedroom and passed out, right after she'd had the presence of mind to call her absent chaperone and pretend she had spent an uneventful evening.

She couldn't stay where she was for the rest of the day. Cassie was due home tomorrow from New York, where she claimed she still had business. These days Mark Westmore's life and death were just items for her stepmother to check off a list, like buying bread or taking clothes to the dry cleaner.

She took a deep breath, unlocked the door and flung it open. Outside the relative order of her suite, all seemed quiet. She ventured as far as the great room, which was the disaster she had expected, but blessedly empty of bodies. If she was lucky, the other rooms were uninhabited, too. She supposed her first job was to make sure.

After that? Something nasty and bitter pooled in her throat again. The last and worst job was the cleanup itself, even though there was no way she could restore the house to anything approximating its pre-party condition. Plants were overturned and potting soil had been tracked throughout. Food was smeared on the walls, and drinks had spilled on formerly pristine sofas and chairs.

Cassie had claimed she was buying this house because she wanted Savannah to have plenty of room and privacy to finish growing up. The furniture was mostly new. Her stepmother had moved very little to Florida that wasn't absolutely necessary, except houseplants. When they had lived in Battery Park City, Cassie had missed the tropical foliage from her childhood, so she had raised what she could indoors to make the New York apartment seem like home. The plants had thrived. Savannah's father had called their apartment Cassie's jungle.

Even though Cassie and Savannah were now living where palm trees grew in every yard and houseplants cost next to nothing, her stepmother had actually gotten a certificate of inspection and moved the plants she'd so carefully tended. They were old friends, she'd said, and both she and Savannah needed old friends.

Right now it looked like most of Cassie's old friends had ascended to plant paradise.

She forced herself to check the house. Luckily, nobody else was inside. The den and extra bedroom were trashed, but Cassie's door was locked. That, at least, was good news.

She discovered her phone in her pocket. She'd probably slept on it, but it still worked when she tried Minh. When there was no answer, she tried Helia. Helia answered immediately, whispering that her foster parents had been waiting up when she got home, and she wouldn't be allowed to go anywhere for the rest of the month or see her brother unless she wanted the caseworker to move her again.

"Good luck cleaning up," she whispered, not sounding like she meant it. "I guess you'll have to get your hands dirty."

Savannah put the phone back in her pocket and looked around. If she worked straight through the next twenty-four hours, she could only make a dent in the mess. When Cassie arrived tomorrow, she would know exactly what Savannah had done.

She wanted to cry, and she was pretty sure she was going to vomit again. She was dizzy and foggy about everything that had gone on the night before, and through it all, one thing stood out clearly.

The zipper pouch had been the start of everything. If her father were still alive, Dr. Mark Westmore would look at the mess, then take her for a walk and ask thoughtful questions about the choices she had made. He would be kind and logical. He had never worn his psychiatrist's hat with Savannah. He had always made it clear he loved her, no matter what she did.

But how much had he really loved her? Had he given his daughter a thought when he risked his life sailing alone in a storm? She had sailed with him frequently, and she knew what a good sailor he was. He believed the sea, like some of the people he treated, could change in an instant. It was important to pay attention and respond with caution. He always had.

Why had he gone out alone that day and ignored weather warnings? Was it the fight he'd had with Cassie right before he left? Was he so angry he'd just forgotten to be safe?

Afterward Cassie had moved them both to Florida because she believed Savannah needed a fresh start in school. Cassie had also said that in Tarpon Springs, they would have family to help, although the family was hers, in no way Savannah's.

She wished her real mother was back in the country, that Gen would fly back to Palm Springs, where she and her partners had a thriving plastic and cosmetic surgery practice, and open her arms to her only child. But Gen, with the blessing of her partners, was spending months doing charitable work at a clinic in Africa so she and her colleagues could score points for the miracles she wrought worldwide.

Of course her mother cared. Gen had flown all the way

from Kenya to New York for Mark's funeral. After the service she had promised Savannah she would always be there for her. Then she'd ended by reminding her that Cassie could provide the stability that she couldn't right now. "We'll talk when I'm back in California," she'd said as she was leaving for the airport.

Savannah had no idea when that would be. Gen texted from time to time when she wasn't out of range of cell phone towers. But for now, Savannah was stuck in Florida.

She picked her way from the great room into the kitchen, kicking aside pizza boxes and half-empty bags of chips. A tub of salsa lay facedown on a new area rug, soaking through it to the wood floor beneath. In the refrigerator a carton of milk lay on its side, the contents forming a puddle at the bottom. There was little else left except undisturbed condiments and nothing she could eat.

Not that eating would be a good idea anytime soon.

She closed the refrigerator and stood with her back to it. When she was a little girl, Cassie had made cleaning her room a game. "Choose a corner and start cleaning there," she'd say, "and then take a step backward, look around and clean everything you can reach." At the end, even if the room was still far from perfect, Cassie had always rewarded her efforts with a treat and lots of praise.

There would be no praise when she came home tomorrow.

Savannah sidled to the sink, skirting another stained area rug. The sink was filled to the top with soggy pizza crusts and other items she couldn't identify. She grimaced, but the sink was the place to start.

She pulled out the wastebasket. The plastic liner was still unused and pristine—possibly the only thing in the kitchen that was. She took a deep breath and began to scoop up the mess in the sink and dump it in the wastebasket. When the sink was empty enough, she ran the hot water and then the disposal.

When she'd made a dent, she reached for the spray cleaner that always sat on the counter. In front of the bottle she saw the zipper pouch, deflated and forlorn in a puddle of beer. Her stomach roiled, but she lifted the pouch and peeked inside. Of course, it was empty. The money was gone forever.

The pouch was the cause of everything that had happened last night. If somebody hadn't been careless enough to lose it, Savannah's life would be a lot different.

She didn't want to look at it for even another moment. She threw it into the wastebasket before she went back to work.

5

CASSIE COSTAS GRABBED HER CARRY-ON FROM THE baggage carousel and hauled it to the floor. The bag was navy blue, exactly like a majority of those traveling along the conveyor belt, and she bent to check the tag just to be sure she had the right one.

"You're in my way," a man said, pushing her to lean over and grab air. "Now I've missed it!"

She had lived in New York for years and she knew how to stand up for herself with strangers, but today that required energy she didn't have. The man was still leaning forward, most likely off-balance. For just a moment she considered giving him a nudge with her knee, so he and his bag could ride the carousel together.

Roxanne probably would have done that, brassy, feisty Roxanne, who had volunteered to provide transportation to and from Tampa. She was meeting Cassie at the curbside to take her home, but unfortunately not right away. According to a text, Roxanne was sitting in a traffic jam.

If Cassie had braved the airport traffic herself and parked

in the garage, she would be back in Tarpon Springs in well under an hour. Her hands might have fused to the steering wheel, foot barely brushing the accelerator, heart speeding as fast as the 18-wheelers whizzing past her, but she would have been on her way.

After years of not driving in Manhattan, her skills were shaky. She was okay in Tarpon Springs on quiet side streets, but not yet on interstates where it was a struggle just to get up to the minimum speed. When she confided to Roxanne that she was booking a ride to go to and from the airport, Roxanne had insisted on driving her instead.

"We haven't had any time alone to catch up," she'd said. "And I love driving. I'll put the top down on my old jalopy, and we'll have ourselves an adventure."

Roxanne was, in fact, Cassie's aunt, her father's much younger sibling, but since the two women were only ten years apart, she had always been Roxanne to Cassie, or more often just Rox. She had acted like an older sister, shielding Cassie from her parents' toxic child rearing whenever Roxanne and her mother, Lyra—known to Cassie and almost everybody else as Yiayia—could find an excuse to intervene.

Now Cassie returned the text to say she had her bag and would be waiting at the curb when Roxanne finally made it.

Outside she filled her lungs with humidity, salt-tinged air and just the slightest hint of decay. Blindfolded, she would have known where she was. She and Mark had brought Savannah back to Florida's Gulf Coast whenever they could to celebrate Epiphany with the Costas clan. No one had kidnapped Cassie after college and dragged her unwilling and protesting to New York. She'd wanted to leave her past behind, and she had loved so much about living in Manhattan—her husband, stepdaughter and their life together. But whenever it was time to return to her roots, she'd walked out of the airport and felt the best parts of her past envelop her.

Today there was no magic in the air, no anticipation of what would be waiting in Tarpon Springs, lamb roasting on a spit, tables laden with pastitsio and moussaka, Yiayia's baked breads, the platters of baklava and kataifi and so much more. The vast Costas clan was scattered now, a few back in Greece, most in other parts of the United States pursuing lucrative jobs. They came together for Easter and sometimes Christmas. As often as possible they stayed through Epiphany, when the city filled up with Greek-Americans from all over the country who wanted to celebrate their culture.

Today Cassie would only be greeted by Savannah, in the new house that had stretched her budget to the breaking point but had seemed so necessary for giving her stepdaughter the privacy and comfort she would need to heal. Savannah wouldn't be happy to see her, in fact far from it. The teen was in turmoil, still raw and bewildered after her father's sudden death and the uprooting that had followed. She blamed Cassie for everything that had gone wrong in her life, and her anger showed no signs of relenting.

There was so much Cassie couldn't share with her stepdaughter. She certainly couldn't share what she'd learned on this trip. The money she'd counted on from Mark's retirement account, money she'd foolishly expected to get them through the next few years, didn't exist.

The words of their financial advisor still echoed. Greg, a man in his fifties, was fit and trim with a luxuriant head of silver hair, the prototype of a Harvard-educated MBA whom a doctor would trust with his nest egg. Greg had made her comfortable with French roast coffee in a china cup and chatted a moment about life in Florida before he told her that all was not well.

"I wish I didn't have to tell you this," he'd begun. "Mark was content to let me deal with his investments, and we were doing well. Then about a year ago he said I was being too careful, that he might want to retire earlier than he'd planned, so he liquidated most of his retirement account to make an investment in a new tech company. There were penalties involved, of course, and I tried to talk him out of it. He lost a lot of money just taking what was left out of the account, but he was sure it was a fantastic opportunity. Only it wasn't."

She had stared at him, bewildered, and he had reached over to pat her hand. "I warned him. I actually pleaded to stay the more conservative course, but he was convinced he was on the road to a windfall. He wouldn't share the name of the company with me. He claimed a prep school roommate was some kind of financial genius and was arranging everything."

"Sim?" she asked. "Sim Barcroft? But he's a financial analyst for some international conglomerate. He's working out of the country somewhere. I don't think Mark had heard from him in years." She couldn't believe that Sim was responsible for hundreds of thousands of dollars disappearing.

Greg shook his head. "He must not have told you, Cassie. I checked out the guy, because that's all I could do, and people practically cross themselves when he's mentioned. He is a financial genius. Only this time, apparently, luck or research or common sense failed him, and he made a bad gamble. The next time I saw Mark, he admitted he'd lost everything. I'm not too surprised he didn't tell you. He was sure he could make up what had been in his account by the time he retired. I think he was hoping you'd never find out."

That and everything else Greg had told her seemed so impossible. He'd showed her papers, reports, promised she could bring in a forensic accountant if she needed to be sure everything was on the up-and-up. But in the end, as she'd taken the elevator to the lobby with its fluted pillars and marble floors, she had known she wasn't being cheated. Because in their final argument she and Mark had fought about money. The missing funds in his retirement account were only the final piece of their financial puzzle. Mark had made other bad decisions, and now she had to figure out how to move forward.

She was still lost in thought when Roxanne finally pulled up in her cherry red Mazda Miata, top down, her hair covered by a black chiffon scarf tied under her chin.

Cassie hefted her carry-on into the trunk and climbed in beside her, tossing a copy of the *Tarpon Times* presently occupying her place between the seats. "Very Grace Kelly," she said, tugging the end of Roxanne's scarf and trying to smile. Her aunt was wearing shorts and a tank top. Her bare arms were tanned, and her face was carefully made up to provide harmony between her olive skin and the blond hair she had chosen without the help of her Creator.

"I was thinking more Thelma and Louise." Roxanne reached down and handed Cassie a gray version of the same scarf. Then as Cassie wrapped and tied the scarf over her own dark curls, Roxanne shifted gears, and they took off, weaving between cars and pedestrians until they were out on the highway and heading north.

"Flight okay?" Roxanne asked when they settled into a lane. "You were probably lucky you got a seat, changing flights and all."

"There was no point in staying longer."

"Did you see your friend?"

Cassie wasn't in the mood to recap her failure, but on the ride to the airport she'd told Roxanne all the reasons she was going back to Manhattan, most probably a mistake since Roxanne remembered every conversation she'd ever been part of and was always ready to hear the next installment.

On the other hand, bold and brassy as she was, Roxanne was also one of the most insightful people Cassie knew. She saw things most people missed, and sometimes Cassie had found Roxanne's homespun insights to be more helpful than those of her well-qualified psychiatrist husband.

"I called Valerie and left two voice mails," she said. "She never returned them. I dropped by her apartment building and found the superintendent. He pretended he didn't remember me. After I gave him my name, he told me she wasn't at home. Without even checking."

"What do the kids call that these days? Ghosting?"

Cassie thought *cruel* was more accurate. Valerie Dorman's husband, Fletcher, had been one of Mark's partners in their practice, Church Street Psychiatric Associates, in Tribeca. Although Valerie was older, the two women had immediately become friends, lunching together, combing through shops, volunteering at museums and local charities.

Once Cassie had learned that her new stepdaughter, three-year-old Savannah, should already be on a waiting list for a pre-K class, the Dormans had recommended the Pfeiffer Grant Academy, where their two daughters were enrolled in the middle school. The Dormans, generous donors to the school's building fund, had twisted an arm or two, and Savannah had started her education there.

"I can't help but wonder if Savannah being ousted from Pfeiffer Grant was the reason Valerie vanished," Cassie said. "Were the Dormans embarrassed that they recommended her? Or was it because Mark left the practice before he died? Or both? Whatever it was, I'd like to know, but it's pretty clear I never will."

"A friend who deserts you when you need her most isn't much of a friend. You're probably better off."

"It's not just about friendship. I was hoping she'd help me

figure out why Mark left Church Street. He left without another position, Rox. That just doesn't make sense." She hesitated. "And that's not the only financial misstep." She gave a
short summary of what Greg had told her.

Roxanne whistled softly. "This isn't good."

"I can't touch Mark's social security until I'm at least sixty,
although I'll get payments for Savannah until she's sixteen.
Luckily Mark didn't screw up his life insurance, too." Once
again strangled by Mark's betrayal, Cassie took a moment
to clear her throat. "But most of that went into buying the
house."

"Selling your condo in New York didn't take care of a
house in Tarpon Springs?"

"Mark took care of all our finances—"

"That was a mistake, Cassie. Why did you go for it?"

Cassie had some theories, none of them flattering. "He liked
doing it, and I didn't. He seemed good at it. Or so I thought
until he died, and I started getting bills from our owner's as-
sociation. Every unit in the building was charged a huge fee
two years ago because they had to reinforce the building's
foundation. I knew about the assessment, but I was sure Mark
had paid our portion. I just assumed."

"Never assume anything with a man."

"He hadn't paid it, so there were fines on top of the assessment and a lien on our condo, and by the time I paid everything, there wasn't that much left. Enough for the move and
setting up the new house, and not much else. I had to dip
into the life insurance for part of the down payment. I wasn't
worried, because I knew the retirement account would come
to me. But I shouldn't have been so naive. We..." Her voice
trailed off.

"More?" Roxanne asked.

"Right before he died, we fought about money. Before he

left the practice, all our bills went to Church Street. He said he worked on them there if he wasn't going out for lunch. Mark loved paper and never really liked paying bills online. But after he resigned, the bank statements were forwarded to the condo. So when I was organizing the mail, I opened one. Our savings account had been closed. And when I asked him what was going on, he told me it was too complicated to explain, but that he had it under control, and I shouldn't worry. We still had lots of money."

"Was that like him? To assume you wouldn't understand something as simple as money disappearing?"

Cassie watched the scenery flying by between 18-wheelers and RVs. "He'd never been like that. In his last year, Mark changed, Rox. He withdrew. He snapped at everybody. He would apologize, and then he'd do it again. He brooded. At first I assumed he was in pain. Remember when he injured his back?"

"Sailing, right?"

"He tripped when he was tacking. Luckily he had a friend on board to help him get to shore. For a couple of weeks he wasn't able to go into work. But eventually with help he improved and didn't need surgery. I assumed things would smooth out, but they didn't. I think I was blaming the accident when it was something else entirely. When I asked what was going on, he'd say it was work, and he couldn't talk about it because of patient confidentiality. And then he quit the practice. Just like that. With no other position in sight."

"He must have given you a reason."

"He said a new doctor was divisive. Some of his colleagues liked the younger man's ideas, but others felt he was trying to change things too quickly. Mark claimed he was trying to mediate, but nobody really supported his efforts."

"And that's why he quit?"

"That was as close as he came to telling me. But at this point all of it's just history. I can't dwell on what happened." Now that she'd explained that much, she hoped Roxanne wouldn't dwell on it, either. At least not today.

Roxanne switched lanes to pass two horse trailers. They drove for a while until she settled back into the middle lane. "So what's your plan?"

This subject wasn't any more pleasant, but it was safer. At least Cassie didn't have to dig deep into her anger at a husband she also grieved. Mark had often talked about emotional ambivalence and the paralyzing effect it had on his patients. Right now paralysis was unacceptable.

"I have to put my energy into finding a job. I need to bring in a paycheck."

Roxanne nodded. "Doing what? Do you know?"

"My marketing degree is as outdated as my experience. I'll put together a résumé and list all the volunteer work I've done, but any job will be entry-level. I guess I'll have to snap up whatever I'm offered. I'll probably be asking if a customer wants fries with his burger."

"You're back in Tarpon Springs, remember? That would be fries with your gyro."

"See, I can't even get that right."

"I seem to remember you liked working at the hospital where you met Mark."

Cassie remembered the heady sense of accomplishment that job had given her. It hadn't been her first, but it had definitely been her best. She'd become confident in her own abilities, and she'd made important contributions. By the time she'd met her future husband, she'd been secure and self-assured.

"I was in charge of the gift shop, remember? They let me close it down, completely redo it, and then open it again. It was fun and successful, too."

"And then you married Mark and quit."

Cassie wanted to hear if her own words still made sense. "Savannah was barely three, and she needed me. When she was older, I looked for another job. But so much of marketing is about products and companies I'd rather not promote. And I guess I believed somebody had to keep things going, make meals, volunteer at school, be there when Savannah got home and then make sure she got to her after-school activities. Besides, let's face it, even then she was a handful."

"Some things never change."

"I should probably go back to school."

"Do you want advice? Because I have some to give."

Despite the air rushing past her, Cassie picked up the newspaper between them and fanned herself for something to do with her hands. "As long as it doesn't involve another husband."

Roxanne reached down and patted her knee. "Do you remember what happened after Gary died?"

Roxanne's husband had died three years earlier, a cancer so rare that by the time the doctors diagnosed it, he was gone. "You came home," Cassie said.

"You visited us in Virginia before Gary got sick. Remember? And you loved Apollo's Café. You thought our food was fantastic."

"I haven't forgotten. You were both so happy." Roxanne and Gary had taken a simple brick building on the edge of the Northern Virginia sprawl and turned it into something special. The food had been Greek with flair, fresh ingredients and old favorites fixed new ways. Most nights the café was filled to capacity.

"When he died, I didn't think hard enough about my future. Gary was gone, and I didn't want to be there alone. So I sold and came home. It was the worst mistake I ever made."

"At the time you said you missed family, that you wanted to be here to keep an eye on Yiayia and cook at the Kouzina. You're not happy?"

"Lord no. I put myself in prison and threw away the key. I expected Mama to let me take over the kitchen. Instead I have no role at the restaurant. On the rare occasions she lets me cook, she stands over me and demands I make everything the traditional way."

Cassie hadn't realized any of this. "She's that bad?"

"Worse. I went from being a successful restaurant owner and chef to Mama's occasional line cook. Now where else am I going to go? These days Apollo's Café is a second-rate sushi bar. Gary Jr. and his fiancée, Patricia, are living in Paris, and nobody knows how long they'll be there, so there's no point in moving closer to them. I made a bad decision on the heels of Gary Senior's passing, and I regret it every single day. So try not to make any big decisions until you have to. You've already made one, a house you bought to make Savannah happy. And now that mortgage is going to eat you alive if that girl doesn't finish you first."

"I've been going on about my own problems. I didn't know you were unhappy here. I'm sorry."

"At the moment your problems are worse than mine. You make me feel better."

Cassie wanted to laugh, but there was no laughter inside her today. "Have you thought about getting a job at one of the other restaurants in town? There are so many."

"Can you just imagine what Mama would do?"

Cassie knew she was right. Yiayia would disown her daughter, and Roxanne's disloyalty would be the main topic at every family gathering until eternity ended.

"At least neither of us has the problems that woman has." Roxanne tilted her chin toward the paper in Cassie's hands.

"What woman?"

Roxanne pointed to a photo on the front page. "Travis wrote that. I brought the article for you to see."

Travis Elliott was one of their distant cousins, so distant in fact that in most families the relationship, complicated by "steps" and "removeds," wouldn't even be noted. But in the same way that Savannah would always be considered a Costas, whether she wanted anything to do with Cassie's family or not, Travis was a Costas and therefore subject to every invitation and snatch of gossip.

Cassie scanned the article. A local woman had stuffed a handmade zipper pouch with money to pay her landlord. She'd been one of those restaurant workers recently struck down by an outbreak of hepatitis A and unable to work for weeks. Not surprisingly the woman had then gotten behind on her rent, but she'd finally managed to pull some money together. Of course, that wouldn't have been much of a story without a sad ending.

"Poor woman," Cassie said, staring at the photo of a pretty embroidered zipper pouch. "It doesn't say who she is."

"I wouldn't want the world to know my name if I was being evicted for not paying my rent."

Cassie had volunteered at a homeless shelter in Manhattan, and she knew how easy it was to end up on the streets. "Travis didn't say what happened to her." She folded the paper and slipped it between their seats again."

"You can ask him next time you see him."

"What kind of person finds and keeps that much money?"

"The kind who thinks they need it. Or the kind who thinks they deserve it, since it was put in their path."

"Maybe the woman will get the money back now. Whoever found it will know where to return it."

"Dream on."

They chatted about the weather and upcoming events until Roxanne pulled to a stop in front of Cassie's new house. Cassie had bought into a gated subdivision, Sunset Vista, on the outskirts of Tarpon Springs, although she'd really wanted something more interesting in the historic downtown, where Roxanne lived. But this house suited their needs and hadn't needed renovation. It had also been in the right district, so that Savannah could attend Coastal Winds, a newer high school with an excellent reputation.

The house itself was beige stucco, with a tile roof of a slightly darker hue, forest green trim and a Palladian window over the doorway. The landscaping was mature and adequate, and while she wasn't allowed to change it, Cassie had already signed a contract to add pavers to the screened lanai that had a lap pool and outdoor kitchen. Once the job was finished, she would take her houseplants out there to preen in the sunlight, adding orchids and bromeliads to her heart's content.

She stripped off her scarf and handed it back to Roxanne. Then she got out of the car and hefted her carry-on from the trunk. "Thanks for the ride. Come in and say hello to Savannah."

Roxanne wrinkled her nose. "I'll reserve that pleasure for another time."

Cassie waved goodbye as Roxanne drove away. Then she started up the sidewalk. She rapped on the door before she unlocked it and called Savannah's name. Finally she pushed open the door.

For a moment she thought she'd ended up in the wrong house. That possibility disappeared quickly. There at the sink, visible beyond the great room, stood her daughter, long brown hair the same cocoa brown of her father's, hanging around her face, thin body hunched forward. And between them a house that looked as if a hurricane had swept through.

She released the handle on her bag, along with a soft cry, and stepped across the floor littered with trash and a puddle of something sticky. One of her houseplants, a tall ficus she'd nurtured for years, a tree she had trimmed and repotted, fertilized and decorated at Christmas, was lying on the floor, the trunk split in two, limbs torn away and pot broken into multiple shards.

She straightened and stared at her daughter. "What happened here?"

Savannah wiped her hands on her jeans. "You're not supposed to be here. You were coming home tomorrow!"

"I texted you. And that doesn't begin to answer my question. What have you done here?"

"Jeez, what does it look like? Some kids stopped by and things got a little out of hand. That's all."

Cassie advanced, which was not as easy as it should have been because she had to navigate past more ruined plants, along with food and dirt ground into area rugs. "You call this a little? Where was Dorian when all this was going on?"

"Off with her boyfriend."

Cassie knew Dorian, a distant cousin's daughter would not have let this happen if she'd been in the house. "And she never came back afterward? I bet you told her not to, didn't you? I bet you lied to her."

"I'm sorry, okay? I was going to have this cleaned up before you got here."

"You think a little soap and water is going to make a difference?" Cassie looked around. Two wing chairs flanking the television had been upended, along with side tables. The sofa looked like somebody had poured a pot of soup on it.

She hoped it was soup.

Savannah rolled her eyes. "People were supposed to help me clean up."

"You must think I'm really stupid, Savannah. You had a party. This was not a few people dropping by. And somehow you convinced Dorian not to show up. Maybe you didn't mean for things to get this bad, but you couldn't control them."

For a moment Savannah's sullen expression changed to surprise. Cassie supposed it had never occurred to her daughter that she had once been a teenager herself.

"I was your age," she said to remind her. "But you know what? I didn't have the money this kind of party must have cost you."

Savannah glanced to one side as if looking for help. "Kids brought stuff. That's all."

Cassie knew she was lying. Savannah was her daughter in every way that mattered. She'd raised her. She knew. "Where did you get the money?"

"Kids brought stuff. I told you. And some of my friends had a little money stashed away."

"Where...did...you...get...the...money?"

Savannah's eyes flicked to the wastebasket at her feet, the one that usually resided under the sink. Then she looked up quickly, but Cassie had seen her expression change again. She could swear she saw guilt.

She strode over and picked up the trash can, peering inside. "What's in here? Did somebody bring drugs? Is that what you're worried I might see?" She brushed aside something slimy and wet and caught a glimpse of bright green.

For a moment she wanted to leave whatever it was in place. Maybe it was nothing. There were a lot of other things to worry about here. Savannah's deceit. The destruction of their new home. The pain of seeing the plants she'd nurtured for years in pieces on the floor. And what else was missing or broken? What other parts of her life were left to destroy?

She was choking back tears, and she couldn't tell if they were from sorrow or fury. Again, as earlier in Greg's office, she was filled with both.

"What's in here?" She looked up. "What am I going to find?"

"Just junk. Trash. If it was anything, it wouldn't be there!"

Cassie knew from Savannah's expression that whatever was there was more than trash. Her cheeks were a deep rose and fear shone in her eyes.

Cassie dug her hand inside the can and pulled out a green zipper pouch. She stared at it a moment. Before she even turned it over, she knew what it was, who it had belonged to, what it had once contained. She also knew who had spent the money and how.

"Jeannie," she read out loud. Then, after a series of shaky, deep breaths she looked up. "Savannah, who the hell are you? Because you sure aren't the little girl I raised, the one who routinely took spiders ten stories down in the elevator because you didn't want them to die. You *stole* this money. There's an article in the *Tarpon Times* about the poor woman who lost it. Did you know she was evicted because you stole her rent money? And now she's homeless! How does that make you feel?"

"I didn't steal anything! I found it on the ground in a parking lot. I waited around—my friends did, too—but nobody showed up to claim it. And where was I supposed to take it? Who was I supposed to trust to take care of it? Maybe it was drug money—"

Cassie waited until the explanation ground to a sudden halt, as if Savannah had run out of excuses midsentence or realized how ridiculous they sounded. "Or maybe you just ruined somebody's life because you could," Cassie said.

"The way you ruined mine?" Savannah turned and fled down the hall.

Cassie watched her go and wondered what Mark would have done.

Sadly she would never know. Now and forever she was truly alone to parent a girl who hated her.

6

ALTHOUGH ROXANNE MADE SUGGESTIONS ABOUT
where Cassie should look for Travis, finding him was anything
but simple. She tried calling, but when her call went to voice
mail, she hung up, because telling him about Savannah was
best face-to-face. The address Roxanne gave her had turned
out to be a vacant lot waiting, alongside its neighbors, to be
turned into a big-box store.

Travis seemed to exist on part-time jobs, some of this, some
of that, none of it regimented. Sometimes he helped a friend
who provided sponge diving tours, but when she checked on
the docks, nobody had seen him. He wrote for the *Tarpon
Times*, but only freelance. Somebody there thought he was
working on a novel and might be tucked away at home but
sensibly refused to give an address.

Whatever he did, Travis was obviously holding body and
soul together, because by the time she tracked him to his real
address, Cassie was surprised to find he lived just steps from
the Anclote River in a small frame cottage with two wings
extending toward the water to hug the backyard. She imag-

ined a dock just beyond that warm embrace, and perhaps a pool, or at least a spa in the center of it surrounded by a patio with a view that she envied before she even caught a glimpse.

The house was a pale gray, with white shutters and a door several shades darker than the magenta bougainvillea on a trellis between windows. Maybe she and Travis were closer on the family tree than she thought, because colorful ceramic pots overflowing with flowering plants adorned a porch and sat under large live oaks shading the house.

She hoped he really was writing a novel, because she couldn't imagine a more inspirational view.

At the front door she rapped softly, then louder when nobody stirred. She was about to add the address to her list of failures when the door opened and a man in shorts and a T-shirt appeared. A moment passed before she recognized him.

She smiled. "Travis. You were hard to find."

He tilted his head, as if trying to place her. "I come and go."

"The last time I saw you, you had a bottle of ouzo in one hand and retsina in the other, and you were pouring both for anybody who held up a glass. Yiayia was beaming at you."

The pieces of a puzzle dropped into place. "Cousin Cassie. How long has it been?"

"More than a couple of years. But that's an easier question than how we're actually related. I have no idea."

He held open the door to invite her inside, and she stepped into a hallway leading into a brightly lit room with French doors overlooking the patio she had imagined. There was a small pool right in the center and more pots adorned the paving stones.

"This is amazing," she said.

"My father bought it as an investment when he was still alive. I moved in a couple of months ago, but I guess I haven't updated the family address book."

Instantly she could picture Travis's father, who had died the previous year. She hadn't been able to get home for the funeral, and Yiayia hadn't yet forgiven her.

"I'm sorry he's gone. I remember him. He and my father got into a huge fight, didn't they? When I was in high school. At a family gathering." She could picture that, too, and the sight of fists flying until family separated the two men. "At Yiayia's?"

He didn't look sorry that she'd reminded him. "I think that fight happened somewhere else. Some kind of cousin or other, at least of mine, if not yours."

She felt the familiar shame that would outlast her days on earth. "He was drunk. My father, that is. I'm afraid drinking too much, too fast, wasn't unusual for either of my parents."

"I do remember he could really put it away, but then so could my father. I don't know what your father said, but it really didn't take much for either of them to get angry."

Cassie appreciated the way Travis was trying to spread the blame, when it was unlikely he needed to. His father had been quiet and thoughtful, only good with his fists when he had to be. "I liked your father." She paused. "I didn't like mine."

He didn't look surprised, because not liking George Costas was commonplace, even among family. "Your husband died recently, too, didn't he? I'm sorry. I can't imagine how hard that must be. I'm glad you came back to be with family. Let's sit."

"It's a complicated time." She followed him to a sofa facing the view and took a seat beside him, refusing his offer of coffee or iced tea. Then she launched into her reason for being there.

"I hate dumping this on you. But I have to because I don't know who else can help me."

"Anything I can do."

"I read your story about the woman who lost the zipper pouch." She watched him nod. "I need her name."

He looked surprised. "She made it clear she didn't want to be identified."

"Let me back up." She looked out at the river rippling beyond his yard and watched a double-rigged shrimp trawler heading out toward the Gulf. For a moment she wished she was sailing away with the crew. "I imagine if somebody turned in the purse filled with cash, you'd tell that person who she was."

"Are you about to?"

She shook her head, and he continued. "If that happened, I would certainly tell the woman the good news and ask if I could give out her name. Although even returning the purse wouldn't change enough. She lost her apartment, and the landlord didn't strike me as the forgiving sort."

Cassie had worked out those details for herself. "I checked with my real estate agent. She said if anything could be found when snowbirds are flocking here, it would be third-rate at best, ridiculously expensive anyway and come with huge security deposits. And under the circumstances, this young woman probably missed utility payments and will have to put down large deposits for those, too."

"That about covers it."

"Does she have another place to go?" Cassie hoped the answer was yes. "A safety net of some kind?"

"Apparently not."

"Did she leave town?"

He frowned. "No, she has a job here and a son in high school."

The son hadn't been part of Travis's article. "A son…"

"What's this about, Cassie?"

She was reminded of the brief eulogy she'd recited at Mark's memorial service. Her next words were almost as hard to get out. "My daughter, Savannah, found the purse. She was with friends in a parking lot downtown, and apparently she tripped over it."

"Then she has it?"

"She *had* it. But she and the others decided that since nobody seemed to be looking, it belonged to them. So they threw a party and spent every penny."

"A party?"

She told him what had happened. The house was still a wreck. She'd hired a cleaning service, who had finished what they could, filling their van with bags of trash and a pickup with furniture that would cost more to repair than replace. But upholstery and carpets were yet to be cleaned.

"Well, that must have been a shock," he said.

She wanted to defend Savannah, but the words were hard to form. "She's been through a lot. But none of that excuses what she did. I still can't wrap my head around it. She's never been an easy kid, but I always knew that at heart she was a good one."

"And now you're not sure."

"I still want to believe it."

Travis rearranged the pillows behind him, as if he needed the time to think. "So what do you want to do about this?"

"I want to pay back what Savannah spent. That's a given. I plan to pay the landlord and then see if he will let this woman move back in. I can pay everything she owed him and give him next month's rent, too."

"Good luck with that. I interviewed him, or tried to. He was furious—one of those people who's sure the world is plotting to bring him down. And he's probably even more that way now that my story's out there."

"I still have to try. That was her home." She tried to think of a way to avoid the next part, but she couldn't. "I can't afford much more than that. My financial situation isn't as good as I hoped when I left New York. I'll do everything I can, but helping her settle back in would be the best solution, if I can work it out."

She made sure he was looking at her as she spoke. "You can trust me, Travis. You've known me since we were kids. Can you give me her name and where she's living? I won't tell anybody else, I swear. I have to talk to the landlord, and then I have to talk to her."

"And if that doesn't work?"

Cassie had considered and reconsidered, but there was only one answer, and she wasn't ready to say it out loud. "We'll see," she said instead.

The sun was close to the horizon by the time Cassie found Sunny Acre Estates, where Amber Blair and her son, Will, were now living. The campground was out of town on a rural road, clean but rustic, with RV sites so close together she was sure everybody knew every detail about their neighbors. RVs nearly as large as a city bus sat next to compact models, and more than a few sites had signs with owner's names and colorful lanterns strung from trees. She spotted a Pilgrim banner in honor of the upcoming Thanksgiving holiday and several bright pink flamingos. The air smelled pleasantly of woodsmoke.

She doubted the tent sites were quite as friendly. She'd been pointed to the back of the grounds, far away from the small pond with signs warning of alligators and the screened pavilion where a bingo game was in progress. The caller was loud and fast, too much of both, apparently, because a woman began to protest, accompanied by the applause of other campers. She wondered if Amber and Will were in there, too, mixed in with the senior snowbirds nesting at the campground for the winter.

Not for the first time she wished that she had insisted Savannah come with her so she could see what she'd set in motion. But surly, defiant Savannah was the last person Amber Blair and her son needed to confront at the moment.

She followed the road until she crossed a low bridge over a creek and came to a stretch of sandy soil. Sites here were numbered but with no electrical hookups and only a faucet for water. They were farther apart than those for the RVs, but haphazardly placed, some under oak trees dripping with moss, some exposed to sun and wind with nothing but scraggly palms and palmetto. Those sites were probably vacant in the summer.

She parked on the side of the road and got out, peering at the numbered posts as she walked past a few and waved a greeting at a friendly family sitting around a picnic table. She finally spotted number six, set back from the others and more private, although that was the only positive. The site was right at the edge of encroaching scrub with no trees and a grill that looked as if a million hamburgers had dripped grease into a million bags of charcoal over the years.

A green sedan was parked beside two domed tents, set close together. A tall teenager with dark hair falling over his forehead was piling sticks into the bottom of the grill, and as she watched he struck a match, sending tendrils of smoke into the air.

She took a deep breath and walked into the site. "Hi, are you Will Blair?"

He looked up and cocked his head. "I'm Will."

She introduced herself. "Is your mother home?"

"She went for a walk. Can I help?"

She imagined what Savannah would say about this young man. He wasn't really handsome, although she could see that he might be by the time he went to college in a year or two. No tattoos or piercings were in evidence, and his hair was too long in the front and too short in the back, as if he'd been the first customer of a beauty school trainee. All in all he looked like an ordinary teenager, but he hadn't lived an ordinary life.

She dredged up a smile. "I need to talk to her. Do you mind if I stay and wait? Or I can come back in a little while."

"She'll be back soon. We're making s'mores. She won't miss that."

"You're not cooking dinner on the grill? I mean I wondered if maybe I was interrupting."

"I might roast a hot dog on a stick to go along, but we already ate. We cook on a camp stove. Canned chili with corn. Are you staying here?"

"No, but I wanted to sneak into the bingo game at the rec center. They were harassing the caller. It sounded interesting." Even though shadows were deepening, she thought his eyes were wary.

"So why are you here?" His voice was polite but firm.

"I'll tell you when your mom gets back. But it's nothing to worry about."

"She doesn't need more trouble." This was even firmer.

"I'm not here to add to her problems, I promise." She could see she still needed to reassure him. "It's about the money she lost. But I'd really rather tell the story once. Will you be okay with that?"

He looked surprised, but then his expression cleared and he nodded toward the road. "There she is."

Cassie turned and saw a slender woman with shoulder-length red-gold hair coming toward them. Amber was younger than she was, but probably not by much. She looked pale and tired, which didn't surprise Cassie. Even under the circumstances, she was a natural beauty. She had small, dainty features, a tiny waist, a loose stride with her shoulders back and her head high.

"Are you lost?" Amber said, once she was standing in front of her. "You've come about as far as you can go. I wouldn't go plowing through the scrub this time of evening."

"We had a bobcat prowling around last night," Will said. "Found the paw prints this morning."

"And heard some fierce growling in the night, too." Amber tilted her head.

"That would scare me to death." Cassie held out her hand and introduced herself. "I'm actually here to talk to you. Travis Elliott told me where to find you."

Amber didn't say anything, but her expression said it all. "He was not supposed to."

"I know. I'm sorry. I really am. But he's my cousin, more or less." She didn't explain what she couldn't. "And the thing is, he knew I had the one good reason to find you and that I won't reveal your name or anything about you to anybody. I promise."

"Reason to find me?"

"Is it possible to sit down? At the table?"

Amber debated, then she nodded. Cassie looked at Will. "You too?"

"I wouldn't miss it."

At the picnic table Will and Amber took one side and Cassie sat on the other. The planks were covered by a plastic table-cloth, red-and-white checks that made her think of an Italian restaurant where she'd regularly indulged in all-you-can-eat spaghetti in the year before she met and married Mark. The cloth was anchored by salt and pepper shakers and a wooden bowl with two apples and a banana.

"I'm going to get right to the point." Cassie looked at her hands, which were twisting on the table, and dropped them to her lap. "My daughter found your missing zipper pouch. In a parking lot downtown."

Amber closed her eyes for a moment, as if visualizing it. "So that's where it was. I don't know how it happened, but I guess I dropped it when I got out of my car."

"Savannah's having a hard time, and I guess she thought giving somebody else a hard time was okay. Because she and her friends took the money and threw a party at our house while I was away. She said she didn't know how to find the owner, and since nobody was looking for it in the lot—"

Amber's voice had an edge sharp enough to slice through metal. "Oh, I looked. As soon as I'd searched the whole store where I thought I'd dropped it, I went out to my car, and when it wasn't there, I looked over the whole lot. Half a dozen times. I got down on my hands and knees and searched under cars."

"You probably just missed them. Anyway, I can't tell you how sorry I am. It's hard to believe she did what she did, that any of these girls thought it was okay." She knew better than to explain how her house had been trashed, because that in no way compared to what Amber had lost.

"So that's it. The money's gone," Amber said.

"Travis also gave me the address and name of your landlord. I went to see Mr. Blevin this afternoon and told him about finding the purse. I paid him the two months' rent you owed and promised that if it ever became necessary, I could pay more in the future. I asked him to let you move back in. But he—"

"He said no. Of course he did. I could have told you he would. But thank you. At least now he won't take me to court while I'm trying to pay him back."

She didn't look grateful; she looked upset, but Cassie was impressed by her good manners. "He gave me a long lecture on how nobody can be trusted, and he's charging three times as much security deposit in the future."

Amber got to her feet. "You went to a lot of trouble to

find me and fix things. A lot of people would have just kept quiet. I appreciate it."

"Can you give me just a bit more time?"

She looked unhappy but she sat again and waited.

"I asked my real estate agent to find you an apartment you might be able to afford."

Amber waved her hand dismissively. "We won't be able to move into an apartment again until at least the summer." She started to list all the expenses involved, but Cassie stopped her.

"I know. And I don't have the kind of money you'll need to restart your life. I wish I did. I do have one thing to offer, though, something I can do. And please don't think this is charity. It's me repaying a debt in the only way I know how."

"You don't have to do another thing."

"Amber, neither of us should have to live with this. You need a real roof over your heads, and I need to help repair what Savannah did to you. I want you to come and live with us. For as long as you need." Somehow she dredged up a smile. "I can't offer bobcats, but there's an outdoor kitchen for s'mores. I promise the house is large enough for all of us. You'll have your own rooms, but you'll be welcome everywhere."

Amber didn't look stunned so much as skeptical. "I'm a stranger. How can you make an offer like that?"

"Because Travis checked your background before he wrote that story. Everyone you work with likes and admires you, and so do your former neighbors. Will has a fan club at the high school among teachers. Everybody thinks you've been hammered by a fate you didn't deserve."

"In my experience, fate's not good at discerning what people deserve."

Cassie silently agreed. "So please let me intervene, for both our sakes? Quietly with no publicity. Say you'll move into my house so we can all move on to better things."

Her gaze fell on Will, and she realized he was the key. "Living closer will be especially good for Will. There's no way he's going to be able to participate in after-school activities out here, and you may even be out of the school district. He'd have to change schools if they found out."

"I could keep my job," Will said, and Cassie knew she had an ally.

Amber stood again, and this time Cassie stood, too. She noticed Will leaped to his feet, as well, a young man who'd been trained to be polite. "How will your daughter feel about having us in your house? We'll be constant reminders of what she did."

Cassie thought that was probably the least of the problems Savannah would face. The biggest was that she would be moved to the small guest room at the end of the hall.

"She's not going to be happy about it," she said carefully. "But at this point in her life she's not happy, period. If she doesn't understand this is right for everyone, she will someday."

"How old is she?"

"Fifteen."

"Savannah Westmore?" Will asked.

Cassie met his eyes. "You know her?"

"I know who she is."

"Please don't let that stop you."

Will smiled a little but he didn't protest.

She turned back to Amber. "You'll think about it?" She really wasn't sure what Amber would say, but the other woman gave a slight nod.

Cassie was prepared. She handed her a slip of paper with her phone number and address. "The offer stands. Whenever you're ready, now or later. Just call me." She started toward the road. Behind her there was no conversation, but she knew there would be plenty after her car had pulled away.

She drove slowly through the grounds and waited until she was on the road to consider everything she'd said. She'd done her best to convince the Blairs to move into her house, and everything she'd told them was heartfelt and honest. Still, not too deep down, just past the layers of guilt and remorse, she hoped Amber and Will could find a better solution.

7

SAVANNAH COULDN'T BELIEVE HOW BORING WORLD History was. She had refused to let Cassie register her for the Advanced Placement class because she wasn't interested in doing more work than she had to. Instead she'd been placed in Honors History. She figured her education in New York had been so superior, she could get through that and high school in general without breaking a sweat.

History had been one of her favorite subjects, but these days she couldn't read three sentences before her mind wandered. And participating in class? Coastal Winds shared at least one thing with Pfeiffer Grant. Every class had the same percentage of dweebs, dorks and know-it-alls. Today when she'd been called on to give her opinion about some stupid Supreme Court ruling, she'd been shot down by the teacher's personal ass-kisser. The teacher had laughed and told him to zip his lips—and how lame was that? But by then, Savannah had lost all interest in the subject.

After the bell rang, she gathered her books and stalked down the corridor to her locker. Unfortunately Helia was waiting for her, about as welcome a sight as Loki in an Avengers movie. At least Helia couldn't teleport or shape-shift.

"You get in big trouble?" Helia was chewing a wad of gum as big as a fist, and it took Savannah a minute to translate.

"Of course I got in big trouble! My stepmarauder came home a day early and I'd just started to clean. Which you and Minh left me to do alone."

Helia chewed faster and louder. "Stepmarauder. That's a good one."

"Stepmonster. Stepbother." She didn't add her favorite nickname for Cassie: Stepmurderer. That one she kept to herself.

Helia shrugged. "I planned to come. I didn't know I'd be under house arrest."

Savannah was surprised. The explanation wasn't exactly an apology, but it was a lot closer than she'd expected.

She thought she had a paper due in some class or the other, but she wasn't in the mood to think about it. She dumped the contents of her backpack inside the locker and turned. "Not one person who showed up Friday night said thanks when they saw me today, or great party, or anything that showed they even noticed I was there."

"Don't be a whiner. It wasn't that kind of party. People came and went, mostly for the beer. We weren't the only game in town."

"Then what was the point? Like my life wasn't bad enough? Now Cassie's not going to let me out of her sight for the rest of my life."

"Yeah, well, welcome to that club."

Savannah slammed the locker door. "I have to meet her outside. She's driving me both ways now."

"My foster father is probably waiting, too. With a car full of screaming brats."

They started toward the front door. As angry as Savannah

was at Helia and Minh—who had avoided her all day—she had to admit it was nice to have somebody walking beside her, even if it was Helia.

Outside, cars packed with juniors and seniors who drove themselves to school zoomed by, kids hanging out the windows and hooting. A group of the popular girls stood off to one side, gesturing in the direction of the parking lot. Ponytails swished and fancy phone cases glinted in the sunlight. At Pfeiffer Grant she'd been one of that group, always with the prettiest or smartest girls, always admired and envied by the hangers-on.

She'd never examined her exalted status, or at least only rarely. She'd just accepted her place, and she'd given little thought to making sure nobody was excluded. She was smart, pretty, funny. Her parents were rich, and girls fought to go to her spacious condo in Battery Park City to hang out in her room and eat Cassie's baklava.

They'd fought for her attention, but only until she was tossed out of school, with a don't-let-the-door-hit-you lecture from the upper school headmistress.

"Yep, there's the man with the van." Helia, who didn't seem to own a backpack, lifted half a dozen books from her side and slipped them under her arm. Savannah saw *The Sound and the Fury* on top.

"You're studying *The Sound and the Fury* in English? Faulkner's pretty dense, right?"

Helia looked like she'd been caught shooting heroin in the teacher's lounge. "It's on our reading list."

Savannah didn't know if she had a reading list. "Is that what I have to look forward to in English?"

"Gotta go."

Savannah watched Helia disappear into the front passenger seat of a rusting van with Comfy-Temps Heating and Cooling painted on the side. Kids were yelling in the back. She wondered how Helia read anything, much less Faulkner, in her foster home.

Cassie appeared a moment later, carefully guiding her clunky blue sedan into a space in front of the school. Savannah would be incensed if the Plain Jane Corolla was the car she was destined to drive herself, but Cassie had paid someone to drive her father's Mustang Shelby coupe, with the racing stripe across the roof, to Florida. She'd told Savannah she wanted her to have it once she was driving, that her father had loved the little Ford, and he would want her to enjoy it once she had her license and was ready for the challenge.

Maybe the fancy Mustang wasn't an Aston Martin or a Porsche, but Mark Westmore had learned to drive in a more basic Mustang himself. While he hadn't used a car much in the city, he'd loved taking it on the occasional weekend when they'd sail over interstates, just the three of them, on the way to a bed-and-breakfast in Vermont or an inn in Bucks County.

Back when they were a family.

In the passenger seat she fastened the belt rather than listen to her stepmother's lecture on car safety. Then she stared straight ahead, hoping to avoid any conversation at all.

Two blocks later Cassie pulled over to the side of the road and parked, turning off the engine. She swiveled to face Savannah.

"I don't feel like talking," Savannah said, heading her off.

"Whether you do or not, talking is on the schedule."

"You've already told me over and over what a loser I am."

Cassie's expression didn't soften. "You're acting like one, but this conversation goes a lot deeper. I found the woman who that purse and money belonged to."

That was a subject Savannah hadn't expected. "How?"

"It doesn't matter. I paid the debt to her landlord, which

she would have done with the money you found. I tried to get him to let her move back in, but he was too angry. So now she and her son have no place to live."

"Why? There must be a hundred places to rent."

"There might be if she had a lot of money. But if you paid any attention at all, you noticed that the purse was filled with small bills, which she collected from tips. She's not rich, and she can't afford what's out there."

Savannah tried not to imagine what that was like.

Cassie went on. "In case you need a pointer, that should make you feel rotten. So now it's time to do something. Her name is Amber Blair and her son is Will. He goes to Coastal Winds, too. I think he's a junior. Do you know him?"

"Like I know anybody. I'm the new girl, remember?"

"Apparently not too new to invite dozens of kids to our house while I was away."

Savannah knew better than to respond. After a moment Cassie filled the silence. "Anyway, I've invited them to live with us."

"You did what?" Now Savannah turned, too, to look at Cassie. "You invited strangers into our house?"

"You'll be moving into the guest room in the back, because they need space and privacy. The guest room carpet has been cleaned, and the room is acceptable, although I had the mattress hauled away, vomit and all. I ordered another. There are stains on the walls, courtesy of your guests. I can't afford to have it repainted, but if you want to do it yourself, I'll buy the paint."

Savannah stared at her stepmother. Cassie had always been on her side, gentle with her, helping her clean up her messes. Even when she thought Savannah had started the fight at Pfeiffer Grant, she'd tried to help her cope with the fallout. Now she sounded stern and, worse, unforgiving.

Savannah leaned forward and narrowed her eyes. "I'm not moving to the guest room, and I'm not living with people I don't know. This woman could be an ax murderer! How do you know she's not?"

"Because I checked. She's a single mom who caught a series of bad breaks, and you were the final one. She's out on the street, and we have it in our power to put a roof over her head."

"Not in *my* power. I don't want her. And I guess you didn't hear me. I'm not moving to the guest room."

"Then I will move you myself."

"I want to live with my real mother!"

Cassie didn't respond. Savannah had made this threat before, and Cassie had always rushed in to reassure her. Today was different.

She finally spoke, spaces between words as if she had to think about each one in advance. "Gen is not home. She's in Africa, and the last I heard, she'll be there at least a few months longer. She expects you to live with me and go to Coastal Winds."

"And I bet she's paying you to take care of me! Paying for my master suite that you're giving to strangers, right?"

Cassie mulled over her answer for a long moment. Savannah could almost see her mind working. "I'm pretty sure you know this, but let's review. Gen and your father had an agreement when they divorced. He took care of all your expenses except your tuition at the academy, which he and Gen split. In turn each year Gen invests money in a college account, so when the time comes, you can attend any college where you're accepted."

"But my father is dead! Who's paying my expenses now, huh?"

Cassie just stared at her.

"Like you would," Savannah said, although with less fury.

"Like I would." Cassie turned back to the steering wheel and started the car again. "The Blairs are meeting us in a few minutes at the house."

"I'm not moving my stuff."

"They'll be moving in tomorrow. And just so you know, Roxanne has volunteered to keep your father's Mustang at her house so Amber can park her car in our garage."

"That's my car!"

"Legally it's mine. You don't even have a learner's permit, and at this rate, you won't get one until I think you're mature enough to get behind the wheel. Where the car is parked is immaterial."

At Savannah's outraged gasp, Cassie's tone hardened in a way she had rarely heard. "Your stuff will be out of your room by the time they arrive, one way or the other. If I have to pack it myself, everything may end up on the front lawn waiting for the Salvation Army truck. Take your chances."

"You're punishing me! I'm fifteen. I don't need to be treated like a preschooler!"

"If I'd been harder on you as a preschooler, maybe we wouldn't be having this conversation. You've gotten pretty much everything you've wanted all your life, Savannah. Maybe your dad and I loved you too much."

"You're not my mother!"

"I was the mother on the premises for twelve years of your life. Whether you can see it, I loved you like a daughter, and still do. But I'm not spoiling you anymore. For the record I'm not inviting the Blairs to live with us to punish you. I'm doing what's right. Someday you may see that, but that will be up to you."

They didn't speak again, which was fine with Savannah. The whole way home she tried to imagine what it would be like to live in a house with Cassie and the strangers whose money she had spent on a stupid, stupid party.

Her life was already hell. Whatever was ahead might even be worse.

Amber stopped in front of the house that, if she had the address right, belonged to Cassie Costas. She left the motor running, in case a reprieve magically occurred to her. "Her daughter has a different last name?" she asked Will.

"Westmore. It's not easy coming in new like she did."

"You should know."

"When you do it often enough, you learn not to care what other kids think."

Will said that as if he really didn't care, but Amber felt a stab right through her heart. Her son had endured move after move into towns that held no family or friends.

Once, as a younger child, he'd sobbed and begged to stay in a popular tourist city where they'd settled. They'd rented the downstairs of a house with a real fireplace and a park across the street. Will had made friends and joined the local Cub Scout troop. But despite his pleas, she packed their car the day school let out and told the sobbing boy they were leaving. They'd driven through three states before she began to sort through small cities that had nothing to recommend them to visitors. She had learned her lesson. With the array of conventions that had come and gone in their previous home, it had been a matter of time before she ran into somebody who recognized and remembered her.

Since then she'd learned to stay away from tourist cities and small towns where everybody knew everybody's business. Somehow she'd succeeded in choosing places where she and her son could fade into the woodwork.

That had changed when the restaurant owner in a central

Florida town had told her he was opening a Dine Eclectic in Tarpon Springs and wanted her to be the assistant general manager. Maybe moving here was a risk because it was a destination on tourist maps. The Greek-American community often found their way to town. But the man she feared, one whose ancestors undoubtedly came from the same Scots-Irish stock as hers, would never look for family here.

Hopefully he would never look for her in Tarpon Springs, either.

"Savannah won't be happy to have us living with her if we decide to move in," Amber said. "Can you deal?"

Will was examining the house, a pseudo Mediterranean in the middle of a gated community of like homes. The yard was small and neatly landscaped, with a driveway paved in hexagonal blocks and concrete urns with the usual petunias and impatiens flanking the sidewalk to the front door. The house was far from a mansion, but it looked large enough for four.

"I would deal with a lot to live here," Will said. "I can walk home from school."

Coastal Winds was probably three miles away, but Amber knew her son would walk if necessary. Right now he had to wait around town until her shift at Dine Eclectic ended. He was doing homework in the library, on park benches, even at a table before the restaurant opened for dinner.

"We won't stay a day longer than we have to." Amber turned the key and waited as the car shuddered into silence.

As they walked up the sidewalk, she thought about the biggest reason she had agreed to this visit today. That morning she'd been outside her tent, making coffee on their camp stove, when an older man, wearing a cap sporting the familiar black-and-gold logo of the West Virginia Power baseball team, walked into their site. "Something smells mighty good," he'd said.

She had forced a smile. "Nothing better than coffee in the open air, right?"

"Except maybe bacon." He'd removed his cap and held it down, and as he did, she noted the Charleston T-shirt with the words *Since 1788* printed on the front. "Do you like camping in tents?" he asked. "There's lot of good campgrounds up where I'm from."

She didn't have to ask where that was. "Charleston area?"

"A bit north, off 77."

She'd held her hands over the burner to warm them, willing them not to tremble. "I've never been to West Virginia." She was hopeful she had lost the Appalachian twang in her voice after so many years and so much effort. "I bet it's pretty."

"A group of us is staying here. Nice place to spend the winters, and we like to set up close to each other. Been friends forever. Winters up our way get colder than blue hell."

Amber clearly remembered her grandfather using the same expression. "So how long do you stay?"

"Oh, we go back about April. Prettiest springs in the world where we come from. You had oughta visit."

"Maybe I will."

He'd turned to start back to the road. "Gotta carry my wife into town this morning for groceries. Good having a talk. We're over by the rec center. You come see us, you hear?"

"Sure will." And at that moment she'd known she was going to take Cassie Costas up on her offer.

Now, looking at the house, she thought about the security guard at the gate two blocks away, and the fact that neither her name nor any identifying details would be on documents related to the house. She didn't even have to give her new address to her boss. Her paycheck went right into her bank account, and she had a post office box for mail. Anyone trying to trace her might find her, but first they'd have to know the name she'd been living under for seventeen years. And if they knew that much, the game was probably up anyway.

At the door she knocked and waited as Will shifted his weight from foot to foot beside her. Cassie, in black capris and a white linen blouse, opened the door, her dark hair curling over her collar and long-lashed hazel eyes searching Amber's face.

Cassie fell somewhere into the gap between striking and pretty, curvy but not overweight, neither tall nor short. Her skin was creamy, but Amber thought her skin might darken after a few months living in Florida. Her teeth were even and white, and right now she had a smile firmly in place, although Amber could read the wariness behind it. It wasn't exactly an "I've had second thoughts" smile, but the woman was worried that by the house tour's end, one or the other of them would realize what a terrible idea this was.

Cassie stepped aside and ushered them in. "We just got home about fifteen minutes ago."

Amber heard loud music from the back of the house. Will might recognize the band or the singer, but she didn't. A young woman was wailing at the top of her lungs about waking in a bad mood.

"Savannah's doing some cleaning and moving," Cassie said. "I'll ask her to turn the music down."

"No, no." Amber rested her hand on Cassie's arm for a moment. "That won't bother us."

Cassie started through the house, and Amber and Will followed. "This is the main living area. There's a small den, too, when you need more privacy, televisions in both. I love the kitchen. Do you like to cook?"

The great room had little character and lacked enough furniture to fill it, but it was bordered by glass doors looking over a pool, which Cassie quickly insisted they could use anytime. Amber followed her past a dining table with only three chairs into a wide kitchen with a dark granite island in the center. Cabinets lined both walls and a lighter granite graced the countertops.

"I would like to cook in here," Amber said. "It's great."

"I like to bake." Cassie leaned against a counter and folded her arms. "Where we lived before…before this, takeout and delivery were a way of life. You name it, somebody within a six-block radius delivered it. So I didn't make meals as often, but I did make dessert."

Amber was beginning to relax. The house had little charm, but it was spacious and open, and she could see how easy it might be to avoid each other. "I don't make dessert, but I do make dinner."

"We were meant to live together." Cassie's smile was a little more natural now. "I expect you to share the kitchen. I'll divide the shelves in the refrigerator. Even if we're both in here at the same time, I don't think we'll be in each other's way."

"I can cook for all of us." Amber ran her fingertips over the cool, smooth granite. "You're not going to let me pay rent. I know that deep in my bones, Cassie, although I'm about to offer—"

"No chance."

"Then I'll make dinner."

"Don't you work nights?"

"Yes, but I make meals for Will to eat while I'm gone, and I eat early. I specialize in things that can be warmed up. Soup, stews, casseroles. I'll make enough for all of us." She looked up. "Not as good as your neighborhood in New York, but you can eat it."

"I'll buy the groceries. You'll give me a list?"

Everything sounded so easy, and none of it would be. But she nodded. "I can shop, too."

"Let me show you where you'll be. Some of Savannah's stuff is still in there, but the room will be ready by tomorrow, I promise. The furniture will stay."

Savannah had brought this on herself, but Amber had been fifteen once, and mistakes were so easy to make. She looked at Will, only Will wasn't where she'd expected him to be.

Cassie read her expression. "I think he went exploring."

"I'm sorry, I—"

"Don't be. He has to be sure this will work for him. Let's find him, and after I show you where you'll be living, we'll find Savannah."

Amber followed her down the hall, where Cassie stopped at an open door. But the room wasn't empty. She heard a girl's voice.

"How does this strike you, Willie boy? It's great, isn't it? Big enough for you and your mother, I guess. Do you like kicking me out of my room? Think you'll like sleeping on the sofa in here or in my bed? I'll be stuck in the back of the house. I don't even have a mattress!"

Amber heard Cassie gasp, but she laid a hand on her arm and held her back.

Will answered, "You know what? I have a blow-up mattress in the tent where we're living now, after, you know, you stole our rent money. Why don't I bring it tomorrow when we move in? I'll let you fill it. It's perfect for somebody full of hot air."

Amber expected Savannah to explode. She'd only rarely

heard her son sound this angry. Will was good at not provoking fights. It was one of the benefits of navigating so many moves, so many schools, so many bullies waiting to take him down.

"You're not living in a tent." Savannah was no longer taunting him, but she didn't sound sure of herself.

"Where do you think people go when they can't pay their rent, rich girl?"

"You could stay in a motel like anybody else."

"If someone hadn't helped herself to all our cash, maybe."

Silence stretched, and finally Amber dropped her hand, and Cassie preceded her into the room.

"Amber, this is Savannah, my daughter."

"Stepdaughter!"

"Savannah, go finish up in your new room, please." Cassie pointed toward the door. Savannah stalked past them and slammed it behind her.

"Can you contend with that?" Cassie turned her hands palm up. "It's a lot to ask when she's already caused you so much trouble. But I'll do my best to make her toe the line."

Amber thought about the man who had visited their campsite. She thought about all the other campgrounds where she'd tried to find a site, only to discover they were overflowing. She thought about throwing herself on the mercy of a charity for the homeless, which she had never done before, and moving into a shelter. But shelters required paperwork, and hers was not above reproach. Besides there was no guarantee she and Will would be allowed to stay together.

"We can contend." She looked at her son. "Can't we, Will?"

He looked less certain, but he gave a brief nod. "With almost anything." His voice was light, but he didn't smile.

Amber wanted to cry. Will's entire life had been about

contending, and no matter how hard she had tried, how far they had run, she'd been able to do damn little about any of it.

She faced Cassie. "We'll pack up tonight, and if you think you'll be ready, we can move in tomorrow afternoon."

"We'll be ready." Cassie looked neither relieved nor sorry. She just looked exhausted, as if Savannah and everything that followed had drained her. "Let's find both of you keys."

8

CASSIE HAD NEVER WORKED WITH A PERSONAL trainer or joined a gym. She had taken the occasional yoga class with her friend Valerie, mostly because of the lunches they indulged in afterward. But her major form of exercise had always been walking. In Manhattan she'd chosen restaurants or stores based on their distances from home and faithfully logged steps and miles on her activity tracker.

Today, by the time she arrived at the staff parking lot behind Yiayia's Kouzina on Dodecanese Boulevard in the Greektown historic district, she was soaked with sweat, exhausted, and ready to toss her tracker under a car because it had no setting to calculate misery.

She had forgotten that in a low-lying city, with water everywhere, walking required sticking to sidewalks along major thoroughfares, in her case in full sun around Lake Tarpon and then along U.S. Highway 19, to get to Dodecanese. Neither had she taken into account the busy morning traffic or the fact that a Florida autumn in no way resembled one in Manhattan. As she'd walked, the temperature had risen to the high seventies, and the humidity had quickly turned oppressive. Trading sandals for walking shoes and grabbing her wallet and smartphone had not been adequate preparation. She didn't want to think about the walk back home.

The Kouzina's kitchen door opened, and Cassie, who was standing with her head down and her hands on her thighs, looked up to find her aunt staring at her.

"Not exactly what I expected to see." Roxanne wore a double-breasted chef's coat, but not the usual white or black. Hers was a bright melon with a black collar and buttons. By no fashion standard should melon work with Rox's skin tones, but like the blond hair she had not been born with, somehow it did.

"I didn't want to come in through the front," Cassie said between pants. "I would scare away customers."

"We're not open anyway. Come inside, and I'll get you something cold to drink."

Cassie straightened slowly and followed. "I wasn't sure you'd be here. I figured Yiayia would be whipping everybody into shape inside."

"She's got doctor's appointments all day, so she left me in charge. Buck's taking her, so I'm allowed to cook." Roxanne gestured toward a small round table in a nook where staff grabbed meals after shifts or paperwork was completed. The table was surrounded by four battered bentwood chairs, and Cassie took the one against the far wall to stay out of traffic. Unfamiliar staff in white coats, a woman and a large man with a blue bandanna over his hair, were chopping and sautéing on the other side of the room, preparing for lunch.

Roxanne emerged from a huge stainless steel refrigerator with two soft drinks imported from Greece, holding them up for Cassie to choose. After she pointed, Roxanne handed her the black cherry and plopped down beside her with a pink lemonade.

Cassie held the cold bottle against her hot cheeks, first one then the other. "Doctor's appointments? She's not sick, is she?" In Cassie's mind her grandmother had been born the age she was now and would usher in the end of time with her secret recipe grilled octopus and platters of Greek salad, Kalamata or Chalkidiki olives and feta, real Greek feta made from sheep's milk.

Don't forget the ouzo.

"She's not sick," Roxanne said. "She schedules all her appointments on the same day twice a year. Internist, dermatologist, ophthalmologist. That way she's not gone longer than the lunch shift. She'll be back tonight after we've opened, checking to be sure I haven't slipped something radical into the daily menu, like the time I featured lamb spareribs glazed with ouzo and honey."

"That sounds heavenly."

"The people who ordered them before Mama snatched them off the menu had good things to say." Roxanne leaned back in her chair and closed her eyes. "She claimed people want to be filled up and not served dainty little snacks at the Kouzina. The dinner plate looked too fussy—Greek food isn't fussy. I should never have added mint to the orzo under the spareribs." She opened her eyes. "Those are the ones I remember. You get the picture. I'll tell you the staff feasted that night after everybody left."

"You're not going to be able to stay, are you?"

"You know how your Savannah is going through a phase?"

Cassie twisted the top off her bottle and took a long drag before she spoke. "Please don't compare my sweet little Greek yiayia to my bratty daughter."

"Daughter? Savannah hasn't been demoted to *step*daughter?"

"Until Mark died she called me Mom. Gen was always Gen—not that she minded. Gen sees Savannah as a friend, a playmate, somebody to hang out with a couple of times a year and take on exciting trips. Anyway, now I'm Cassie."

"And has Gen become Mom?"

Cassie gave a weary smile. "I think Savannah knows Gen would not be pleased or even comfortable with *Mom*."

"And yet you like her."

"Savannah? Not right now I don't."

"You know who I mean."

"Everybody likes Gen," Cassie said. "She's lovely, brilliant, devoted to changing the world one cleft palate and facial reconstruction at a time. She's just not good with intimacy, which is why her marriage to Mark only lasted until Savannah was born and they finalized their divorce. She's utterly and profoundly thankful that I've supplied our daughter with love and rules. Last Christmas she sent me a Fendi watch dripping with more diamonds than a coronation crown. She said it would help me keep track of our daughter's schedule. How can I not like her?"

"Similar situation here. How can I not love and stand by Mama as she ages? And she is aging, although she tries hard not to let it show. She shouldn't be running the Kouzina. It's much too hard on her body and heart. And her spirit? She makes mistakes, and when she realizes it, she feels so terrible about herself that she lashes out at everybody around her."

"Mostly at you, right?"

"The spareribs were more than a new dish. They were a symbol. She knows I'm the obvious person to take over the Kouzina after she leaves. But the easiest way to fight change is to treat me like the lowest level of hired help, so I'll take off my chef's coat and saunter into the sunset."

"She doesn't want that."

"Of course she doesn't. But what her head knows, her heart doesn't."

"I understand the divide. Intimately."

Roxanne put her hand over Cassie's. "I'm sorry things are rough. How are the roommates working out?"

Cassie didn't know how to answer. Two weeks had passed since Amber and Will had moved in, and ever since they had made themselves scarce. Sometimes she heard the hum of laughter or voices from what was now their suite, but for the most part their door was closed and silence reigned.

The situation, though, went beyond awkward. They were two families coexisting in a space meant for one, trying to stay out of each other's way.

"Savannah doesn't speak to any of us. Will is polite but clearly uncomfortable." She searched for positives. "Amber's a good cook. I filled the refrigerator and cupboards, so she takes what's available and makes something delicious. In one of our rare conversations she told me she learned to cook in restaurant kitchens."

"I think I'm jealous. How's her moussaka?"

Cassie managed a smile, because Roxanne, who had been educated at the Culinary Institute of America, was a talented chef. "She knows better than to try Greek. She makes things that can be warmed up while she's at work. Will takes his and disappears. Savannah only eats if I'm not in the room. I'm left to sit at the kitchen table with a plate of food in front of me and nobody to talk to."

"Have you found out more about them?"

"I asked her about herself. She says she left home when she got pregnant, and she's made it on her own."

"Where was home?"

"Arkansas, but she's been all over. She says she's been chasing the American dream, but she's never caught it."

"She raised that baby alone."

"Apparently. Maybe Will's father came along, too, at least at first. She's vague. I get the feeling her past isn't something she wants to dwell on. Travis says she flies under the radar, but everyone has only good things to say about her. One restaurant manager told him that once Amber brought back her paycheck because he'd calculated her hours incorrectly and overpaid her. He was so impressed he hired her as his bookkeeper."

"So she probably won't slit your throat or steal your family heirlooms."

"The only heirloom my parents left me is a strong desire not to live my life the way they lived theirs."

"And you haven't."

Cassie finished her drink and reluctantly got to her feet. She had her phone, and the minute she could sneak around the corner, she was going to call Uber for a ride. "I'm sorry I missed Yiayia, but I'm glad I saw you. I think I'll head home before it gets any hotter."

"I'm driving you, so don't argue. Ten minutes at most each way and still plenty of time here to get things going." Roxanne disappeared into the pantry but continued to talk. "Mama made me promise no specials today, and the three of us can turn out lunch with our eyes closed. We don't get as many customers for lunch as we used to. Hell, we don't get as many customers, period. The place needs sprucing, and so does the food. We need a website, a mailing list, yada yada."

Cassie knew Roxanne was talking to keep her from arguing. By the time she was out of the pantry, Roxanne had her car keys and was waving them in Cassie's face. "Let's go."

Before leaving, she introduced Cassie to the two cooks, Oliver and Kristina, who were chopping like their lives depended on it. "You notice how crowded it is in there?" she asked as they headed toward her car, parked behind the restaurant. "The kitchen needs an update, too. I'd kill to open it to the dining room so customers could watch us cook."

"But it's always been that way and should stay that way," Cassie said, filling in the last part of the sentence in Yiayia's high-pitched voice.

"You got it. I drew up a sketch and showed Buck some changes that would make it easier and more efficient."

"Did he like them?"

"Whenever I ask he just smiles. He's so crazy about Mama, if she told him we were serving poison mushrooms for lunch, he'd clean and cook them himself. Probably take a bite to be sure they were tasty enough, too."

"Buck? Yiayia?"

Roxanne unlocked the doors of the Miata, which had the top up today because seagulls flourished this close to the water. "How'd you miss that? Buck's been in love with Mama since the day he took over as chef. Why do you think he stays on cooking the same boring menu? He's been ready to retire for years. He has family back in Kalymnos and Rhodes that he never gets to see. He'd love to go back, spend a few months now and then, maybe more. But he stays around because Mama's here."

Cassie was still processing this as Roxanne screeched out of the parking lot. Buck Andreadis was a quiet, gentle soul, portly and balding, but with a rare smile that lit up a room. He, like Yiayia, was probably in his mid-seventies. But where Yiayia was always bustling around the kitchen snapping orders, Buck seemed rooted to the spot, moving his hands with such measured grace it was easy to miss how much he did and how quickly.

"He told you how he feels? Does she know?" Cassie asked at last.

"She's never let on, but remember what he's doing today? He's chauffeuring her from appointment to appointment, listening to excruciating rundowns of whatever the doctors tell her, buying her lunch somewhere nice outside Greektown. You'd have to love Mama to put yourself in that position. And the biggest clue? He cooks what she thinks he ought to. He's actually a wonderful chef. Everything he does, he does well. He just doesn't get to make his own choices."

Cassie thought about Roxanne's theory. "Tell me, whose idea was it to have him chauffeur Yiayia today? His? Hers?"

Roxanne didn't answer, and Cassie laughed. "It was yours, wasn't it!"

"Well, I might have mentioned it."

"You're cultivating a romance. You're hoping if the two of them get together, he'll whisk Yiayia back to Greece to meet his family and leave you in charge."

Roxanne tossed her hair. "The thought crossed my mind, but only when I realized how much he loves her."

"The very *moment* you realized it."

"Well, I think she's sweet on him, too. I really do. Only she's sure that part of her life is over. She's been a widow for more than twenty years."

"At least she's not wearing black and covering her hair with a kerchief. Doesn't this seem a little late in her life for another love story?"

"No such thing as too late for love."

Cassie wondered about that as Roxanne rounded the lake, finally pausing at her neighborhood security gate until the guard saw and waved them through. "Gary's been gone for three years now," she said. "Are you ready to fall in love again?"

"Maybe. But I've said my final farewells. You're not close to saying yours."

"I may never be." Cassie still had moments when she forgot her husband wasn't alive. When the phone rang, too often she expected it to be Mark.

"Take it slow, honey. When and if you're ready, you'll know."

When they reached her street, Cassie unbuckled her seat belt. "Come in and meet Amber. You'll be in and out, and later you won't have to convince her you are who you say you are. I have a feeling she's careful about strangers. The pest control guy showed up, and she made him wait outside until I approved him. Even though he was in uniform."

At the front door Cassie found Travis standing in the entryway talking to Amber. "Hey." She leaned over and kissed him on the cheek. "You found us."

"I wanted to see if Amber was doing okay, and if she and Will needed anything."

"I told him you're treating us like honored guests," Amber said.

Cassie wondered how many of the people Travis interviewed got this kind of treatment. He was a great guy, compassionate and thoughtful, but she guessed, most of the time, a brief follow-up phone call was his go-to. The difference? Few of the people he interviewed were as pretty as Amber. Today her new housemate was wearing faded jeans and a gauzy white blouse with a beautifully embroidered yoke. Her red-gold hair was loosely pinned so wisps fell around her face.

Roxanne stuck her hand out. "I'm Roxanne, Cassie's aunt and some relation or other to this guy." She inclined her head toward Travis.

Amber took her hand, and while they shook, Roxanne continued. "See, the time's passed for honored guest status,

Amber, so I propose an upgrade. Come have Thanksgiving at my mama's house and graduate to honorary family."

Cassie was embarrassed she hadn't asked first. "That's a great idea, and eventually I would have thought of it." She watched Amber's expression, which seemed to be an equal mix of gratitude and horror.

"I'll be there," Travis said. "I'd love to have somebody to talk to who doesn't sketch our family tree on a napkin and show me where his branch converges with my twig. I can guide you and Will through the crowd."

"I may not have the day off," Amber said, the first chance she'd had to speak. "Dine Eclectic is planning to stay open, but you're so kind to include me."

"Come if you can," Roxanne said. "Cassie will bring you."

Cassie stepped in to make sure Amber knew she was welcome. "I'm making baklava. I hope you'll come. I haven't been home for Thanksgiving for years. It's…" She ran out of words and shrugged.

"Noisy and crazy," Travis supplied. "The food is unbelievable, though. And when Yiayia can't host anymore, some of the traditions will disappear. So this is your chance to be part of something different and special."

Amber's expression lightened. "Different? No construction paper turkeys decorating the table?"

"We have those, along with name tags in Greek."

Roxanne opened the front door. "I've got to skedaddle." She said her goodbyes and started down the walk. Cassie trailed after her, to leave Amber and Travis alone.

"That girl's seen a world of hurt," Roxanne said, as she slid into the driver's seat. "You did the right thing to bring her here. Let's just hope she can keep whatever it is away from this house. But if I were you? I'd keep my eyes open. Not because she's trouble, but because it might be following her."

She was gone with a wave, leaving Cassie to wonder what Roxanne had seen and how, if it was true, each of them would be affected.

9

AMBER HAD CONSIDERED AND RECONSIDERED WAYS to avoid attending the Costas family Thanksgiving. She couldn't imagine an entire day spent with Cassie and Savannah trying to be civil and interested in what was going on when the distance between all of them showed no signs of narrowing.

Neither could she imagine a day spent with Travis, who thought of her as a human-interest story or a charitable endeavor. Worst of all, she couldn't imagine a day spent at Cassie's grandmother's house.

Lyra Costas was well-known in the restaurant community as a staunch defender of traditional Greek cuisine. She was well-liked but also feared because she had widespread support in the city's Greek community, which was ten percent of the population. Local leaders consulted her on issues ranging from Greektown sidewalks to the best candidates for mayor. When she spoke, people listened.

Unfortunately there was no way to get out of attending this celebration. Dine Eclectic had decided not to open after all,

and when she told Will about the invitation, he had been delighted. They had rarely celebrated Thanksgiving with other
people. Wherever they'd lived, she'd tried to make the holiday special, but she'd never been able to make up to him for
their lack of family. And she had never been willing to explain how lucky he was not to be with them.

As she followed Cassie into the garage, she wished she could
avoid Thanksgiving entirely.

"Yiayia won't like my baklava." Cassie, who was carrying a sheet cake pan, followed by Will, carrying a second,
didn't sound concerned. "I used chocolate-hazelnut spread
along with hazelnuts and pistachios. I made this recipe once
in New York for a party and it was the hit of the night. But
there is not here."

Amber cradled a large casserole dish with traditional sweet
potatoes topped with miniature marshmallows. Despite living in the same house, she and Cassie rarely conversed, and
she had to rake through possibilities to politely continue the
conversation. "Why did you make it that way, then?"

"I'm half-Greek. *It's* half-Greek. I figured that made it perfect." She paused while Amber obligingly managed a polite
laugh. "And the family will like it, even if Yiayia doesn't, especially the younger crowd."

"Half-Greek?" Amber followed Cassie's lead and stowed
their dishes in the trunk before she climbed into the car.

"My mother's ancestors were from somewhere else in Europe. We existed on the outskirts of the Costas clan because
my parents didn't want anything to do with anybody. Roxanne and Yiayia swept me away from home as often as they
could, but I never went to Greek school—"

"Greek school?" Will climbed into the back, and at the same
moment the house door slammed, and Savannah stalked out
and got in beside him.

Cassie turned to tease him. "Will, don't tell me you never went to Greek school, either?"

Savannah, who had been informed that no, she could not stay home alone, made a sound of pure disgust. Despite the havoc she'd wreaked, Amber felt sorry for the girl. She was clearly miserable and trying to drag everyone down as she sank even lower. Amber had been a rebellious teenager, too, and every single day she remembered how it had affected her life.

"I missed Greek school somehow," Will said. "What do they learn?"

"The language, church holy days, Greek culture and religion in general. It's usually a couple of hours twice a week at the church."

"So *you* didn't learn Greek." Will sounded disappointed.

Amber explained, "Will loves languages."

"You've come to the right place, then," Cassie said. "A lot of people in town still speak it at home. You may hear it today. Anybody you ask will be thrilled to teach you a few words."

"Jeez," Savannah said. "Greek's nothing to get excited about."

"I love hearing it spoken. Even if I've only learned a little."

Savannah wasn't finished yet. "If you weren't really part of the family, Cassie, then why are we going today? I don't want to be there!"

Cassie remained calm, but Amber saw her hands tighten around the steering wheel. "I never said I wasn't part of the family, Savannah. I said my parents didn't attend a lot of the family events. If you don't want to be with us and enjoy the party, maybe you can find a quiet spot by the water and sit by yourself all day."

The rest of the drive was blessedly short and silent. Amber paid attention to street names and turns, something she did almost without thinking. By the time they parked at the end of a long driveway with cars extending past nearby houses, she could find her way back to Cassie's on foot if the need arose.

"You can tell which house we're heading for by the bouzouki music." Cassie got out and Amber and Will did, too. Savannah stayed in her seat, but Cassie ignored her. The temperature was soaring toward eighty, so Amber had chosen to wear a sundress and sandals. Cassie popped the trunk and together they removed the food. Then they started toward music that reminded Amber of mandolins.

A memory swept over her. It was both unexpected and sweet, one of the few she was glad to recall. Her "papa," her father's father, had played a mandolin on his wide front porch on summer evenings, and whenever she visited, he would lift his granddaughter to his lap so Amber could pluck the strings. For a moment she could almost smell the honeysuckle climbing up his trellis and feel the brisk mountain breeze.

Then the memory was gone. Because even good memories were too often gateways into places her mind didn't want to go.

"You really didn't have to bring anything," Cassie said as the three of them walked down the street skirting parked cars. "But they'll love you twice as much for bringing food. This family loves to eat. You'll see what I mean in a minute."

Amber was relieved when the conversation ended and they reached the end of the block, which was directly on the water. She followed Cassie up a path to an unpretentious concrete block house with a million-dollar view. The house itself was painted white with robin's-egg-blue trim and a blue tile roof unlike any Amber had ever seen before. Porches and decks flanked every side, and across the road, a row of mangroves stretched down to the water. The landscaping was simple. Palms and live oaks. Colorful shrubs and patchy grass.

"That's Spring Bayou," Cassie said, pointing to the water.

"It's a big deal on Epiphany. You'll see why when the holiday comes around in January. We'll have a ringside seat."

Amber was trying to note everything without being obvious. As soon as they came into view, people streamed over to hug Cassie and meet her guests. Amber shook hands, accepted hugs from people she'd never met, a few whose English was generously accented, and tried hard to respond when people spoke to her.

Worn out immediately, she felt a hand on her elbow and turned to see Travis. "I'll help you put your food on the table."

Amber smiled, naturally this time, and thanked people. Then she let Travis lead her to the back of the house where three long tables, placed end to end, were already sagging with food. Will, still clutching Cassie's baklava, stayed behind to talk to a boy he'd recognized from one of his classes.

Amber set her sweet potatoes in one of the few empty spots. Travis wore a tropical shirt and shorts with deck shoes and no socks. Thanksgiving was clearly not a time to dress up at Yiayia's house. She felt the stiffness in her spine loosen just a little. "How many people are here? Will all this food get eaten?"

"They'll come and go, but probably close to seventy," he said. "Maybe a lot more. And the food will be gobbled."

"The family is that big?"

"You missed the memo? Living next door makes somebody family. Living *with* one of us definitely makes somebody family. It's not just a joke that I don't know how I'm related to most of this bunch. It doesn't matter."

She thought how easy it would be for strangers with ill intent to insinuate themselves into the crowd. She kept her voice light. "How do you weed out the people who have no right to be here?"

"I guess we go on the theory that everybody has the right."

She wondered if anyone had ulterior motives for being

here today. At this point she wasn't feeling paranoid enough to think the motives had anything to do with her. Still she planned to stay alert.

Cassie and Will arrived together and set the baklava on the dessert end of the table. Before they could regroup, a woman probably in her seventies broke away from a group of laughing men and headed their way.

"Yiayia," Cassie warned.

Lyra Costas held her arms wide and enfolded her granddaughter. "You look so pretty today. I see your father in your eyes and your mother in the way you hold yourself and move. Like a dancer."

Cassie winked. "I think I look more like you."

Yiayia was clearly delighted. "And that beautiful daughter of yours?"

Cassie didn't miss a beat. "Savannah is sitting in the car brooding."

"Ah, girls that age. How well I know. And what did you bring today?"

"My special hazelnut chocolate baklava."

"You are so clever. You were always such a good baker. But I taught you baklava. I remember teaching you. How is it you've made something that's not real?"

Cassie laughed. "Yiayia, let me introduce my new friend Amber and her son, Will."

Amber was suddenly and completely folded into the older woman's arms, and then quickly Will was given the same treatment.

"You are taking care of my Cassie? Living with her so she won't be lonely?"

Amber hadn't thought about their arrangement that way. When she allowed herself to think about it at all, she visualized herself being stretched on the rack. But she'd already decided this was not a woman one disagreed with. Lyra Costas was short and comfortably round, with abundant silver hair piled on her head and dark eyes that never stopped darting from one face to another. She had a warm, gracious smile, but Amber was sure that when it drooped to a frown, everybody paid attention.

"Cassie has been incredibly generous with Will and me," Amber said.

"Yes, I know what my great-granddaughter did."

For a moment Amber wasn't sure who she meant, then she realized Lyra was talking about Savannah. She glanced at Travis, who raised one eyebrow, as if to say, "See, I told you."

"Girls that age are faced with so many decisions," Amber said carefully.

"You are kind, kinder than most people would be. I like you and your handsome son." She patted Will's cheek. "I hope you will be happy today and eat some of everything from our table."

"Amber made sweet potato casserole with marshmallows," Cassie said.

Lyra looked startled, but her smile broadened. "I will eat anything with marshmallows. You must have known. You are a woman of great sensitivity and consideration." She hugged each of them again and then waltzed over to another group.

Cassie watched her go. "In case you didn't know? You two were just ushered into the Costas family. Yiayia liked you."

Savannah was hot and hungry, both of which she was trying to ignore. After abandoning Cassie's car she had commandeered one of the many folding chairs set up for Yiayia's guests, dragging it across the street and down a few houses to the edge of the water.

She wished she could find a better place to hide out, since

sitting by the water was Cassie's suggestion, but she had nestled the chair behind some kind of spiky shrub. Unfortunately the shrub offered little respite from the sun, nor was it foolproof as a hiding place. A quartet of little boys had come down to the bayou to throw sticks, and an older couple had strolled over to entice her to go up for dinner. She'd insisted she wasn't hungry, and they'd finally taken the hint.

Cassie hadn't appeared, and neither had Cassie's aunt or grandmother. So much for so-called family.

She was bored out of her mind. Yesterday Cassie had taken her phone after the high school called to report that Savannah was skipping classes, so now she didn't even have texts from her friends in New York to fall back on. She'd skipped out on History a few times, yeah, but only because she hated the teacher's pop quizzes, which required detailed analysis of assigned readings. She might remember history from her "real" education in New York, but this teacher assigned pages from original sources. Of course these were pages Savannah never read and certainly wouldn't remember if she did. The whole class was high-key lame.

The air smelled of roasting meat and the sulfur of rotten eggs from wells dug deep into the sandy soil. As the afternoon had progressed, she'd peeked at a group of men at Yia-yia's who appeared to be roasting turkeys on spits and what she was afraid might be a lamb, as well. Now the spits had been cleared away and the men had moved on, and the last time she'd peeked, everyone was clustered around a long row of tables dishing up massive amounts of food.

In New York Cassie had frequently dragged Savannah and her father to Zorba's, a neighborhood restaurant that had reminded her of home. Savannah liked Greek food, but not at Thanksgiving.

The music was getting louder now, so it seemed like maybe

the meal was over and she could finally go home. She turned to peek through fronds, cringing at what she saw. A long line of people of all sizes and ages were holding hands, arms held high, and moving back and forth, then slowly to the right. From what she could tell, the music was recorded, but one old guy was standing with something that looked like a gourd with strings, playing along.

She started to turn back until she saw a familiar figure coming toward her.

"Will..." The word tasted bad. The worst kind of geek was living in her house, sleeping in what had been her bed. When she moved back into her suite, she would fumigate the mattress.

She had more reasons to dislike him than she had fingers. Among other things he didn't seem to care what people thought. He wore pants that were too short. No guy would dress like that on purpose, but if he noticed, he didn't let on. He was an overachiever, too. He had some kind of after-school job stocking shelves, but he still made top grades. Not that she cared. Not that she'd checked. And, of course, Will was a mama's boy, always doing little stuff for Amber, like fixing her a plate and leaving it in Savannah's refrigerator.

He and his mother were like twins. They had some weird psychic understanding of each other's thoughts. Or maybe they were aliens.

She watched him coming closer, carrying something in front of him, and when he got too close, she turned back to stare at the water. He didn't take the hint. Will came around to stand in front of her and held out a plate overflowing with food.

"If I'd been out here as long as you have, I'd be hungry."

She shrugged. "Too bad I'm not."

He turned and lowered himself to the grass beside her with

athletic grace, not even using his hands. He set the plate on his lap. "I don't think I've ever seen that much food in one place before."

"Go eat more then."

"I couldn't eat another bite. Your mom made this amazing good baklava that—"

"She's not my mom! She's my stepmother. And maybe not even that, since my father's dead now." Savannah wondered if that was true. The idea that she and Cassie might no longer be related legally should have made her happy, but instead she felt oddly uneasy.

"She puts up with you," Will said, staring at the water. "That's what mothers do."

"Like yours puts up with you."

"Mine doesn't have as much to put up with."

She stared at the plate on his lap. The scent of garlic, of onions and oregano, of roasted meat, was tantalizing, and despite herself, her mouth watered. Will had plopped a portion of pastitsio on the plate, a pasta and meat dish topped with something rich and cheesy that she remembered from Zorba's. She'd always ordered it. Whenever they ate there, her father had called her Pastitsio for days afterwards. She wanted to dig her fingers into it and suck off the sauce.

"Wow, it's hot out here in the sun," Will said. "It's cooler up there. You could sit in the shade and eat."

"Why are you trying to be nice to me?" The words were out of her mouth before she'd thought about them.

"I'm not trying. I am nice to you. Even if you don't make it easy."

"You moved me out of my room!"

"Well, we both know why."

She opened her mouth to reply, but this time no words formed. Instead tears threatened to fall.

"I hate everything about my life," she managed at last. "I hate this place. I hate my stepmother. I even hate my real mother because she won't leave Africa to come and get me. And I hate having strangers living in my house. I hate it!"

"Summed up, your life sucks."

She swiped the back of her hand across her eyes. "Don't make fun of me!"

"I'm not. You think your life sucks, so I guess it does. That's how that works. I've been there. You can always find a reason to be unhappy, if you need one."

"Who are you, Dr. Phil?"

"Please. I'm much better at figuring out things than he is." Will lifted an arm in emphasis, nearly upending the plate. "You've been dealt a bad hand. There's no getting around it. And we shouldn't be living in your house. It's awful. Everybody's tiptoeing around trying to be quiet, to be nice." He paused. "With one particular exception."

She wanted to stay angry, but something about the way he said it eased the pain in her heart. "I don't want to be nice."

"And you have succeeded. So can you call that a win and go eat some dinner to celebrate? I could use some more of your...Cassie's baklava if any of it's left. And if it's not, there is so much other stuff. I've had a break. I think I can take on a small plate."

She watched him rise with the same weird athletic grace. He held out the plate. She got to her feet, too. "I still don't like you."

"What's there to like?"

"Cassie just left me here to bake in the sun." Savannah didn't know why she'd said that. Who cared?

"She doesn't know what to do with you. Nobody would."

"My father would have. He always knew." This time the tears spilled over.

Will didn't touch her, and he didn't sympathize. "I've never had a father."

"So?" She scrubbed at her eyes again.

"Tell me about yours. I don't get fathers. You can explain."

Somehow they were walking up toward the others. Savannah grabbed the plate and held it against her waist. "You must have had a father."

"Yeah, it's biologically impossible not to, right? But I guess I just had a sperm. An unidentified sperm. The positive? I've got a great mother."

"But you're poor."

"And humble. Incredibly humble about everything, but never resigned."

"You know everybody thinks you're weird, right?"

Will looked down at her and gave a small smile. "I put on a good show. But somebody else in Cassie's house is every bit as good an actor. People think I'm weird, and they think you're mean. We've probably performed beyond our own expectations."

"Getting weirder," Savannah said, but she felt her tears drying up because a smile was trying hard to peek out of her misery. "Weirder all the time."

10

"IS IT OKAY BEING HERE WITH EVERYBODY TODAY?"
Roxanne, in leggings and a blue silk cheongsam from a trip
she'd made to China, joined Cassie in the kitchen, where the
women had gathered to clean up. Her hair was braided back
from her face and fastened in a bun at her nape, with a silk
flower tucked inside the knot for accent. She looked pretty and
festive, like someone who had spent time choosing her outfit.

These days Cassie ran a comb through her hair when she got
out of bed and shrugged her way into whatever happened to
be clean in her closet. Today she'd followed that pattern again,
grabbing a black knit dress that never wrinkled and pairing it
with a string of pearls and a swipe of lipstick to show she was
in the holiday spirit. Of course, she wasn't.

"I'm doing okay," she told Roxanne. "First Thanksgiving
without Mark."

"What did you usually do?"

"When Savannah was small, we always drove to Connecticut to eat with his parents." She forced a smile. "Then, blessedly, they moved to Seattle."

She remembered how annoyed Mark's parents had been during their Connecticut days whenever Savannah made noise or forgot her manners. At their final Thanksgiving dinner together, Mark's mother had hired a bored teenager to take Savannah to the local playground so the adults could eat in peace. Eight-year-old Savannah's only taste of the holiday was a plate of microwaved leftovers at the kitchen table when she returned. The whole awful day had been a glimpse into Mark's own childhood and the reason he was so devoted to being a good parent himself.

Luckily Seattle had been too far away for holiday weekends, which had saved Cassie from telling the senior Westmores she would not share Thanksgivings with them in the future. From that year on their family had celebrated with staff from Church Street Psychiatric.

Now she was surprised how comforting it was to be with her own family. A few at a time they had sought her out during the afternoon to tell her how sorry they were about Mark's death and share what memories they had. One of Yiayia's contemporaries remembered how Mark's eyes had crossed the first time he slugged down a shot of ouzo. A woman who was only vaguely familiar to Cassie shared that Mark had taken her aside during a visit to ask about her husband, whose depression had been so obvious that he'd wanted to be sure the man had at least spoken to their family doctor.

"I made an appointment the next morning," she said softly, "and they put him right in the hospital. He's much better now, but only because your husband paid attention."

Cassie hadn't realized that Mark had made such an impression, or that people she'd become so distant from would make such an effort to comfort her. She wished she could share some of those good thoughts with Savannah, but the teen had spent the afternoon aiming her iciest stare at the poor fish in Spring Bayou.

Now Roxanne put a hand on Cassie's shoulder. "Do you miss New York?"

"Not as much as I expected. And having the dinner here is great. Everything's running so smoothly."

"I haven't seen any blood. No fistfights, no kids jumping off the roof into Mama's pool. It's probably too much to hope there won't be any before—"

Roxanne's words were interrupted by the scurrying of footsteps and a screech. "What is wrong with those people! My Kouzina is not even among the top five restaurants in Tarpon Springs? My Kouzina needs updated menu and decor? They couldn't send a Greek to write their reviews?"

Cassie turned in time to see Yiayia, who had just come into the room, slam down a copy of the *Sun Sentry*, the daily newspaper for a wide swath of Florida. The kitchen table, worn from countless meals, shuddered.

"Oh, Lord." Roxanne rolled her eyes. "Who showed her that?"

Cassie moved closer to whisper. "Who showed her what?"

"Yesterday's *Sun Sentry*." Roxanne whispered, too. "Their food critic did a review of local restaurants and ranked the top five."

"And the Kouzina isn't among them?"

"In the 'other possibilities' section it says that while the Kouzina once flourished, now it's tired and dated."

"Who's the critic?" She hoped he slept with a gun.

"The name's Dallas Johnson. Nobody knows who he or she is. They sneak around doing reviews and nobody even knows a critic's been there."

"What are you saying over there?" Yiayia demanded.

"I was telling Cassie that nobody knows who this Dallas Johnson is, Mama."

"He's a bad man, that's who he is."

"We don't know it's a man."

"You think a woman could write this trash?" Lyra pounded a fist between her breasts. "Women have hearts and souls. We cook out of love. Of family. Of food. Of home! You think a man understands that? This Dallas person is a man!"

Roxanne held up a hand. "Mama, the restaurants he or she named are good ones. You have to agree they were good choices. This person was probably limited to only five. It would be hard to choose."

"No, it would not! And he did not eat at my restaurant, or he would know that Yiayia's Kouzina is the best in town, in Florida. The things he said about us? He could not have eaten our food or visited our beautiful dining room. Best of everything, I serve. Freshest fish brought to our door, special delivery every day of rich cream from a dairy in Odessa. Your uncle Felix himself brings me tomatoes. From his own garden patch. And his oregano?" She rolled her eyes. "It's so fresh it doesn't know it's been picked!"

"Don't worry, Mama. Opinions are subjective."

Cassie watched the other women in the room. Four—two she recognized as possible relatives—had been chatting happily among themselves when she came in. Now they were pressing against walls and into corners. The one who had been at the sink was drying her hands, as if readying for a quick escape. She hoped they left a clear path for her.

"You are sure you didn't talk to this man? That you didn't tell him what to say? That you are not trying to tell me what you think through this…this back door? This piece of trash?" Yiayia grabbed the paper and shook it in Roxanne's direction.

"The *Sentry* is a good paper, and it's one review. And no,

I have never talked to a person named Dallas Johnson that I know of, and I have never seated a food critic at the Kouzina. Okay? Enough!"

"But you agree with him. You say as much when we are alone, and I try to reason with you. You want to fix dishes no Greek woman has ever made in her kitchen. This is not why people come to my restaurant."

Roxanne was losing patience. "You no longer know what Greek women make in their kitchens, Mama. You haven't been home for at least a decade. So maybe if you took a nice trip there, you would see that there are a hundred wonderful new things to do with lamb and octopus, and women and men all over the country are doing them. You'd see that moussaka can be made in new and interesting ways, and fresh fish? The things we could do with it. Cassie's chocolate baklava would be a hit in Athens, or on Hydra or Santorini, but it wouldn't be new to people there. Because things have changed in Greece, too."

"You think she's right?" Lyra turned to Cassie. "You think my daughter knows more about Greece than her mother, who was born there?"

"I think my name should never have entered the conversation." Cassie stepped forward and wrapped her arms around her grandmother. "You and Rox are fabulous cooks. And both of you know how to run a restaurant. I see no reason why both of you can't have your way. You can make some of this, some of that, and together decide what customers like best. Why not?"

"I want to find this Dallas Johnson. I want to make him eat my food while I sit there watching, and then I want to hear him squeal like a little girl and say how good it is!"

Outside the window the loudspeaker, which had been playing music all afternoon, screeched. Then a man spoke, twice, because the first time there was too much feedback for anyone to understand him.

"Before people begin to leave, we want to have a time to remember our loved ones who have passed on. Will you join our circle?"

Cassie released her grandmother and looked at Rox. "What's this?"

Lyra answered. "It's a thing the Costases do on this day. We are thankful for so much, and thankful for those who were with us but have left. When your father died, we did this. You weren't here?"

"I haven't been home for Thanksgiving since before I was married."

"Then it's past time." Lyra straightened her shoulders, sent a glare in her daughter's direction and stalked out of the kitchen.

Cassie looked at Roxanne. "Do I have to stay?"

Roxanne put her arm around Cassie's shoulders. "One year Mama convinced a priest to sprinkle holy water on anybody who spoke. Unfortunately nobody opened their mouths after the first person got splattered."

"How many people will be remembered?" she asked. "I probably ought to get Savannah and the Blairs back home. It's been a long day."

"If you don't mind upsetting Mama…"

The other women had already abandoned the kitchen, which was looking well on its way to clean. "You know how to turn on the guilt, don't you?"

"Guilt about disappointing Yiayia is a sure thing." Roxanne raised her hand and left for outside.

Cassie debated, but in the end she had no choice. She couldn't wander the grounds looking for Amber and Will and then corral Savannah while Yiayia's family and guests were remembering their loved ones. She started outside, and in the hallway nearly bumped into a man she'd seen at one of the tables but hadn't recognized.

"Whoa, sorry," she said. "I guess I need to watch where I'm going."

He didn't move away. "Cassie Costas. You don't remember me, do you?"

She stared a moment. He was taller than she by at least six inches, broad shouldered and muscular. His hair was cut short and already turning gray, although they were probably close to the same age. He had olive skin and dark eyes that looked as if they'd seen more of life than they should have. The creases around them hadn't been caused by laughter.

"I'm afraid I'm on information overload," she said. "You look familiar and that's as far as I can take it."

"It's been a while. Nicos Andino. We went to high school together."

"Nick." Suddenly she remembered all too well. Nick Andino had been a year ahead of her, popular with everyone, but never full of himself. They had both been in drama club, with roles in *Our Town* during Nick's senior year. She had played Julia Gibbs, the mother of one of the main characters, and Nick had been the milkman. While they'd never shared more than a casual friendship, she'd had a secret crush on him. Unfortunately Nick had never lacked for girlfriends. She hadn't stood a chance.

"I heard you were back," he said. "Are you settling in again?"

"Trying to. Looking for a job and taking care of my daughter. You stayed in town?"

"I came back after college to join the police force. Their dive team convinced me that was the thing to do."

She remembered now that Nick's family had been spongers, too. Diving for sponges was a large part of the history of Tarpon Springs, and Greek divers, considered the best and most knowledgeable in the world, had been brought in as early as the late nineteenth century to help with the harvest. At one time, sponges had been the largest industry in Florida, larger than tourism or citrus. The divers had stayed and raised their families here and sponging was still part of the local economy and culture. In the old days her family and Nick's had probably vied for the same underwater treasure. Of course his presence here was proof nobody held that rivalry against him. It also made sense he spent some of his time underwater. He'd been born to it.

"It's nice to see you after all these years. Tell me, you're not a long-lost cousin?"

"My wife maybe, but your grandmother's not into specifics. Last month I escorted a customer out the door at the Kouzina when he started causing trouble, so now she has me picking up the night's receipts and depositing them."

"She'll be your friend for life."

"That, and I think she was hoping a cop at the dinner today would be a subtle reminder to keep things friendly."

"You can never be too careful, huh?"

"There are a lot of people here. Not to mention a lot of ouzo and beer." He smiled. "It's nice to see you again. Call me if you run into any trouble settling in." He continued down the hall.

Outside the sun was sinking, and the sky, streaked with clouds, was a shimmering wash of bronze and rose. Those who hadn't yet gone home were gathering loosely into a circle, about fifty stalwart souls who'd had a long, happy day together.

She headed toward Roxanne, who was standing cattycornered to Yiayia. Cassie looked up the bayou, where Savannah had fumed alone, but she was no longer there. She wondered if her daughter had walked home, and what she'd done when she got there. Cassie had wanted to go to her a dozen times during the day and carry food. But not only would she have been soundly rejected, catering to her daughter's tantrums was unwise.

"Those who've lost someone always stay. It's a comfort to bring their loved ones back into the family circle," Roxanne said, when Cassie reached her.

"All these people?"

"Some are here to offer support."

Grief felt so individual, so impossible to share. She and Savannah, who had been closest to Mark, hadn't been able to share anything, because Savannah had shut her out completely. Then Valerie had abandoned her. Cassie had felt completely alone.

Across the circle she saw Amber and Will slip into an empty space. She knew so little about Amber. Will's father wasn't in the picture. Maybe Amber needed to honor him, too.

Cassie's grandmother was standing beside Buck, who had entertained them through the afternoon with bouzouki music and Greek folk songs. Today he wore a Greek fisherman's cap with dress slacks, and he and Yiayia made a good-looking couple. He removed the cap and held it over his heart.

When they were all gathered, Yiayia stepped forward. She motioned, and two men came around the circle with plastic glasses and bottles of wine, pouring and nodding as they went.

Like everyone else, Cassie held up her glass for wine. "Just a bit," she whispered. She would only raise her glass in toast and touch it to her lips. As a heartbroken teenager whose parents had lapsed so far into alcoholism they never found their way back, she had made a vow. Inside the house just behind her she had sobbed in her grandmother's arms and told Lyra that she would never take a drink.

The man on the loudspeaker, whom she recognized as

someone she simply called Uncle, held up his glass and took a step forward. "Let's drink a toast to the good health of all who are here today. *Yiamas*."

Cassie repeated the word, and then Uncle began to speak. "My sister Mary, who lived in Detroit but visited me often." He held up his glass. "We are thankful, and we remember." He stepped back into the circle.

Everyone repeated this and raised their glasses to their lips. Then there was silence. Finally someone else stepped forward and spoke, a woman Cassie didn't recognize. "My best friend, Alice, who was like a sister to me." She held up her glass. "We are thankful, and we remember."

Cassie felt a lump growing in her throat when Roxanne stepped forward and lifted her glass. "My husband, Gary, who I will miss every day for the rest of my life." Everyone repeated the now familiar refrain.

Ten steps, ten names and ten sorrows passed around the circle. But the names were said with love and gratitude. Those who had passed on were remembered, the lives they had lived still vital to their loved ones.

The next voice was newly familiar. Nick had been standing to her right, blocked from her sight, and now he moved forward.

"To JoAnn, my wife and friend, who loved this town and would have loved being here with us today. We are thankful, and we remember."

Earlier Cassie had jumped to the conclusion that when Nick had referred to his wife, the woman was still alive. They shared another bond neither of them had acknowledged.

His simple words were the key to unlocking her own grief. For a moment she couldn't breathe. Swallowing her emotions, she looked across the circle to see that Amber and Will had stayed, and just past them she glimpsed Savannah, hanging back, but not far. She looked bewildered and unhappy, but she was there, not hiding down at the water's edge.

Cassie stepped forward, locking eyes with her daughter. "My husband, Mark, who had more love to give as a husband and father than I had ever hoped for." She raised her glass. Everyone spoke with her. "We are thankful, and we remember."

Savannah turned and walked away, but not fast and not far. Cassie knew better than to follow and alienate her further. She wished that she and Savannah could mourn without questioning what had happened on the day of Mark's death or who was to blame. She wasn't sure either of them would recover fully unless they really understood why Mark had died in the storm.

And nobody was going to look for the truth and tell them.

As others finished memorializing their loved ones, the full weight hit her. There was only one person who could determine why remembering Mark today was necessary, only one adult who cared enough to dig through the past for answers.

She could no longer sit back and mourn for her husband. It was time to find out if the man she'd loved for so many years was really the man she'd thought him to be.

11

THE DAY THEY MOVED INTO CASSIE'S HOUSE, AMBER had insisted Will take the suite's bedroom so he could enjoy more privacy. She usually came home from Dine Eclectic well after ten, and hours passed before she unwound enough to sleep. The sofa bed in the sitting room was comfortable, and she could wash up for the night in the powder room off the great room without disturbing her son. The suite was tight quarters for a teenage boy and his mother, but they'd shared tight quarters before.

Now Amber looked up as Will came in from the bedroom. The door between had been open since they returned from Lyra Costas's house hours ago, but Will had been so quiet she thought maybe he'd fallen asleep.

She smiled a welcome. "Quite a day, huh? You seemed to have a good time."

He flopped down in the armchair across the room, stretching his long legs in front of him. "Those people are great. Did you like the…" He paused, and then he grinned. "The *galopúla*."

"Did I what?"

"Did you like the *galopúla*." He pronounced the last word slowly. "And how about that *sáltsa apó fígi*. Although Yiayia—that's what I'm supposed to call Mrs. Costas—said they don't really eat *sáltsa apó fígi* in Greece."

"Don't eat what?"

"Cranberry sauce! And *galopúla* means turkey."

"Wow. Not only did you learn that, you remember it."

"I probably didn't pronounce it right, but I'm going to study Greek when I get to college. If you really want to understand the origins of language, Greek and Latin are important. Maybe Hebrew, too."

She nodded, knowing as she did that Will changed his mind every week about what he wanted to study in college. He never changed his mind about wanting to study, though, and she never changed hers about finding a way to make sure he could. Even when they might be dangerous, like staying in Tarpon Springs until he graduated.

"So Mrs. Costas taught you that?"

"You're supposed to call her Yiayia, too."

Amber tried to imagine. "Every time I looked for you, you were with a different group of people chatting away like you'd known them forever. It's so great to see how easy conversation is for you."

"The Costases?" he said. "They're exactly the kind of family I wish we had. They're nothing like perfect, but they're real, like right down to the bone. They're involved in each other's lives—"

"Maybe too much so."

"They're involved because they care. And they made me feel like I was part of that."

"I'm glad."

"Savannah and I hung out for a while."

The change of subject was so abrupt, she couldn't think of anything to say, but that didn't stop him. "I know she gave you a hard time, but I think maybe hers is harder. She's miserable. She's never learned how to get up after she's been slugged. It's tough to watch."

She tried not to swell with pride at his kindness. "Did you talk about why?"

"Her dad's only been dead a little while. And I think moving here was hard because she had to say goodbye to all the places that connected her to him."

"You could be right."

"Come on, Mom, when you say that, it's the same thing as when people say 'that's interesting,' or 'why didn't I think of that?'"

"Okay, I'm trying not to be judgmental, but I am impressed at your ability to forgive and forget."

"We talked a lot about dads."

She couldn't think of a thing to say that wasn't simply a reflection of his words, and Will had just proved he was too old to let her get away with that anymore.

"I told her I didn't have a father," he said after a while. "Not that I know about, anyway. I asked her to tell me what it's like to have one."

She took a deep breath. "That was a hard conversation, I'm sure."

"I've been thinking about it ever since we got home." He had been looking down, but now he looked up. "I think it's time you told me the truth about mine. When I was a kid, it felt okay not to have a dad. I had friends whose parents were divorced, and some of them just saw their dads for a week or two a year. So not having a father wasn't that weird. Now I realize not even knowing your father's name is plenty weird.

I think I'm old enough to accept and understand the truth. Don't you?"

Amber had dreaded this moment, which had occurred before but with less thought and much less interest.

"Being at the party stirred up a lot, I guess."

"Please don't change the subject."

She formed her words slowly. "Telling you details won't accomplish anything, Will. Your father is dead. You've always known that. And while I understand you want to know more, there's nothing I can tell you."

"And you can't tell me *why*. I've heard this before. It's burned into my brain."

"Your father was a good man, intelligent, kind and sensitive, who would have loved you dearly if he could have helped raise you." She'd always told him that, and she searched for something new to tell him, something that helped him see she was trying to be honest. "Are you worried that maybe he was somebody you would be ashamed of? Because he wasn't. You'd have been proud to be his son."

"Was he married to somebody else?"

She was stunned, but why? Adultery was a reasonable assumption. She was glad she could erase that possibility.

"He wasn't married, and neither was I. And that's all I intend to say, except that not a day passes when you don't remind me of him. And that's a good thing."

"I'd like to know his name. I'd like to know who my family is. Don't I deserve to know?"

She got to her feet, a signal that the conversation had ended. "You deserve everything and anything, Will. I'd give you the moon if I could. What I can't give you is more information. Not tonight. Will you please understand and let this go?"

He looked as if he didn't want to, but after a while he got up, too. "I'm going to bed."

"Sweet dreams."

He closed the bedroom door behind him, leaving her to contemplate their conversation and the inevitable fallout. Will was not going to stop asking about his father, and in the next weeks she had to come up with a story, a perfect story with no holes, that explained everything to him in such a way that he would stop asking once and for all.

A story that in no way was based on the truth.

12

ON THE MONDAY MORNING AFTER THANKSGIVING,
knuckles white and heart pounding, Cassie pulled up in front
of the Boardwalk Grand, a five-star hotel not far from Disney
World in Orlando. The hotel was a conference hub for well-
to-do professionals whose families wanted to visit the parks
while Daddy MD or Mommy Esq., attended workshops and
meetings.

She'd made the decision to drive here on Saturday while
going through the mail. In the pile was a professional journal
Mark had received. After his death she had spent hours notifying all his contacts and canceling subscriptions, but this
one had slipped by.

Cassie had identified Mark's body herself, and there had
been no possibility of a mistake, yet a piece of mail with his
name on it was still a knife in her heart. Every time, for just
an instant, she wondered if the sender knew more than she
did, and her husband was alive after all.

Opening the pages she'd found a cancellation address, and
right below it a half page announcement for a conference be-

THE HOUSE GUESTS · 125

ginning the following week in Orlando. Dr. Fletcher Dor-

ginning the following week in Orlando. Dr. Fletcher Dorman, of Church Street Psychiatric Associates in Tribeca, was listed as one of the speakers.

At the end of the Thanksgiving celebration, she had looked across the memorial circle into her daughter's eyes and known that to heal, both she and Savannah needed nothing so much as the truth. She didn't want Fletcher's advice or even support. Today she wanted information.

The hotel catered to small conferences. The lobby, which was right in the center of things, had soft gray walls, with mulberry and teal upholstered furniture. After watching and waiting an hour with no sign of a familiar face, she gathered book and purse and asked a front desk clerk where she might find information about the conference in progress. The clerk sent her down the hall to a large meeting room. A registration table staffed by two chatting women was stationed not far from the door, and another held pamphlets and themed giveaways. In the corner she found a signboard that detailed the day's schedule.

She noted that Fletcher's workshop—on the ramifications of changes in mental health law—would take place just before the dinner break. The better news was that a luncheon was scheduled in the conservatory in little more than an hour with a guest speaker and "important announcements."

Hoping the announcements were so important every registrant would be there, she checked the map, then crossed the lobby to look for a place where she could unobtrusively watch for the Dormans.

An hour later conference goers streamed into the conservatory, which was partially open to a patio and the lush grounds beyond. The conservatory ceiling was domed, with filtered glass and beneath it, dozens of plants basking in butterscotch-hued sunlight. Cassie had tucked herself into the space beside the elevator that led to an emergency stairway. While she pretended to talk on her phone, she could see most of the people who were going inside.

The crowd thinned to stragglers, and then the hall emptied completely. Someone inside the conservatory closed the doors to the hallway, and she heard the screech of a microphone and a woman's voice welcoming attendees. Either Fletcher was not attending or he had entered from the patio.

She was contemplating what to do next when she heard footsteps. A man hurried down the length of hall from the lobby toward the closed doors. Her heart sped into action mode. She had seen him a thousand times, entertained him at her home and partied at his.

Right before Fletcher reached his destination she stepped into his path. For a moment he seemed confused, like anyone encountering something familiar in an unfamiliar place. She saw when he made the connection, along with shock and, sadly, dismay.

"Cassie." He cleared his throat. "What are you doing here?"

"I came to see you."

His laugh was thin and false. "Most people make appointments."

She cocked her head. "I'm not in the market for meds or counseling, thanks. I'm here as the wife of your best friend. I thought we were friends, too."

"Well, of course. I didn't mean as a patient. I just wish you had called. I would have arranged some time."

She let that hang a moment, then she shrugged. "I think now is as good a time as any."

She watched him consider ways to refuse. Fletcher Dorman held himself as straight as an army drill sergeant, which still only gave him an inch over her five-five. While these days he needed glasses, his blue eyes were still clear, and the skin around them largely unwrinkled. Today the eyes were wary.

"I'm sorry, but I'm supposed to be at that luncheon." He nodded at the door.

"And I'm supposed to be at home looking for a job, Fletch. But here I am instead because this is important. Any chance Valerie is with you?"

"She hates Florida."

She hadn't remembered. "I was hoping to talk to her, too. I was in New York not long ago, but she never returned my calls."

"Val is busy these days. She's taking Spanish three times a week so she can converse with more of the women at the local food bank. She does a lot of volunteer work there."

"Let's stop pretending that ignoring me is normal and acceptable, okay?"

"You sound upset."

She shook her head, to dislodge an angry response and buy a few seconds. "Listen, I was married to a psychiatrist for twelve years, remember? I know the tricks of the trade. Take off your doctor's hat and let's just talk like regular people who used to be friends. Do you want to do that here, where we might be overheard? There's a restaurant off the lobby where we would have more privacy."

He inclined his head toward the conservatory. "I already paid for my lunch. Let's figure out another time to get together."

She took a step closer and tried to keep the mounting anger out of her voice. "Do you think your workshop might be a good time for a conversation? I'll be polite. I'll even wait until you're done speaking. I can tackle what I need to know during your Q and A. Would that be better?"

She probably wouldn't be allowed into the workshop, but

she'd made her point. His shoulders drooped. "You don't have to threaten me. Let's get this finished now."

"Lead the way."

She followed him back through the lobby, and they didn't speak again until they were sitting in a booth in the farthest corner of the restaurant. She ordered iced tea and a chicken salad sandwich. He ordered coffee.

"How is Savannah?" he asked.

"Devastated. Her whole world collapsed. And I don't have any good explanations."

"One of the hardest lessons for an adolescent is discovering that not every problem or question in life has answers."

Cassie took a moment before she spoke. "One of the hardest lessons for an adult is discovering how often people make useless conversation when they want to cover up what they think or feel. You don't want to talk to me because you don't want to talk about Mark. I don't have to be a psychiatrist myself to see that."

"I'm not trying to marginalize you, Cassie. I was just..." He shook his head.

"Wasting time?"

"You seem determined to pretend we're adversaries."

"You're still wasting time. So let me tell you what I want, and more insightful comments about my state of mind are not on the list. I want to know why Mark resigned from Church Street. The real reason. Not the one he gave me—"

"What did he tell you?"

Their server arrived with the iced tea and coffee, and she waited until the woman was gone. "I'd rather start fresh."

"So you can see if our stories match?"

She ignored that. "I also want to know your personal take on why he left, not just the official line. And who else, if anyone, was involved in the decision. I would like to know if

Mark was ousted without a fair financial settlement. Although I'm not sure I'll believe whatever you say about that."

The last request seemed to surprise him. Mark had always said that Fletcher's major professional weakness was his inability to keep his expression neutral. Patients were led to say what he wanted them to, simply by watching him carefully. Now he looked genuinely perplexed.

"The settlement was completely fair. You don't have details?"

"Mark was in charge of our finances. He said something to the effect that the attorneys had come to an agreement, and he was just glad to be out of Church Street. When I asked for details, he told me they were complicated, but I didn't have to worry."

"Do you have records?"

She had records, a ridiculous number of boxes that had arrived along with everything she had moved to Florida. Mark, who had never kept a sock with a hole in it or a shoe that was scuffed, had hoarded paper. She had despaired when the movers asked if she wanted them to pack all the contents of filing cabinets and bookshelves. Without time to go through the papers, to toss out years of receipts, ancient bank statements and sentimental birthday cards, she'd had to bring it all along.

"I have records," she said. "But it's going to take a long time to sort through them."

"Then I'll send you what I can about his settlement from Church Street. Once I get back."

"I would appreciate that."

Her sandwich arrived, and wordlessly she offered him half, but he shook his head. She took a few bites to give him time to consider the other items on her list.

It didn't take long. "I'm not sure where to go with this, Cassie. Mark was a fine psychiatrist, a great member of the team, and all of us were surprised when he resigned and didn't give a good reason."

"You were surprised?"

He hesitated a second too long. "Yes."

"You weren't."

"Somewhere in between yes and no, then."

"Why?"

"You really want to hear all this? It won't bring him back."

"I'm not here for a resurrection."

He spoke hesitantly, as if he was feeling his way from word to word. "In Mark's last year at Church Street, he seemed to be burning the candle at both ends. He was stressed. He had a few confrontations with colleagues, which was not like him. Suddenly he had no patience with discussions, and apparently no time for them, because he ignored other people's opinions and did whatever he felt was best. Even when it wasn't."

Fletcher's story felt too close to home. Mark had been stressed at home, too. "Was there somebody in particular he clashed with?"

"When we brought Mark on board, he was the youngest psychiatrist on staff. He came in with a lot of new ideas and opinions, and people well along in their careers weren't always happy to hear them. The same thing happened when we brought Tom Wallings into the practice."

Tom Wallings was the latest doctor to come on board, the one Mark claimed he'd tried to help. Cassie liked the young man, although he could be brash, even hotheaded.

"So Tom was the problem?"

"Mark was the problem. He had no time for Tom, not for anybody, as a matter of fact. But Tom came in with lots of ideas and energy, and that irritated Mark."

"And you think that's why he bailed?"

"I think Tom's unrestrained enthusiasm was an addition to

Mark's stress but not the root. If Tom had come in a year before, I think Mark would have enjoyed him, mentored him, even mediated. Instead Tom constantly irritated him, and he overreacted."

Cassie was aware there was more Fletcher didn't want to say, that he was parsing his own sentences, making sure he didn't lead her in a direction he didn't want to go.

"What was his official reason for leaving?" she asked. "What did he say?"

"His written resignation expressed gratitude for all we had accomplished together, and then he said he felt he was growing in new directions as a doctor. He wanted a different platform to explore them."

"Did he talk to you about those different platforms?"

"Not really, no. He left it up in the air."

Cassie sat back and lightly slapped the table. "I want the real story, Fletch. Not a sanitized version. Why didn't you talk? You had always been so close."

"There's nothing else concrete I can tell you."

"Then tell me what everybody was thinking. Not what you could prove in court, okay? You're supposed to be masters of insight. What did all those psychiatric heads come up with when you put them together?"

His shoulders sagged, as they had in the hallway. He really was easy to read. This time he spoke as if he was no longer forming every sentence ahead of time. "Things deteriorated faster than I've indicated. And when the whole staff got together without Mark to discuss the problem, collectively we thought something was going on in his personal life, maybe at home, that was causing him stress. Because his short temper, his impatience, were so uncharacteristic."

"Nothing new was going on at home." She paused. "Except that Savannah and I were seeing the same things you saw at the office."

"And that's what he said when we met to discuss our concerns. That everything at home was fine."

"*We* met? You and Mark?"

"No, by 'we' I meant all the doctors. Nobody wanted to be the one to go out on a limb alone, because quite frankly, nobody was sure how he would react."

She tried a deep breath and discovered her chest would not allow it. Her heart was taking far too much room, beating too fast and squeezing painfully. "And he didn't tell you anything more?"

"We tried to go deeper, and that's when he resigned. Not after some well-thought-out planning, but during that conversation. He resigned effective immediately and claimed that if his own partners didn't trust him, what was the point of being in the practice?"

Mark had worked long and hard to become a psychiatrist and join the others at prestigious Church Street, yet he had been willing to throw it over without an in-depth discussion. She didn't know what to say.

"In a way it was something of a relief when he decided to go," Fletcher said. "I hate saying that, but the air immediately felt lighter and easier to breathe. We're always on guard with our patients. We didn't like being on guard with each other. Not to that extent."

"Who is *we*? You mentioned staff, not just the other doctors. What did you hear from them?" She named the people she meant. The staff social worker. The occupational therapist who was their usual referral. The two physician's assistants and office managers. "And what about the nurses?"

She stopped, because she was thinking of others. The small behavioral unit at Riverbend Community, the hospital where

Cassie had met Mark, was often filled with patients sent there by Church Street. The hospital staff's insights might be valuable.

"Ivy Todsen from the behavioral health unit worked hand in hand with Mark," she said. "Sometimes she even called him in the evenings to update him on patients they were worried about. And how about Zoey Charles? He liked working with her because he said she always went the extra mile. What do they say? Or any of the others?"

"I don't know what staff at the hospital were thinking, Cassie. We didn't take a poll of everybody he knew." Fletcher sounded annoyed.

She lifted a brow. "You didn't talk to the staff members who might have the most information?"

"I didn't say that. I just don't remember how much if anything Ivy or any other hospital personnel had to say. It was a difficult time." He looked at his watch. "I've missed the meal, but I can still hear the luncheon speaker. Are we good now?"

She held up her hand when he started to get to his feet. "Was all of this so traumatic, Fletch, that you couldn't face me after Mark died? I'm having problems understanding why everybody connected to Church Street, including your wife, distanced themselves so thoroughly. That just doesn't add up."

"I'm sorry you felt abandoned. We sent flowers, cards. We were there for the memorial service."

"And so were the people who cleaned our condo." She knew better than to belabor the personal. She might never know why Fletcher and the others had backed away, and in the long run what did it matter?

She had put so much of herself, so much energy and love into relationships that had been severed with little thought or concern. She contrasted that with her family, who she had often given little thought to, but who had welcomed and comforted her since her return. In the future she would need to be more careful.

Fletcher stood. "Please tell Savannah that Valerie and I are thinking of her. And take care of yourself, Cassie. We hope you'll find peace here."

She watched him walk briskly away. She wondered if he was really going back to the conservatory, or off to the bar for a double shot of a top-shelf Scotch. Fletcher had told her some of the truth, but she was no fool. He had not told her everything.

Today was only the beginning of her search for answers.

13

WHEN SAVANNAH EMERGED FROM HER ROOM ON
Monday morning, Will was already in the kitchen finishing
a bowl of cereal. Over breakfast in Manhattan she'd always
sprawled in the chair across from her father, who read her interesting tidbits from the *Times*. In his final months he'd often
been too busy or preoccupied to talk, but most of the time
he'd still sat at the table. Now facing breakfast without him
made her stomach hurt.

She had dreamed about her father last night. It hadn't been
one of her worst nightmares. She hadn't been thrown out of
their sailboat to drown, or swimming toward him as he went
underwater for the final time. This morning they'd been on
land, no place she recognized, and he'd been trying to explain something in a language she didn't speak. He'd waved
his hands, and finally he'd pointed in the direction she'd come
from. She had tried to tell him she couldn't understand, but
he'd continued speaking anyway.

Cassie seemed to know Savannah no longer wanted a sit-
down breakfast. Most mornings she put out something Savan-

nah and Will could eat on the way to school, like a homemade muffin or peanut butter toast. This morning Savannah found a plate of her favorite oatmeal cookies, spiked with lots of almond butter and dried fruit, sitting on the counter.

Will took his bowl to the sink, then grabbed two cookies, taking a big bite of the first before he spoke. "I love the stuff your mom makes for us in the morning."

"She is my stepmother, not my mom, and baking gives her something to do besides hassle me."

"You don't like her much, do you?"

"She dragged me here. What part of that am I supposed to like?"

"I like living here."

"You've never lived anywhere better."

Her insults never seemed to faze him. "One person's better is another person's worse. And my mom's waiting outside."

Last night Cassie had explained she'd be gone today by the time Savannah woke up, and Amber had agreed to do school transportation. Cassie hadn't said where she planned to go, nor had Savannah asked. She hoped the final destination was so far away her stepmother wouldn't be home again for days.

She took two cookies and followed him out the front door, wincing at a blast of cool air. She tugged the hoodie over her head as Amber pulled her car out of the garage. She stepped out and greeted Savannah with an apology.

"I'm sorry. You both have to sit in the back today. I didn't realize the passenger window in front was cracked open when I washed the car yesterday. The seat's damp."

Savannah wanted to find a reason not to like Amber, but so far, despite what Savannah had done to ruin her life, she didn't seem to hold her actions against her. Amber treated her with warmth mixed with an appropriate level of caution.

Will climbed in beside Savannah and struggled to curl his

long legs into a comfortable position. He smelled like soap and laundry detergent, and she could see he'd shaved this morning, although most of the time he didn't bother since there wasn't much need.

"Do you two have tests today? Anything special?" Amber asked from the front.

"Who knows," Savannah muttered.

Will took up the conversational slack and chatted with his mom. They were almost at school before Savannah realized that the bracelet she was wearing under the hoodie had snagged on something. She carefully rolled up her sleeve until the bracelet was exposed. The clasp was caught on a thread. She noticed Will was watching.

She unfastened it and picked at the thread until it was free. "What are you looking at?"

"That's just a pretty bracelet."

She clasped it in place again and turned away. She rarely wore the bracelet. She had a good idea how much it had cost, and she saved it for special occasions. But that morning, on impulse, she had opened her jewelry box and pawed through rings and chains until she found the drawstring pouch of robin's-egg blue with a Tiffany logo. The bracelet was a gold chain with one simple stylized heart. Her father had given it to her on her fifteenth birthday and told her she would live in his heart forever.

Maybe she still did. Maybe that's what he'd been trying to tell her in the dream. Maybe somehow Mark would see that they were still connected. Maybe he would come to her again when she slept, and this time she would understand.

Two hours after Amber dropped them off at school, Savannah was struggling to bluff her way through another stupid chemistry quiz. She reached under the hoodie's sleeve to finger the bracelet for good luck, then farther up her wrist. Finally she rolled up her sleeve and shook her arm. But even after she slid her hand all the way up to her shoulder, the bracelet didn't materialize.

After class she carefully slipped off the hoodie while she was still at her desk and turned it inside out. She looked under the desk and then, more frantically, in her book bag, in the pockets of her jeans, even inside her high-top sneakers. But the bracelet was gone.

Out in the hall she saw Helia and Minh coming toward her from the other direction. Minh stopped. "You okay? You don't look too good."

"I lost something, that's all."

Helia chewed the inside of her cheek, then she shrugged. "I guess we could help you look since it's lunchtime."

"You should go to the office and tell them," Minh said. "If somebody turns it in, they'll know who it belongs to."

Helia punched Minh's shoulder. "That's always your answer, isn't it? Tell an authority figure and everything will be okay."

"If we'd told the police about that money we found, the way I wanted to, maybe things would have turned out better. None of us would have gotten in trouble with our families."

"Stop it!" Savannah took a deep breath and fought back tears. "I'll look myself. I don't need your help!"

Helia stared at her, but instead of leaving or yelling back, she shrugged again. "Okay, it's gotta be a big thing. What are we looking for?"

Minh put an arm around Savannah's shoulder. "And where do you think it might be?"

"I don't have a freaking clue." Savannah described the bracelet without adding it was from Tiffany's. "My father gave it to me." She remembered Helia pointing out that she'd never had a father, and Savannah should get over herself. But this time Helia looked like she was thinking things through.

"So how'd you get to school?" she asked after a moment. "Then where did you go and what did you do from there?"

"And on our way to all those places, we will stop by the office," Minh said.

Helia rolled her eyes. "Like good little girls."

Savannah hoped three sets of eyes would be better than one. "Thank you."

"I figure I'm open to one good deed a year, and the year's almost up," Helia said.

At the end of her Geometry class Savannah stared out the window as rain whipped across the glass and skies grew darker. She had one more class after this one, and afterward she intended to spend another hour scouring the school for her bracelet. The office had taken the information and promised they would let Savannah know if anybody turned in a bracelet. Helia had come up with several places to look that Savannah hadn't even considered. But even three sets of eyes hadn't turned up the bracelet. Somebody had probably found it and planned to keep it. That sounded disturbingly familiar.

When the bell rang, she gathered her books and stood to leave, but her teacher, a woman about Cassie's age, beckoned Savannah to stop by her desk on the way out.

She winced at a thunderclap before she spoke. "Savannah, there's no reason you shouldn't be making As in this class. You seem to understand everything we cover, but you're about to fail because you aren't turning in your homework. What's up with that?"

Savannah turned up her hands, as if she had no idea what the answer was. "I just forget to do it."

"I'll be calling your mother to discuss the necessity of doing homework."

Savannah nodded as if she agreed. "You can try, but I doubt she plans to do homework, either. I think she already passed Geometry."

She scooted out the door and wondered what it would feel like to fail a class. Maybe somebody in the office, the principal or a guidance counselor, would decide she should become a hairstylist or a cook, although both of those things probably required classes, too. Maybe somebody in charge would help her plan a life cleaning houses or picking up trash in the streets.

Maybe she'd find her bracelet while she was dumping cans into a garbage truck.

She looked up and saw that Will was waiting for her just a few doors away. She rarely saw him during a school day, but now he grinned when he saw her. She almost turned in the other direction, but she was blocked by a group taking up most of the hallway behind her.

"What do you want?" she demanded.

"My mom texted to say she can't pick us up."

"Oh, goody."

"She has an emergency meeting at the restaurant, and she wouldn't be able to get here until close to five."

"Did I ask why?" Savannah cocked her head. "I don't think so."

"She said we should walk home together."

The house was at least a couple of miles away, maybe farther. Savannah couldn't believe this. "Walk? In this weather? You're kidding, right?"

"The rain's supposed to stop about four. We can wait until then and do our homework in the meantime."

Even though she'd planned to spend time after school looking for the bracelet, she glared at him. "I'll find another way."

Will looked uncomfortable. "Mom kind of promised Cassie she'd make sure you got home safely."

"You don't mean *safely*. You mean without getting into trouble, right? Like I'm in jail because I made one mistake, which I've paid for and paid for!"

"Hey, this isn't my fault."

"Don't look for me after school. You won't find me." She started past him, but he grabbed her arm.

"That's not the only reason I'm here."

She shook off his hand. "No? What else?"

"I found something of yours." Will reached in the pocket of his jeans. He held out her bracelet.

Savannah snatched it from his hand. She knew what must have happened. When she'd slipped the bracelet back on in the car that morning, she hadn't clasped it correctly, and it had dropped on the seat between them. Will had seen and taken it without telling her. Maybe he'd planned to pawn it. Maybe he'd figured out that it was real gold and worth some money. Or maybe he'd just wanted to get even with her for what she'd done to him and his mother.

She stared at the bracelet and then at him. "You had it all day?"

"I didn't have a chance to return it until now," he said. "I found it—"

She didn't let him finish. "You had it all this time! What did you plan to do with it, Will? Why didn't you find me right away unless you were trying to figure out how to make this work for you?"

He stared at her, then he shook his head, but his eyes were blazing with anger. "You really are a brat, a spoiled brat who thinks everything that happens in the world is about you. Just because you steal things from other people doesn't mean everybody else will, too. Walk yourself home today and every day. And the next time I find something that belongs to you, I'll leave it right where I find it." He turned and pushed his way through the group in the hallway.

She watched him go, so upset she was riveted to the spot. One of the girls in the group, a popular one who never paid any attention to Savannah, came over to stand beside her. She was ridiculously pretty, a brunette with the kind of figure boys always followed with their eyes.

"I'm Madeline," she said. "Madeline Ritter. They call me Mad. And right now I'm not the only Mad in the hallway, right?"

Savannah blew out a long breath. "I'm Savannah Westmore."

"Yeah, you're new to Winds, right? From somewhere up north?"

"New York. Manhattan."

"I live a couple of streets over from you. I've been meaning to introduce myself. We should get together sometime. There aren't too many Coastals in Sunset Vista."

"Not a lot of sunsets or vistas, either." Savannah realized that maybe Madeline was a fan of their stupid housing development, and she'd just ruined any possibility of a friendship.

But Madeline laughed. "Lots of old people, though. Did I see you talking to Will Blair?"

Savannah knew she had to be honest. "Will and his mother are staying with us for a while. My stepmother invited them. He's the most annoying boy that ever lived."

"A dweebster for sure."

"He just told me I'm supposed to walk home with him after school. Not much chance of that."

"You don't have a ride?"

"My ride bailed."

Madeline assessed her. "Meet me out front after school. You can ride with me."

Savannah couldn't believe her luck. "That would be great."

"Gotta protect you from the weirdos. I saw him digging around by the front steps at lunch. Maybe he was looking for worms?" Madeline raised a hand and started back the other way.

But Savannah hardly noticed. She was picturing the moment she and Will had gotten out of Amber's car that morning. When she got to the bottom of the steps she decided not to wear her hoodie inside. Few others were bundled up against the cold. In fact some of the kids hurrying to class were wearing shorts and tank tops that were barely long enough to pass the dress code. Embarrassed, she slipped the hoodie over her head and folded it against her, only later giving in and putting it back on when the temperature dropped even more.

She hadn't noticed the bracelet was gone until Chemistry. Had she lost it in the car, the way she'd imagined the scene when she accused Will? Or had the bracelet slipped off when she pulled the hoodie over her head before classes began? Had Will seen it at lunchtime, after the bracelet had been trampled into the ground by other kids hurrying to homeroom that morning? Had he seen something glinting in the dirt, unearthed it and realized who it belonged to?

Not worms at all. Something treasured and valuable. Something he had returned at the first opportunity. She had an awful feeling that when she asked him, that was the story he was going to tell her. If he ever spoke to her again.

Apologies were not her thing. For most of her life she'd only rarely needed to make them. She'd tried not to hurt people, and when she screwed up, people had quickly forgiven her.

Who had she become? This morning in a dream had her father warned her that she was heading in the wrong direction? Did she need his warning?

Didn't she already know it was true?

14

AFTER MARRYING MARK, CASSIE HAD GIVEN UP HER job at Riverbend Community, where they'd met. Bonding with her adorable new stepdaughter felt more important than coordinating events or writing news articles presenting the hospital in a favorable light. The gift shop, her most important project, was finally running well, and she was ready for more intimate challenges.

Savannah had needed a hands-on mother, and Cassie had been ready for a daughter. She and Mark had expected to add new little Westmores to the family, but that had never happened. Savannah's status as an only child had made her that much more precious. But twelve years of raising her hadn't done a thing for Cassie's résumé.

"I've included all my volunteer positions," Cassie said, as she handed a job application to the librarian behind the counter at the Tarpon Springs Library. The young woman had promised she'd file it in case any marketing jobs for libraries became available in the county.

The librarian's gaze flicked over the top page. "Look as far afield as you can. And be open to starting positions."

Cassie tried to imagine a long drive to work for a job that probably paid little more than minimum wage. She was still the slowest driver on the road, and she needed health benefits, a decent salary and daytime hours so she could keep an eye on her daughter after school.

And if she found a job, it wouldn't leave her the time she needed to pursue the mystery surrounding her dead husband.

She thanked the young woman and prepared to leave when she saw a familiar face. Amber, in a flowered shirt and rust-colored capris, was sitting under the etched glass panels above one of the library's computers.

Since Cassie's return from Orlando two days ago, they'd only seen each other in passing, and Amber had seemed preoccupied. Cassie's own life was already too complicated, and the last thing she wanted was to be more involved in the Blairs' troubles. But how possible was it to share a house and not be some part of each other's lives?

Amber looked up from the screen and saw her. She looked back down, and after a moment the screen went blank. She stood and Cassie met her in the middle between them.

"You didn't have to stop what you were doing," Cassie said softly. "I don't want to disturb you."

"I was about to leave and get some lunch."

"I just dropped off an application, in case jobs come up through the library. I haven't had lunch, either. Would you like to join me?" She noticed Amber's hesitation and could guess the reason. "I'm going to the Kouzina for a gyro so it's my treat. Yiayia always gives me the family discount, whether I want one or not. I can drive and I'll drop you back here to pick up your car."

Amber smiled without enthusiasm. "That would be nice."

In the car Cassie wondered if Amber had agreed because she felt obligated to the woman who was essentially her landlady. She tried to turn the tables. "This is my thank-you for taking Savannah to school Monday. And for supervising."

"I guess she didn't tell you."

Cassie imagined a catastrophe. "She doesn't tell me much. What happened?"

"I only took her in the morning. She found her own ride home. I had an emergency meeting at work, and she didn't want to wait or walk home with Will. But she was home when I got back, or I'd have gone looking for her."

They parked in the Kouzina's lot and Cassie turned off the engine. "*Emergency* doesn't sound good."

They had rounded the corner to enter through the front door when Amber elaborated. "The restaurant's closing. We never recovered after the bad publicity. People were afraid to eat there, even after the owner did everything to make sure it was the healthiest restaurant in town. By the time diners started filtering back in, it was too late."

"I'm so sorry."

"Yeah, me, too. And now it's going to be longer before I can move out of your house. I hate to do that to you."

As they neared the corner, music wafted through the Kouzina's open doorway. The building was two-story with a derelict apartment taking up the top floor, but between the poor condition, and the noise and smells from downstairs, the apartment wasn't easy to rent. It was vacant now and had been for months. Yiayia refused to spend the needed money for renovations.

Today half a dozen tables on a covered porch were empty, because they wouldn't be completely out of the sun until later in the day. Upbeat Greek music played from the speakers. As they went inside, she was comforted by the familiar shabby mural of a Santorini hillside covering one long wall and the goddess statues flanking the doorway. Tables were covered with blue vinyl cloths topped with white paper and an arrangement of plastic daisies in the center of each, paired with a bottle of olive oil.

They were greeted and seated by a pretty young woman with a long dark braid who gave them both a warm smile. "I'm Dorian's older sister, Maria Sostratos, a Costas a couple of generations back," she said, when it was clear Cassie hadn't placed her. "But don't hold that against me."

Before hightailing it back to college in Tallahassee, Dorian had apologized profusely for taking Savannah's word that all was well on the night of the party. "Savannah was at her worst that weekend," Cassie said, not looking at Amber.

"I'm filling in for Nani today. Her baby came early. A little girl."

Cassie remembered a pregnant young woman at the Thanksgiving celebration, someone else she should probably know. "I hope they're okay."

"Great, but she's going to be super busy for a while." She seated Amber and Cassie with no problem, since the restaurant was only half-full, went to fetch ice water and menus, and promised to send a server before she headed back up to the hostess stand.

"Are you related to everybody in town?" Amber asked.

"It's kind of amazing, isn't it? When I lived in New York, I was completely invisible. Of course being Yiayia's only granddaughter makes me more visible because she's so well-known."

"The only granddaughter?"

"Yiayia had two children, my father only had one child, me, and my aunt Roxanne has one son. Most of the family comes from my grandfather's side. Yiayia was born on Kalymnos but Pappou was one of fifteen children from a local sponge diving family. A lot of her extended family still live in Greece, but they visit when they can, and send children and grandchildren to stay. Which is why it's so confusing."

"I can't imagine."

They waited until another unfamiliar woman came to take their orders. Amber asked for the chicken souvlaki and Cassie the gyro. Both women ordered iced tea and waited for their server to leave before Cassie cocked her head in question. "Do you know what you're going to do now that Dine Eclectic is closing?"

"I've already started applying to other restaurants." Amber hesitated, as if deciding how much to share. "It's sad, because I came here especially for that job. I was the assistant general manager, with a promise I'd be made the general manager in a year. It was a step up careerwise from floor manager and server. After the meeting Monday the owner offered me a job at one of his other restaurants, but the closest is West Palm Beach. I want Will to stay here. He's doing so well at Coastal Winds, and his best shot at a college scholarship is to stay until he graduates."

"Like you needed this."

Amber waved that away. "I just hit the bottom of the employment barrel again, but at least I know how to land."

"So we're both on a job search."

"Good servers are always in demand here, although maybe not at the really popular restaurants. What about you?"

Cassie explained her job history. "The thing is..." She took her first sip of the iced tea their server had dropped off. "Working full-time, if I can find a job, and then trying to ride herd on Savannah won't be easy. You have Will, so you know, although I hesitate to equate the two. But truthfully Savannah used to be a lot like Will. She did well in school. She was happy at home. She wasn't perfect, but we could talk, and she would see my side of things even when she didn't agree. Now we never get that far." She paused. "She used to call me Mom. I miss that. Gen, her birth mom, has never really been in her life for more than a week or two a year. I was the go-to mom, the one who took care of her and held her hand when she was sad or angry. These days she's angry a lot, mostly at me."

"It has to be hard for her. I take it she and her father were close?"

Cassie wasn't sure how the conversation had turned to her problems, and she wasn't sure who was at fault. "They were. Mark's death is obviously the worst thing for Savannah. But the problems started a while ago. I won't bore you—"

"Please do. Misery loves company." Amber waited as their server delivered their sandwiches, then she leaned forward. "Maybe it will help me understand Savannah better. She's clearly having a bad time. Will says…" She stopped.

"What?"

"Well, not a lot since Monday, actually. He's avoiding her, like she developed smallpox. Something happened, which may be why he walked home without her. But whatever it is, he's not talking."

Cassie mulled that over. "What did he say before that?"

"What you probably already know. That she's not doing homework, and she's in danger of failing a couple of classes."

"She told him that?"

"I doubt that, but people know they live in the same house. Maybe other kids or a teacher?"

This wasn't news, it was just more corroboration for what Cassie already knew. "I'm getting regular phone calls from teachers and Miss Simmons at the school. She's the assistant principal for tenth grade. I took away Savannah's cell phone after she skipped a few classes. I make her sit at the dining room table at night to do homework, but the guidance counselor, her teachers? They don't see it. It's like she wants to fail, like she wants to prove something, only I don't know what."

They were interrupted by clapping and a "there you are!"

Cassie got to her feet just in time to fall into Yiayia's arms for a hug. "You were going to eat lunch and not see me?"

"Of course I was going to see you."

Yiayia released her and bent to hug Amber, who looked surprised but pleased. "And your pretty roommate is with you?" She addressed Amber. "I looked up your name after our Thanksgiving. In ancient Greece the word for amber was *elektron* and some people think it came from the Phoenicians. So your name means beautiful light, like electricity. Perfect for you."

Cassie suspected something had been lost in translation, but she loved the smile that Yiayia's explanation brought to Amber's face. "Our lunch looks delicious, Yiayia."

"Many more people will be coming. We will fill up soon."

"Is lunch a busy time for you?"

Yiayia drew herself up. "Busy enough."

Obviously the restaurant was not busy, and no one was streaming in, even though it was closer to one than twelve. "You make the best gyros. Everybody knows."

"And no one makes salads like we do. I will send out our best horiatiki. And Greek fries. Nobody makes those the way we do, either." She bustled back toward the kitchen, and Cassie took her seat again.

"Actually everybody makes them exactly the way the Kouzina makes them," she said, leaning across the table. "Which is why only half the restaurant is full today. People come in if they're family or loyal customers. Or if they're visitors who get hungry as they walk by. But there's nothing to draw them in, is there?"

Amber looked sympathetic. "You started to say something about problems before your husband died?"

"This can't be interesting."

"Relevant, though, and honestly? Somewhat familiar. Not because of Will, but because I was a rebellious teenager, too. I knew what was right for everybody, even when it wasn't."

Cassie gazed at the other woman. Amber had the dewy, rose-tinted skin of a woman in her twenties, but Cassie knew she had to be older. She wore little makeup, but even the minimum effort succeeded because she was naturally lovely. She'd clearly had a difficult life, but it didn't show.

"You must have been very young when you had Will," she said without thinking. When Amber didn't pick up on that, Cassie backtracked to her own history. "Savannah was a student at a private girl's academy in Manhattan from the time she started school until the last year we lived there."

She debated how much to say but decided on a condensed version. "The year before Mark died, things were tense at home. He was injured in a sailing accident, and it took time to recover, so I thought that was probably why his mood spiraled downward. Mark hated illness. It seemed like a personal affront. Anyway the problems continued after he was back on his feet. Something was going on with him, and I think Savannah felt the tension. She started acting out, and for the first time she seemed to be having trouble at school. Then one day Mark and I were called in to see the headmistress. Savannah had been expelled for fighting and injuring another student. The school had a no tolerance policy for physical fights. The headmistress had no choice."

"What a setback."

"It was awful. That was midyear, so she finished at a public school. Then her father died in July. You can imagine how that affected her. Two huge losses, back to back."

A large salad arrived, made with cucumbers, tomatoes, red onions, olives and a square of feta on top. Cassie often made horiatiki at home. The fries were sprinkled with feta and Greek seasoning.

Amber took one from the plate between them and bit into it, and Cassie followed suit. "Do you know why she was fighting?"

"Savannah claims she was protecting another student, a younger girl named Liza, who was being bullied. She said one of the really popular girls, a star student and former friend named Gillie, kept shoving Liza and ridiculing her, and Savannah got sick of nobody doing anything about it. Gillie's parents were big donors to the building fund, and Savannah claims that teachers looked the other way and let Gillie get away with things nobody else would have been allowed to."

"Could that be true?"

Cassie didn't know. A part of her still wanted to believe her daughter, despite all evidence to the contrary. "Mark said it wasn't at all likely, that I just wanted Savannah's version of events to be true, so I weighed the facts to point that way. He said the term for what I was doing was 'motivated reasoning,' and it didn't help Savannah to deny the truth."

"He was a psychiatrist, right?"

Cassie smiled a little. "Can you tell? And one with little patience by that point. Savannah said that when Gillie started in on Liza that day, she grabbed her and pushed her away from Liza, and unfortunately Gillie fell against a stone wall. Her head snapped back, and she was knocked unconscious."

"Badly hurt?"

Cassie really didn't know. "There's some dispute. Mark talked to the doctor who examined her. Apparently there was no bump, no bruising, no signs of a concussion. Gillie may have pretended she was hurt to get Savannah into more trouble, but it didn't really matter. Savannah told her side of the story, and not one of the girls who witnessed the fight, including Liza, agreed that's how it had happened. Everyone said Savannah pushed Gillie because they were arguing about plans for a school dance. Four girls to one. Out Savannah went."

"Earlier you said she *claims*, not claimed. She's sticking to her story?"

Cassie spooned extra tzatziki sauce on her gyro and then added fries for good measure. She was impressed with how carefully Amber listened. Roxanne was the only one who had listened to her like this since Mark's death, and she was warmed by the attention.

"I doubt she's willing to admit she was at fault, even now. Besides it's too late to make a difference."

"Did you stick up for her? Did her father?"

"What kind of parents make excuses and let a child get away with something like that?"

"I can see that."

"Anyway, from the time she left Pfeiffer Grant until now, Savannah's made sure no one has a reason to question that she injured another girl. She's making a career out of injuring people, you among them."

Amber shook her head, which surprised Cassie. "Cassie, I don't see that. I've never had the feeling that Savannah took the zipper pouch to injure me or anybody else. I'm no expert, but I think if she'd known how to return it, she probably would have. She was with friends, and I think they egged each other on to throw that party, like girls do at that age. Like the girls probably did the day Savannah pushed Gillie."

"That's very nice of you."

"I think she's paying a big price."

"Maybe what she's going through will help." Cassie looked up from her sandwich, which was already half gone. "And for what it's worth? I don't think having you and Will living with us is a big price, even though it felt awkward at first. Don't worry about moving out right away. This arrangement could work for both of us when we find jobs. We can watch out for each other and each other's kids. We'll probably be in and out at different times. It was a relief on Monday to know you'd be doing school transportation."

"Even if it didn't quite work out the way it should have," Amber said.

"Savannah got home safely, and you came home to keep your eye on things. Maybe two sets of eyes watching them will keep things on a more even keel."

"We can hope."

The conversation felt finished, and they ate the rest of their lunch, dividing the salad, and talking about nothing important until they were done, and Cassie dropped Amber back at the library.

As she watched Amber heading to the parking lot, she made a decision. Instead of going home, she circled back to the Kouzina and parked in the spot she'd just vacated. This time she entered the restaurant through the back door.

She wasn't surprised to find her grandmother in the kitchen. Yiayia was sitting at the table, resting her face in her hands, and she looked exhausted. Everyone else was busy, but Cassie noticed that Buck was watching her with concern between preparing orders.

A moment passed before Yiayia even realized Cassie was taking a chair across from her. She sat up straighter. "You enjoyed your lunch? Your friend did, too?"

"It was delicious. Thank you for adding the salad and fries. We ate every bite."

"You can see I still know how to run a restaurant? Your

food came quickly? You were seated quickly? The food was hot when it was supposed to be and cold when it was not?"

Cassie knew a little truth was called for. "You will always know how to run a restaurant. No one can change that, but I know how to braid a little girl's hair. That doesn't mean I have to find a little girl to practice it on every day. Now I have more time for other things. You would, too, if you'd be a little easier on yourself and let others do more of the work."

"What would I do instead? This is what I know."

"Go home to Greece? Read a book, listen to music, knit a little. You used to love to knit. Remember the doll clothes you made me? When was the last time you made something?" Cassie gave a sly nod toward Buck, who was pretending not to listen. "Find a friend to enjoy your time with."

"I am happy just as I am."

Cassie didn't want to risk alienating Yiayia. "Maria told me about Nani and the baby."

"We haven't had time to find a replacement."

"Maria said she was only filling in today."

"Maria's sister-in-law might want the job until Nani comes back, although she is clumsy and lazy. Maria says she is looking for a job where she can sit all day. But this is to help family, right?"

Yiayia always hired family when she could. She never opened jobs to the general public, never advertised. Everything was done by word of mouth in family circles.

"I have someone better." She squeezed Yiayia's hand again before she dropped it. "Someone who is experienced and smart." She paused. "Amber."

"Your friend Amber?"

Cassie nodded. "Dine Eclectic is closing. Did you know? Apparently they're not doing enough business to stay open."

Yiayia put her hand over her heart. "A failure?" Cassie could almost read her mind. Her grandmother wanted to know exactly what failure meant. Because, despite everything she'd said, the Kouzina was in trouble.

"Everyone who works at my restaurant is Greek. You've never noticed?"

Cassie laughed, then she cast the line with the hook that would reel in her grandmother. "I do know she's had a hard time, and this is just another blow. Didn't the Greeks coin the word *philanthropy*? Isn't this a good thing for her? Besides, you liked her the moment you met her." She waited a moment for emphasis before she spoke again. "And she has a son to feed."

"You have been taking lessons in manipulation from Roxanne."

"They're good lessons, but you have to pay attention while I practice."

"I will give it some thought."

Cassie stood and bent over the table to kiss her grandmother's cheek. "You'll call to let me know?"

Yiayia waved her away. But the wave was for show. Both women knew what the answer would be. Cassie just wished her own job situation could be so easily fixed.

15

SAVANNAH HAD BEEN WRONG TO ASSUME WILL HAD taken her bracelet. And she'd figured out the truth quickly, hadn't she? But two weeks later he was still avoiding her.

Part of the problem was that Will didn't like Madeline, who she was hanging out with more and more. The day of the missing bracelet the heavens had opened just as Madeline pulled away from the high school curb. Two blocks away they'd passed Will, who was walking home without even a rain jacket, and Madeline had tooted her horn and zipped right by, making a point to splash him.

Savannah hadn't exactly apologized for the suspicions or the splashing, but ever since she had made a point of being more polite to him. If he'd seen the difference, he hadn't responded. She doubted they had exchanged more than a dozen words since.

Not that she had any reason to care.

Today, before the last class of the day, Savannah noted the admiring looks of other girls as she and Madeline walked to the far end of the hallway. "I can't believe you have to live with Will Blair," Madeline said.

"I hardly see him."

"We're in a couple of AP classes together. He's always asking questions. Of course he just does it because he wants teachers to think he's something."

The old Savannah had asked questions, too, but never because she wanted to impress teachers. She had a feeling Will asked, as she had, because he was interested.

"I guess Will makes good grades," she said. "He sure studies enough."

"Yeah, he's probably trying to get somebody else to pay his college expenses. The way poor kids always do."

Madeline's opinions about the world and its problems were miles from Savannah's own. Madeline didn't like a lot of people, but wasn't that her right? So far she had taken potshots at Helia and a few at Minh. The way she looked and acted, Helia might as well have a target drawn on her back, but Minh was pretty and nice to everyone, so it was harder to understand. Savannah was afraid that Madeline might not like Minh because she'd been born in Vietnam.

They reached Savannah's World History classroom, and Madeline stopped, too. "Look, you don't like Miss Simmons, do you?"

"What's there to like?"

"She's giving Lolly trouble."

Lolly was Madeline's best friend, a bra-busting, dimpled blonde, whose father owned car dealerships and had promised his daughter her pick from his lots when she turned sixteen.

Savannah could see where Lolly might get in trouble with Miss Simmons. The assistant principal had a perpetual squint, as if she was trying to read what was going on inside every student's head. Lolly was sassy and sure of her status at the school—especially with guys—and she knew how to make anybody feel lower than pond scum, even adults. She'd probably worked that magic on Simmons.

"Simmons gives me trouble, too," Savannah said. "She and my stepmother are on a first-name basis."

"You know Mr. Jordan's her husband, right?" Madeline nodded toward the History classroom Savannah was about to enter.

"I don't know which of them I dislike more."

"Really? Well, I have an idea about that. Meet me at my house after school." Madeline headed for her own classroom.

For once Savannah had studied the assigned material and found it oddly absorbing. She wasn't surprised when Mr. Jordan announced a quiz. She decided she might as well show him she could do the work, so she answered every question in detail. He gathered the papers and looked them over as one of the other students read a report he'd finished on a war that didn't interest Savannah at all.

After class Mr. Jordan crooked his finger in her direction. He waited until the other students were gone before he looked up again. "Did you copy these answers from somebody or something?"

She stared at him. "Like who or what?"

"Another student? Your phone?"

"Did anybody else have exactly the same answers?"

He didn't respond. He just continued to stare at her.

She narrowed her eyes. "Did you see me take out my phone? Because, you know, I don't have it with me, so that would be tough. Besides, how would I get the answers if I didn't know what you'd be testing us on or even that you would be?"

"This isn't like any other quiz you've turned in."

"It won't be like any other quiz I turn in for the rest of the year, either." Furious, she flounced out of the room.

Helia was leaning against a locker in the hall. "Wow, I heard you all the way out here."

"I hope they heard me in the office! Mr. Jordan just accused me of cheating."

She started down the corridor, and Helia joined her. "He said that?"

Savannah was too upset to dissect the nuances. "He as much as said it."

"Maybe you just surprised him. I had him last year for another class. He's not so bad."

Savannah thought about Madeline. "I'm not going to let him get away with it."

"You gonna go running to Mommy and make her stand up for you?"

Savannah faced Helia. "No, I'm going to get even with him and that storm trooper he married. With the help of a friend. A real friend."

Helia didn't look upset at the cut, but she did look troubled. "Look, Savannah, I'm the last person to butt in. I have enough problems, you know? But if you're talking about Madeline Ritter, I'd be careful. She and her squad really like to mess with people and get them in trouble. Okay?"

"She doesn't say anything good about you, either."

"We went head-to-head in Jordan's class last year, and I roasted her. Nothing she says matters to me because she's total bad news, but she's done a couple of things since then. I almost got kicked out of school for one of them."

Savannah tried to reconcile Helia's story with what she knew about both girls. Madeline was from a wealthy family, pretty, popular and smart. She was Savannah's entrée into a new circle of friends.

Then there was Helia, who was generally snubbed or ridiculed by everybody. Helia was mostly in advanced placement classes, despite her difficult home life, but she could be snatched out of Coastal Winds at any moment and sent God knows where by an unfeeling foster care system. And where would that leave Savannah?

The choice wasn't hard. "I can manage my own life," Savannah said. "Mad's been great to me."

Helia didn't look impressed. "Watch your back." She turned and started down an intersecting corridor, and after a stop at her locker Savannah headed to the front of the school, where she was supposed to meet her stepmother.

Will was already waiting when she joined him on the steps. Cassie hadn't arrived, and Savannah was in no mood to talk to him.

He glanced at her, then at his watch. If they wore watches, the guys at Winds wore smart watches, and sometimes stainless steel sport watches with fancy chronographs and subdials. Will's watch, like everything else about him, was unassuming and plain, and knowing Amber, it had probably come from a garage sale.

"Would you tell your mother I had to head for work?" he asked.

"Stepmother!"

He shook his head. "That's all you got out of what I just said? I need to go into work early, but I didn't want to leave Cassie waiting. Now that you're here, can you tell her?"

She lifted one shoulder, like she was too bored to treat him to a full shrug.

He started down the steps, then he turned. "Your new friend said to remind you to come to her house."

She was surprised Madeline had even spoken to him. "I didn't forget."

He chewed his bottom lip a moment. "You two are planning something big?"

"Nothing you need to worry about."

At that, he did look worried. "She likes to play people one against the other."

"Yeah, you would know because the two of you are so close."

"Madeline Ritter isn't someone I would be close to."

She twirled a finger in the air. "Because she would never let you near her. Is she too much competition?"

"I don't want to be good at the things Madeline Ritter is good at." He started back down the steps. This time he kept going.

Five minutes later Cassie pulled up, and Savannah got in beside her and buckled her seat belt. Today Cassie was in jeans and a red camp shirt. Her hair was combed but had needed a trim for weeks, and her nails had been cut short but not filed into any discernible shape. Cassie was nice to look at when she tried, which she didn't anymore. For a moment Savannah felt sympathy, because when they had lived in New York, Cassie had always gotten regular haircuts and manicures, and she had worn attractive clothing that looked good on her.

Then she remembered the fight she had walked in on the day her dad died. Sympathy vanished.

She issued the Will report in one long breath. "Will's walking to work. He has to be there early."

Cassie pulled into the street and asked the usual questions about her day, although Savannah usually answered with a grunt. Unfortunately today she needed her stepmother in a good mood so Cassie would allow her to go to Madeline's house.

She stared out the side window to hide her distaste. "School was okay. I think I did well on a History quiz."

"Did Will help you study?"

She glared at Cassie. "Are you kidding? I don't need Will to be my tutor."

"Sorry. I know History is one of his favorite subjects."

"I studied—" She caught herself before she could say "by myself," because she had a better idea. "With Madeline. You know the girl who lives a few streets over? She had Mr. Jordan last year, so she knows what kinds of things he wants us to learn from the material he assigns. She was a big help."

"That's great. It's nice to have a friend nearby."

"She offered to study with me again this afternoon, if that's okay. I'll be home before dinner."

"That's fine with me. And since I didn't get any bad reports from school this week, how about if I give you back your phone? I don't like you going places without it, in case you need to call in an emergency."

Savannah wondered if her stepmother had any idea how unlikely it was that she'd call her for any reason. But she said thank you, like good Savannah would have in New York.

At home she dumped her books in her room except for a history text and a notebook, which looked like enough to pass inspection. Cassie was in the kitchen baking. Savannah remembered when she used to come home and their Manhattan condo had smelled like chocolate or cinnamon. Most afternoons she would sit to report what had happened at school, a cookie in one hand, a glass of milk or mug of tea in the other.

"Would you like to take some of these to your friend's house?" Cassie waved at the counter, where her special Greek butter cookies were cooling on a rack. She made them for Christmas every year. Savannah remembered they were called kourabiedes, because as a little girl she'd liked to say the word, and the cookies had been one of her father's favorites. In those days when she'd helped Cassie bake, Savannah had been in charge of adding a thumbprint before they went into the oven and then coating them with powdered sugar when they emerged.

Nostalgia warred with anger. "I don't think so."

Cassie looked up, her expression sad. "I wasn't sure whether to bother this year, but they're part of our tradition. It's getting so close to Christmas already, and we haven't done anything to mark the holiday."

"I just want to forget about it."

"I don't think your father would want us to."

"How does anybody know what Daddy would want? He's dead!"

Cassie took a deep breath. "I know, Savannah. I wish none of this had happened. I wish we could go back three or four years and start up a different path. But now we have to figure out the best way to walk the one we're on."

"Well, don't include me on your Christmas path, okay?" Savannah started out of the kitchen, grabbing her phone as she left.

Outside she stowed her book and notebook under the bushes by the driveway and walked to Madeline's house empty-handed. The day was warm, and she wondered what the weather was like in New York. She thought about texting a friend to find out, but she might sound pathetic. She planned to move back to Manhattan as soon as she was legally allowed to, but she wondered who would be left? The girls she'd been closest to would be at universities somewhere else, and at the rate her grades were plummeting, she'd be lucky to make it into a community college herself.

Madeline lived in the part of Sunset Vista where larger houses were set farther apart. Madeline's car, a snappy blue-green MINI convertible with black trim, was parked in the circular driveway in front, and her new friend didn't take long to answer the door.

"Lolly's already here. We're ready to go." Madeline winked. "I'll tell you where in the car."

"I have to be home before dinner."

Lolly appeared from somewhere behind Madeline, and they both came out, slamming the door behind them.

"We have to get an ice chest from the back," Madeline said. "Let's go."

Savannah wondered if they were off on a picnic, and the ice chest held beer. She knew better than to ask. Madeline obviously liked suspense. Lolly, who didn't greet her, was still in her school clothes, a barely legal top cut in a sharp vee that plunged just to the top of her ample breasts and skin-tight shorts. Savannah wondered how she'd managed to sit through classes.

The ice chest was only half-visible under shrubbery beside a small potting shed. Madeline grabbed a handle on the side and pulled. Once it was out, she motioned for Lolly and Savannah to carry it to the car. She was putting the top down when they arrived.

"Put the chest in the back seat. Savannah, I hope you don't mind keeping it beside you. It'll be a little cramped."

Savannah climbed in beside the chest, and Madeline clicked her seat back into place before she got into the driver's seat.

"Better you than me," Lolly said, speaking for the first time. Then she giggled. The sound was somewhere between the bray of a donkey and the screech of a siren. Savannah hoped she wouldn't be treated to Lolly's belly laugh anytime soon, because she could only imagine the horror.

"Let's go." Madeline waited just long enough to be sure Lolly was sitting and then screeched out of the driveway. Savannah grabbed her hair with one hand and her seat belt with the other.

"We have to do this quick," Madeline said. "Everybody listening?"

"Aye aye, Captain." Lolly gave a mock salute followed by another ear-shattering giggle.

"Jordan and Simmons are in a faculty meeting until at least four o'clock, probably later. So we have until then. My uncle owns a seafood distributing business, and I know where he dumps all his waste until it's picked up. We're going to fill up the ice chest, then take it to their house. Savannah, you'll go around back with a trash bag of fish heads and guts. There's a hand shovel on the floor under my seat. See if you can bury what's in your bag in their flower beds or better, flowerpots, if they have them. That way they'll smell the fish in a day or two, but they won't be able to figure out where the stench is coming from. At least not for a while. Lolly and I will hide the rest of it around the front porch. Agreed?"

Savannah took a moment to put this together, but unfortunately she'd heard Madeline right. She struggled for something to say. "Like, isn't that a bit extreme?"

"It's dead fish, not a nuclear bomb. But they'll sure know they've been pranked."

Lolly didn't seem surprised. "You afraid to get your hands dirty?"

Savannah wondered if Madeline had shared the plan with her earlier. "Dirty, no. Smelly? Yuck!"

Madeline made a right turn so quickly Savannah fell against the ice chest. "If you think it's yucky," Madeline said, "imagine what they'll think."

Savannah was still trying to form what to say when they slowed in front of a warehouse near the Sponge Docks. Madeline screeched into a driveway that skirted the building, ending in an asphalt parking lot, and turned off the engine.

"There are plastic bags in the ice chest," she said. "You can use them like gloves. Scoop up whatever you can. Lolly and I will fill the ice chest, and, Savannah, you fill one of the two black trash bags, because you're the one who will be carrying it. Take out the other trash bag and put it at your feet before you put the filled bag on top of it. I don't want anything leaking in the car. Grab anything that looks disgusting enough to make somebody sick."

Savannah was feeling a little sick herself. Nothing anybody had done to her deserved this kind of payback. The assistant principal was probably required to report bad behavior, and maybe Mr. Jordan had cause to wonder why she was suddenly doing A quality work. This whole thing felt like some kind of initiation rite.

"You with us or what?" Madeline stepped out of the car without waiting for an answer.

"Yeah, but it's sick."

"Absolutely. So get with it." Madeline pulled back the seat, and Savannah climbed out. The next few minutes were hideous. Savannah loved seafood, but she wondered if that was about to change. They couldn't reach anything in the small dumpster behind the building without climbing inside, but there was a heavy lidded can filled with waste beside it. Madeline said it was emptied into the dumpster at night.

"There's another on the side near the front door. Lolly and I will fill the ice chest from that one. Get busy."

Savannah tried not to gag as she removed the top of the can and scooped up fish waste and threw it into her bag. Even if the other two girls had been right there, nobody would have talked, because that required breathing.

In a few minutes the chest and bag were back in the car and closed tight, but despite having double bags around her hands as she'd scooped, Savannah could still smell the disgusting odor of fish guts all over her.

"I have wipes up here, but let's wait until we're done at the house. Then we can clean up and finish at my house. You can take a shower if you need to. Agreed?"

Savannah felt too sick to talk. She wasn't sure which was worse, the smell or the sense that she was sinking to a new level of depravity. She wondered what her father would think.

Madeline knew exactly where she was going, and they arrived in less than ten minutes. The neighborhood was old, with pickups in driveways and dogs barking inside fences. They parked under a canopy of oak trees at the end of the block. The hedges between houses were tall, but the houses themselves were tiny. Luckily the lot across the street was vacant, which meant no one was there to watch them.

"Okay, everybody out," Madeline said, nodding to the house in front of them. "We don't want neighbors to get interested in what we're doing."

The chest was on the ground in moments. Madeline and Lolly each took a handle and hauled it toward the front porch, which was only a step above the sidewalk. They were flanked by trees, and Savannah was hopeful nobody would see them.

"Savannah, grab your bag and go around back."

The other girls were already rooting around in the chest. Savannah grabbed the bag and hauled it around back, hoping it didn't split open before she got there, because by now she was sure she wasn't going to spread the contents. She was going to find a way or a place to get rid of the fish waste without opening it.

Salvation, when it came, was in plain view beside the rear steps. A garbage can sat there waiting for her to dump her bag inside—tied tightly to disguise at least some of the smell—and head back around front.

She did exactly that, shoving down the lid until the can

looked as if it had been welded shut. Then she counted slowly to five hundred before she circled to the front of the house.

The next moments ran together in her mind, like a television screen showing multiple programs at once. Slowly she registered that Madeline's car was no longer in front of the house. In its place another car had just pulled in. Helia and Will jumped out of that one, a beat-up Ford with a dented passenger door. With visible alarm they surveyed the front yard, which Savannah hadn't had time to do. Now she saw what they were gaping at and registered the fish waste scattered in plain view. Fish heads. Fishtails. Bones, slime. The mess was dribbled over the yard in a disgusting display.

"Get inside," Helia said, pointing at the car. Savannah realized the driver was Helia's brother, who had been granted the right to spend time with his sister once again by her foster parents.

"Where's Madeline?" Savannah was bewildered. "Where's Lolly? How did you find me?"

Will grabbed her arm. "You have to get out of here. Now."

But Savannah was beginning to understand what had happened. Madeline and Lolly hadn't brought her here to prank high school faculty. They'd done it to prank *her*. They'd seen how happy, how grateful she was to be Madeline's new friend, and they'd probably thought that was hilarious.

She didn't pull away from Will. "They left me, didn't they?" They'd probably left her the moment they'd dumped the contents of the ice chest on the lawn. They were counting on Savannah getting caught. There probably wasn't even a faculty meeting today.

A red sedan pulled into the driveway and her stomach sank as Miss Simmons got out and came to stand beside the three students. Helia's brother remained behind the steering wheel of his car but didn't drive off.

"What's the meaning of this?" She slapped her hands on her hips as Mr. Jordan came around to stand beside her.

"You were that angry?" he said to Savannah. "You needed to get even this badly?"

Savannah had been living on borrowed time at Coastal Winds, and it was nobody's fault but hers. She had been expelled in New York for something she hadn't done. Now she was about to be ousted in Florida for something she had. Revenge was not sweet; it was sickening. Nobody deserved this mess.

"It wasn't Savannah," Will said, stepping forward. "She told me how upset she was at…at the way she was being treated. So I did this because…" This time he fumbled too long, trying to think of a good excuse. "Because I was trying to help her," he finished.

Savannah turned to stare at him. Will narrowed his eyes as if to say shut up and let me take the blame.

He obviously thought he had a much better chance of surviving this fiasco than she did. But Savannah had never allowed anyone else to take the blame for her mistakes. It was time to reclaim that virtue, as insignificant as it seemed at the moment.

She held up her hand. "Will and Helia just arrived. Somehow they figured out I was about to get into big trouble, and they were just trying to stop me."

She wondered how Will and Helia had known or suspected, but now was not the time to ask. "None of this was actually my idea, but I went along with it. I realized how stupid and mean the whole thing was, but I went along."

"It's certainly both," Miss Simmons said. "And you're not out of trouble. Misconduct off the school grounds aimed at a faculty member can still be punished."

Savannah nodded.

172 · EMILIE RICHARDS

"What was the point?"

"There was no point. It was pointless." She looked up. "I'm sorry. And I mean that. I think I've been sorry since the minute I learned what was supposed to go down."

"Who talked you into this?"

Savannah closed her eyes. "I can't say. I'm sorry, but they'll just deny it anyway. It doesn't matter who had the idea. This is on me."

"It matters," Miss Simmons said, but she didn't pursue it.

"I'll clean this up with my bare hands, and then you can do whatever you want. There's more fish waste behind the house in your trash can. I couldn't make myself spread it, like I was supposed to. But you'll want to get it out of there as fast as possible."

Miss Simmons turned to Will. "You shouldn't have tried to lie for her."

He didn't answer. She turned to Helia. "And what are you doing here?"

Helia shrugged. "It was something to do."

Mr. Jordan stepped closer. "Helia, you might fool everybody else in the world, but you don't fool me. Take yourself out of this. You and Will go and wait by the car."

Will hesitated, but Savannah touched his arm. "Go. And Will? I'm so sorry. For everything."

She waited until they'd both headed toward the street. "Please don't punish them. They were trying to help me. I don't know why—"

"Frankly neither do I," said Mr. Jordan. "Because you make helping you just about impossible. You've built a wall around yourself that's a mile high. And those two climbed over it anyway, at their own risk." He left to talk to Will and Helia.

"I hate being me," she said. "You have no idea how much I hate it!" And despite herself, she began to cry.

"We know you've had a tough time this year," Miss Simmons said, her voice gentler. "Things aren't easy for you right now."

Savannah wiped her eyes. "It's no excuse. I get that."

"I hope you see what real friendship looks like. I think I know who talked you into this. The girls you were apparently trying to be friends with are users. They've been in trouble before. They hurt people for fun. You aren't the first."

Savannah remained silent.

"I'll call your stepmother and talk to her. She needs to be involved."

Savannah felt no pleasure. She would be yet another problem for Cassie to handle. And what good did that do either of them? More problems wouldn't bring back her father. Fresh tears sprang to her eyes.

"I'll get you something from the house to clean this up," Miss Simmons said. "Then I want you to go straight home. Will you do that?"

Savannah wiped her eyes again. "Yes, thank you."

Surprisingly, after his wife went into the house, Mr. Jordan came over and touched her shoulder. Just the lightest touch to get her attention. "Was the quiz the thing that pushed you into this?"

"My whole life is the thing."

"I'm sorry I questioned you this afternoon. But after the way you've behaved in class and your other test scores…"

"I get it. It's just… It's hard to study, you know? It never used to be, but things are so different here." She sniffed hard, because she was tired of crying.

"Let Miss Simmons figure out what to do with you. But when she's done, I want you to see me after school a couple of times a week to catch up. You could be one of my best students if you'd try."

Savannah couldn't imagine that, but she nodded. "Can I ask Helia if she'll wait while I clean up?"

When he nodded, she went to face her friends, the ones who had come through for her. The two loners whose lives had been difficult for years and had still showed up anyway.

16

THIS YEAR CASSIE COULDN'T ABIDE CHRISTMAS
carols on the radio. While she'd grown up with Florida Christmases, getting reaccustomed to palm trees with colored lights
and Santas in bathing suits and sunglasses was harder than
she'd expected. Getting used to Christmas without her husband was hardest of all.

The Westmore family had always celebrated the holidays in
Manhattan with tourist-like enthusiasm. Over the years they
had ice-skated in Central Park with snowflakes falling gently
around them. They had watched the lighting of the Christmas
tree at Rockefeller Center, seen the Empire State Building
dressed in red and green lights on the skyline and the Rock-
ettes' Christmas show at Radio City Music Hall. At home
they'd decorated a Fraser fir with ornaments she and Savannah made themselves, adding to the collection each year with
new ones that grew more elaborate as Savannah grew older.

She wasn't sure the ornaments had made it to Tarpon
Springs during the move. The garage was still lined with
boxes, and when the one marked Christmas hadn't leaped

into her arms with a glad cry of reunion, she'd given up. Still, could they just ignore it?

On Tuesday, after she delivered Will and Savannah to school, she sat at the kitchen table with Amber, drinking cups of freshly brewed coffee. They had already covered Amber's week of training at the Kouzina. As approachable and competent as she was, she'd make good money in tips once she had all her hours. Especially with the tourist season taking off.

Their morning coffee ritual had begun tentatively with plenty of opportunity to pull back. But a couple of mornings a week had increased to more. Whichever of them wasn't doing car pool made a fresh pot to enjoy together when the driver returned. Although Cassie had never expected it, she and Amber had become more than each other's captive audience, a bonus so new that she still didn't know what to make of it. She just knew she looked forward to this chance to chat, as much as she could look forward to anything. Amber seemed to enjoy it, too.

Now the conversation drifted to Christmas.

Cassie was still trying to imagine how to celebrate with a sullen teenager who wanted to be anywhere except with her. She said as much.

"Savannah went to school without a problem this morning?" Amber asked.

"She did." Cassie hoped Savannah had finally discovered that if she didn't shape up, every day of her immediate future was going to be a nightmare she created herself.

Amber helped herself to one of the kourabiedes that Savannah still refused to enjoy—as if a taste would be disloyal to her father. She licked the powdered sugar off her lips before she spoke. "Will thinks she's really sorry for the things she did. He believes her."

Cassie had learned most of the story of Savannah's "prank"

in bits and pieces, as well as the way poor Will had gotten involved. A girl named Helia, whom Cassie had yet to meet, had seen Will walking to his job and stopped to tell him Savannah was about to make a big mistake. Apparently they had accurately guessed where to find her, because Savannah had said something about getting even with the principal and her husband.

"Will has such a good heart," Cassie said. "Miss Simmons told me he tried to take the blame, but Savannah said no, it was her fault. And considering that when she got back home she smelled like something that had washed up on the beach, I guess it wasn't hard to figure out."

"What happened to the other girls who were there?"

This was the only part of the story that Cassie could repeat with enthusiasm. "Savannah refused to name them, but their identities were solved by the glories of technology. Miss Simmons and her husband have a doorbell with a camera. The other two girls were caught on it, and the school's dealing with them now."

"Do you think seeing the guidance counselor will help?"

Cassie and Savannah had spent an hour with the guidance counselor and the assistant principal working out the consequences of her behavior. After all the bad reports, the school was still willing to discuss and plan strategy together.

In the end Miss Simmons had pronounced her verdict. Savannah would spend an hour after school every day for two weeks, beginning when winter vacation ended. Some of that time she'd spend with the guidance counselor. The rest she'd receive tutoring from the teachers whose classes she had routinely blown off.

To her daughter's credit, Savannah had accepted the decision without complaint. Maybe she really was trying to put everything behind her, and if her relationship with Will was evidence, maybe it was working. Last night they had sat together in the den, chatting as they watched television. She'd heard them talking as if they actually had things they needed to say.

Maybe it was a Christmas miracle.

Cassie took a cookie, too, and not her first. "I wanted her to see a counselor after Mark died, but try telling a psychiatrist's daughter she needs therapy. She has a lot she needs to talk about. And she certainly isn't talking to me."

"Would you send Savannah to California if you could?"

Sometimes Cassie wondered, too. "Savannah's never been with her mother on Christmas. Gen gets her for part of the summer. Savannah flies to California over Easter or spring break. But that's it."

Amber didn't reply, and Cassie knew what she was thinking. "Yeah, I know. Savannah's father is dead, but Savannah's still living with me, a woman who has no legal claim to her. If it came to some kind of ridiculous custody battle, I'd lose. Mostly because Savannah would be given her choice. In the meantime it's not an issue because Gen is out of the country."

"So Savannah doesn't want to celebrate Christmas," Amber said. "What shall we do about that?"

Cassie pulled herself out of her own problems and focused on Amber. "What do you and Will usually do for the holidays?" She watched Amber sort through her answers. Cassie was used to how much Amber hid about her past.

She finally turned up her hands like she was making an admission of guilt. "I usually wait until Christmas Eve, hit the dingiest lot and find the worst tree. Then I bargain the salesperson down to whatever I have left in my pocket."

All the elaborate, expensive Christmases the Westmores had celebrated in Manhattan flashed through Cassie's mind. During her marriage she had lived in a dreamworld. "Then what?"

"We made decorations ahead of time. We moved too often to take things with us, so every Christmas we tried something new. One year we covered the lids of tin cans with felt and pasted magazine photos on them. Another we turned Popsicle sticks and straws into gold and silver stars. That was probably our prettiest tree." She looked up. "Will and I used to spend the whole year leading up to Christmas coming up with ideas. It became a game to see how little money we could spend."

Cassie thought of all the expensive craft supplies and kits that she and Savannah had purchased. "Savannah and I made decorations every year, too. Only I can't find them."

"Are you going to have a tree?"

Cassie wanted Amber to be a part of the decision. "Are *we* going to have a tree? Do you want one? Does Will?"

"Will makes a point of not asking for things."

"Then guess for him." When she saw the answer in Amber's eyes, she nodded. "What's on your calendar today?"

"Since the Kouzina's closed tonight, I was going to take care of odds and ends. I've about run out of fabric for my zipper pouches, so I want to go to the thrift store to see if I can find more."

Cassie finished her coffee and stood. "I need to find curtains for my bedroom. Would you like company? Maybe we can find a Christmas tree to bring home."

Amber looked both surprised and pleased. "The thrift store may have decorations and lights. They may even have trees."

"This will be the first time I've actually had enough room to store a Christmas tree. Wouldn't that be perfect?"

Amber rose, too. "Don't expect perfect if the tree comes from Things From the Springs. It's somebody's reject."

"But good enough. That's what we're shooting for." Cassie felt a small sliver of Christmas spirit chipping its way through the ice around her heart. Maybe that's all she'd get, but that, too, was good enough for now.

They didn't come home with curtains but they did come home with a six-foot artificial blue spruce from Things From the Springs, marked down because the box was missing and two branches were damaged. Since it was easy to set the tree against a wall, Cassie had grabbed it. They also took a chance on strings of lights, which she tested in an outlet by the door. The lights had twinkled, and the store manager, wearing a Christmas sweater complete with Rudolph's blinking nose, had applauded.

At the next store Amber bought yards of white satin ribbon on clearance to make bows with long streamers, and at another, Cassie found red satin balls the size of grapefruit, along with glass icicles.

"Let's wait until Will gets back from school to get the tree out of the car," Amber said, once they were inside with all their packages. "We might damage it even more if we don't have help."

Cassie left to change. Shopping with Amber had been more fun than she'd anticipated, and Things From the Springs had been a revelation. While she had found beautiful curtains, they had been the wrong size. However now that she knew about the little store, she could check back frequently until the right sizes appeared.

She'd had to restrain herself from reorganizing the whole place, aisle by aisle, which badly needed it. She had been reminded of the hospital gift shop and the fun of changing it into an attractive, financially stable enterprise. Imagining how to remodel Things From the Springs had been the most fun she'd had in months.

There had been one odd moment, though. A man came

into the store and stood at the front, arms folded, as if he were searching the aisles. Amber had moved to the side, just far enough, Cassie thought, that she wouldn't be seen behind a rack.

Cassie had lowered her voice. "Problem?"

Amber didn't answer.

"Is the man who just came in somebody you know?"

Amber looked at her, then back toward the front. The man was now laughing with the manager. He was tall and broad shouldered, like someone who might be formidable in a fight. His head shone under the fluorescent lights, and then, when he leaned against the front counter, Cassie saw he was wearing a priest's collar.

Amber relaxed. "No, I don't know him."

"But he looks like somebody?"

"Just a guy I went out with on a date and would rather avoid. The most boring date of my life."

Cassie didn't quite believe Amber was telling the truth. Her friend's reaction pointed out something she had noticed more and more. Amber was good company. She knew how to listen, and she always had something good to add, but whenever she was out in public, she was constantly scanning the landscape, looking closely at people coming toward them. In comparison Cassie, who had considerable street smarts, was as trusting as a lamb. She wondered if she needed to be more observant or if Amber needed to relax.

Her cell phone rang as she zipped a pair of well-worn jeans. She dropped to the bed without snapping them and checked the number. The area code was Manhattan.

"Cassie?" The woman's voice at the other end wasn't familiar. "This is Ivy Todsen. I don't know if you remember me..."

Cassie sat up straighter, placing her immediately as the hospital nurse Mark had often mentioned. Ivy was tall with a boyish figure and hair so heavily highlighted it was mostly blond. She sported a year-round tan, usually only seen south of the Mason-Dixon Line or in a tanning salon.

"You worked on the behavioral health unit at Riverbend," Cassie said. "Mark sang your praises."

"I am so sorry for your loss, and for ours, as well. He was the best psychiatrist on the unit. I always thought the patients under his care did better than others." She added the next part as if she felt obligated to. "Of course the whole Church Street practice is excellent."

Cassie wished she could ask if Ivy really meant that. Sometimes lies were about plugging conversational holes or saving face.

She scanned through her memory for facts she knew about this woman. Mark sought out Ivy when he needed a favor on the unit and consulted her about patients. On a personal level Cassie knew little, except that Ivy had taken time off while she was going through a nasty divorce. Mark had been forced to forge new working relationships in the unit because Ivy was gone.

She propped pillows behind her back and settled into the conversation. "Did you know I'm living in Florida now?"

"I'd heard. I found your number because all the staff list their emergency contacts, and you were Mark's. I was reorganizing the list, and when I saw his name, I realized we'd never, well..."

They'd never deleted him. Cassie wondered how long it took before a person was erased completely, as if they'd never lived at all. "I'm glad you found me," she said, to ease the strain.

"I wasn't able to attend Mark's memorial service. I was on duty that day, and I decided that taking care of his patients was the best way to honor him. Of course the staff on our unit sent a card and flowers, but not speaking to you bothered me. I know this must be such a hard time. Tell me how you're doing."

Cassie thought how much that question would have meant from Valerie. "It is hard. You probably deal with grieving patients all the time."

"And families. It helps to talk."

They chatted easily, moving past the subject of Mark and into a comparison of life in New York and Florida. Ivy asked about Savannah, and Cassie found herself telling the other woman how hard the adjustment had been for her daughter.

By the time they were ready to hang up, she was happy she'd been able to talk to someone she'd known in Manhattan. She felt as if a chapter that had been ripped out of her life had been reclaimed.

"It was so thoughtful of you to call," she said. "I can see why Mark liked working with you."

"Do you mind if I check back now and then? Just to see how you're doing? I can save hospital gossip for you if you'd like."

Cassie's mind was already whirling with possibilities. "Perfect. I miss knowing what's going on at Riverbend." She thanked Ivy and hung up.

The day spent with Amber and the call from Ivy had pointed out how much she needed friends. Being Ivy's would have another benefit, too. Once they were more comfortable with each other, Cassie could ask the RN about Mark and his relationship with the others at Church Street Psychiatric. Ivy would have an insider's view. Cassie was still determined to find out what had really happened, and why he had resigned. Maybe Ivy could be a stepping-stone to the truth.

Nothing was clearer than the fact that she couldn't do this alone. She needed all the help she could get.

17

AMBER GOT OUT OF HER CAR AND LEANED IN TO say goodbye to her son, who was in the driver's seat. Will was wearing a crisp white dress shirt and black slacks and looked, in her unbiased opinion, amazing.

"Don't forget. I'll find my way home when I'm done here, or I'll wait for you at the Kouzina if I can't," she said. "But you'll call if you have any problems?"

"I'm not going to have problems." Will's smile was so dear it almost sucked the air out of her lungs. "And I can see why Yiayia wanted me to start training on your day off."

"Well, I'm a Mother Hen, and you're my only hatched egg, kid." She straightened and thumped the top of their car and watched him pull away from the curb. She was still surprised that Will was driving, and driving well, to boot. Their life together had flown by so quickly, and as tough as it had been, she wished she could do it again.

Of course, even more she wished she could have done it differently the first time.

"Billy, you would be so proud," she whispered as she

watched the car disappear down the road. Unexpectedly tears filled her eyes. She wasn't sure they were prompted by pride or sorrow, but her feelings didn't matter, hadn't mattered for years. Survival had demanded that she push everything aside except the rules she'd made for herself. Stay under the radar. Move often and without fanfare. Keep to the simplest facts about who she and Will were and where they'd come from.

Inside the library she saw several empty computers and chose one, keying in the number from her library card when prompted. Once her number was accepted, she knew she only had ninety minutes on the internet, but despite that, she had trouble settling in. Will's delight at having a new job, where he would make better wages and interact with people instead of unpacking cartons and stocking shelves, was catching. At the oddest times she found herself smiling. Their life since they had moved in with Cassie had improved immeasurably.

Since Cassie refused to accept even pocket change, Amber was rapidly saving money. She'd paid off outstanding bills and begun to replenish her bank account so she could afford rent again someday. Her new job as a server at Yiayia's Kouzina was more fun than she'd expected. Yiayia and Roxanne too often went head-to-head, but the rest of the staff got along surprisingly well. Since Amber liked both the Costas women, she stayed away from them during arguments and managed the restaurant until they were finished knocking heads.

None of the other servers had aspirations toward management. If Amber had been in charge, she would have talked to each about their commitment to their job. But she wasn't in charge. Truthfully no one was. Roxanne and Yiayia were in constant negotiations. Roxanne was trying to manage the back of house and help Buck cook, but her hands were often tied. Yiayia tried to manage the front, but she was more interested in socializing with customers—and giving too many discounts.

As an outsider, Amber had discovered she was able to make suggestions if she couched them as casual conversation. Sometimes Yiayia even took her advice. Roxanne had noticed, and now she fed Amber ideas for things to discuss with her mother. Sometimes it was a definite benefit not to be a real Costas.

On the way to the library today she had counseled Will to stay out of family squabbles. No one had been more surprised than her when he'd come home on Monday and told her that after the grocery store had refused to raise his hourly wage, he'd applied at the Kouzina and been hired immediately.

"I didn't want you putting in a good word for me, or Cassie doing it, either. I wanted to get the job on my own." His grin had poured sunshine into her world. "So I did."

Amber was sure that Will had sold the deal himself. While there was nothing easy about busing tables, he knew that the two afternoons and evenings he was scheduled at the Kouzina would give him extra time for schoolwork. For now he was in training while he also served out the two weeks he owed the grocery store. She hoped today went well for her son, but she suspected that by night's end, Will would have established himself as someone to be counted on.

She finally logged on to the internet and geared up to conduct two different searches. She and Will owned a computer, a clunky laptop so old they were lucky it hadn't self-destructed. But age and unreliability weren't the only reasons she was at the library. While she doubted her son would check the browser history, she also knew if he accidentally came across something he didn't understand, he might be curious.

So when necessary she used the library computers and sometimes even public ones farther away, like Tampa or St.

Petersburg. If anyone was trying to trace her, she wanted to make her hometown difficult to pinpoint.

She was at a crossroads. Settling permanently in Tarpon Springs would be so easy. Gambling that after sixteen years no one was actively searching for her might be easy, too. She had covered her tracks more than a dozen times and taken twists and turns on the journey. She had changed her name and appearance. She had a son—only one person from her past knew about Will, and Betsy Garland would rather die than betray her. She could make a life here and a place for Will to come back to on breaks from college.

Sadly, easy was never going to be safe, not for her.

She spent the next thirty minutes checking websites and making a list on a steno pad of towns to investigate in case she had to pull up stakes quickly. If she saved enough money, they might be able to move to a small city in Arizona or Utah that had good restaurants but was far away from major tourist attractions.

After six cities made the cut, she took a deep breath and switched to her second reason for being there. She had an hour, but she hoped she wouldn't need that long, because there was no news to report.

"Darryl Hawken," she said under her breath, as she typed in the name. Then, as distasteful as it was to see the name in print, she went slowly down the list of results.

She conducted this search whenever she could, but never at home. As the sheriff of Croville County, the smallest county in West Virginia, Darryl Hawken was something of a public figure. His name was mentioned often in passing, and she quickly paged through former mentions. Toward the bottom of the page she found a recent newspaper article about impaired driver enforcement. Sheriff Hawken was quoted as saying he was proud of his department's arrest record.

Amber wondered how many of Croville County's impaired drivers had simply driven away after paying the arresting officer a bonus at the roadside. She found it hard to believe that any honest man or woman who worked under Darryl Hawken would be allowed to remain.

She moved to the second page. She was particularly interested in finding anything about trips Darryl might be taking out of town, or places he'd been seen. But halfway down, after checking several unhelpful websites, she stopped.

Sheriff Darryl Hawken was considering a run for the House of Delegates.

She'd probably taken a civics class that concentrated on the state where she'd been born and raised, but now few facts came to mind. She did more digging and discovered how little money a delegate made. Why would Darryl consider running for state office? It didn't take more than a moment or two to answer her own question. The House of Delegates was a stepping-stone to power. Darryl was a man bent on grabbing more of everything for himself. Who knew what he had in his sights?

She wondered what his candidacy might mean for her. Would he be more desperate to hide his past? More determined to rid himself of people who knew him for the man he really was? More intent on finding them?

She wrote the headline and name of the paper for future reference and made notes from the article before she continued to page down.

She was on the third page when someone spoke behind her.

"Are you busy? I don't want to bother you."

She recognized Cassie's voice, and without having to think about it, she instantly closed down the search engine and turned off the computer. Then she got to her feet and faced her friend.

"Hey, I didn't expect to see you."

Cassie's gaze flicked to the monitor, then up to Amber's face. "Amber, you didn't have to stop. I won't take up your computer time. I just saw you here and thought I'd say hello."

"Not to worry. I was all finished. Will dropped me off on his way to the Kouzina. I was just checking…" Her mind whirled and settled on a story. "The news in Kentucky. In my hometown."

"Kentucky? I must have jumbled that in my head. I thought you said you were from Arkansas."

Amber nodded, as if nothing was wrong. "Born in the Ozarks, but my family moved to Kentucky when I was little." She realized her newest mistake when Cassie looked even more confused. Had she told her that she'd left her home in the Ozarks when she was pregnant with Will? She'd told that story often enough that she probably had. At some point a year or so ago she had scrambled to change her life history for a while, and now she couldn't remember why or when. Someone she'd met. Something that had been said. Someone who'd wanted to trade stories about life in the mountains. She had broken her own rule, which was to keep everything simple and the same. Now she was paying the price.

She took a chance and tried to glue it all together with more lies. "My parents moved back to Arkansas when I was in high school, but Kentucky still seems most like my home, which is why I like to check the news there. We Blairs are wanderers, I guess. It's in my blood."

"They're still there?"

For a moment Amber was so rattled she wasn't even sure where "there" was anymore. She shrugged. "I don't know."

"You don't look them up?" Cassie inclined her head toward the computer. "Online?"

"Some things are better left alone. Sometimes it's the right thing to just make a clean break. I know how you feel about family, but these were not people I'd want Will to know."

"Oh, I'm sorry. That's hard."

Amber thought she was probably in the clear now. "Are you by any chance heading home from here?"

"I'm just picking up some books I reserved. Do you need a ride?"

"That would be great. I'll let Will know he doesn't have to pick me up."

Amber started to leave, but Cassie stopped her. "You forgot your notebook. Here." She reached around to the desk and picked up the steno pad. Amber saw what Cassie just glanced at on the front page, the notes on the newspaper article she'd read about the West Virginia House of Delegates.

Amber snatched the pad quickly and slipped it into her purse. "Do you have any thoughts about dinner? I took chicken out of the freezer this morning."

On the way out they chatted about everything except the truth. But Amber worried about the things they weren't saying. If Cassie had paid attention to her notes, now she knew that Amber had not been catching up on news about a hometown in Kentucky. Even worse? She might also be wondering if everything else Amber had said that afternoon was a lie.

18

CASSIE HADN'T BEEN SURE WHAT TO GET SAVANNAH for Christmas, because whatever she bought would be wrong, simply because it came from her. She settled on a smart speaker Savannah could program to play music and follow simple commands. She finished with a few smaller gifts so inexpensive that she didn't care if they landed in the garbage that night. She fully expected them to.

On Christmas morning she got up early and put gifts under the tree, flipping on the lights so they would greet the others when they joined her. In addition to gifts for Savannah she'd bought Will Bluetooth headphones to go with the new smartphone his mother was giving him.

She'd intended to buy Amber a gift card for something practical like oil changes for their car, but instead she'd found herself at the outlet mall clutching a deep violet rain jacket with a pillowy zip-out lining that was perfect for the changeable local weather and her new friend's coloring. Amber's own jacket was thin and showing wear, and by now Cassie knew it would have to self-destruct before she replaced it. She was sure Amber would love this one.

When the gifts were all in place, she busied herself in the kitchen, filling the coffee maker with freshly ground beans. She slipped the cranberry Christmas bread that she made every year into the oven to warm and took a citrusy fruit salad from the refrigerator to sprinkle coconut flakes on top.

By the time the coffee was ready and the house was stirring, she'd whipped a dozen eggs to make omelets and set out shredded cheese and crumbled bacon. Amber was the first to wander into the kitchen. They exchanged Christmas greetings as Cassie pulled the bread from the oven to slice.

She and Amber hadn't been alone together since the day at the library. She wasn't sure if Amber was avoiding her, or if their schedules just hadn't meshed. Cassie had given their encounter some thought. Before Mark's death she had taken people and what they told her at face value. These days she found herself evaluating everything. The person she'd been closest to had lied in the months before his death. Now she looked for lies in every sentence.

At the library she hadn't had to look hard. She had caught Amber in a lie about her family. As Cassie had watched her flail through an explanation about where she'd grown up, she had realized that Amber's reaction was both important and troubling. Clearly fear lay behind the jumbled story. And if Amber was afraid, did Cassie need to be afraid, too, that whatever boogeyman was pursuing her new friend might find its way to the house in Sunset Vista?

Then there was the memo pad and the words West Virginia. She'd seen nothing but those, but she had noted the way the words were gouged into the paper, as if Amber had been chiseling a headstone.

She had considered and reconsidered whether to talk to

her friend, to point out what she'd seen and encourage her to share her real story. But in the end? She had stayed silent. She wasn't really sure she wanted to know Amber's secrets. More important she didn't want Amber to leave. Amber and Will were buffers between her and Savannah, giving them the space they needed to heal their relationship. And having a friend was pulling her out of the depression she'd sunk into after Mark's death.

"When do you think the kids will get up?" Amber poured coffee for both of them without being asked and went to the refrigerator for cream to add to Cassie's.

"As a little girl Savannah was always up by five. I'd double that today. How about Will?"

"I think he'll be up earlier. But he and Savannah were banging around last night, and he went to bed late. I heard him tiptoeing around my bed."

"What do you think they were up to?"

"Will's good at keeping secrets."

"Like his mother."

Amber didn't tense as much as grow absolutely still, as if she was waiting for the next sentence. Cassie let the silence extend just a moment. "You can't hide anything in this house. You've been up late, too."

Amber relaxed a little. "I haven't kept you awake, have I?"

"I stay up late, too, to keep from tossing and turning even longer. Your light's been on as late as mine."

"Well, the reason won't be a secret after this morning."

Cassie looked up at a noise. Savannah, in soft flannel pajamas and fuzzy slippers, was in the doorway. "Can we get this over with so I can go back to bed?"

Cassie measured her daughter's tone. It was more promising than her words. "As soon as Will gets up, too."

"Stay out of the living room. And I'm going to go make a lot of noise outside Will's room."

Cassie noted it was no longer "my suite." Now the suite belonged to Will and his mother. Another change.

"Want a couple of pot lids to clang together?" Amber asked.

"Nope. Got it covered."

Cassie watched her daughter disappear down the hallway. Then, the air was filled with the strains of "Santa Claus is Coming to Town," screeched at top volume.

Amber screwed up her face, but Cassie only smiled. The morning showed no signs of being a storybook Christmas, but it was much more than she'd expected. She was happy to take it exactly the way it was.

Later that morning, after a nap on her sitting room couch, Cassie stared across the room at the lemon tree Savannah had given her for Christmas. She had placed the Meyer lemon in a spring green ceramic pot that had survived the disastrous party, even filling in the gaps with potting soil.

Cassie had been too disheartened to begin a new plant collection. Even tending to the party's survivors hadn't given her much comfort. But this new tree, small in stature but dotted with scented flowers? And the thought behind it? She smiled. When they had exchanged gifts that morning, Savannah had acted as if the tree was nothing, but Cassie was clinging to it as a sign that things could change again. Maybe they already were.

The gifts under the tree had all been selected with care, and now she knew what Amber had been doing late at night. Her housemate had bought and repurposed the curtains Cassie had admired at Things From the Springs so they would fit her windows. A new border ran along the sides and hem of each, highlighted with tasteful machine embroidery that made the curtains look like they'd come from a designer boutique. Will had given presents, too. He had visited the local used bookstore and bought half a dozen books he thought Cassie might like, because he remembered her saying she'd had to leave most of hers in New York.

Both of them had appreciated their gifts from her, and Savannah had added a gift card to the local movie theater for the Blairs to share. Will and Amber had gone in together to buy Savannah a Himalayan salt lamp shaped like a crescent moon. The morning had passed without the drama she had feared.

Savannah was now at Helia's foster home for the family's annual Christmas party. Helia had arrived with her brother and another girl, Minh, to collect Savannah and finally for introductions to Cassie and Amber.

Afterward Amber had said how much Helia reminded her of herself at the same age, a surprising slip from a woman who rarely admitted to having a past. The girls were all strangers at Coastal Winds, and each, in her own way, seemed to be particularly perceptive. Both had arrived with small gifts for Savannah, and to her daughter's credit, Savannah had bought gifts for them, as well.

Cassie had the afternoon free because Amber and Will were making dinner. Her sitting room had been neglected, and she hated for Amber to see the stacks of mail and magazines when her friend came in that evening to help hang curtains. She carried all the piles to her sofa and set the mail on the coffee table, moving magazines to one side and bills to another.

She had missed a few Christmas cards, mostly the kind sent by service providers. She opened one from her pest control company and another from her accountant in New York. The next card-sized envelope had an address label, which meant it was probably a mass mailing. She expected an advertisement, but she was wrong.

Five minutes later she was connected to the local police station.

"I'd like to leave a message for Officer Nick Andino. I'm sure he's not there today, but I need to talk with him when he is."

She listened and nodded, as if the woman on the other end could see. Her hand was trembling, so she clutched the phone harder. When the woman fell silent, she gave her phone number and name and hung up. Cassie had explained this was not an emergency.

It just felt like one.

She sorted the rest of the mail to make sure nothing from the same person was lurking in the pile. Once finished, she was staring at the windows that would sport Amber's Christmas curtains when the phone rang. Nick was on the other end.

"Not in a million years did I expect to hear from you today," she said. "I told them it wasn't an emergency. Are you at home with family? We can talk—"

"I cover for the officers with children who need the morning with their families. I'll see my brothers and sisters later this evening at my mother's house. What's up?"

"I got something…in the mail." She realized she didn't want to describe the letter. "May I bring it by for you to look at?"

"Why don't you meet me for coffee. I'm about to take a break anyway. McDonald's is open and not far away. Can you come now?"

"I'll be there in ten minutes."

She wasn't surprised at how good Nick looked in his uniform of dark slacks and a short sleeved shirt with patches on both sleeves. She remembered, looking at him now, how she'd always yearned to have those beautiful brown eyes focused on her.

She took a deep breath and handed him the coffee she'd insisted on buying, then retrieved slices of cranberry bread she'd brought. "You don't have to eat that now. It's my traditional Christmas breakfast."

"I may swallow it whole."

Cassie knew she had to get straight to the point. "I left the message for you just to get in line. I figured I'd hear later this week."

He sat back. "So tell me about your mail."

She pulled out the envelope and handed it to him. "I'm not sure when it came. I haven't been good about keeping up with things. I was sorting mail today and found it in the pile."

"It looks like it was postmarked on December 18."

"I saw that. Who knows how many people handled it before or since. The woman who delivers our mail. My roommate. Her son, who usually gets the mail, or my daughter."

He opened the envelope and held the piece of paper by the corner.

She knew exactly what it said. Whoever had sent the note had kept it short. It was printed on standard-issue computer paper and unsigned.

She recited as Nick read silently. The words were burned into her brain.

"Your husband had all kinds of secrets. Do you want the world to know them now? How about that daughter of his? Is she old enough to understand? Are you safe enough in that cozy little town not to bother protecting yourself from the truth?"

He slipped the letter back into the envelope. "You always were good at learning lines. *Our Town*, remember? I struggled with mine. I think you helped me."

"At that point in my life I would have shined your shoes. I had such a crush on you."

He looked pleased. "Did you?"

"Oh, yeah. But so did half the girls in the school. You were a charmer."

"My charming days are gone. Now when people see me coming, they run the other way. Tell me about your husband."

She knew he was referring to the note. She wasn't sure how much to say about Mark. Did she talk about the old Mark? The one she'd married, the generous and kindhearted man who had been devoted to his wife, daughter and patients? Or did she talk about the one who, in the last year of his life, stormed away from the practice he'd worked so hard to establish? The Mark who had dismantled his family's financial safety net and left his widow and daughter scrambling?

"Mark was a psychiatrist," she began, and then continued on to tell Nick about his first marriage and the custody arrangement.

"Could the letter be from his ex?"

"No chance. She's unfailingly supportive of me, and she was of Mark, too. Plus she's in Africa at the moment."

"Someone could have mailed it for her."

"She has no reason to make threats. She might be a distant mother, but she loves Savannah. She wouldn't hurt her."

"The letter mentions secrets. Did your husband have them?"

She sipped coffee and tried to think how much to say. "We had a good marriage. I would have said a great one until about a year before Mark died. Then he changed. He was irritable, and suddenly we went from talking about everything to only talking about what we were going to watch on television. He was away more often, too, and he got annoyed if I questioned him. Then he quit his practice. He had an excellent reputation, got along with everybody. In fact he was the one who smoothed over bumps they encountered. Then, one day, he came home and said he'd quit."

"Just like that."

"I've spoken to one of his partners. He wasn't interested in rehashing it, but in the end he said they were seeing the same things at work that I was seeing at home. The other doctors were relieved when Mark left. They thought he was bringing personal problems into the office, and when they tried to talk to him, he just blew up and resigned."

"Do you have any theories why?"

She knew she should mention the sudden holes in their finances and the lies that Mark had told his financial advisor. But she wasn't ready to make any of that public yet, not until she could do more investigating on her own. She didn't know how much Nick was required to report.

Instead she moved to the explanation she favored most. "Like I said, Mark was a psychiatrist. He got death threats a few times. One from a former patient who was in prison, another from a patient in a locked ward in a psychiatric hospital across town. There might have been verbal threats, too. In fact, I'm sure there were. He worked with very difficult cases. You can't do what Mark did without stirring up all kinds of problems. I'm just not sure how anybody like that could get my address."

"Have you ever googled yourself? Your address probably took whoever sent this letter about one minute to locate."

"Life was probably easier before the internet."

"How did your husband die?"

"Sailing. He loved the water, and he'd been sailing since childhood. But one afternoon he took his boat out when he shouldn't have, got caught in a storm and drowned."

"He knew about the weather ahead of time?"

There was so much she could say about that, so many fears

she harbored. She took a moment to compose herself. "He should have. I guess we'll never know."

He drummed his fingers on the table. Nick had wide, strong hands, and he still wore a wedding ring, as did she. She wondered if he sometimes woke in the night and reached for the wife he'd lost.

"I'm sorry, but was there any chance his death was foul play?" he asked.

"Would a medical examiner look for that?"

"Depends. They did an autopsy?"

She shuddered. "Yes, but if there was anything out of the ordinary, I never heard about it. His body was found less than twenty-four hours after I reported he didn't come home. I expected him for dinner that night, and he said he'd be back. They found him the next afternoon." She looked up. "It was so unexpected, Nick. I keep asking myself if it would be easier to accept what happened if I'd had time to say goodbye."

"Don't count on it. I had months to say goodbye to JoAnn."

He had opened the door, so she walked through. "How did she die?"

"Breast cancer. We thought she was clear. She was in remission, and then she wasn't. At that point nothing helped. I'm not sure I'd trade one ending for another."

"I'm sorry."

He nodded, his lips a grim line. "Same here."

"Shouldn't *Our Town* have been more of a warning?"

He closed his eyes a moment. "That play was a downer, wasn't it? We were too young to really understand what it means to lose someone we love."

"I think maybe we're always too young."

He leaned forward and held up the envelope. "Would you like me to take this and start a file? This borders on extortion—for all practical purposes we lump extortion and blackmail together in Florida—but no demands have been made. There's nothing we can really do at this point, and to be honest, I don't think you need to worry. There's no overt threat here. It's more like somebody is hoping or guessing there were problems in your husband's life, and they're striking out at you because they need to hurt somebody. Maybe they had unfinished business with your husband, a patient he couldn't help, or one who took his death personally. But at the worst this looks like a setup. So keep your eyes open and call if you notice anything unusual. If you get more mail? Let me know immediately."

She got to her feet. "It was more than kind of you to take time to go over this with me on Christmas Day."

He got up, too, and held up the cranberry bread. "I feel well paid."

"I hope the rest of your day feels more Christmassy."

"Yours, too." He took her hand and squeezed it. "It was good to be with someone who understands how hard losing a life partner can be."

"I just hope the next time you don't have to examine my mail."

"Next time I'll buy the coffee."

She watched him head to the counter, most likely to buy lunch. She hoped Nick's time with his family that evening would ease the ache in his heart, just a little.

19

CASSIE KNEW SHE SHOULD PUT THE LETTER OUT OF her mind. Undoubtedly Nick was right, and there was no threat to worry about. But one day later she was still wondering who could help her discover the author's identity. The Manhattan friends who'd sent Christmas cards had no connection to Mark. Lines of communication with Valerie had been nailed shut, and everyone at Church Street would cite confidentiality.

While Ivy had only worked with Mark at Riverbend Community, she was still Cassie's best possibility. They had talked twice, and Cassie found her both compassionate and accommodating. This afternoon Cassie hoped she would be both.

Ivy was working twelve-hour shifts at night in order to have long breaks at the weekend. When four o'clock arrived, Cassie punched in her number, hoping to catch her after she'd had some sleep.

Just after a voice mail message began, Ivy answered. She didn't sound like someone who'd been forced out of bed, which was a relief.

Cassie greeted her. "Is this a terrible time to talk?"

Ivy assured her she was heading out for dinner with a friend but wasn't in any hurry to dress. They traded Christmas stories. Then Cassie got down to business.

"Something happened, and I want to pick your brain." She explained about the letter, quoting a part of it. Nick was right. She was good at learning lines, and she hadn't forgotten those.

"Wow, that's ugly," Ivy said. "Who would send something like that at Christmas?"

Cassie pulled up the covers and told herself she was just cold, not frightened. "Somebody who wanted to upset me, I guess."

"You have no idea who?"

"That's why I'm calling. It's a long shot you might be able to think of possibilities, but if this is a patient of Mark's, maybe he or she was on the behavior health unit with you. I wondered if you remembered anybody who had real issues with him?"

"Transference is a reality," Ivy said slowly, as if thinking out loud. "You know, when somebody treats their therapist the way they'd like to treat someone else in their life or their past. A father, a teacher."

"Mark didn't talk a lot about what went on in therapy."

"He was a real professional. He wouldn't." The warmth in Ivy's voice was unmistakable.

"I know I'm asking a lot, but is it possible you can think of somebody who might still be this angry with him, even after his death, someone who would write a letter like that to me?"

"To vent, you mean? To make somebody who loved Mark unhappy?"

Mark might not have talked much about what he faced every day, but Valerie had told a story about the patient of another doctor who had come to the office with a handgun.

"It's an odd way to get even," Cassie said, "but the people

Mark dealt with ranged from mildly depressed to raging psychotics. They weren't always thinking clearly."

"One person's odd is another person's go-to," Ivy said. "Remember when Mark was laid up at home that time? While he was recovering, one old guy kept insisting Mark was in jail, and we had to rescue him. One night he managed to get off the unit, and an orderly found him on another floor trying to steal clothes so he could take a bus to Rikers Island and free Mark."

Cassie felt a stab of pity for the old man. "At least he was trying to rescue him."

"I wish somebody with darker motives would spring to mind, but unfortunately no such luck."

Cassie was disappointed but not surprised. She felt better after Ivy's next comment, though. "How about if I nose around a little? I have to be careful, because I don't want to get in trouble. But I may be able to single out patients Mark worked with and look through their records. A couple of people might have ideas if I can figure out a good way to approach them."

"That would be great if you're not putting your job on the line. And I have another question, if you have time."

"You're giving me the excuse I need to sit instead of clean the apartment."

"This one may be even harder. I'm trying to find out why Mark left Church Street. I cornered Fletcher last month and asked him point-blank what had happened. He was vague—"

"That doesn't surprise me."

Cassie waited, but when Ivy didn't go on, she asked. "Why not?"

"Fletcher Dorman couldn't take a stand or be straight about something if his life depended on it." She paused, then said something under her breath that was distinctly profane. "Listen, I didn't really say that."

"I didn't hear a thing."

"What did Dr. Dorman tell you when you asked?"

Cassie gave her a condensed version of that conversation. She explained that near the end of his life, Mark had been short-tempered and hard to work with, and that the staff had been surprised but also relieved when he resigned.

"That's not the way I heard it," Ivy said when she'd finished.

Cassie sat up a little straighter. "What did you hear?"

"You really have to keep this to yourself. Obviously I wasn't there when any of this happened. But I heard snippets of conversation between some of our doctors, and so did other nurses. So..."

"So?"

"I heard the problem was between Dr. Dorman and Mark. Mark challenged him, effectively saying his treatment of patients no longer met the standard of care. He said Dr. Dorman needed to bone up on new thinking, even do some additional training, because he was failing his patients. Everyone knows Dr. Dorman is pretty old-school, but that was the first time his methods were talked about openly. Dorman had been there longer than Mark, and people were forced to take sides."

Cassie tried to remember if Mark had ever expressed qualms about Fletcher to her. In the months before the resignation, their relationship with the Dormans had declined, although she hadn't seen it at the time. Now she recognized a pattern. The Dormans had made excuses and refused invitations to dinners and excursions that Cassie had tried to set up, including a birthday dinner for Valerie. Tickets they'd bought together had been exchanged and reservations canceled.

"I'm going to have to think about this," she said. "I can't

think of a single time that Mark talked about Fletcher's skills or lack of them."

"Did he ever bring problems home?"

"Never." Mark had never asked her for help. The psychiatrist who was supposed to have all the answers had always lurked in the background.

"Well, that's the kind of man he was," Ivy said. "Professional to the core. I promise I'll see what I can discover, but a change of subject while I still have you? I had an idea after our last conversation, so see what you think. I know Savannah's not happy being in Florida, and she misses New York."

"She's doing a little better. I'm not running it up the flagpole yet, but I'm hopeful."

"If you and Savannah want to visit over the holidays, I could get reservations and tickets. It's nice to have someone on-site to coordinate."

Cassie was touched and thanked her. "But I think we'll be here until after winter break. Savannah and her friends have plans to celebrate Epiphany on the sixth. It's a big deal in town."

They said their goodbyes, and Cassie hung up. If Fletcher and Mark had quarreled, that could well explain why the Dormans had distanced themselves. Maybe it also explained why Fletcher hadn't wanted to discuss other staff members. He'd known why Mark left, and perhaps he'd also known that if Cassie began to ask around, the truth would come out.

Ivy had been exactly the right person to consult. Valerie and Fletcher may have disappeared from her life, but Cassie still had someone she could count on in New York. Thanks to Ivy, she and her daughter hadn't been completely forgotten.

Both Will and Amber were working a holiday party at the Kouzina that evening, and Savannah had left for Minh's to eat a traditional Vietnamese meal and spend the night. Cassie had planned to spend the evening alone, but instead, after a phone call, she was heading to nearby Palm Harbor for dinner.

Dr. Lawrence Steele had been Mark's psychotherapy supervisor and mentor during his psychiatric residency, and he had remained a close friend through the years. Larry was now retired, living in Clearwater, and he'd called to tell Cassie he had the evening free. They arranged to meet halfway, and he was waiting in the foyer when she arrived, a distinguished-looking man with a head of silver curls and a waistline that showcased his love of good food.

Before they had time for more than a peck on the cheek, they were shown to an attractive wooden booth in a room with dark paneling and lighting courtesy of a brightly lit aquarium and stained glass panels.

She'd last seen Larry at Mark's memorial service, and there hadn't been an opportunity for more than platitudes and sympathy. But after she'd moved to Florida, a package had arrived in the mail. *A Grief Observed*, by C. S. Lewis, written after the death of the author's wife. A note from Larry had accompanied it. "When you're ready," the note said, and now the book was waiting on her nightstand.

He didn't comment on her appearance, which was too often the first thing out of people's mouths. She was tired of being told she looked good, as if she was the one who'd drowned and her apparent good health was shocking. Instead he smiled and asked how she was.

If she'd had to choose a psychiatrist from the many she'd met, Larry would be her choice. Not only was he infinitely kind, he was interested in the whole person, who they were and had been, all the way down to their marrow. Larry believed he was no better than his most troubled patient.

Now she felt his warmth as she told him about the past

months. He listened closely, nodding as she spoke. He understood her wide range of emotions because he had lost his wife ten years before and never remarried.

"We'd better look at the menu," he said when she'd finished. "Our server looks like he's about to pounce. Then we can talk."

She ordered salmon, and after a host of questions about the way items were prepared, Larry ordered the duck breast and a glass of rosé from Provence for himself after Cassie told him she was fine with water.

"I've never seen you drink," he said, after the server left to put in their order.

She explained, then smiled. "Mark thought my not drinking was a bit obsessive."

His eyes twinkled. "Are you thumbing your nose at your parents?"

"I would if I knew which direction to aim, up or down. But no, it's a disease. I've just put myself on permanent quarantine."

They chatted about both their lives until the salads arrived.

"Do you miss your students?" Cassie asked after the salads were replaced by their entrées. "Mark thought you were the best. He said anything he learned to do right was because of you."

"I don't work with students, but I still take a few clients now and then. I've also met someone, and I'm relearning how much time a relationship takes."

She was delighted for him. "It's hard work until you fall into predictable patterns."

"I do miss supervising. Not all my residents were as superior as Mark, but I rarely found any that didn't improve over time."

"Mark put so much effort into everything he did."

"Was that hard to live with?"

The question surprised her, but it shouldn't have, considering Larry's profession. "At times."

He continued, "He wasn't really an overachiever, because he had the talent and drive to achieve anything he wanted. No 'over' about it. But he couldn't let go. Nothing he achieved was ever good enough."

She suspected there was a point here and it would become clear. "It was a little intimidating to be with someone who was always pushing himself," she admitted.

"Because then you had to push yourself to keep up?"

"There was no hope of keeping up. Instead I just found my niche, taking care of Savannah, making sure our lives ran smoothly and happily. I made that my contribution. It seemed to work."

"You were happy?"

She'd always thought so, although lately she'd begun to wonder. "Until I left for college, I was the caretaker in my family. So when I married Mark and he asked little more than to love him and Savannah and keep our home life running smoothly, it was like being in heaven."

Larry sat back from his meal, as if taking a break. "It's not surprising Mark asked very little. He was excellent at seeing the needs of other people, but not at understanding his own."

"You're trying to tell me something, aren't you?"

"Did you know at one point during Mark's supervision I considered demanding he go into therapy, intensive therapy, and delay finishing the program? I was talked out of it by others who felt he was doing well. And they were right. On every level except his ability to confront his own demons, Mark was the best."

"Demons?"

"Maybe an overstatement. Since he hid what he was feeling so well, I never got close enough to find out whether the problem was demons or just annoying mosquitoes buzzing in his brain."

"Was this about the time he and Gen got married?"

"The marriage was a good example. Mark decided to do the right thing for Gen and their unborn baby. I don't think she necessarily wanted it that way, but Mark had his say and his way. He could be very persuasive."

"I'm glad. I don't know what I'd do without Savannah in my life." Although lately she'd wondered, but that was beside the point.

"You rescued all of them. You made it work. But having Savannah was part of Mark's pattern. If he made a mistake, he made up for it a hundredfold."

"Again, I think you're trying to tell me something."

He reached over and took her hand. "You would have been a good therapist, Cassie. And if Mark had allowed it, you could have taught him so much. But I don't think he ever let you, did he?"

She waited but he didn't go further. He was waiting for her, and she took the leap, squeezing his hand as she told him about Mark's final months and all the unanswered questions he'd left behind, ending with a plea. "If you have answers, I'd like to know them."

He squeezed and dropped her hand, but his eyes continued to show concern. "I don't have answers, but if I did, I would give them all to you. I will tell you this. Mark came to see me a few weeks before he died. I was in Manhattan, and we went for a drink. His need to tell me something was painfully obvious…" He shook his head. "Whatever it was? It was so important that despite his great reserve, he sought me out, hoping he could put it into words. But in the end, he wasn't able to. I let the situation sit a few days and then got back in touch with him. But by that time his defenses were so high, there was no way to reach him. Then he was gone."

Cassie felt tears on her cheeks, unusual and disconcerting. She took her napkin and dabbed them. "Mark was as at home in a sailboat as most people are in front of their television set."

"But he went out with a storm approaching."

"Do you think the accident was suicide?"

"I have no idea. It might have been. Or a need to challenge God, the final showdown to see who would come out on top. But we'll never know."

"You guessed I might have questions, didn't you?"

"Of course."

She took a deep, shaky breath. "I keep asking myself if I should pursue this, or just back off. He's gone, and maybe I should concentrate on moving forward."

"It's too late to make a difference for Mark, but maybe it's not too late to make a difference for Cassie. You two were very different. You confronted your problems, and he kept his inside. You're open about what you went through and how you've coped. I don't see you wanting to bury this. I don't see you able to."

"Larry, are you giving me your blessing?"

He picked up his fork, as if to say, we're done with this now. "My blessing's not worth the paper it's printed on. But I want you to know you have my support. Anytime you need me. I'll be there."

20

ALMOST TWO WEEKS LATER ON EPIPHANY MORNING,
Amber watched Will finish getting ready for the day. He was
so excited that he'd been talking nearly nonstop since breakfast.

"We'll probably go to Yiayia's house at some point." As he
spoke, he shrugged his shoulders into a navy blue hoodie that
fit perfectly, but would be too short at the wrists in another
month. He was almost as tall as his father at the same age, and
Amber suspected Will would stop growing about the time he
hit Billy's height.

Amber resisted the urge to reposition the hood so it rested
flat against his back. She could just imagine the conversation
that would follow if she tried. "I told Yiayia I'd stop by, too.
Cassie's working at the festival afterward—they call it the
Glendi. And I don't know when or if she'll get off to make
it to Yiayia's."

Somebody rapped on the sitting room door, and Amber
found Cassie with her fist raised to knock again. "Travis
stopped by to see if we wanted to watch the boys dive for the

cross with him. I'll be tied up preparing food, but you might want company."

Cassie looked past Amber to Will. "You're invited, too, but Savannah says you're meeting Helia and Minh to go off on your own."

Amber still couldn't believe how quickly things had changed between Savannah and Will. Since the afternoon he had tried to rescue her, they'd moved from a guarded truce to what was beginning to look like friendship. Will was especially glad to be included in Savannah's activities if Minh was there, too. She saw the way her son looked at Savannah's friend, and was pleased at his good taste.

Amber liked both Minh and Helia. Helia, despite sarcastic comebacks and floundering attempts to reinvent herself, had proved she was good-hearted and above all smart enough to learn from her mistakes. Minh was kind and insightful, devoted to her family, while forging her own path in her adopted country. Maybe the girls had banded together because the high school viewed them as outsiders, but their relationship had deepened into friendship, and now it included her son.

"Why don't you find out what Travis is planning?" Cassie started back down the hall before Amber could reply.

"Why don't you, Mom?" Will favored her with a grin. "He's from here. He'll be able to explain the whole thing to you."

"I thought I might stay home and enjoy the silence."

"You can have silence anytime you want it. Epiphany is once a year."

Amber hadn't taken her son to church often, at least partly because too many congregations, no matter the denomination, tried to involve newcomers in their activities. Neither had she wanted to form friendships or learn more about the God who had abandoned her when she was just sixteen.

Reluctantly she slipped her feet into flip-flops so she could tell Travis to go ahead without her. "How do you know so much about Epiphany?"

"Savannah told me. In the Orthodox church, Epiphany honors the day John baptized Jesus in the River Jordan. In other Christian churches, it's the day the Wise Men visited the baby Jesus. So it's a two for one."

"Well, I do know a bunch of young men are going to get wet today."

"It would be nice to be part of something like that. To know all your life that you had today to look forward to."

She wasn't surprised by his wistful tone. "At least you can enjoy it this year and see the dive first hand," she said, before she went in search of Travis.

She found him standing by the sliding glass doors in the great room, looking over the lanai with Cassie. He was dressed casually in a button-down shirt, khakis and leather jacket. She really wasn't sure what it was about Travis she found so attractive. The way his sandy hair waved back from a slight widow's peak. The deep brown of his eyes and the darker brows arching over them. He had the long legs and trim physique of a runner, along with the relaxed movements of a man comfortable with his body. The whole package was appealing.

"Travis just offered to share some of his plants with me," Cassie said, as Amber joined them. "He's going to give me cuttings and extras."

Travis pointed to a corner of the lanai. "If you want to go to the trouble, you can grow tomatoes, lettuce, anything you can pot. It looks like that area gets plenty of sun."

"Cherry tomatoes would be great," Amber said. "Perfect for pasta sauce. I'd help with that."

Cassie looked at the clock. "The food at the Glendi sounds

good. Roxanne signed me up to make salads. I'd better head out in a moment."

"Greek salad with potato salad?" Travis asked, and Cassie nodded. Often Greek salad was served on top of potato salad in Tarpon Springs.

"It's not served that way at the Kouzina." Amber knew from experience, because she'd had to disappoint more than a few customers. "Yiayia's determined to keep potato salad off our menu. She says it's not really Greek."

"She has firm opinions," Travis said.

"I hope she doesn't see me making salads. Warn me and I'll hide under a table." Cassie got her purse and keys and started toward the door. "You two better scoot if you want to see the procession. Amber, make sure to catch it, and Travis probably knows a good place to see the dive."

Amber started to protest until she realized she wanted to go. Who knew where she would be next year? Travis wasn't acting like a man who expected more than someone to enjoy the day with.

"Do I have a few minutes to change?" she asked him.

"Take your time."

Will passed in the hallway with Savannah, and both teens waved goodbye as she closed the sitting room door. She took a cue from Travis and slipped on a casual denim skirt and peach-colored tank top with a darker peach sweater, ending with comfortable shoes.

The others were gone by the time she joined him a few minutes later. "Perfect," he said when he saw her. "It may be cool until later this afternoon. It's a good thing the divers won't be in the water long."

She locked up and followed him to his car, a small sedan that looked well broken in. "Did you ever dive?"

"No, I did the whole Greek school thing, learned some of

the dances, met pretty Greek girls..." He smiled and so did she. "But I was never involved enough. I was always more interested in watching and writing stories about the things I saw." He opened the car door to usher her inside, an old-fashioned courtesy she hadn't experienced in a long time.

"Always the journalist?"

"My life's path. I took leave from a large paper last year when my father fell ill. My mother died when I was in high school so I wanted to be with him. I started freelancing to make ends meet, and by the time he was gone, I realized how much more I liked living here. So here I am. Still. Probably permanently."

"I'm sorry about your father."

"He was a great guy. I wish you could have met him." He didn't follow up and ask about hers. Travis seemed to know that her past was off-limits. Instead he switched to a rundown of the day.

"They're expecting twenty thousand people or more. I thought we'd park a few blocks from the church in a friend's driveway, and we can walk over to hear a little of the liturgy from outside. There'll be a crowd around the cathedral. We should probably leave for Craig Park and the bayou before the service ends and the procession begins, but we can find a good spot to see the dive and watch the procession arrive. Sound good? There's some walking involved."

It sounded like fun and she told him so.

The walk only took a few minutes. The sun poured over them, but Amber was glad she'd added the sweater. As they neared the cathedral, the crowd grew. People chatted quietly, and some stood transfixed as chants from inside serenaded the crowd through loudspeakers.

"St. Nicholas watched over and protected sailors," Travis said as they got closer. "He's the patron saint of Greece, so it made sense for the sponge divers and fishermen here to name their church for him."

She'd seen the cathedral, of course. The building of tan brick with dozens of stained glass windows was magnificent, centered in town and impossible to miss. "It's outstanding, isn't it?"

"The architecture is a combination of Byzantine elements, like the mosaics inside and the domed rotunda at the center, with more modern elements. One honors the faith's origins, the other honors its home here in America. The cross on the tower—" he pointed up "—is illuminated. You've probably seen it at night. It's a beacon for the faithful."

"The cathedral must be beautiful inside."

"I'll show it to you sometime."

She smiled, because a smile could mean anything and never be called a lie. They stood side by side listening to singing, to people chatting in both Greek and English in the crowd around them, and then prayers and readings from the cathedral in both, as well.

"You went to Greek school. What are they saying?" she whispered.

"The Greek the clerics use is an older form. Most people in this crowd couldn't translate, even if they speak Greek at home. Tradition changes very little, which is important to the Orthodox religion." He turned to see her better. "You probably grew up with something different."

She knew better than to answer in monosyllables or to be vague with a man who made his living digging for facts. She followed her own rule and told as much of the truth as she could. "My parents weren't religious. But when I visited my grandparents, I attended a one-room church on a dirt road with a preacher who hauled hogs to market the rest of the week."

"Where was that?"

She remembered how she'd changed the story she'd told Cassie and then had to cover up her mistake. "They lived in Kentucky. We did for a while, too."

"This must feel very different, then."

A moment later a line of young men wearing white T-shirts and blue swim trunks walked out a side door and through the crowd. They looked to be Will's age, and they were all barefoot.

"The divers," Travis said.

She could picture her son in this crowd of handsome young men. He wouldn't dive just because it might be fun or because his friends were doing it. He would be as determined as these divers to follow tradition and do his best for something he believed in. That was the young man she'd raised, and she was sorry that she hadn't, couldn't have given Will the sense of continuity and belonging these barefoot young men probably assumed were normal.

"Heard enough?" he asked after the divers had disappeared inside the cathedral.

She nodded and he took her arm to guide her out of the crowd and down the road where police had set up roadblocks. He dropped his hand once they were able to move freely, and they walked side by side.

"So tell me what's going to happen," she said.

"The boys were chosen by the nine Orthodox churches in the area to dive. They'll walk from the church to the bayou in a procession. They always walk barefoot."

"Why?"

"Humility? Because Jesus was probably barefoot when he was baptized, and the event symbolizes Him going into the river that day? I'm not sure. The church tries to make certain the dive doesn't become a sporting event, so the divers spend time learning about themselves and their religion."

"And then they dive?"

"Not quickly. Wait and see. The boy who retrieves the cross is supposed to receive blessings for the next year."

"All boys, no girls?"

"Fifty-five boys this year, but girls are allowed to dive in other places, including Greece."

"Yiayia's convinced that Greece is holding steady on all traditions, and nothing's different there than it was when she was a girl."

"When Yiayia was a girl? As traditional as she is, it goes further back than that for her, maybe as far back as when the Greeks worshipped Zeus."

Amber could sympathize. "Most of the time fear is the motivation for keeping change at bay, isn't it? Anything new can feel dangerous. I'm not sure what Yiayia's afraid of, except maybe becoming irrelevant. If she holds on to what she's sure of, time will slow. She'll remain young."

His eyes were warm with approval. "Handing over a life's work to the next generation must be hard."

"She's right about one thing. Every time we make a change, it does feel dangerous." She thought about her own life.

"Is that why change is hard for you?"

She came to a stop. "I change all the time, Travis. Jobs. Towns. I'm always looking for something new."

"From my perspective? Staying put would be the biggest change of all. From what I know of you." He held up his hands when she frowned. "And clearly I don't know a lot. That probably came out of hope that you're going to take a chance and hang around Tarpon Springs."

"Why?"

"So I can show you the inside of St. Nicholas." He smiled. "And get to know you better."

"I've never wanted anybody to know me better."

"Then that would be a big change, too, wouldn't it? And frightening. But I promise it wouldn't be dangerous."

She started walking again but tossed him a warning. "Danger, like beauty, is in the eye of the beholder." She hoped he understood.

After another block he pointed to an area around the bayou, which was more similar to a lake than the murky, sluggish water Amber associated with the word. Yiayia's house wasn't far away, but the platform where the archbishop would throw the cross wouldn't be visible from her yard. Dinghies, tied together, formed a half circle in front of it.

Travis led the way to a stretch of grass where people were already lounging in chairs or on blankets. "This is my favorite spot. Once the procession arrives, the shore will be crowded right up to the water. Let's get as close as we can."

The ground was cold, but Amber's skirt offered enough protection. They positioned themselves so they could see around the people just in front of them.

"Are they in the water long?" she asked. "How long does it usually take them to find it?"

"At least one time a second cross had to be tossed. Then a boy found the first one buried in mud after the second was claimed. So they were both declared winners."

She hoped that the year of two winners had been warmer than this one.

They chatted until the procession appeared. Travis held out his hand and helped her up to see better. As they watched, children in traditional dress walked abreast, holding hands, and other groups followed. She smiled at the young boys carrying a banner that read Future Divers, and then clapped along with others for a pretty teenage girl wearing a white smock over her dress, who was strolling side by side with a young man the same age.

"She's the dove bearer," Travis said. "She was specially chosen from girls in the choir. Can you see the dove in her hands? She'll release it during the ceremony. If I'm right, the man beside her is the diver who found the cross last year."

The present year's divers followed, and then bearded clerics in gold cloaks, some studded with jewels, who were preceded by altar boys carrying lanterns and other items Travis described, one of which was an ornately carved box holding an icon of the baptism of Jesus. An older man wearing a high gold crown and a white-and-gold robe climbed up to the platform, followed by others.

"The archbishop. He'll bless the water with sprigs of basil that were consecrated inside the cathedral. Watch the boys swim out to the boats." Travis pointed, and Amber watched as, evenly divided, the divers who had jumped into the water climbed on board and positioned themselves along the gunwales.

More prayers followed, and at last the dove bearer released the dove into the air to applause from the crowd, which had grown exponentially as the procession arrived. The dove flew up into the sky and disappeared, glad, Amber thought, to finally be free. More prayers followed, and just when Amber wondered if they'd forgotten the dive, the Archbishop stepped forward and threw the cross into the water.

A terrific splash followed as each boy dove in, hoping to be the lucky one.

"Well, it's a fast year," Travis said after a few moments, pointing into the middle of what looked like a whirlpool. "That took less than a minute."

She could see one of the boys waving something in the air,

and then they were all climbing a ladder out of the water to be wrapped in towels.

"He'll receive a trophy. The other boys will carry the winner through town on their shoulders. And then the Glendi begins." Travis brushed off his pants. "And there you have it."

Amber had been unexpectedly moved. Not by the liturgy, since she'd understood little of it, but by the adherence to tradition, the sense of being part of something that had been happening for years.

"Thanks for explaining. You made it so much more interesting."

"So we have choices now. I need to stop by Yiayia's."

"Me, too."

"Perfect. And then we can head over to the park for the Glendi. They'll have food, dancing, lots of families hanging out together. But I have another idea, if you're interested."

"What are you thinking?"

"When we're done at Yiayia's, let's ditch the crowd and go to a quiet little restaurant I've been wanting to try. Then I'll take you home."

She knew better than to say yes. Attending this celebration together had been one thing, but eating at a restaurant felt like a date. She started to refuse. The words wouldn't form.

"That sounds good," she said instead. Because, despite warnings zinging between her heart and brain, it did.

She liked this man. She liked his warm, easy smile, the way he listened to her opinions, the way he'd gone to bat for her when she'd been evicted. Travis was different from the other men who had tried—and failed—to get close to her. Reporter or not, Amber had never been just a good story to him. From the beginning he had recorded her plight but seen her humanity.

He took her arm so they could stay together as they wound through the crowd. And when he didn't drop it right away, she didn't protest.

21

SAVANNAH HAD ALWAYS TAGGED ALONG WITH HER parents if they came to Tarpon Springs for Epiphany. They hadn't made it every year. Sometimes at Christmas they'd had to visit her grandparents in Seattle, a long flight and a short stay. Her grandparents liked their quiet condo better than they liked their son and his family. They tidied their guest room and came along for the obligatory day or two of sightseeing, but their farewell was always more enthusiastic than their welcome.

She'd spoken to them twice since her father's death. Her grandmother had advised her to put the past behind her and get on with her life.

Savannah didn't like her grandmother.

Yiayia, on the other hand, was hard not to like. Savannah and the others had seen the dive and been to the Glendi. Now Yiayia's house was their last stop.

Yiayia greeted them immediately, raved about Helia's hair, which was now cotton candy pink on top and shaved on the sides, and welcomed Minh as a fellow immigrant.

She embraced Will right before she left to greet more guests, and Savannah watched his cheeks turn red. "Your mother was already here," Yiayia scolded. "She did not eat enough. You make her a plate to take home."

Savannah was relieved to have the introductions over and no crisis—at least she hoped not—from anything Yiayia had said. Yiayia shooed them to tables loaded with food and insisted they pile their plates high.

The yard looked much the way it had at Thanksgiving, and once again loudspeakers were belting out Greek music. The crowd was a little smaller because people were coming and going.

"Does she always do this?" Will asked, when they were out of earshot and Helia and Minh were filling plates. "Have a party for every holiday?"

Savannah didn't know. "We only came for Epiphany, but somebody told me this is nothing. Easter is supposed to be twice as festive."

"You're so lucky."

"I'm not related to her. She just pretends. She's related to Cassie. That's all."

"Yiayia isn't pretending." He glanced sideways. "Do you have other family? You know, blood family?"

"Grandparents on my father's side. Gen's parents are missionaries who run an orphanage in Nigeria. I met them once, and Gen says one day we'll go there and visit. I have doubts. They weren't exactly friendly the first time."

"Why?"

Savannah usually didn't talk about the strange custody arrangement her father and mother had worked out, because it was too hard to explain. But for some reason she wanted to tell Will.

"Nobody's ever really said so, but my parents only got married so I wouldn't be illegitimate. You know, a bastard."

"Not a good way to think of yourself, Sav."

"Yeah, but almost correct. They split up pretty much right after I was born. My father wanted to raise me, so that's how they worked it out. They were on different coasts, so, like, shared custody was impossible. Anyway, my grandparents are super religious. Missionaries, right? And I think they're still angry at Gen for the whole setup. I'm thinking I won't be visiting them anytime soon."

"Maybe I'm lucky I don't know my family."

Savannah thought about that as they dished up plates and later after Helia and Minh had gone off on their own and Will was driving back home.

"So...you don't know your family at all?" she asked, as if the conversation had been just a moment ago.

"Just my mother. I've never met her relatives, and she doesn't talk about them."

"You really don't have a father?"

"My mom says he's dead, but I remind her of him. He wasn't married, so it wasn't adultery. That's about all I know."

Savannah watched as he turned into Sunset Vista and waited for the security gate to open before he continued at a snail's pace. "I guess you don't know his name?"

"I don't."

"I'm sorry, but that's weird, Will. Was he a serial killer or something?"

He strangled a laugh. "I don't think so. She says he was a good man."

"Well, what else would she say?"

"I doubt he was Ted Bundy."

"I didn't mean to make it sound like he was."

"I like it when you apologize."

She tossed her hair over her shoulder. "Don't count on it ever happening again." She saw they were nearly home. "You really deserve to know more, don't you? You're old enough to drive this car and work part-time and, well, everything else. If you want to know, shouldn't you ask her?"

"You think I haven't?"

"You're just such a goody-goody, I'll give you some advice. If you want something, you keep asking. Maybe with Amber you have to phrase it differently every time. You know, ask it this way and that. In different places, maybe. Casually and pointed. That kind of thing."

"Wear her down, you mean?" He sounded skeptical. "Is that working for you?"

Savannah considered. "I haven't measured my success rate. But yeah, sometimes. Mostly I didn't have to find out big stuff like you do. I knew who my parents were. Mine was little stuff. Like curfews and going to parties."

"My mom's life has been tough. I don't know what it was like before I came on the scene, but I'm pretty sure it wasn't good."

"Your father had to be part of it."

"Yeah, that's obvious. But if she doesn't want me to know more, do I want to make her life harder with demands? I mean, I'm all she's got."

"Doesn't that seem kind of weird, too? I mean, your mom's gorgeous. She's smart and funny. Wouldn't any man want to be with her? Or...woman?"

He snorted. "Man."

"You know for sure?"

"She goes out with men." He pulled into the driveway and clicked the garage door opener. "Sometimes."

"You're going to move away one day." She frowned and gave that some thought. "I hope you are, right?"

"She wouldn't want it any other way."

"Then she'll be alone, and her life might be tougher. So if you make it a little tougher now by asking about your father, maybe asking will, you know, make her tell you. And maybe that will free her a little to have a social life."

"That makes no sense at all."

"I just think you have a right to know exactly who you are, even if it hurts your mother a little. I read this article about adopted kids and how important it is for them to find out about their birth parents. Not all of them, maybe, but a lot."

"Even if the news is bad?"

"At least they know. It's better than living with secrets and wondering the worst. And I think maybe if your mother finally tells you, she'll feel better and be able to move on."

He pulled into the garage and parked as Savannah finished up. "If you're old enough to help support your little family, you're old enough to know its history."

"You don't let up, do you?"

She considered. "I'm demonstrating."

"I got the picture." He reached around and took the plate he'd heaped high for his mother at Yiayia's insistence.

They both got out. "Hey, we have the stuff for ice cream sundaes," Savannah said. "I could make them."

"You didn't eat enough at Yiayia's?"

"You're probably already hungry."

He smiled just enough to let her know he wasn't holding a grudge.

The sun had set by the time Travis walked Amber to the door of Cassie's house. They'd had so much fun at the restaurant that she hadn't even realized how late it was. Tonight she'd learned that Travis had worked in food service during college, and as a bachelor, he tended to eat out a lot. So he was something of a connoisseur.

"And another thing," she said on the front stoop. "Four different people checked on us. From my perspective, that's excessive and pushy."

"And our server only checked once. The rest of the time they were strangers."

He had a journalist's eye. She was impressed he'd counted. "A lot of restaurants are trending away from having their servers establish a primary relationship with customers. Some of it seems to be the way they organize the dining room and scatter servers from end to end. One person takes an order, then someone else delivers the food, and managers or assistants or even the host who seated them stop by to be sure all is well. I've never thought that was a good idea. I like to be the one they ask if they need something or have a complaint."

He laughed. "You want them to complain?"

"We make our living from tips. If people feel they know us and can depend on us, they're more generous. The best dining rooms keep servers in their own section. Tickets are printed wirelessly. Bills are presented and credit cards swiped at the table. Tonight I was waiting for the bartender to show up and ask how you liked your Manhattan."

"We both liked the food, though."

"If I hated it, I would certainly have had lots of evidence to back me up. You ordered enough for an army."

He put one hand on the door and leaned against it. "It will all get eaten eventually. And aren't you glad I ordered the pasta with artichokes, even though you thought it was too much, on top of the grouper?"

"And the three appetizers and the extra sides. Oh, and different salads."

"Seems to me you ate your share and mine."

"I'm not going to eat again for a week. I've done nothing all day but eat."

"Except the seafood salad. You only ate one bite."

"I'm not a fan of calamari."

"You're living in the wrong town."

"It didn't feel like it today," she said, before she could consider her words.

He was pleased. "So you had fun? You like being with me?"

She had liked it, although she wondered how a man who made his living as a freelance journalist could afford to entertain her that well. She hoped they hadn't eaten their way through his entire monthly food budget.

"No?" he asked, tilting his head in question when she didn't answer.

She couldn't do anything but smile, because he was so appealing as he tried to get her to confirm what had been perfectly obvious. "Travis, you are really hard not to like."

"Which means you might be willing to enjoy my company in the future?"

She searched for an answer that wasn't a commitment. "Stranger things have happened."

He pushed away from the door and opened it. "And you're sure I can't pawn off some of the doggie bags? Will would probably love what we had."

"Nope. This way you won't have to cook all week, and these days we eat a lot of our meals at the Kouzina." She started inside, and then she turned to face him. "Thank you for a wonderful day."

He rested a hand on her shoulder and leaned forward, brushing his lips against hers, so fast she wasn't prepared. Not quite like a friend, but not like somebody determined to become her lover. He understood her well, which concerned her.

He straightened. "You're welcome." And then he was gone.

She was smiling when she closed the door behind her. There were no lights on in the great room, so either Cassie hadn't made it home yet, or she was in her suite washing off the remnants of a day serving food under a tent at the park. She thought she heard music coming from Savannah's room.

At the door of their suite she knocked to let Will know she was entering. Inside, the door between the sitting room and the bedroom was open, and she crossed to peer inside.

Will was sprawled on the bed using the laptop they shared. He didn't look happy.

"Hey, did you have fun today?" she asked.

He looked up. "It was good."

"Did you get enough to eat? Or do you want to make something now?"

"I'm full. Look what I'm doing." He turned the laptop to face her. She couldn't tell what was on the screen from that distance, so she walked closer and bent over.

The last website she'd visited was on the screen. She remembered now that she'd closed the computer without getting off the site and erasing her history. She'd done exactly what she tried so hard to avoid. She had left a footprint for Will to follow.

Had she left more? Her mind raced through the websites she'd visited lately. But here? At the library? At the community college?

"Are you looking for a new place to move?" His tone was just short of a rebuke.

The page read "Small Towns, Big Rewards." Now she remembered that she'd been checking out some of the places she'd investigated the day Cassie showed up at the library. Frantically she continued to search back through her mind, praying that this was the only site she had checked on this computer.

She perched on the edge of the bed and tried to look relaxed. "Not seriously," she said, with a smile. "But you know me. I'm always looking for the next great opportunity."

"Mom, a lot of your so-called great opportunities weren't. You know what I mean? And I thought we were staying here until I graduate."

Will was rarely angry. She didn't know how she'd given birth to someone so even-tempered, since neither she nor Billy had come from easygoing families. Many times she'd tried to imagine their life together if Will had been prone to acting out or temper tantrums.

He was angry now, though. She could see it in his eyes. He was angry and hurt that she was looking for a way out when he was growing happier and happier here.

She formed her next sentences slowly and carefully. "You're right. I guess I've found enough not-so-great opportunities that I keep expecting the roof to cave in here. We came close, remember? When we were evicted?"

"Yeah, well, we have a roof over our heads now, and Cassie and Savannah really want us here. So why are you looking for the next town?"

She made herself comfortable against the footboard of the bed. "Habit?"

"You're making friends, and Yiayia thinks you're great. She sent home a big plate of food for you."

Her stomach turned over. "It's really nothing for you to worry about," she said. "I was just fooling around on the internet. Wasting time, I guess."

"You could have a real life here, if you just made up your mind to stay. Travis likes you a lot. That's pretty obvious."

"Don't play Cupid."

"I'd like a father, you know?" He narrowed his eyes. "As far as I can tell I'm a frigging miracle."

She wondered what had brought this on, but hadn't she known that the confrontation would come at some point? Hadn't she stayed awake at nights preparing what she should say?

She schooled herself to sound calm. "You're angry that I've told you so little."

"You think?" He sat up straighter, crossing his legs campfire style. "It's my past you're keeping secret. And what will happen if you die suddenly? How will I know if I'm going to be prone to certain diseases? Or—"

"You're worried about your health? You've hardly ever been sick, Will. Anything serious would have shown up by now."

"I'm worried about my mental health. Not knowing who I am isn't good for it, you know?"

She pressed her lips together and tried, just one more time, to think of a better way out of this. But nothing occurred to her now, just as nothing had on all those sleepless nights.

"I'm sorry," she said at last. "I really am. I… It's not a pretty story, sweetheart. And nothing good can come out of it. When I'm done, you still won't have a family." She paused. "But maybe you'll understand why not."

"I'm all ears."

He was so rarely sarcastic that stopped her. "For the record, you're not the only one this has been hard on. Okay?"

He nodded after a moment.

"You have to promise that whatever I tell you will be between us. And that you won't go to the people I'm going to tell you about, looking for more answers. Otherwise I'm not going to tell you a thing."

"That's not fair."

"If you don't think so, then we're done here. Do you want to hear this or not?"

He considered. For a moment she thought he might say no. But finally he nodded again. "Your terms."

"Your father was my high school sweetheart, Will. He was two years older than I was, and his name was Roger Hart. He enlisted in the army right after graduation. He wanted an education and a way for us to be together, and he thought that was his best option. Then 9-11 happened and our country went to war. I'm so sorry to tell you that he was killed almost immediately after being deployed to Afghanistan."

He looked so sad that she wanted to hug him close, the way she would have when he was much younger. But an embrace would not soothe his pain.

"You knew he was dead," she said softly.

"Not how."

"No, and I doubt you feel better for knowing."

He cleared his throat, but his eyes were filmed with tears. She hated herself.

"So why is that such a secret?" he asked.

"Because of our families. That's the worst part. The Harts and my people had been bitter enemies for generations. They fought over land, and both sides still thought they'd been cheated even when I was growing up. Roger and I knew the score, so our relationship had to be a secret right from the start. But we were young and in love. We couldn't help ourselves."

"Where?"

She had done her research, and she knew what to say. "A small town where everybody knew everybody else's business. That's all you need to know. But if either of our families had learned that we'd fallen in love, they would have been furious, and who knows what they might have done to one or both of us."

"This is like Romeo and Juliet," he said.

She hoped the similarity didn't make the story ring less

true. "We didn't marry, the way they did. We really couldn't. Between us we had no resources and nobody to help, and we were too young to marry without our parents' consent. So Roger joined the army after graduation. The plan was for him to come for me once he could afford to, marry me, then together we would go to each of our families and tell them what we'd done. By then I would be through school and able to leave with him. He wanted a career in the armed services. We thought we had it all figured out."

Will was way ahead of her. "I guess you didn't figure out that I was on my way into the world."

She made herself meet his gaze. "Unfortunately your father was sent to Afghanistan right after training and killed in action. Before he deployed, he came home for a visit. We spent as much time together as we could in secret. Then he left and weeks later I realized I was pregnant."

She let that sink in a moment, hating herself the whole time. "I'm not even sure he got my letter telling him about you because he was killed very soon after he left. I knew that, at best, my parents would force me to give up my baby once it was born. I was also afraid that Roger's family might some-how find out the baby was his. And then what would they do? They wouldn't have welcomed us into their family, that was certain. So I left and never looked back."

"You never tried to work this out?"

"My family held grudges for decades. There was no hope of that. Growing up there was like walking barefoot over a volcano, Will. My parents had no understanding of love or compassion, and Roger's were the same. Both families are dead to me."

"Maybe you're wrong. Maybe they've forgiven you, Mom. Maybe they would like to get to know me."

She covered his hand with hers. "No, sweetheart. Neither

family would want anything to do with us, even all these years later. Trust me on this. They will still be angry, because that's the kind of people they are. Read about family feuds sometime if you have to. This one began generations ago. All through history and over the centuries, too many people have been hurt or even killed just because they have the wrong last name. I had to protect us both."

"This is hard to believe."

She hoped he was wrong and that he *would* believe it once the story settled in his mind. She hoped that now that he had facts, he could put the whole issue of his parentage behind him. She hoped she had painted Roger Hart's family and her own as so unforgiving and hateful that he would never look for them.

She was not optimistic.

"Why didn't you tell me before?"

She had an answer for that, too. "I believed that no family would be better than the real ones. And I've been keeping you from trying to make contact. Because everyone would suffer if you tried, Will. Most of all you and me. And I hope you're old enough and smart enough to take me at my word and leave this alone."

"Are they the reason we've moved so much?"

She almost said yes, but she was afraid that would open a whole new avenue of questions. More important, she needed for him to feel safe.

"Like I've always told you, our moves have been for better opportunities. I don't think anyone's looking for me. I left the family fold, and that made me a traitor. I think my family would walk a mile in the other direction if they thought I was suddenly going to pop up in their lives."

He didn't say anything, and suddenly bone-tired, she got to her feet. "I know that's a lot to think about. Promise me again that you won't contact the Harts, or the Blairs. Let sleeping dogs lie." She paused. "And it would be best if you just laid this to rest and didn't try to find out more. Because nothing you'll find out will be good or helpful. Leave it all behind us. That's where it belongs."

He looked like he was trying to master a host of feelings. "Was my father the good man you always told me he was?"

The names might be counterfeit, but now, at least, she could be truthful. "He was wonderful. I'm not sure how we both fell so far from the family tree, but your father was nothing like his family. You would have loved him. I did."

"I think I'm going to take a shower." Will swung his legs over the other side of the bed.

She gave his back a pat before he stood. "I would rather not talk about this again. Can you see why?"

"I guess." He left for the bathroom and she watched the door close behind him.

She hoped that the bathroom door wasn't the only one to be securely closed that night. She prayed silently that Will would now bury his questions and move on.

22

CASSIE COULDN'T BELIEVE SHE'D FALLEN FOR A
scam, but early that morning she'd seen an advertisement in
the *Tarpon Times*, and she hadn't taken the time to do research.
She dived in without checking for sharks because she wanted
to be the first applicant in the water.

Now she closed her front door and leaned against it, arms
folded. She was angry, exhausted and, for the moment, just-
hit-bottom hopeless.

Amber, toweling her hair, came into the great room and
stopped when she saw her. "Uh-oh."

Cassie closed her eyes. "Do I look like a pushover to you?"

"This can't be good."

"Well, do I?"

"Of course not. Even if you did bring a stranger with a
teenage son into your house and refuse to charge them rent."

"The correct answer is just plain no." Cassie opened her eyes
and pushed away from the door. "Worst job interview ever."

"I bet I can top you."

"You start."

Amber stopped toweling her hair long enough to lay a finger on one cheek, as if she was trying to choose. "Two years ago a restaurant owner told me I would get the floor manager job if I agreed to have breast augmentation surgery. He said he'd front the fee himself—and yes, he phrased it that way—but I had to promise I'd stay until I worked off what he paid. For both of them. He was very specific, right boob, then left."

"You're making that up."

"Nope. Then he said if I wanted to get out of debt faster, he'd be happy to pay me for other services I could render after work. He promised I would love every minute of our time together. In fact, I would want to pay him."

"Did you report this guy?"

"That would have increased the fun a hundredfold, right? Police, prosecutors, lawyers. But I did tell the next three women waiting to be interviewed they should run like the wind. Two got up and came with me. One was thinking it over when we left." She cocked her head. "Your turn."

"The ad in today's paper said the job was an immediate hire in the arts and entertainment field. They wanted someone with general marketing experience but would train for specifics. I made an appointment, and that's where I've been. The guy conducting the interview told me I'd be promoting major entertainment figures who were coming to a variety of venues in the area, and before we talked specifics, he wanted me to see where I'd be working."

"Tell me you didn't get in his car."

At least that part of her hadn't been suckered in. "I knew better, so I followed him. We ended up in a housing development about thirty miles from here. When I got out of the car, he handed me a stack of printed announcements that contained a two-dollar movie coupon at the bottom and told me to go door to door and hand them to the homeowners. Get it? Promoting major entertainment figures at a variety of venues?"

"That was it?"

"He said he wanted to see how I conducted myself with people, if I was friendly and knew how to push buttons. And if I did well, every time somebody used one of my coupons I'd earn a percentage. The percentage would depend on how many coupons other 'marketing pros like myself' had success with each week. There was only so much money to split up, so it varied."

Amber finished rubbing her hair, and then flung the towel over her shoulder. "Do people fall for that, do you suppose?"

"If they travel there in the guy's car, they probably can't get home until they comply. Or if they're desperate and willing to work for next to nothing."

"You win because you had to drive all those miles and waste so much time. My boob interview was blessedly short. I was already at the door by the time he mentioned the other services."

"I should get a bonus. I ripped the flyers into pieces and dropped them at the guy's feet. He said he was going to have me arrested. I told him I'd seen a 'No Solicitation' sign as we drove in, and I would be happy to stay until the police arrived so I could explain why he was there."

"We need T-shirts. Badass Women Unite."

"At the rate my job search is going, I have plenty of time to hand paint a hundred."

"There's no reason I shouldn't be paying rent."

"Sure there is."

Amber shook her head. "I've got to finish getting ready for work. What about family—can they look out for job prospects?"

"Carefully chosen family members already are. Roxanne.

Travis—" She saw the subtle change in Amber's expression at the mention of the name. "A few others. Try not to mention this to Yiayia. I can wait forever for the kind of job she would find for me."

"Mum's the word."

Cassie stepped out to the lanai and checked her fledgling plants. Savannah's lemon tree was flourishing, scenting the air with blossoms and already forming fruit. Travis had dropped off half a dozen good-sized starts, an orchid already loaded with blooms, a spider plant and a variety of succulents that she'd transferred to pots. It was no accident that he'd made sure Amber was home the day he arrived. He'd wangled an invitation for dinner, too.

Afterward she stretched out in a lounge chair and gazed into the pool. Half an hour later she was still staring at the water when Amber came out to say goodbye. "I got the mail, and I'm on my way to the Kouzina. I'll bring home dinner. There's leftover pizza for the kids." She handed Cassie a stack of what looked like junk mail and went back into the house.

Cassie paged through and dismissed most of the mail, but the final envelope was the size of the one she'd opened on Christmas Day. The address label looked the same. Her heart sped faster. She held it up to the sun streaming overhead, but the envelope revealed nothing.

She debated, then she hit Nick's phone number, which she'd added to speed dial. As before, she expected to leave a message, but he answered.

She identified herself and told him about the envelope in her hand. "Should I open it, or would it be better to let you or somebody there do it?"

He hesitated, said something to someone nearby, then came back on. "I'm down at the docks. Want to meet me at the Limani for lunch?"

"Only if I can pay."

"Great. That way I can order Greek fries, too."

"Only if you share." She had struggled to sound casual but apparently hadn't succeeded.

"Hey, it's okay," he said, his voice reassuring. "We'll get to the bottom of this."

She hoped he was right.

Today Nick wore jeans and a long sleeved polo shirt. The Limani was on the Sponge Docks, a walk-up window with wire mesh tables in the back looking over the river and boats docked on both sides. The air was scented with salt breezes, fish and grilled meat. Cassie ordered a pork souvlaki plate for Nick, and asked them to make the fries Greek style. She added a fish pita for herself and more fries so she wouldn't be tempted to steal his.

Nick lounged in the sun as they waited to pick up their order. "I love this place. It's real taverna food. *Limani* means *port* in Greek and every port in Greece has a taverna."

She watched a sponge boat docked just beyond them. One crew member sprayed water over the harvest, cleaning the black "skin" off the sponge, which was really a skeleton of an animal that could regenerate from whatever the sponge diver left behind. Sponges that had already been cleaned during the trip swung in long strings from poles and every surface high enough to move them out of the way. As she watched, the other crew member took down one string and began stuffing the sponges into a net bag.

She remembered when there had been more sponge boats. Late in her childhood, beds in Greece had suffered, and the world had looked to Tarpon Springs for its harvest. Like a gold rush, men had streamed in, many with no idea what to do, and underwater deaths had followed. Today natural sponges were still needed. Among other uses they had antibacterial properties and were softer for bathing delicate skin or washing cars or boats. Shoe manufacturers used them for applying color and restorers preferred them when dry-cleaning works of art. But the fleet was smaller, the divers used scuba gear, not helmets and suits, and boats often stayed in the Gulf for weeks at a time. This was a smaller craft with two burly and obviously competent men, and watching them work was a pleasure.

"Have you been to Greece?" she asked Nick.

"During the summer after high school I worked for an uncle on a fishing boat in Thessaloniki. JoAnn didn't like to travel, but I went back after she died and rode ferries from island to island to try to put myself back together."

"Did it help?"

"I saw her in every sunset."

She understood completely.

"You've been?" he asked.

"I've always wanted to. Mark liked to travel, but he also liked to choose where we went. Greece was never on the menu." Now she wondered why she'd let him get away with that. She wondered what it would be like to travel there now that Mark was no longer calling the shots. If she and Savannah could heal their relationship, would her daughter accompany her? It would be an exceptional graduation present.

They picked up their order. Water was sluicing across the deck of the sponge boat, and gulls and other seabirds were circling.

They chatted about high school, and Nick caught her up on friends they had shared. He ate efficiently and quickly. When he'd finished, he pushed his plate to one side. "Show me the letter."

She dug it out, and he pulled on disposable gloves and held up his hands. "So you'll think I know what I'm doing."

"Will you have the letter dusted for fingerprints?"

He smiled a polite no. "Let's see what it says this time. The last one just fell into the despicable category."

"I guess you can't charge anybody for despicable."

"We all have a little despicable in us. Unfortunately some have more than a little."

She handed him the envelope, and he took a plastic knife he hadn't used with lunch and carefully slit the envelope. He unfolded the paper and read out loud.

"I'm sure you've been thinking about my last communication. It has to be eating at you. How important is your dead husband's reputation? How much do you care if people know who he really was and what he did? And that sweet daughter of his? How will she feel if the news gets out? I bet you're trying to figure out what to do and how to stop that from happening."

Cassie took a sip of the bottled water she'd bought with lunch. She waited, but Nick had fallen silent. "Does it go on? Does this maniac say what I have to do to stop whatever it is?" She'd read up on Florida's extortion laws. She knew this didn't qualify.

Nick shook his head and carefully folded the letter and put it back in the envelope before he stripped off the gloves and shoved them in a pocket. "I still think somebody's toying with you. There's no information on the so-called secrets. No hint they really know anything. It feels like someone trying to get under your skin. Maybe to make you do something foolish."

"Like what?"

"Make enemies by asking questions that don't need to be asked? Or maybe someone wants you to ask questions because they want you to find things you don't know. Maybe, once you do, they plan to make some kind of offer."

It was all so vague. They. Maybe. Some kind of offer.

"So." Nick sat back and tented his fingers. "Do you know more about your husband's last year than you've told me? You don't have to answer. No crime's been committed, so I'm not asking as a police officer. Just a friend."

"A police officer is a good friend to have right now." She stalled. "Do you like what you do, Nick? I thought you'd end up as a lawyer. Don't I remember that was your goal?"

"Good memory, but after college I was tired of classrooms, so I decided a few years of working in law enforcement would be a good thing for law school applications. In just months I realized I was happy right where I was."

"The dive team was a bonus, right? Not a lot of underwater action for lawyers."

He smiled in answer to hers. "Some attorneys probably make enough money to dive all over the world. But I wouldn't have the thrill of recovering murder weapons or finding hidden drug caches. And I wouldn't be able to give a family closure who lost a loved one in deep water and needed to bring the body home."

She had asked about his job to buy time, but she hadn't thought ahead. Mark's body had been found by the Coast Guard, although divers hadn't been needed. She could see Nick had just realized he'd hit too close to home.

"Cassie, I'm sorry…"

She held up her hand. "No, it's okay. Really. I'm glad there are people like you, Nick. Mark's body was found very quickly, washed into shallow water, but I can't imagine how much more awful it would have been if I'd had to wait for days or even forever. Everyone I dealt with couldn't have been kinder. You're doing something important."

"Next of kin notifications are the hardest things we do. I feel like I'm digging a hole under their feet and shoving them in."

She liked this man and she realized she could trust him. "I told you that Mark changed significantly in the last year of his life. But I didn't tell you the kicker. He was a psychiatrist, remember? And the practice he was part of catered to a lot of affluent patients. He always saw people who weren't rich, too, but the upshot is that Mark made a lot of money."

She explained how carefully their money had been invested. She paused, because the next part was hard enough to believe, much less recount. Then she told him what she'd learned from Greg.

Nick finally spoke. "An investment with a prep school roommate? Was it a scam?"

"I don't know. The roommate, Sim Barcroft, really is a genius. He's a financial analyst for some international conglomerate. I've seen articles, and he's brilliant at predicting the market. I guess this time his genius failed."

"Leaving you with nothing?"

"Leaving me with a fraction of what I thought we had." She told him the rest, including the fight over the savings account. "When I confronted Mark, he got angry and blamed me for snooping. We had a huge fight about it right before he went sailing."

He reached over and covered her hand with his for a moment. "And now you feel responsible?"

She was grateful he understood. "Late at night the fight haunts me, but to be honest I've been too busy trying to pick up the pieces of our lives to regularly beat myself up."

"That's some story."

She nodded. "If there are secrets to be exposed, they probably revolve around the money that disappeared."

"So what have you done about that?"

She told him about her conversation with Fletcher and then with Ivy. "Greg, our financial advisor, assured me I can get a forensic accountant to look at his records. I haven't done that yet because I think he told me the truth."

Nick balled up the trash from their lunch, scooping up hers to add to his. He left to dump it in a waste receptacle, but when he came back, he leaned over the table, resting his palms against it. "Hire the accountant. What about the prep school roommate? Have you talked to him?"

"What could he tell me?"

"Whether your husband's story was true. Can you trust him?"

"I guess it would depend on what he said."

"Start there, then."

Cassie got to her feet knowing that Nick probably had to get back to work. "You think this whole financial thing could be what the letters are about?"

"Find out what you can. But if it turns out that your husband didn't lose everything in a bad investment, then you have to ask yourself where all the money went. The letters may refer to whatever your husband did with it. If the way he spent it was aboveboard, like buying rental properties or funding a fledgling charity, he would have told you, probably even if he was afraid you would disagree. But since he didn't..."

"I don't have any ideas. Not one."

"Ask yourself how people spend money. And I mean in ways they shouldn't. Make a list, Cassie. You knew him better than anybody. What were Mark's weaknesses?"

She didn't have to give that any thought. "His conviction he wasn't allowed to have any."

"A man like that would have a lot of trouble when he realized he had given in to a weakness, wouldn't he?"

He was warning her. She might not like what she found. She might learn things about Mark she didn't want to know. She might learn answers about his death she would rather keep as questions.

"You're very kind to help," she said, holding out her hand.

He shook his head, then he came around the table and pulled her close for a quick hug instead. "You know, I actually wanted to do that in high school. Call it delayed gratification. You get more letters, or find out anything you want to share, you can always find me. I'll help if I can. That's a promise. Thanks for lunch." He gave her a casual salute and headed down the dock.

Nick had warned her about the road ahead, and with good reason. Unless the letters turned into full-blown extortion, she could set the past aside. She could move on with her life as she'd told him she was trying to do.

Instead she sat at the table they had shared and began to scroll through her list of contacts, looking for somebody who might know how to get in touch with Sim Barcroft.

Finally, with seagulls cawing behind her and the sponge boat crew taking more strings of sponges from hooks, she punched in a number and waited.

23

AMBER WASN'T MAKING AS MUCH MONEY AT THE Kouzina as she'd made during the pre-hepatitis days at Dine Eclectic, but she enjoyed the job more. The other servers were friendly, as was everyone back of house. Unfortunately the Kouzina was competing with so many other "authentic" Greek restaurants, they weren't attracting the tourists they needed. Yiayia's solution was to turn up the music and dust off the fading plastic flowers on the tables.

The restaurant needed serious renovation. The wallpaper mural of Santorini, with its blue domed churches and colorful houses clinging to the hillside, had been in place for decades. The white plaster buildings in the foreground were turning yellow, and the setting sun looked as if it planned to sink into the ocean and never come up again. Half the chairs needed seat repairs, and wobbly tables were steadied by Yiayia's Kouzina matchbooks, left over from the days when smoking was allowed inside.

Amber had a surprise to spiff things up.

"This is for me?" Yiayia asked, reaching for a huge gift bag Amber had purchased at the Dollar Store.

Everyone in the kitchen stopped to watch. Roxanne looked most interested. Amber was sorry she hadn't consulted her first, but Yiayia had to be in charge, even when, these days, she really didn't have the energy or flexibility.

"I can't imagine." Yiayia grabbed Amber and kissed her on both cheeks.

Amber tried not to appear as flustered as she felt. "The gift is really for everyone. But you'll see. I just hope you like them."

"How could I not like them when you brought them to me?" Yiayia began to pick at the ribbon tying the bag. "What could this be? It's heavy. Like a bag of rocks."

Roxanne had a brow cocked. Amber gave the slightest shrug, since Yiayia wasn't looking her way.

She finally got the bag open and began to pull out the contents. She stopped with the first item, peering inside, where Amber knew there were a dozen more just like it.

"What is this?"

"Shake it out and see."

Yiayia did. "Oh, it is beautiful!"

Amber felt her entire body relax. She'd made the server's apron in Yiayia's hands from white duck canvas she'd found at Things From the Springs. Someone had donated multiple yards to the shop, most likely left over from a work project, or mill ends. She'd taken the whole lot for very little money. She still had enough remnants to make half a dozen canvas bags for her Etsy shop.

"It says Yiayia's Kouzina! And the pockets!"

Amber had used the embroidery feature on her sewing machine to add a Greek key design in bright blue along the top of both sizable pockets on the bib-style aprons. Yiayia's Kouzina was embroidered in script across the apron's top. She'd designed them to look sleek, swooping along the sides to full coverage from the waist down.

"They are beautiful! You did this for us?"

"Nobody else." Amber submitted to another cheek kissing. "There are twelve, enough for every server to have their own, so they can take them home to launder when neded."

Yiayia rubbed the fabric against her cheek. "They must have cost so much."

"Not a thing for you." She explained about the fabric. "And I made them in the evening while I watched television. My gift to the Kouzina. A thank-you from Will and me."

Half an hour later Yiayia was still crowing about the aprons when Amber, wearing hers over the required uniform of blue slacks and white shirt, got a phone call. She was filling saltshakers and setting the tables for lunch, and since the restaurant hadn't opened, she still had her cell phone in a pocket. She raised it to her ear without looking at Caller ID.

At first no one answered, then there was a screech, and a voice that sounded like someone screaming underwater. "Who is this?" she asked.

Something which might have been a laugh was her answer, but the sound, which was drawn out and increased in volume until it was painful, was followed by a loud click, then silence.

She immediately checked Caller ID and saw "Unknown Caller," a popular telemarketer ploy. By the time she slipped the phone back in her pocket, her heart was speeding.

Roxanne, wearing a bright emerald chef's coat, was lending a hand at setting up the tables. Before the call she had complimented Amber on convincing Yiayia that the aprons were nothing more than a thank-you gift instead of an attempt to raise the bar. Now she frowned when she noted her staring into space. "You okay?"

"Fine. Just a weird phone call."

252 · EMILIE RICHARDS

"These days I don't even answer a call unless I'm sure it's somebody I know. Legitimate callers can always leave a voice mail."

Amber was only half listening.

"For someone who's fine, you don't look fine," Roxanne said.

Amber had gotten so good at lying she didn't hesitate. "You have a son, right? Gary? Did you worry about him the way I worry about Will? I was afraid that might be the school with bad news."

"You never stop worrying, but you're raising that boy right. He's a trouper."

Amber retrieved a smile from somewhere. "I'm being silly. Thanks."

The second call came when she was taking her first order of the day. Normally once the restaurant started to fill, her phone went into her purse hanging from a hook in the kitchen, but because of the strange call, she still had it with her. She could feel it buzzing against her leg, although she couldn't answer. Once she'd placed the order, she stepped into the hallway in front of the coatroom. Again the screen read "Unknown Caller."

She checked her voice mail and listened, breath held. Again the caller sounded as if he—she thought it was a man—was drowning. She couldn't make out a word.

She told herself this had to be a telemarketer in a call center somewhere across oceans and continents. She hoped maybe now that a message had been left, the person would move on.

By the end of her lunch shift, though, she knew better. She'd gotten two more calls. All similar, all inaudible and all frightening.

Darryl.

By now her hands were trembling. She'd bought and registered her phone in Alabama years ago, right before leaving the state on her way to Baton Rouge, where she and Will had lived for a year. She'd thought that registering the number in a state where she no longer lived would protect her. But since then she'd learned about radio signals between cell towers, triangulation software and the way law enforcement could track almost anyone.

She wondered if making call after call helped pinpoint the phone's location even more closely. She wondered if that was why she had now gotten a total of four. As sheriff, even sheriff of the smallest county in West Virginia, Darryl had access not only to advanced technology, but to people who knew how to use it.

None of that addressed how he'd gotten her phone number, but the possibilities were endless. The most likely was the woman who had helped Amber from the very day her nightmare had begun. Betsy Garland was in her seventies now. While she'd promised she would never write down Amber's number, had she grown afraid that one day she might not be able to remember it? Had she jotted the number somewhere and Darryl had found it? He would know how to search a house without detection.

"You know, you're not looking too good," Roxanne said.

Amber realized Roxanne had probably been standing there awhile. This time she didn't have to lie. "I'm not feeling that great. And it's not going away."

"Do you have a shift tonight, too?"

Amber nodded.

"Want me to see if I can get somebody to cover for you? Maria likes to sub. If she's not able to, we'll find somebody else."

Amber needed the money, but she was afraid she might

need to pack even more. "That would be great. But I can do it if nobody else comes through."

"You just go home and take care of yourself."

Amber thanked her, hung her apron on its hook and grabbed her purse.

At Cassie's house she checked her surroundings, then quickly drove into the garage and let herself in. She was relieved to see she was alone inside. She was already heading toward the bedroom when she remembered she'd better check the house phone, too. If Darryl was her caller, then he might know everything, starting with the name she'd adopted the day she left Croville County forever.

The phone was blinking, and she punched in the code, although the first time she was shaking too hard to do it correctly. Finally, she fell to the chair by the phone and listened.

The same underwater voice sounded over the line, but this time the message was cut short. She sat still listening to the dial tone and tried to decide what to do. Could she drag Will away from Coastal Winds and Tarpon Springs because the caller might be Darryl? And if this was Darryl, wasn't it already too late to make an escape?

She'd made emergency plans for this situation, and for years she'd honed them. She had the name of a man who could provide her with more false documents. She had a folder of information on Darryl she had gleaned from the internet, including the names of other law enforcement personnel who had gone head-to-head with him. Betsy, who still lived in the town of Chaslan, Croville's county seat, had helped with that.

As a last resort Amber had nudged Will to take Spanish as his foreign language, and she'd signed up for free classes herself wherever they were given, in case they had to cross a border and disappear. But moving to Central or South America was a pipe dream. The tidal wave of immigrants heading to the United States was proof that heading the other way was pointless. Even though she'd been able to save money since moving in with Cassie, she still didn't have enough for a safe and comfortable transition to another culture.

And what would a move like that do to Will's life?

Even though she wasn't sure what to do or where to go, she began to assemble basics. Paperwork they would need anywhere they moved. Shoes and underwear. She divided clothes into piles so when she figured out where to go, she would be ready to pack.

Most important she tried to figure out what she would tell her son. She was desperately afraid the only explanation that would satisfy Will was the real one.

Somebody wanted to kill her. And when they found out about him…

The doorbell chimed, and she stifled a moan. Even though she told herself Darryl wouldn't bother with the bell, she couldn't make herself move. When it chimed again, she forced herself to step toward the front window of the suite and peek through the curtains.

Travis was just turning away and heading back up the sidewalk.

Her legs were shaking so hard it took twice as long as usual to get to the door and open it. She called his name and the squeak that she pushed out didn't sound like her voice. She was surprised he heard her.

He turned, smiled and raised his hand in a wave. "Hey, did I wake you? Roxanne said you weren't feeling well. I was checking to see if you needed anything."

She had never been happier to see anyone. She pulled him inside quickly and closed the door, leaning against it because she wasn't sure she could stand without support. She tried to come up with something to say, and nothing occurred to her. Her mind continued to spin.

"You do look pale." He reached over and laid his palm against her forehead. "You're not hot. That's good. Did you get lunch? Shall I make you something? Soup maybe?"

"I'm fine. I think I need a good nap."

"I'll leave you alone, then. But I've tried calling all morning—"

"What?" She stood a little straighter.

"Yeah." He looked perplexed. "Is that okay?"

"Sure, of course... But I didn't get..."

"Yeah, that's what I thought. I switched service providers and there seems to be some kind of glitch. I hear a click, and then the line goes dead after I start to speak. You didn't get messages either? I called here, too."

She was breathing deeply now, trying to calm herself. A moment passed before she could answer. "I did get a few strange—" She frowned as she pictured her Caller ID. "Every one of those calls said Unknown Caller. Have-you-changed-your-name-to-Unknown?" The last sentence came out as one angry word.

He looked surprised. "My name is blocked on all outgoing calls. As counterintuitive as it sounds, more of my article sources will answer if they don't know who's calling. Even when I'm just writing fluff pieces, people still don't want to talk to a reporter."

"They would rather talk to a telemarketer?"

"Sounds crazy, I know."

She closed her eyes. She was beginning to breathe more normally now.

"Did I scare you?" He sounded concerned.

She knew better than to pretend otherwise. "A little. The calls were really eerie, like someone was drowning. It sounded like something from a horror movie, some monster from the deep." She opened her eyes. "You need to get your phone fixed."

"I will."

By now her heartbeat was slowing. And she was so glad the calls had come from Travis, she wanted to throw her arms around him. "So, why was the Loch Ness Monster calling in the first place?"

He laughed. "Probably not the best time to ask now."

"Try anyway."

"I'm covering a charity event on Valentine's Day. It's a fancy bash, dancing, door prizes at a local country club. Swanky, not to mention a great cause. They're trying to raise funds for a new women's shelter. Will you be my date?"

She noticed, not for the first time, how long his eyelashes were and how the broad sweep of his brows drew more attention to the rich brown of his eyes. She also saw that he had one deep dimple in his cheek. She was so relieved that Darryl had not found her, her good sense fled.

She stepped forward and kissed him, and not all that casually, before she stepped back. "I'll clear my schedule. I would love to be your date. I'm assuming I have to get dressed up?"

He looked ridiculously pleased. "Do you mind?"

"I'll find something worthy."

"Hey, should I always catch you when you aren't feeling well?"

"Apparently."

"Should I push for more?"

"Not on your life."

He laughed. "Worth a try."

She reached around and opened the door. He passed her and then paused in the doorway, before leaning forward to brush her lips with his. "Feel better."

"I already do."

When he was gone, she went back to her suite determined to put piles back into drawers and reorganize her life. Instead, and for the first time in a long time, tears spilled down her cheeks. With her head in her hands she fell to the bed and cried for the woman she could have been if she hadn't spent the past seventeen years afraid that she and her son were both going to die.

24

SAVANNAH'S JAIL SENTENCE AT SCHOOL WAS OVER.
For a week now she'd been able to leave after the end of classes.
No more counseling sessions or tutorials. She had expected the
two weeks to crawl by, but surprisingly they hadn't been bad.
None of her teachers had resorted to busywork. Instead they
had pinpointed her problem in their class, which, of course,
didn't take massive amounts of brain power. She wasn't paying
attention and she didn't care. All rolled into one bad attitude.

The surprising part was that nobody really lectured. They'd
presented her with material to help her catch up, but nobody
had stood over her and insisted. Her counselor—a hipster with
black-framed glasses and a crew cut—had asked her to dia-
gram her future, devoting one side of the paper to what might
happen if she continued to blow off classes, and the other side
to what might happen if she decided to use her abilities and
talents. Clearly she wasn't dumb—just acting like it—so she
had a choice to make.

Every day Cassie had picked her up, and after the first afternoon, when Savannah had told her to butt out, she had

stopped asking how things were going. At first Savannah had been glad, but then she'd sort of missed Cassie's questions. Cassie asked different questions than Gen. Cassie knew Savannah's friends, her classes, her likes and dislikes. She never pried, but she always seemed to know what was on Savannah's mind and to find a way to help her explore it.

In contrast Gen never quite got her. Savannah understood it was easy to lose track of somebody you didn't see often. Gen tried to keep up, but sometimes the questions were so out-of-date, Savannah had trouble finding a polite response.

She had to tiptoe with Gen. Not that Gen had ever threatened her, but she was so rarely available that Savannah didn't want to take chances. She didn't know her mother well enough to be sure that if Gen was hurt or angry, she wouldn't disappear entirely.

Today, with school out and kids leaving, Savannah actually considered popping in to see her counselor, just to say hello, although she didn't, because how wack would that be? Instead she slouched on the front steps waiting for Will so they could walk to Roxanne's, where Cassie had promised to pick them up after five. Her stepmother was going on an afternoon job interview, and Savannah was hoping she would start working evenings. How perfect would it be to have her gone whenever Savannah was home?

Nobody else could provide transportation because the Kouzina was hosting an elaborate baby shower, complete with rented Greek columns, gilded clusters of grapes and laurel wreaths for the head of every mother in the room. Roxanne had volunteered to let Savannah and Will hang out at her house, which was only half a mile from the school. Yesterday she'd dropped off a key, and now Savannah had plans. She couldn't wait to share her idea with Will.

As she waited, Madeline and Lolly zoomed by with Madeline's mother at the wheel. After the fish guts incident the best friends had been suspended for two weeks and were only recently back in classes. According to rumors, Madeline's parents had taken her car keys until spring.

A familiar voice sounded behind her. "It's gotta be hard to be them. Up on top and then slapped down to the bottom. And, you know, it takes practice to make a good life down here. I don't know if they've got it in them."

Savannah glanced at Helia, who was now beside her. The pink topknot was history, and these days she rocked a buzz cut. Savannah had been surprised to discover that her friend's real hair color was a pretty golden blond, although at this point it was more like duck's down. Helia had said getting rid of the topknot was nobody's idea but hers. From what Savannah could tell, that was true. Her foster parents had turned out to be surprisingly cool, only insisting on rules that mattered. Helia hadn't said as much, but Savannah thought her friend liked living with them. She even seemed to like the younger kids, who swarmed through every room.

"Will and I are going to my aunt Roxanne's house," Savannah said. "You met her at Yiayia's, remember? Want to come?"

"I can't, and I feel sorry for you."

Savannah didn't get the connection. "Why?"

"Will's in a mood. He didn't turn in a paper in our Spanish class. He gets marked down one grade for every day it's late."

Savannah was surprised. Will was such a goody-goody. Missing a deadline seemed unthinkable.

"You haven't noticed how crabby he is these days?" Helia asked.

"He's kind of been locking himself away." Now that Savannah thought about it, that was unusual. "Did he tell you why?"

"Like we talk about feelings?" Helia snorted. "Minh says he seems different, too. And she should know."

Minh and Will weren't exactly hanging out, but Savannah had seen them together in the halls and sometimes after school. "Are they fighting or something?"

"Didn't sound that way. She says he's quiet, like he's thinking about big stuff but doesn't share."

Savannah wondered if she had set this in motion herself when she pressed Will to talk to his mother about his father. "Well, maybe he'll talk to me today," she said.

"What is he to you anyway?"

Savannah stared. "Are you kidding? He's like a brother, or a cousin you have to be nice to. Anything else would be creepy!"

Helia held up her hands. "Okay."

"So how do you get your brother to talk to you?"

"He's hard to shut up. It's not a problem." Helia lifted her hand in goodbye as her foster family's van drove up, children hanging out every window as far as their restraints would allow. They began shouting her name.

She stepped to the sidewalk and turned before she went to the van. "Do you believe it? These poor suckers claim they want to adopt me." She shrugged, and before Savannah could respond, she took off.

Savannah was still smiling when Will came up beside her. "Are you ready?" he asked with no preliminary.

"Hello to you, too, Mr. Grouchy."

"Don't start on me, okay?"

They started down the sidewalk with Savannah leading the way. "Guess what Helia told me," she said, wanting to share Helia's good news—she hoped it was good.

"So what? I forgot to write a paper. It happens. I'll write it at Roxanne's."

"That's not what I was talking about." She decided to keep Helia's news to herself until he was in a mood to appreciate it. She tried a new topic. "There's something at Roxanne's I want you to see."

He just kept walking.

Savannah tried again. "She keeps a six-ton elephant in her bathtub and a giraffe in her pantry to help her reach the cans on the top shelf."

Will didn't respond.

"So today they made me homecoming queen, even though I'm only a sophomore," she said. "I told them I wasn't interested, but they insisted."

"Homecoming's over."

"You are alive. I wasn't sure." She fell silent, and they stayed that way for the next few minutes until she turned into Roxanne's driveway. He followed her to the front door, where she unzipped her backpack to get the key.

Roxanne's house was a concrete block bungalow she'd painted a soft turquoise on the outside, adding coral-colored trim and a door the color of ripening lemons. The exterior was sedate compared with the inside and extended all the way to the back of the lot.

Savannah opened the door and ushered Will inside. Color blared from every surface. It was like stepping into a box of crayons, the supersized pack of two hundred she'd always begged for as a child.

"Holy cow." Will whistled.

"You're the only sixteen-year-old in the world who says *holy cow.*"

"This is a rainbow on steroids."

"It's hard not to be cheerful here."

"It's hard not to get a headache here."

"Yeah, sometimes I have to go outside and stare at a tree. But it's a good house. It's got a lot more room than it looks."

"I might have to go outside to write my paper."

"Before you do, I want to show you something."

Will was walking around the room touching things. A lipstick-red pillow on a cobalt blue sofa with lime-green arms. Brightly patterned glass bowls on a coffee table. A wall of artwork so wild that Savannah had to look away after a moment.

"I have to get to work," he said, turning back to her.

"This'll only take a minute. Do you have more to do than the Spanish paper?"

He looked away. "I have a test on genetics in Biology on Thursday, another paper for Composition. I'll be up all night."

"Take a minute and come with me." Savannah tossed her backpack on the table between the kitchen and living room and went to the door going into the garage. She unlatched and flung it open.

"Ta-da!" She stepped inside and Will followed. Roxanne's car was gone, but Savannah's father's Mustang was parked in the second bay. "Get in."

The 2012 Mustang Shelby GT 500 was in pristine condition. Low-slung and shiny black, the car sported flashy aluminum five-spoke wheels and a red racing stripe. She especially loved the silver cobra on the back and the smaller ones on the front grille and in front of the side door. The cobra was even embossed on the front seats and floor mats.

She walked around and opened the driver's door, sliding behind the wheel. Will hesitated, but after a moment he got in on the passenger side.

Savannah introduced the car. "It's like a special, elite kind of Mustang, not new, but the mileage is low. It's been serviced regularly so it's in top condition. This little angel has fog lights, power everything, rear spoiler, eight speakers. Eight!"

"Why doesn't Roxanne drive it?" Will ran his hand over the gleaming dashboard. "I mean, her other car's great, but this...this is classic."

"She does once in a while. To keep it charged or whatever. But she doesn't drive it much because it's not hers."

"Whose is it?"

"Mine." She twisted to look at him. "My dad always said he wanted me to have the Mustang once I got my license. When I was old enough and we were somewhere out in the country for a weekend, he would take me out on a deserted road, just us two while Cassie slept in. He taught me about the clutch and brake and how to shift. I got to practice."

She usually tried not to think about those times because she was afraid she might cry. "When we moved, Cassie had someone drive it to Florida. When you and your mom moved in, Roxanne said we could park it here, because she wasn't using this side of the garage. Sometimes in New York we used to take off down the highway and turn up the sound system…" Her chest tightened at that memory, too.

"Cassie doesn't want it?"

Savannah took the Mustang's ownership for granted. She supposed the car might belong to Cassie if her father hadn't specifically mentioned it in his will. She wasn't exactly sure how her father's possessions had been divided, but she was sure he hadn't expected to die so young. He'd probably expected to sign the car over to his daughter in a year or two.

She wasn't sure why a doctor at a prestigious hospital had left his family in debt, but she knew Cassie could really use the money that she would get if she sold the Mustang. Right now her stepmother was out scrounging for a job she probably didn't want. She'd bought a basic car for herself, and as far as Savannah could tell, she wasn't buying much of anything else. She hadn't even replaced key furnishings that had been damaged during the party-from-hell.

When she didn't answer, Will tried again. "This car's kind

of a classic. She could probably sell it for a lot. But I guess she doesn't need the money."

Savannah tossed her hair over her shoulders. "She knows I'd never speak to her."

"There's a problem with that?"

She socked him on the shoulder. "How would you like to take it for a ride?"

"No way. You don't have your license."

"I mean with you driving."

He rested his hand on the gearshift with its bright red knob. "I'd have to check my insurance to make sure I'm covered."

Savannah blew out a frustrated breath. "Do you ever, like, take a chance on anything?"

"You mean when somebody else could end up in big trouble if I did? Not usually, no."

She heard the drip of sarcasm. "Fine. Don't bother. You probably can't drive a manual transmission anyway."

"I learned on one." He hesitated, then he smiled at her. "It's nice of you to ask, though. It really is. Are you trying to cheer me up?"

"Like I care." She made no move to get out. Sitting behind the wheel felt amazing. Even if the engine wasn't running.

"I asked my mom about my father," he said after a minute.

Savannah's irritation was gone in a flash. "What did she say?"

"She told me his name. She said their families were enemies, and they couldn't tell either side that they wanted to get married. After high school my father—he was named Roger Hart—joined the army and went to Afghanistan. She was supposed to finish high school, and then they were going to elope once she turned eighteen. Instead he was killed by a roadside bomb. And she got pregnant when he came home on leave before he was shipped out."

He told the story so quickly it took Savannah a few moments to process. "Wow, but why did she keep it a secret? I mean, okay, they weren't married, but lots of people have babies without getting married, and nobody's making them wear a scarlet *A* on their chests. The thing is your dad was a war hero. Didn't she know you'd be proud of him?"

"It's more like she was afraid I'd go looking for the families. She says they can't know, that they're not good people, not either side, and even now they would be furious. I guess she doesn't want me to feel rejected, because that's inevitable. Or maybe she's afraid my surprise appearance would give them more reasons to feud."

Savannah tried to imagine how she would feel if she were Will.

"I promised her I wouldn't tell anybody, but you were the one who convinced me to push," Will said. "You deserved to know. Just don't let on that you do, and please don't tell anybody else."

"Sure." She angled so she could see him better, the steering wheel pressing against her side. "Did you look him up? Roger Hart?"

He nodded. "He was one of the first to die in Afghanistan, so that was a long time ago, you know? The internet wasn't what it is today. So there's not a lot."

"What do you mean?"

"Today fallen soldiers have their own webpages or Facebook pages put up by their families or friends to honor them. They have good photos, and tributes and stuff. But not back then. And I guess nobody's thought to add all that, because Roger Hart's been dead as long as I've been alive. Longer."

"So?"

"So there's just one bad photo online, in his uniform, and a small notice. But I do know where he was from. It's a small town north of here, Blayney, Georgia, just over the Florida border."

"Could you tell anything from the photo?"

"Not much. He's in uniform, wearing a hat and frowning. It's not a good photo. From his expression…"

"What?"

"I'd guess he didn't want to go."

She felt awful, and she wished she'd just stayed out of this. Maybe Will was better off not knowing and not wondering all his life how his father had felt right before he was blown to pieces.

"I'm sorry," she said. "When my father died, as awful as it was, I got to say goodbye. Not you. Even your hello is kind of messed up."

"I can't go back and talk to his family. I want to know more, like what he was like as a kid, and if I look like him, but I'll never be able to. I'll never even stand by his grave. He's buried in Blayney. It said so online. One of the only things it said."

She thought about that. "How much better would you feel, if you got to do that? Say goodbye at the grave? What do they call that?"

"Closure." He grimaced. "It doesn't matter because it's not going to happen."

"Why not?" She was thinking faster. "Will, we have a day off coming up in a couple of weeks, and it's right before a weekend. We could take off for Georgia then, or, if we have to wait, at spring break. It can't be that far, right? Like no more than eight hours? We could see Blayney and the cemetery, maybe do a little research, but not enough to alert anybody. We could be super careful."

"How would we even get there?"

She tapped the steering wheel with both hands. "We can

take my car. We can tell Cassie and Amber we're doing something else, and then go there. If we plan carefully..."

"You don't think Roxanne will notice the car's gone?"

"She's flying to Europe soon to visit her son. If we're lucky, she won't be here to know it's gone."

"And if the dates are different?"

"I don't know. Then maybe I'll tell her it's time to have the car serviced and you're going to take it to the garage and leave it there."

"And you don't think she'll mention this to Cassie?"

"I don't know! Would you stop throwing up roadblocks? One thing at a time. First we see if the dates coordinate, and if they do, we can stop worrying about that and start planning what we're going to tell our mothers—" She realized what she'd said. "Your mother, my stepmother."

"I know who you meant." Sarcasm again.

"Do you want to go or not? Is it worth maybe stretching the truth a little?"

"A little? Stretching it as far as Australia."

This time she slapped the steering wheel with her palms. "Fine, Will-the-Pill. Don't do it." She opened her door and swung her legs to the ground. "I've got a test to study for."

Will was still sitting in the car when she went into the house. It was impossible to tell what he was thinking, but she'd done all she could and probably more than she should. Now it was up to him.

25

CASSIE WAS BAKING, A SURE SIGN SHE WAS TRYING
not to sink into a sea of depression. She only turned on the
oven for a handful of reasons. Either she baked to celebrate,
the way she did during holidays, or she baked to make sure
Savannah ate something moderately healthy before she left for
school. Finally, like today, she baked when she had to keep
busy or dissolve into wrenching sobs. During prolonged ep-
isodes of drinking, her mother had sobbed over hangnails
and wet newspapers, and as an adult, along with renouncing
alcohol, Cassie had made a conscious decision to renounce
tears, as well.

In the past hour she'd mixed up batter for zucchini muffins and whole wheat oatmeal cookies. Now the muffins were
cooling on a wire rack, and the first batch of cookies was in
the oven while the rest waited their turn on shiny aluminum
sheet pans. Since she felt only marginally better, she was pon-
dering whether to start on chocolate chip scones or attempt
mini quiches. Before long she'd have to leave baskets at midnight on neighbors' doorsteps.

Instead she made a pot of coffee, and when Amber came into the kitchen dressed in her Kouzina pants and shirt, Cassie automatically held out a mug. "Time before you leave?"

"Just a few sips. I'm going to need it. Roxanne just called. Yiayia mistakenly booked two events at the same time today. A bridal lingerie shower and a men's club luncheon—which wouldn't have happened if we had a reliable management system."

As she filled the mug, Cassie tried to picture the upcoming nightmare at the Kouzina. "Are they small groups?"

"The men alone would take up most of the room. Then top that with twenty-five women. Can you imagine how much fun the guys are going to have when the bride starts opening gifts and pulling out babydolls and G-strings?"

Cassie whistled softly. "Hold the corsets and push up bras."

"Yiayia's insisting it's not her fault, and Roxanne is recruiting everybody to help. She's trying to put the men in the front and on the porch. And if she can rent folding screens, she'll sequester the women in the back. But this is going to take a lot of cooks in the kitchen and servers on the floor."

Cassie looked away, but not quickly enough. Amber set her mug down with a thump. "Didn't you work at the Kouzina when you were in high school?"

Cassie was still examining nothing. "Maybe I hosted a little."

"No *maybe*. You could do it again today. We need somebody to seat and greet and make nice with everyone. Come with me. Do you have something you can't cancel?"

"I'd love to help, but, you know, I have to—" Cassie couldn't think of a single word to finish the sentence.

Amber's smile could trap honeybees. "Hey, no problem. I'll just tell Yiayia I tried to get you to help during her hour of need, but you were busy doing something you couldn't remember."

"Use my sweet little yiayia against me?"

"Say you'll come." Amber walked around to stand in front of her so she couldn't look away.

"I'm baking cookies," Cassie said.

"Then come when they're finished. You have blue pants and a white blouse, right?"

Cassie gave up. "If they're clean, I'll come as soon as I pull the last batch of cookies out of the oven. Will that suit you?"

"I won't have to tattle to Yiayia."

"You wouldn't have anyway."

"You'll never know." Amber checked the clock, finished two gulps of coffee before she plopped her mug in the dishwasher and headed for the garage.

"I'm supposed to pick up the kids after school," Cassie called after her.

"One of us can swing by and bring them to the Kouzina."

The door closed, and Cassie was left alone. The timer sounded and she took out the first batch of cookies, sliding in the next two trays before she closed the oven door. As much as she hated to admit it, working at the Kouzina sounded more promising than baking scones, cleaning the pool—she'd let the pool guy go—and especially more promising than making phone calls.

In the past weeks she'd been on the phone so much she was considering a career in telemarketing. She'd spent hours following up on job leads, broadening her search to office management. Now she was looking into getting a certificate in web development at the local community college. When she wasn't scouting jobs, she'd made at least a dozen phone calls to reach out to Sim Barcroft. As one of the contacts had said— with unmistakable arrogance—nobody as overwhelmingly successful as Sim was available for just anybody. Cassie had explained that her husband and Sim had been roommates at Farum Hall, a prestigious New England prep school, but the man's snort had been unmistakable.

The calls weren't finished. One woman had hinted Sim was living in Asia. At least Cassie had narrowed his location to the largest, most populated continent on the globe.

Unfortunately, her other phone calls had been equally frustrating. Two evenings ago she'd checked the Riverbend Community website, hoping that the roster of staff in the behavioral health unit might turn up more people willing to share information with her. A nurse named Zoey Charles had also worked hand in hand with Mark, but Zoey was no longer listed. More disconcerting, neither was Ivy.

So Ivy had been on her call list, too, and so far with no results.

While the last batch of cookies baked, she headed for her bedroom to change. She was half-undressed when the phone rang. She almost didn't recognize the sound. She grabbed it with one hand, and the waistband of her pants with the other. She succeeded in pulling them past her hips so she could perch on the edge of the bed as she answered.

"Cassie? It's good to hear your voice. It's Sim. Sim Barcroft."

The call was so unexpected, she was at a loss for words, but that didn't stop Sim. "First, I am so, so sorry I couldn't come to Mark's funeral. I really wanted to be there, but I'm working in Hong Kong now, and by the time I learned what had, well, happened to him, it was too late to book a flight in time for the service. Can you forgive me?"

She was still too disoriented to say what she really thought, that she wasn't surprised that Sim, who had cost their family an untold amount of money, had stayed on the other side of the world. "Of course," she said automatically, while she tried to pull together a more pointed response.

"Dave gave me your phone number. I'm so glad he did. I wanted you to know I gave a donation in Mark's name to Farum Hall. They're going to use it to fund a new chemistry lab. Chemistry was Mark's favorite class. I'm surprised he didn't go into medical research instead of psychiatry."

Apparently Dave had stopped snorting long enough to dial Sim. "That was very kind of you," she said.

"You probably don't know I talked to Mark before he died. We had one of our knock-down, drag-out fights about the economy. I wanted him to get his financial guy to invest twenty-five thou in a new IT startup that I knew was going to be a huge success. I told him if he invested even more, he could retire young and sail around the world, the way he always said he wanted to. But you know Mark..."

"Apparently not as well as I thought."

Sim didn't seem to find Cassie's response odd. "Well, I wish he were still around to gloat. I really do, even though it would be at my expense. Mark wasn't one to take chances or spend needlessly. Honestly, I think he got that from his father. The Westmores used to invite me to come to Connecticut for holidays if my parents were abroad. Mr. Westmore would make us rake their yard—and trust me, it was some yard—to earn money to buy gas so we could use the family car."

She had never heard that story, because Mark had only rarely spoken about his childhood.

"Mark internalized those lessons, I guess," Sim went on. "So he refused to invest, and you know what? This time he was right. My sure thing went south two months ago. Luckily I saw the signs and pulled most of my money out in time, so I didn't lose my shirt. But if the company had tanked when he was still alive, Mark would never have let me forget it. What a guy. I'm sure going to miss him."

Cassie cleared her throat. "Sim, you're saying you suggested this investment to Mark, and he turned you down?"

"Yeah. You know the bit about a prophet having no honor in his own country? Well that was me and Mark. I guess when two guys spend their teens in the same dorm room, they know every wart and pimple on the other one's—well, you know. Trust me, he was the last person I'd have gone to for analysis, too. I understood."

"Sim, did you invest *any* money for Mark? Especially in the past few years?" She scurried for an excuse for asking. "I'm still trying to make sense of his portfolio, and what's what."

"Never a penny. His financial advisor was good. Greg something, right? I checked him out. He was a good fit for somebody like Mark who was risk adverse. Through the years I looked over a few things when he asked, but that was it. I never saw a need to suggest he and Greg make any big changes—except for that IT company. He was happy, and if I thought the growth was too slow, that was just the difference between us."

With her mind whirling, she could only pull together a one-word answer. "Thanks."

"I would be happy to look at what you have, Cassie, and help you understand whatever you need to. But Greg should be able to do that, and he's a hell of a lot closer. I'm surprised he hasn't."

Sim didn't need to know that Mark had blamed him for the destruction of their retirement portfolio. She could imagine how upset he would be. "Don't worry. Apparently Mark mentioned you and the IT thing, so Greg just wondered whether Mark had put some money into it that he didn't know about. That's all. Otherwise I think I'm set."

They chatted for a minute about Savannah and the move to Florida, and then Sim wrapped up the call. "Well, it's midnight here, and I'm falling asleep at my desk. But this is my direct number. You can call me anytime. Anything I can ever do for you, don't hesitate to ask."

She thanked him and hung up, but if the kitchen timer hadn't gone off just then, she might not have gotten up. She zipped her pants and grabbed the shirt, buttoning it as she walked down the hall, but once the cookies were out and the oven was off, she stood in the middle of the kitchen for a long time, staring at nothing.

Mark had unfairly blamed Sim for a bad investment and the resulting loss of almost everything they had saved so carefully. Nick had suggested she hire a forensic accountant to be sure that Greg Gleason was on the up and up. There was no question she had to do just that and confirm that Sim was being honest, too. But she already knew what even the most scrupulous investigator would eventually tell her. Greg and Sim were telling the truth, and Mark was the liar.

Not only had he lied about the money, it was possible the same person who was sending Cassie letters might know where it had gone. No huge leap of logic to postulate a theory. The money that was missing may well have gone into the blackmailer's pockets.

There were still so many questions, but the two most important? What had Mark done that he'd needed to hide? And who knew his secret?

The garage shelves were stacked with boxes of financial records dating back to the beginning of Mark's career. Now Cassie was glad she hadn't been foolish enough to discard them. The day she'd learned how much moving so many boxes to Florida would cost, she'd briefly considered dumping the whole lot. Instead, in the next weeks, she needed to take down each one and conduct a thorough search. She needed answers, and she was the only person dogged enough to find them.

Maybe the fact she hadn't yet found a job was a good thing. It looked as if she had one after all, unpaid and tedious beyond measure. But by the time she finished, hopefully she would have the answers she needed to finally move on with her life.

26

HOURS LATER CASSIE WAS EXHAUSTED. SHE HAD been on her feet since arriving at the Kouzina, and now that the lunch guests were finally gone, she estimated in addition to standing for hours, she'd probably walked the equivalent of home and back performing her hostessing duties. Luckily, she'd had fun, largely due to Roxanne and Amber, who had pulled off the dual luncheons with no hard feelings and gales of laughter. The high point for both men and women was when Buck came out of the kitchen with his bouzouki to sing a naughty song in Greek wearing one of the bride's new red bras as a headband. Buck was the hit of the afternoon.

Amber was a star, too. There was no other way to describe her. Cassie had watched as her housemate did complicated math in her head to tell Roxanne how much she should charge for a special that night—all while making up mezze platters for each table. She had rearranged seating and headed off myriad problems before they developed, including gracefully fending off the advances of one of the older members of the men's club while signaling the bartender to substantially water down the old guy's drinks. When Cassie hadn't been able to figure out a difficult check, Amber had swept in and fixed it. Best of all, early on she had convinced Yiayia to go home and sleep off the headache that had developed when she realized what a big mistake she had made.

"I still say it's something of a miracle she got Mama to leave," Roxanne told Cassie. "But she does things for Amber she won't do for the rest of us. Like those aprons. Do you know how many times I suggested we buy new, prettier ones? And did you notice that the tables now have fresh flowers? Amber started washing the plastic flowers every time she came in."

"Washing them?"

"She told Mama they might harbor germs. Next thing I knew, we had these pretty little vases she found for practically nothing and fresh daisies every morning. The florist gave her a deal, too."

Cassie finished counting the contents of the cash register drawer and made notes before she closed it. "Do you mind?"

"Mind? I want to clone her. I love this old place. I want it to stand long enough to become the new Yiayia someday."

"Won't you need a grandchild to be a yiayia?"

Roxanne winked. "Gary Jr. says he and Patricia are going to the town hall to tie the knot when I get there next week. I think they want children sooner than later."

Cassie held up her hands and they slapped palms. "No big fat Greek wedding?"

"They want a small, skinny wedding. Just them, me and Patricia's parents and her sister. I'm heading over the end of next week."

"No Yiayia?"

"I asked her to come, but she says we can't both leave the restaurant." Roxanne lowered her voice, even though Yiayia wasn't there. "She's been afraid to fly ever since 9-11.

You didn't know? That's why she never goes back to Greece. Whenever flying is mentioned she tells the story of Icarus. Like we're demanding she strap on wax wings and soar to the sun."

Cassie hadn't realized Yiayia was afraid of anything. "I guess she's never going home again, then."

Roxanne lifted one brow. "There are boats."

"That would be one long cruise."

"Wouldn't it, though?" Roxanne smiled and let the silence stretch. "Wouldn't it just?"

Amber came out of the kitchen. She'd removed her apron and now she stretched her arms over her head and swayed back and forth. "We did it, ladies."

"Couldn't have done it without you." Roxanne grabbed her for a quick hug. "You are something special."

Amber looked pleased. "I hate to spoil this lovely moment, but Buck just gave me bad news. Somebody defrosted the rest of his lamb shanks. They moved them from the freezer to the refrigerator this morning and forgot to move them back."

Cassie didn't voice what all of them were thinking. Yiayia, who felt it was her job to rearrange and keep track of supplies, was the most likely culprit.

Amber went on. "They're fine but can't be frozen again. Anyway the shanks go on the menu tonight, and he wants to make stew but he's out of canned tomatoes. Should I run to the market?"

"Lamb stew is perfect," Roxanne said. "Even Mama can't argue with that. I'm sure we have extra cans of tomatoes in the storeroom, if I can get to them. It's a mess in there."

"Let me guess," Cassie said. "Yiayia knows where everything is and doesn't want anybody else to organize it."

"You know your yiayia." Roxanne beckoned and started across the floor. "And she refuses to buy a real point-of-sale computer system that would track everything, along with, oh, a hundred other important parts of running a restaurant. You two help carry what we need."

Cassie hadn't realized the Kouzina now had a storeroom, since there hadn't been one when she worked there during high school. The kitchen wasn't large, and the space wasn't well utilized. She visualized frequent trips back and forth, but even that was better than it had been, when cans and bottles were piled into pyramids in corners and someone always needed to shop for whatever was missing.

She and Amber followed Roxanne to a doorway on the side of the dining room. She had assumed the door led to an employee restroom or an office, but when Roxanne unlocked it and swung the door open, Cassie saw a space the size of a small living room, cluttered and crowded but considerably more expansive than a kitchen pantry.

She joined Roxanne, and Amber squeezed in behind her. "Wow, where did all this come from? What was here before?"

Roxanne was moving cans from side to side with the toe of her shoe. "It was a newsstand. Do you remember? Books and newspapers from Greece? Souvenirs and penny candy?"

Cassie couldn't. "I guess not."

"When the property came up for sale, my father bought it. He always intended to expand the restaurant, put in more tables, maybe display baked goods in a case along one wall. But he never had the money to expand, and more restaurants were being added nearby, so it didn't seem sensible to him. He gave the space to Mama instead. You don't remember this?"

"Before my time? After?"

Roxanne moved more cans, bending over to clear a path. "He wanted her to make it into a souvenir shop, not that there weren't already a ton of those, but I honestly thought he believed a shop would keep her out of the kitchen. At least some of the time."

"Did it work?"

"Not for long. The shop was a disaster. He wanted low priced items she could sell for more than they were worth, and sponges. She wanted nothing but the best—real souvenirs straight from Greece, which people only want to buy in Greece. Here they want nice little souvenirs they can afford. He convinced her the space was needed for storage, so Mama went back to the kitchen, and he walled over the door to the street. For once she didn't disagree. It's not as sad as it sounds. She was bored standing here waiting for customers who didn't buy anything."

"It's been a storeroom ever since?" Amber asked.

"More like a dump. It matches the apartment upstairs," Roxanne said.

The other two women each grabbed a can of tomatoes and left, discussing the server schedule. Cassie was dusting off another of the giant tomato cans to bring along when her cell phone rang. She perched on the crates Roxanne had just vacated and saw the call was from Ivy.

She answered immediately. "Ivy?"

"Hi, Cassie."

"I've been trying to reach you for a couple of days. Are you all right?"

There was a pause, and then a little laugh. "As well as I can be, considering I've lost my job."

"I'm sorry. I saw you were no longer listed on the website." She thought she ought to explain. "I was checking for Zoey Charles, but then I realized that you were..."

"Kaput? Yeah, that's me. Wednesday was my last day. Zoey's been gone for a while. She was Dr. Dorman's go-to, like I was Mark's, and I think he found her a supervisory position in Michigan somewhere."

"Do you want to talk about this?"

"There's not a lot to say. Dr. Dorman has pull at Riverbend, and I guess we went head-to-head about a patient one time too many. He went over my head, and then over my supervisor's. I was told if I left without a fuss, I'd get a good recommendation and the administration would be sure I was eligible for unemployment. Potential employers would be told that fewer patients were being admitted to behavioral health. I was the most recently hired, so reluctantly they had to let me go."

"Will you be able to find another job without a lot of trouble?"

"I'm probably going to take a break first. Between unemployment and savings, I'll be okay for a while, and I need a month or two to unwind before a new job gears up again. I have to decide what kind of setting I want to work in next time. Time off will help."

Cassie was only half listening. Fletcher Dorman had been the one to oust Ivy. Of course that would never appear on a document or even, most likely, in any conversation Ivy was privy to, but her friend sounded certain. When she finished, Cassie encouraged her to take the time off, especially since nurses were so badly needed, and she wouldn't have a problem finding something else. Then she decided to take a chance.

"You said you and Fletcher went head-to-head." She waited.

"That's not unusual. He's very old-fashioned. Even the meds he prescribes are older ones he falls back on. This time he overmedicated a young woman and then tried to send her home when she could barely stand upright. I protested, and I guess that was the last straw."

From conversations with Mark, Cassie had been left with the idea that Fletcher was always trying new approaches.

"Was that all?" she asked. "Just a disagreement about medication?"

Ivy was silent so long Cassie knew she wasn't finished.

"What else?" she prompted. "Please tell me this didn't have anything to do with the reason Mark left Church Street."

She was still silent.

"Okay, obviously it did," Cassie said. "You can tell me, Ivy. I'm sitting down."

"I can't say for sure. But I think Dr. Dorman discovered I was asking questions. Another nurse told me he asked if I'd been sticking my nose into office politics."

"Who would have told him?"

"Anybody who wants to be the next Zoey Charles. Doctors have a lot to say about the shifts we work and the pay we receive. They aren't really supposed to have that much impact, but that's the way it works. And there's no better way to get what you want than to make sure somebody else doesn't get it first."

Cassie couldn't blame Ivy for sounding cynical. "I am so sorry. This is my fault, because I was the one who asked you to probe."

"You can't blame yourself. Apparently I'm not good at the cloak-and-dagger stuff. Besides, without Mark on staff, it was harder to be sure things ran the way they should have on my floor. I know I'll find a better job when I start looking."

They chatted a little longer, and then Cassie hung up, promising to call again soon. Even though she was scrambling for some way to fix what she'd broken, she knew there was absolutely nothing she could do to help her friend.

Amber appeared in the doorway. "Turns out I'm not on tonight, and I need to do a little shopping so I'm getting out of here. Do you have the energy to come with me? I could drop you back here to pick up your car when we're done."

Shopping was only a little less effective than baking as a mood lifter. Cassie got to her feet. "Be careful," she warned. "I just got somebody fired. As a friend, apparently I'm lethal."

"You can tell me about it on the way."

Cassie realized with startling clarity how glad she was to have Amber in her life.

27

SAVANNAH NO LONGER THOUGHT OF THE BEDROOM
in the second suite as hers. Will's stuff was scattered all over
the room now, even the bed where she sat cross-legged as
she read a packing list out loud. The room smelled like sweat
socks and deodorant spray, and if she ever moved back in, she
would need to do an exorcism first.

Today was Valentine's Day, and now that school was out, the
afternoon marked the beginning of a long weekend for students because teachers had a workday tomorrow. She and Will
had plans for exactly how to spend it, but once she finished
reading the list she'd prepared, she realized he was frowning.
Doubt could derail the entire weekend.

She didn't waste time easing into a pep talk. She started
full throttle. "Everything's falling into place, Will. Like we're
supposed to do this. Don't wimp out."

"About a million things can go wrong."

Savannah dropped the list and held up one hand, tapping
her thumb with the other. "Roxanne left for Paris, so nobody
will know we took the car. It's mine anyway, so it's not like

we're stealing it. Plus I have a copy of her house key, so getting in and out will be easy."

She tapped her pointer finger. "We have tomorrow off, kind of a miracle, wouldn't you say, so we don't have to kill ourselves driving to Georgia and back in two days." The third finger was next. "We both got permission to do Coastal's annual field trip to remove non-native plants in the Ocala National Forest. We'll let Cassie or Amber drop us off at school in the morning to catch one of the buses, and your mom and Cassie will think we're pulling weeds and learning birdcalls instead of heading for Blayney. They'll never figure it out."

She still had two fingers left, but she'd finished, so she rested her hands on the bed. "See? We're set. We pack light. Just a change of clothes, something to sleep in and toiletries. I have money saved from checks Gen's sent me, and you have some from your job. We leave early tomorrow, drive all day, sleep somewhere, and then start back Saturday, after you've had time to look around and visit your father's grave. We stay overnight on the road, repark the car and then walk to school Sunday morning to arrive at the same time the buses do. My mom or yours picks us up and we tell them what a great time we had. Nobody will find out, and you'll feel a lot better."

"You're sure about that last one? Like you can tell how I'm going to feel when we're back home again?"

She held up her hand again and pointed to her fourth finger. "You get to drive the Mustang. Maybe that won't cure your guilt, but it should cushion it."

"I told my mom I wouldn't take this whole thing with my dad any further. This is further."

"She shouldn't have asked. She doesn't seem to get how important it is for a boy to know his father, or at least everything he can find out."

"What if I don't like what I find?"

Savannah folded the list into quarters, shoving it in the pocket of her jeans. "You know what I think? I think you can face whatever you learn a lot better than you can face not knowing. Don't you?"

He didn't answer, but she could tell by his expression she'd made headway.

Amber chose that moment to come into the suite. "Hey, you two. What's up?"

Savannah took the initiative, so that Will didn't confess. "We were just deciding what we'd pack for the field trip."

"Did the school give you a list?"

"It didn't include important stuff like snacks and battery packs for our phones."

"The trip sounds like fun. Campfires and cookouts."

"Outhouses and wood ticks." Savannah got off the bed. "Scorpions and rattlesnakes."

Amber laughed. "Not much of a camper are you?"

"Will promises he'll teach me whatever I need to know."

"I think it's great you two volunteered," Amber said. "But I bet you'll sleep most of Sunday once you get back. I don't think you'll get much rest on the trip."

"Helia probably snores," Savannah said. In reality Helia wasn't going on the trip, either, but Savannah had told Cassie they were in the same tent to make her own attendance more believable. She wasn't worried that Amber or Cassie might run into her friend that weekend because Helia was going to SeaWorld with her foster family.

Savannah started through the sitting room and stopped. An incredible dress hung from a hook beside the door.

Amber came up behind her. "What do you think?"

"That is, well, completely amazing. That's not the dress you showed me—that rag you and Cassie brought home last week."

"She didn't believe me when I said it was perfect, either.

I told you the fabric was gorgeous. Just because the designer was an idiot shouldn't mean the fabric has to go to waste."

The original dress was a wedding gown no bride would wear down the aisle. The transformation was unbelievable.

"I took it apart, and then I dyed the lace and the silk separately. And while you don't always know what you're going to get when you dye old fabric, the two shades of butterscotch were exactly what I wanted, darker lace, lighter silk. I made a sheath out of the silk and then covered it with the lace, using the prettiest panel in the front. I decided against sleeves, so I made thick straps to emphasize the plunging neckline."

"Well, you can carry it off." Savannah wondered if she'd ever be able to fill out a dress like this one.

Amber took the dress off the hook and laid it over her arm. "I made the underskirt shorter than the lace, see? So the dress is knee-length, but the inner skirt is shorter and flirty, plus it's split up the back just far enough to make walking easy. I had all kinds of ideas for trim, but in the end I didn't need them. The fabric said it all."

"You're going to be gorgeous."

"You could do this. I could teach you to sew."

Amber was being so nice, Savannah felt bad that she and Will were about to deceive her. She even felt a little bad about lying to Cassie.

"Maybe you could," she said, forcing a bright smile. "The party's tonight, right? Have a great time." She called into the bedroom behind her. "See you in the morning if not before, Will." She winked at Amber. "I'll take good care of him."

On the way to her room her pocket vibrated, and then her cell phone began to play Ariana Grande's "Break Free." She held the phone to her ear without looking at the caller. "What's up?"

"Vanna?"

Savannah held the phone at arm's length for a moment and saw that yes, the call really *was* from her mother. "Gen! I can actually hear you. You must have a primo connection today. Are you in Nairobi?"

"No, I'm back in California."

By now Savannah was in her room. She closed the door and fell into her desk chair. "You left Kenya? I thought you weren't coming back for another month or two."

"That was the plan, but we finished what we needed to at the clinic earlier than expected. And one of the doctors in the practice here in Palm Springs is having surgery. He'll be out for a while, and they really needed me to come back. I have to say, I'm happy to be home, in my own place. I had a lot of work done by a decorator while I was gone, and it's really gorgeous. I can't wait for you to see it, Vanna."

Gen was the only person in the world who called Savannah Vanna. She might have liked the pet name better if it hadn't reminded her of Vanna White on *Wheel of Fortune*—which she watched religiously if nobody was around to catch her.

"I can't wait, either." Savannah wasn't sure what else to say.

As it turned out, it didn't matter. Gen chatted about what she'd done in Africa—reconstructive surgery, mostly on children with birth defects—the condo renovations, the weather in Palm Springs, which was nearly perfect this time of year.

Savannah liked Palm Springs. Deserts fascinated her, and sometimes she thought she might like to do something desert-related as a career. Geology maybe, or desert ecology. Of course the area where Gen lived wasn't all that deserty because the towns and suburbs had grass even greener than the yards in Tarpon Springs. Her mother was always lobbying people to pull up their turf and put in desert friendly plants, and now, as part of her monologue she touched on that, too.

She finally ground to a halt. "I've gone on and on about me. I want to hear all about you. I just wanted to catch you up."

Savannah wanted to please Gen. She had wanted to as long as she could remember, even during early visits to California when she'd been so homesick for Cassie and her father that she'd counted hours until she could fly home again. But Gen was her mother, the real deal—not like Cassie.

Unfortunately, she couldn't think of much that would impress her. She made an effort. "Changing schools was tough, but I'm making progress. She hoped Gen wouldn't ask for specifics. "I've made a few friends." She hoped Gen wouldn't ask for photos. "I'm getting to know my teachers better, too." She hoped Gen wouldn't ask why.

"Not a lot going on," she finished. "Same old stuff."

"What's your favorite class?"

Savannah knew "none" wasn't going to fly. "Probably History." She realized it was true. Now that she was paying attention and speaking up once in a while, it wasn't too bad.

Gen told a long story about her own History class in boarding school. Savannah was always relieved when her mother took the conversational reins.

The story finally ended. "I've kept you long enough," Gen said, "but I just want to be sure I have the dates you're coming to visit. When is your spring vacation now that you're in Florida?"

"Um, I think it starts the second Saturday of March."

"You have a week?"

"Yes, but I didn't think you'd be back. I didn't, you know, think I'd be seeing you."

"I always intended to be together, even if I had to fly back from Africa just for that. Check and send me the exact dates, and we'll work out details so I can buy your ticket. I thought we'd just stay around here, maybe do some day trips but nothing crazy. I have to get back in the swing again, but one of my partners has a granddaughter about your age. We'll have to get you two together so you can hang out when I'm working."

Savannah rolled her eyes. She didn't want to spend days with a girl who probably hated being paired up with a stranger. She, Helia and Minh had made all kinds of plans for that week. Right now she couldn't recall them, but that didn't matter. She wanted to swim in the pool, bike to the beach. And Will had volunteered to help her paint her room. She was thinking navy blue.

Gen was her mother.

She didn't sigh, although she felt one building deep inside her. "I'll work out the dates and text them to you." She forced enthusiasm into her voice. "It will be great to talk to you, Gen."

"You, too, Vanna. I can hardly wait."

Savannah slipped the phone back in her pocket and stared into space. Flying coast-to-coast to perform the role of perfect daughter was exhausting. Still, she hoped everything she did or didn't do in California would make Gen love her a little more.

Her father was dead, her stepmother's actions had killed him, and Gen was all she had left.

28

AMBER PRESENTED HER BACK TO CASSIE. "I JUST couldn't ruin this beautiful fabric with a zipper. Thanks for coming to my rescue."

Cassie began to button the back of Amber's dress. "I always wanted a sister. You know, somebody I could talk to about boys. Somebody to zip or button a dress. I had friends, but I wanted somebody right there in my own house."

Amber held up her hair as Cassie got closer to her neck. "I've met more than a few women who are barely speaking to sisters because of things that were said or done when they were thirteen."

"Not always. I had a neighbor in New York. Every July she and her three sisters take a long vacation together. Somewhere amazing, too. I remember one year they spent months planning a trip to Tahiti, and I wanted to stow away. I could hear them in the hallway, laughing and teasing on their way to her condo to make plans. Actually, though, now that I think of it, there was a fifth sister, too. I never saw her."

"See, you could have been that sister. It could mess you up for life."

"Maybe, but I think I remember she lived out of town and just couldn't attend the planning sessions."

"Kind of an optimist, aren't you?"

"I have a feeling you're not. Did you grow up with friends you were close to instead?"

"Some, but I don't have a lot of practice making friends as an adult." Amber found Cassie's hand, and squeezed it. "The good news? Here we are, you and me. It's nice, isn't it? I always need somebody to button a dress."

Cassie squeezed back before she let go to finish the last two buttons. "This would have been a much harder time without you."

Amber cleared her throat. "I suggest we change the subject or I'll be a weepy mess when Travis shows up."

Cassie finished and stepped back. "You're all set. And for the record Travis will take you any way he can get you. In case you haven't noticed, he's got a thing for you."

"I bet you can tell me a lot about him." Amber cocked her head in question. "A lot."

"There are no deep, dark secrets to uncover with Travis. So you can ask away, and I bet he'll tell you."

"You've probably figured out that I don't need a journalist in my life."

"Travis isn't interested in you as a story. You do see that, right? He'll take no for an answer until you're ready to say yes."

"I will never be ready."

Cassie didn't look so sure. "Then I guess at some point you'll need to tell him and just see how he does with it. But tonight? Go have fun. You deserve it. The kids are gone for the weekend, the party will probably last until the wee hours and if you don't come home? I won't be keeping track."

Amber could feel her cheeks warming.

"It is Valentine's Day," Cassie said, "and romance is in the air."

"Tell me one thing. How does he support himself? He has a nice car, and you told me his house is wonderful. I honestly can't believe he makes a lot freelancing. From the little I've picked up, he does some of this and some of that, but I think that's more because he likes variety."

"You will have so much to talk about."

"You're not going to tell me?"

"I've probably seen more of him since you moved in than in all the years before. I just know he's a good guy. Everybody likes him, and Yiayia has tried to marry him off for years."

"I suppose that's something of a recommendation."

"Just don't tell her you went out with him tonight. She'll convince you to join the church, and then she'll start planning your wedding." Cassie looked at the clock. "I think I heard the doorbell. You'd better finish up. Just stop worrying."

She left and Amber went to the mirror to fluff out her hair. She'd worn it many ways since leaving home, but the changes had begun before she fled into her new life. As a teenager she had hated everything about herself, so she'd dyed a short bob black and adopted spiky bangs to emphasize the layers of eye shadow and false lashes she applied every morning. Even though her grades were excellent, most people hadn't looked beyond the surface, which was the way she'd wanted it.

Billy hadn't let fashion stop him.

These days her hair was its natural color, although she'd been both a pale blonde and a brunette along the way. At the moment looking the way Mother Nature intended was as safe as looking like somebody else. If old classmates thought about that Parsons girl, who "ran away with her boyfriend," most likely they remembered a sixteen-year-old with three-inch silver nails and red lipstick, a girl with one massive dragon earring and three diamonds glued over a heavily penciled eyebrow. Her teenage insecurities had been beneficial after all.

Finished with her hair, she straightened her skirt, slipped a gold chain over her head and added gold hoops to her earlobes. She grabbed a small gold purse that looked good with sparkly pumps from the shoe table at Things From the Springs and a shawl she'd found there made of fine velvet. She was ready.

Travis was in the great room talking to Cassie when she walked in. He got to his feet and smiled. "You look amazing. What a great dress."

Travis looked pretty amazing himself. His hair was a little shorter, his shirt was snow-white and he wore a British cut dark suit, obvious to the seamstress in her because of the structured shoulders, special cuffs and double pleated pants. With the suit he wore a wine-red tie, and a handkerchief the same color peeked from his pocket. She knew the invitation said Black Tie Optional, but as good as Travis looked, she was glad he'd opted not to wear a tux. Although he would have rocked that, too.

"You two have a great evening," Cassie said.

Amber realized Cassie would be alone tonight. "What do you have planned?"

"Paperwork. With you gone, nobody will have to watch me tear out my hair. But first a glass of wine and some of that moussaka you brought home last night."

Outside in the driveway Amber let Travis install her in the passenger seat of his Subaru sedan. "That's a great suit," she told him when he pulled into the street. "Beautifully cut."

"I was on vacation in London last year and pitched a story to a magazine about Savile Row today. I let myself be measured at one designer's store to learn the difference between a bespoke suit and a made-to-measure. After the piece was published, the designer was so pleased by the space I devoted to him that months later this suit arrived."

"Couldn't that be construed as a bribe?"

"I didn't accept it. But since I couldn't bear knowing it might be trashed, I bought it. He sold it to me at his sale price, and that satisfied my editor."

She realized how much she liked talking to Travis, something she hadn't experienced often with men. "Did anybody tell you about the cuffs?"

"I don't recall."

"They're called surgeon's cuffs. They have real working buttonholes and buttons at the wrist, not just for decoration. That's a sign of real quality."

Travis lifted his arm and looked. "Why are they different?"

Four-H, where she'd learned everything from sewing and cooking to raising animals, had been the teenage Amber's passion and salvation, as well as an occasional ticket away from her unhappy home. Betsy Garland, the advisor, had become her role model.

"I studied menswear for a 4-H project in high school. Some people think real buttons and buttonholes made it easy for nineteenth-century physicians who were operating on battlefields to roll up their sleeves for surgery. Savile Row was home to many doctors' offices, and as the tailors moved in, they probably made suits for them."

"You've got a great memory."

"Here's the last little thing you should know about your suit. It's fashionable to leave that last button unbuttoned. And in a climate like this one? It's good ventilation."

"Remind me not to watch *Jeopardy* with you."

They chatted comfortably until he turned into a wide drive lined with moss-draped oaks and wound through a golf course with water glinting in the distance. A two-story building of rose-colored brick and long, narrow windows sat at the end of the drive. Travis stopped in front and gave his keys to a valet.

Inside they were directed through the lobby to a spacious covered patio with tables set up on the grass beyond. Five musicians played golden oldies from one side of the patio, and long tables with silent auction items adorned the other.

"They want to raise at least forty thousand tonight," Travis said, guiding Amber toward the name tags. "They've done a first-rate social media blitz. They'll easily get that and more."

She'd served at enough of these events to know that donors also came to be seen and admired, and fundraising was only a part of it. She watched people embrace and pretend-kiss old friends, and after she'd pinned her tag in place, she walked down the steps to the lawn to find a table.

They chose one on the outskirts and set their programs and Amber's purse on the far edge, so they could look out over the crowd. Travis left temporarily and returned with drinks and a small plate of hors d'oeuvres.

"Bad news," he said. "I just heard that dinner is scheduled for late. I think they want people to drink and bid, likely in that order and on an empty stomach."

Amber, who planned to drink the wine Travis had set in front of her and no more, wondered how they would spend their time until dinner was served. She certainly wasn't going to hover over the silent auction, and she didn't know a soul except Travis, although a couple of people looked familiar enough that she guessed she'd waited on them at one time or another. There were four extra seats at their table. She envisioned a long night of small talk with strangers she had little in common with.

He nudged her, as if he had read her thoughts. "We'll enjoy the beautiful weather, maybe dance a little?" He waited for a nod. "I'll talk to everyone I have to, and then we'll sneak

out. I know a great little place for dinner, unless you're holding out for roast beef."

The evening suddenly seemed brighter.

They nibbled from the plate, and when Travis was half-
finished with his drink, he invited her to meet some of the
partygoers he wanted to interview.

"Or not," he added.

"You'll go quicker without me."

"Smart move. Good people, good cause, goodbye faster."

She watched him go. She loved the way he walked, long,
determined stride. She wondered how many people got away
from Travis when he wanted an interview.

As she had a hundred times before, she asked herself why
she'd let herself get involved—even at a casual level—with a
journalist. Of course Travis wasn't Woodward or Bernstein
ferreting out a big national story, and her story was small,
anyway, with only three characters on its pages. One was
dead, one was still on the run after nearly two decades, and
the other?

She wished she knew for sure how to characterize Darryl
Hawken's role. Was he still the pursuer? Or, after all this time,
had he decided he could turn his full attention to running
for the West Virginia House of Delegates? Could she settle
into life in Tarpon Springs, safe to make a real home for herself and her son? Was she safe to enjoy her time with Travis
without apology?

By the time he came back, all the chairs at the table were
filled and she was already out of small talk. "Get everything
you need?" she asked, after he introduced himself to the others.

"Plenty for a couple of paragraphs. They have a professional
photographer, and they'll send photos to choose from. Now
I'm going to claim one dance before we head out."

She smiled goodbye to the two couples who were happily chatting with each other.

Up on the brick patio they joined other couples who were dancing in the area just in front of the band. Without a break the band finished one song and swung right into "I Can't Help Falling in Love with You." She tried to remember the last time she'd slow danced with a man.

"I set this up ahead of time," Travis said, pulling her close.

She took one hand and rested the other on his shoulder, but not for long. Somehow, without conscious permission, her arms slipped around his neck and he pulled her even closer.

"You feel as wonderful as you look tonight."

His hips were against hers, her breasts pressed into his chest. He didn't grasp or pull. He was just there. Close. Sure. Delightful.

Her body was thrumming in ways she recognized but hadn't experienced in a long time. She hadn't gotten emotionally involved with a man since leaving West Virginia, but she'd invited a few into her bed. This felt different. New, and special—which meant it felt wrong. *Fools rush in*, she thought. How appropriate.

The song ended too soon or too late, she couldn't decide. She stepped away from Travis and touched his cheek. Lightly. Briefly. "Did I hear something about dinner?"

They drove without much conversation until twenty-five minutes later he pulled up in front of a ramshackle building near the water, more bait and tackle shop in appearance than restaurant. The windows looked new, but the rest of the building was weathered—an unfortunate mixture of concrete block and in places, rough textured wood shingles.

"Havana Seafood," Travis said. "As beautiful as you look tonight, I should really take you somewhere fancier, so it's your call. But this place hasn't been discovered yet, so we can probably get in without a reservation."

"We already did fancy. I'm all in."

Inside they waited to be seated. "Mr. Slade, welcome back," a middle-aged woman in a black dress said when she returned to the hostess stand. "We love to see our diners return."

Travis smiled and put his hand on Amber's back to guide her to a table in the corner. The room wasn't full, but most of the tables were occupied. Since Valentine's night was often celebrated at restaurants, it should have been more crowded. But for a new one, it seemed to be doing okay.

"Mr. Slade?" Amber said, once they were seated.

He turned up his hands. "I don't care what they call me as long as they feed me."

As he had before, Travis asked what she wanted from the short but innovative menu, then he suggested additions after she chose the blackened pompano.

Amber wondered if he was purposely trying to send her home with leftovers. "You know, I've caught up with the worst of my bills, and I'm even saving a little money. We have a refrigerator filled with food, so I will have other meals."

He smiled as he continued his examination of the menu. "Cedar Key clams are delicious cooked in white wine and butter sauce. I've had them on Cedar Key, but I haven't had them here yet. Let's try them."

"Travis, we already have enough food for an army."

"You don't want to miss a chance to try these. It's exactly the right season. For the pink shrimp, too, and they grill those. I had them last time. They were perfect with the black beans and rice."

She could tell arguing wasn't going to deter him. Maybe he was planning to take the leftovers home again.

Their server, a pretty young brunette with a shy smile,

took their order and suggested they might also want a salad of roasted beets, oranges and almonds. Travis complied.

"She's the youngest daughter of the Diaz family, who owns this place," he said after she left. "And that was her mother who seated us. They came up from Miami a year ago to open Havana, and their extended family joined them to make a go of it. Everything from supplying seafood to renovating the building, an ongoing project."

He was sitting beside her in a comfortably padded booth, and she shifted to poke his middle with a finger. His abdomen was hard and flat. "Where do you put all this food? Not an extra ounce anywhere."

His smile widened, as if they were sharing a joke. "I eat out a lot."

"I guess cooking for one person isn't much fun."

"Actually I like to cook. I tested recipes for a newspaper in San Antonio right out of college and I can make some mean Tex-Mex. But I love trying new things and seeing if the old ones are as good as I remember."

"So food is your hobby?"

"I'm a down-home guy. I cook. I eat. I garden. I sit by the river and wave at passing boats. Some people think I'm boring."

She was definitely not one of them. "And you write."

"That, too."

Amber trusted Cassie, but something seemed odd here. "So how many different jobs do you have?" She listed the ones Cassie had told her about.

"I love how these stories get started."

"Finish then. I'm curious."

"Curious or suspicious?"

"More the first than the second. But truthfully I do have a suspicious nature. I've had to develop one."

"Why?"

"Are we going to trade Q and A?"

He thought it over. "Okay. At the moment I freelance for both the *Tarpon Times* and the *Sun Sentry*. It looks like I might get a permanent spot at the *Sentry* if the managing editor likes the next story I submit. Right now, though, I also help a cousin on his boat, but only if he really can't find anybody else, and I stay strictly above the water."

She supposed there was enough income in what he did to keep body and soul together, although restaurant bills had to take a fair share of it. "Do you want that permanent spot?"

"I'm hopeful."

"What kind of reporting would you be doing?"

"You're avoiding my question now. Why did you have to develop a suspicious nature?"

She considered what she could safely tell him. Once again a portion of the truth was easier to remember. "When I was a teenager and pregnant with Will, I was forced to leave home. I've been on my own ever since, and like every young woman making her way through this world of ours, I had to learn quickly who to trust. Not trusting anybody was safest."

"That covers a lot of time and an entire philosophy of living. What it's short on? Details."

"I didn't promise details."

The expression in his dark eyes was warm and concerned. "I can make an educated guess. You're still suspicious because you have something to fear."

She supposed fear as a motivator really was clear to anybody who could put two thoughts together, and Travis could put together many more.

"I practice caution," she said.

"Are you in touch with your family?"

This time she could be perfectly honest. "Both my parents are dead. There's nobody else."

He didn't ask about Will's father, although it must have been obvious that if she was still suspicious of others, there must be someone or something from her past that was haunting her. Will's father was the obvious choice.

Travis rested his head against hers for a moment to make sure she knew he wasn't blaming her. "I think if we slowly peel back these layers, one at a time, we might actually get to know each other sometime in the next decade."

Their server returned with a local beer for Travis and club soda with lime for Amber, followed quickly by ceviche, which they shared. She was glad they were finished sharing life stories along with it.

"Like the ceviche?" he asked.

"A little more lime than I'm used to, but I like it anyway. What about you?"

They finished the ceviche and discussed the simplicity of it as compared to more elaborate versions. They chatted easily about the restaurant's decor and the food. When the clams arrived, Amber found them delightful, sweet and juicy with nothing hiding their natural flavor.

"I have this feeling you like discussing the food as much as you like eating it," she said when the next dish arrived, a seafood soup with rum that Travis had ordered and shared, analyzing each swallow.

"Nothing ever beats good food." His smile was sly. "Well, some things do, actually. One thing comes to mind."

She smiled, too. "Both pleasures of the flesh."

"But unlike food, you really can't get too much of the other."

"I've never tried. Have you?"

Now he laughed. "To get too much? I never set out to.

But like food, when sex just isn't right, you don't want a second helping."

"Are you feeding my appetite so I can feed yours later tonight?"

"We aren't mincing words. I brought you here because I wanted to spend time with you. The rest of the night is a mutual decision."

The server returned, and with her, a man wearing a chef's apron. "Mr. Slade, are you enjoying the food tonight?"

Amber waited for Travis to correct his name, but he didn't. "It's as good as it always is."

"The pompano was an excellent choice. I know your friends enjoyed it the last time you were here, too." He and Travis chatted, and Amber listened. It was clear from their conversation that Travis had brought a large party with him recently.

She waited until the chef disappeared. "Mr. Slade again?"

"It's impolite to correct people."

But her mind had been spinning as he and the chef discussed his last visit, and from that, an idea had taken shape. "Who comes back to the same restaurant with different people and gives a false name? And who orders practically everything on the menu at one visit or another."

"Is this a riddle?"

"Humor me."

"A man with lots of friends who like to eat out?"

"How about a man who doesn't want his real name to be known because maybe..." She covered his hand with hers just as he reached for his fork again. "He writes restaurant reviews?"

He didn't say anything. He just waited.

"As Dallas Johnson?"

"You really do have a suspicious nature." He grinned.

"Travis!"

"It wasn't my job to fool you, Amber. It's my job to fool *them*, the cooks and the servers. Some of my friends know what I do, but you work for Yiayia. And this is not something I want her to know. So I had to keep it to myself."

"Yiayia!" Amber had seen the *Sentry*'s mention of the Kouzina, and she knew Yiayia was still furious about it.

He watched her expression, as if wondering just how much trouble was in store. "Most food critics use their own name on their reviews and fake names at restaurants. Some critics even wear disguises because their photos are posted on the wall in the kitchen. I may have to resort to that if I get bumped up to full-time critic at the *Sentry*. I can't follow the norm and use my real name on reviews because I've lived here most of my life and too many people know me. But for now, nobody but my closest friends know I'm writing them. So far no restaurant has moved me to their best table and tried to interest me in their tastiest morsels. No bottles of expensive champagne have appeared mysteriously."

"Cassie promised me you had no deep, dark secrets. Boy, was she wrong."

"Deep maybe, but not dark."

"How did you fall into this?"

"A short trip. I told you I worked on the food section in San Antonio. When I came back to Florida, it was on my résumé. I freelanced at the *Sentry* doing other things, and one day they asked if I wanted to work on their new restaurant column. From there, eventually they started asking for reviews. I like to tell the stories of the restaurants, how they started, what they felt like, not just a list of what foods I liked or didn't, and the managing editor enjoyed the way I presented them. Now the food critic position is opening up and I hope it will be mine if I want it."

One fact stood out for her. "Wait a minute. I'm the perfect

date, aren't I? Because I know the restaurant business backward and forward, and you know whatever I say will have merit."

"Amber... That's not why you're the perfect date." He leaned over and kissed her. She didn't move away. Only when their server returned did they straighten. The salad was served, and with it, Amber's pompano and the roasted red snapper Travis had ordered.

"Dallas Johnson?" Her hand was trembling just a little as she cut a piece of the pompano and set it on his plate for a taste. "How'd you come up with the name?"

"Right out of college I moved on to law school in Dallas. I was ambitious, to say the least. Even though I didn't really love my classes, I thought a law degree would get me where I wanted to go. Big city. Big money. Big dreams. Then one day in my second year I tried to cross a street while I was texting somebody in my study group. I was nearly mowed down by a pickup truck and ended up with broken this and sprained that. I couldn't finish the year so I had to withdraw while I recovered."

"And you want to remember that awful moment every time you sign a review?"

"It sounds crazy, but after I adjusted—and I'll confess that took a while—I realized I'd let ambition consume my life. All the other things that really mattered to me had almost slipped through my fingers. My family and friends, my hometown, my writing. I'd majored in journalism in college because I liked digging for facts and reshaping them in interesting ways, but I let that drop in favor of law school. So now when I sign Dallas Johnson on my reviews, it's a reminder that life goes on, and sometimes even unwelcome changes work in our favor."

"I wish I could say the same."

"I get a strong feeling you can't."

"I do have Will. But he was never unwelcome."

"Then how about *unplanned* changes."

The time had come to be absolutely honest. "You're an unplanned change, Travis. And you need to know something before the evening goes any further. Nobody will ever be able to count on me staying around, not even for a day. And I absolutely cannot hook up with a journalist if I think he's going to dig for answers. Can you promise you won't take it on yourself to nose around in my life because you think you can help? Because you can't. Nobody can."

"How can that be true?"

"Trust me."

He took a few moments to answer, obviously running through the ramifications. "You're living with Cassie. Are the police going to show up on her doorstep looking for you? Could she be charged for harboring a fugitive?"

"No."

"Then are she and Savannah in danger?"

"I've never put anybody in danger." And it was true, as far as she knew. Would it always be? The moment she had reason to suspect that fake IDs and constant moves were no longer protecting the people around her, she would vanish again. She just prayed that if that moment ever came, she would recognize it.

"You drive a hard bargain." Travis put his arm around her and pulled her close. "If anything changes and you're ready to include me in this, you'll let me know?"

She nodded.

"I don't want it to be this way," he said, "but I have to believe what you say."

Travis didn't like being kept in the dark, but he was willing to respect her wishes. He hadn't tried to draw out the truth. He'd only made certain that the people around her were safe from whatever haunted her. He had faith in her, and that was better than any spoken promise that he wouldn't interfere.

She made her decision. "How much more do we have to eat so you can do your review?"

"Maybe they'll pack dessert to go."

She touched his cheek and turned his face to hers. "Then maybe they should."

29

THE TOWN OF BLAYNEY WAS IN THE RED HILLS region of Georgia, north of Florida's state capital by an hour. Or it would have been an hour if Will had exceeded the speed limit at any point.

The brakes had been thoroughly tested by the time they drove past a sign that read "Welcome to Blayney," and below that "Y'all Come Set a Spell at the Hulk Hogan Film Fest."

"Cute. Very down-home," Savannah said.

"Local. Hulk Hogan's from Georgia."

She had learned the hard way just how many useless facts Will kept in his head. Either he had a photographic memory, or he was an even bigger nerd than she'd realized.

"Too bad a film fest's not as exciting as the Rattlesnake Roundup back in Whigham," she said. "Maybe we can go next year."

Will pulled into a parking spot about three blocks down the main street and turned off the Mustang's engine. His head flopped back against the seat, and he closed his eyes. Will's little naps were another reason a trip that should have only taken five hours had taken more than eight.

Savannah had envisioned their trip to Georgia like the ones she'd taken with her father and Cassie through upstate New York and New England. Adorable little towns. Scenic roadways. Quaint tourist attractions. Instead Will's eyes had been riveted to the road when he wasn't napping at rest stops. He'd only left the car to use the restroom. He'd insisted on eating drive-thru burgers in the car.

She felt like a vampire who had sucked all his blood so she could watch him deflate like a limp balloon. The combination of a long drive in an unfamiliar, not-quite-stolen car and the reality of a past he knew little about had done the poor guy in.

"We have about an hour and a half until sunset," she said, after a few minutes. "We have tomorrow to explore, too, but if the trip home takes another eight hours, and we need to be back in Tarpon Springs when the buses are supposed to arrive, then we'd better start back tomorrow afternoon so we can get to Roxanne's by noon on Sunday in time to stow the car and walk to school."

He didn't open his eyes. "You must be a whiz at word problems."

She dug into a store of patience fast approaching empty. "Look, that gives us options. We can look around town now, and then go out to the grave tomorrow. Or we can do the cemetery first."

While she waited for him to decide, she examined the street. Blayney's downtown was dusty and old-fashioned, not exactly Mayberry R.F.D., but with touches of the same dubious charm. She noted old brick buildings with trim painted white or green, huge shade trees and paved sidewalks with newish lampposts mimicking vintage models.

Unfortunately, two of the nearby storefronts had "Closed"

painted across their windows. The road they'd come in on had been filled with potholes, and the first stop sign they'd reached had been bent double, like a man with an overpowering bellyache. Obviously, effort had been expended to make Blayney more welcoming, but she saw no signs that additional work was in progress.

From research she had read aloud to entertain Will, she had learned that agriculture was a big part of the local economy, with peanut, cotton and pecan production near the top. She wondered how many of Blayney's college graduates returned to live and raise their families here.

"Do you suppose the internet makes it easier to live in a place like this?" At least Will's eyes were open now. "Maybe people move here and start businesses from home. They can be in Atlanta in half a day if need be. But I guess it wouldn't have been all that exciting when your parents lived here."

Will didn't answer. She shifted so she was facing him. "Look, we need to do something, okay? You need to decide."

He heaved a sigh. "Let's walk around and see what we can find out. We passed a diner when we turned onto Main Street. We can eat dinner there and maybe figure out a place to stay."

Will had packed sleeping bags for both of them. She had a bad feeling that the "place to stay" was going to be a clearing somewhere. Or the car.

She got out, and he followed, carefully locking the car behind them. "We ought to stay close," he said. "The car's kind of exposed."

They started down the sidewalk looking into store windows. Savannah didn't know what she'd expected. A friendly old general store with an old man behind the counter who had grown up in Blayney and knew everybody? With the exception of a drugstore with a soda fountain along one wall and no customers, the majority of buildings housed offices and a few discount stores Savannah had never heard of.

"I think we ought to try the library," Will said. "They might have phone books or old newspapers online or on microfilm."

She was relieved. Back at the car she looked up the address and saw that the downtown library was open until six. They covered the required blocks and parked beside the building, which was small but modern. People were still going in, and she and Will joined them.

The reception desk was just to the left with two grand-motherly women standing behind it. Will had agreed that Savannah should do the talking. Both of them knew she was a better liar.

She waited her turn in line, and then she beamed her most winning smile when the older of the two women, wearing a bright red flowered blouse that complemented her dark skin, asked if she could help.

"My brother and I are just passing through. We're meeting our parents in Atlanta tomorrow, but we'll probably stay here for the night. I remember Mom telling me she had relatives in Blayney. We thought it might be fun to see what we could find and surprise her tomorrow."

The woman asked exactly what Savannah was looking for, and she pretended to think for a moment. "Well, her maiden name was Blair. I think she said there were a lot of Blairs in the area."

The librarians exchanged shrugs. The second librarian, as pale as the other was dark, answered. "I've lived here all my life, but I can't remember a single Blair, except maybe one who came from somewhere else and ran the State Farm agency for a while. Mary Blair? Marilyn?" She looked at the other librarian, who shrugged. "Maybe ten years ago?"

Savannah hadn't smiled this much in months. "Mom left like twenty years ago."

Will stepped closer. "I think she might have been related to some Harts, too."

The woman in red was nodding now. "Now those we've had plenty of. Harts all over the place."

"Good people, the Harts," the other woman said. "They been farmers, preachers, teachers. One Hart was a war hero. We lost him just about the time you're talking about. Young man named Roger. My daughter went to school with him, which is why I remember. A nice boy, too. He died in Afghanistan sometime right around then."

"That's so sad," Savannah said without missing a beat. "He's probably buried in Arlington Cemetery?"

"No, he's buried right here. Just outside town. Which way'd you come in?"

Savannah pointed and the librarian explained they'd passed the cemetery a few miles from town.

"I don't suppose you have newspapers from that time?" Will asked. "I doubt she's related to this Roger, but she'd be interested."

"We might find a Blair or two," Savannah added.

The librarian in red took over again. "The *Blayney Independent* was still being published. We have all the issues on microfilm, but somebody digitized the paper copies we had from 2000 to 2005. Who was that again?" The librarians consulted each other, and the first woman nodded. "Yep, high school journalism class did it for a service project. We don't get much call for it, but it's there. You could check on one of our computers. I'll set you up. You're supposed to have a library card, but since you're from out of town, you can just show me your driver's license."

"While we're at it, how about phone books?" Will pulled

out his wallet so she could note his information. Savannah was impressed.

The library was small, but one wing had six computers, two of which weren't being used. The second librarian settled them at one and helped them get to the *Blayney Independent* site, while the first went to retrieve phone books. "We do close at six. You're staying in town tonight?"

"We haven't decided," Savannah said. "We thought we'd make it to Atlanta today, but there was so much to see along the way. We'll look for a place to stay near here and head that way tomorrow afternoon."

"Your parents won't worry?"

"We stay in close touch. And they don't get to Atlanta until tomorrow, either."

"My, they seem to have raised two considerate, levelheaded children. If you want a place to stay, the Sinclair Motor Court just beyond town is cheap and clean. You'll be safe there. Just call ahead and explain the situation and tell 'em I sent you. They won't get fussy that way."

Savannah thanked her. When the woman was gone, she pulled up a chair beside Will, who was already starting a search.

"Sounds like we have a place to stay tonight," she said.

"I thought we'd sleep in the car."

"This was my doing, and I brought plenty of cash. But no hanky-panky."

He looked at her like she'd lost her mind. "Ew." He made a face.

"Well, I don't think of you that way, either."

Will clicked on the magnifying glass to enable the search function and typed in Hart for the first issue. There were six separate results. He and Savannah scanned each one. Two were ads for Hart Backhoe and Dump Truck Services. Two more mentioned a cafeteria worker named Rose Hart at a local elementary school, who had received an award for saving a student with a peanut allergy.

"That poor kid sure lived in the wrong part of the country," Savannah said. "Good old Rose."

The last two Harts were high school students. Roger Hart was not among them.

"Try Blair before you go to the next issue," Savannah said.

He did, with no results.

The first librarian arrived with a stack of local phone books. Savannah thumbed through them noting the addresses of half a dozen Harts and the absence of Blairs.

"Here's a Blair," Will said. "Ted Blair, from Austin, Texas. He was in an accident out on the highway. Sounds like he was just driving through on his way somewhere else." He was quiet a moment as he kept looking. "Hey, here's a couple of hits for Roger."

Savannah pulled her chair closer and read the text. "'He received an award for participation in the U.S. Army Junior Reserve Officer Training Corps at the high school.'"

"That makes sense since he went right into the military." Will found another mention in a list of graduating seniors. "There he is, but my mom was two years younger. So she's not listed."

Savannah was beginning to wonder if that was the only reason.

The biggest success came with a slightly different version of the article about Roger's death, complete with the same grainy photo in black-and-white.

Will quietly read it out loud and paused at the end. "His birthday is tomorrow."

Savannah sat back. The online article hadn't listed a birthday. "Talk about being here on the right weekend."

"He would have turned thirty-six tomorrow. Mom's thirty-four." He paused. "I'll be seventeen in a couple of weeks."

Savannah hadn't realized his birthday was so close. "When?"

"The twenty-sixth. Roger was only a little older than me when he died."

"We should take flowers to the cemetery or something." Savannah knew that was inadequate, but she didn't know what else to say.

By the time six o'clock arrived, they had done what they could. Savannah had noted addresses for Harts. Will had found nothing more of interest.

"We should have asked if they had high school yearbooks!" Savannah couldn't believe she hadn't thought of that. "I bet they did."

"We can come back tomorrow."

Only as it turned out, they couldn't. When they turned in the phone books and asked about the yearbooks, they were told the library was closed on weekends that month.

"Shortfall in the county budget," the librarian in red told them. "We're the first thing they cut."

They thanked both women for their help, promised they would be careful on the road and went out to the car. On the way Savannah motioned for Will to stand in front of the library for a photo. "To remember today by."

He didn't look happy, but the setting sun was positioned just right to beam down on him like a halo. When she told him, he laughed and she caught the photo at exactly the right moment.

"I'll send you this one," she said, after she checked it. "You actually look half human."

"What would I do without your love?"

She made a face. "Since there's still light. Some of the Harts in the phone book lived along Satwiller Road. I found it on Google Maps. We could drive that way and see what it looks like."

"This feels like a wild-goose chase."

"Let's give it a try. Then we can eat and I'll call the motor court."

Satwiller Road was only five miles from downtown, a long, windy road lined with cotton fields and acres of trees that Will identified as pecans and maybe peach. Gardens were freshly plowed in front of brick or frame houses. The light was fading and there were no Harts on mailboxes.

"Is it weird to think your father might have lived out here?" Savannah asked as they headed to the diner.

"You want to know what's weird? My mom made it sound like the Blairs had been in Blayney practically forever, like a big clan of feuding Hatfields and McCoys. But those librarians didn't know any Blairs, and no local Blairs showed up. Wouldn't the kind of feud my mom told me about be news? People arrested maybe, or at the very least remembered? She said both families had lived here for generations."

Savannah had been mulling that over since they left the library. "Maybe the feud seemed like a huge deal to her and your dad, and their immediate families were still hanging on to bad feelings. But maybe nobody else in town really knew or understood."

"That doesn't say a thing about why no Blairs are showing up."

"Maybe we'll find out more when we ask around tonight."

Unfortunately they didn't. They ran into more dead ends, and after a fried chicken dinner with crowder peas and corn bread, after they had checked into the motor court and were both trying to fall asleep on opposite ends of a stuffy dormitory-style room, they didn't discuss what was beginning to seem obvious.

They might leave Blayney tomorrow afternoon knowing as little as they had when they drove out of Tarpon Springs that morning.

By the time they got to the cemetery the next afternoon, they hadn't learned much more. The morning clerk at the motor court, who had been every bit the gossip they'd hoped for, didn't know any Blairs, but she, too, remembered Roger Hart.

"He was such a fine boy," she said. "From a good family, not one that put on airs or walked around with noses in the air, if you know what I mean? They were down-home folks, and we were all broken up when Roger was killed."

"I guess the Hart family had been here for generations?" Savannah asked.

"Well, there have been Harts here awhile, sure. Good solid folk who just do what they have to. I'm not all that sure he was related. He was a town boy, and most Harts lived out in the country."

After checking out, they'd walked around town again. Nothing else had turned up, and while Savannah had wanted to buy flowers for Roger's grave, even the downtown grocery store was closed for the morning. They headed to the cemetery empty-handed.

She was beginning to realize how far her imagination had carried them with very little payback. Roger Hart had lived here. They'd known that. Roger Hart had died in Afghanistan. That, too, was a given. All they were really taking away from this trip was the absence of Blairs in Blayney, and questions about the so-called feud.

The medium-sized cemetery was divided by a circular road around most of the grave sites, which, like a pie, were divided into eight sections by narrow paths. The site was well tended with neatly trimmed grass and shade trees. Simple headstones appeared to be clustered in family groups.

They weren't alone, but the sky was clouding over, and Savannah guessed that most visitors had already come and gone. The few people she could see were some distance away.

"I thought maybe the veterans' graves would all have flags. I don't see any." Savannah started down one of the paths, gazing at headstones. She stopped in front of two graves, John and Sylvia Grady, and at their feet the smaller grave of baby Jesse. She no longer saw this trip as an adventure.

"I think they only put flags on veterans' graves on special days, like the Fourth of July or Veterans Day," Will said. "Let's stay in the same section, but take different sides, fan out and come back together until we finish it."

The idea was as good as any. She wondered how many other tiny graves she would encounter. She thought of Gen, who had willingly given up her own baby to be raised by its father, and realized she could more easily imagine how Sylvia had felt than how her own mother had coped. Neither of her parents had ever discussed their feelings.

They were walking through the third section, nearing the point of the triangle, when she noticed Will had stopped in front of a marble headstone not far from a maple tree. She waited, and when he didn't move away, she walked along the path between rows of graves and joined him.

"Find something?"

He nodded. She had a feeling speaking wasn't on his immediate agenda.

She looked down and read "Roger Sawyer Hart, 1983-2002." And under that: "Beloved son of Matthew and Theresa Hart." Farther below, attached to the headstone, was a small bronze medallion featuring a flag folded into a triangle with the word *Veteran* at the top and *U.S. Army* at the bottom.

Will swallowed hard. "I read that when a soldier dies, an honor guard conducts a ceremony and plays taps at the funeral. Afterward they fold the flag the way it's folded there and present it to the next of kin."

Savannah took his hand and squeezed it, dropping it after a moment because she suspected he might need it to wipe his eyes. "I remember how I felt when it was my father in the ground. Like the bottom had fallen out of the world."

"I wonder, you know, would he be proud of me? Or would he think I didn't measure up?"

"Why would he think that? You're, like, perfect. Smart and nice. Sometimes too nice, but I bet college will take care of that."

He gave a strangled laugh. "Or you will."

"He would love you."

"I missed out on all the dad stuff. My mom tried to fill in, and she did a great job. But it wasn't the same."

Amber had devoted her life to raising Will when surely she'd had other plans before Roger died. And she was a great mom. Savannah didn't question that. But she did question how honest Amber had been. Because while Roger Hart was lying in the ground at their feet, just the way they had expected him to be, nothing else Amber had told her son rang true anymore.

They were still standing quietly side by side when she heard footsteps and turned to see a middle-aged man in jeans and a dark jacket over a dress shirt coming toward them. He wore a ball cap and dark sunglasses. The man seemed focused on Roger's grave, and she only had enough time to whisper: "Company. Let me do the talking."

Will looked surprised and turned, but by then the man was almost on top of them. He stopped a few feet away. "I'm sorry. Did I give you a scare?"

Savannah smiled. "No, but hardly anybody's here today, so I was surprised."

"I won't ask if you knew Roger. You're way too young for that."

She made up a story. "We're doing a school project on the war, you know, in Afghanistan. And Will here thought it might be a good idea to get a photo of the grave of a soldier, a real one, who died there. We just found it. Did you know him?"

"He was a fine young man. The kind you hope your daughter will marry."

Savannah felt a chill run up her spine. "Would you mind telling us about him? We were going to look him up online. But it would be great to talk to somebody who knew him."

He seemed pleased, almost as if talking about Roger was a way to honor him. "Rog was a smart boy. I always thought he ought to go to college before he joined the service. But you know, 9-11 changed everything for a lot of young men. He signed up right away. They sent him to Afghanistan, and of course, he was so young, with no skills, no technical education to keep him off the front lines. Anyway, he fell quickly."

They stood in respectful silence. Finally the man put out his hand. "Peter Drake."

They both shook hands with him, and Savannah gave her full name. Will only gave his first, but Mr. Drake didn't seem to notice.

"You know, today is Roger's birthday," he said. "I mean, if he'd lived. I come here on this date every year if I'm in town. I travel for work, but I try to be here."

"You must have been close to him," Savannah said. "I mean, to try so hard to come to his grave."

"He was quite a young man. But, of course, my daughter was the one who was close to him. They were going to be married. For a while she was the one to visit on his birthday, but a few years after Rog was killed, she met and married another fellow and moved to California. So I come here to honor him and to pay tribute to his service to our country."

Savannah hadn't breathed during this recital of facts. Now she gulped in air. "Your *daughter*? He was your daughter's fiancé?"

"Quite a coincidence you came today, isn't it?"

"Definitely," Will mumbled.

"I'm curious," Savannah said. "Is his family still in town? Because I wonder if they would let us interview them. Unless you think it would be too painful."

"They moved away not long after he died. I think being here was too much of a reminder. And every time they saw my Lucy, they were reminded all over again of the wedding they never got to see."

"I can imagine," Savannah said, although her imagination had officially been stretched to the limit.

"They were quite a couple," Mr. Drake said.

Will was silent, so Savannah continued the conversation. "It's such a small town. I bet they knew each other for practically forever. Unless one of them moved here later."

"No, they were friends starting in sixth grade, and it just grew from there. By the time they were in high school, it was pretty clear how it would end. Lucy started saving for their wedding when she was a junior. Awful, awful shock for her when the news came."

Savannah understood more about shock than she had an hour ago. "I'm so sorry. It's all terrible."

Mr. Drake smiled sadly. "Would you like to see a picture of them? It's like a little piece of our past that's still precious, despite everything that followed. The photo was taken the day they got engaged, right before he left for boot camp." He gave a little laugh. "He still had his hair that day. He sure looked different with a military haircut."

"I'd love to see it," Savannah said.

"So would I." Will sounded as if he was choking on the words.

Mr. Drake pulled out his wallet, opened it and dug deep behind a couple of credit cards in one of the slots. Finally, he took them out and then felt around until he was able to tug out the photo.

He started to hold it up, as if reluctant to hand his precious memento to a stranger, but finally he held it out to Savannah.

She squinted down at the photo. Two teenagers stared back at her. The girl had long blond hair, pulled back at the top and fastened with a barrette or a clip. She was so happy that her smile gave her face a certain beauty it might not have otherwise had. The boy, Roger Hart, had a mop of red curls falling over his forehead and collar, curls a much brighter red than Will's mother's hair. He was a true redhead with freckled skin and a prominent nose.

He looked nothing like Will.

Will had been peering over her shoulder. She offered him the photo, but he didn't seem to notice. He kept staring.

"Quite a redhead," she said, when she finally handed it back. "What a beautiful couple. What a loss."

"I try not to imagine what their children would have looked like. Lucy has two now, ten and thirteen. Boys. They're dark-haired, like their father. She would never have had dark-haired children with Roger. Mother Nature wouldn't have let that happen." He slipped the photo back into his wallet.

"We'll go now," Will said, before Savannah could speak. "I know you'll want some time alone. Thank you for talking to us."

"Do you have everything you need for your paper?"

"More than enough," Savannah said. "We appreciate your time."

They left Peter Drake at the graveside and started toward the road. They didn't speak until they were far enough away that he couldn't overhear what they said.

"Was he right?" Savannah asked. "Wouldn't it be possible to have a dark-haired child if the father had red hair like Roger Hart?"

Will was silent so long she wasn't sure he was going to answer, but when he did, his voice was choked with emotion. "We just finished a long unit on genetics in biology. I can tell you for certain, two parents with red hair could never have had a son who looks like me."

Savannah had studied enough genetics at Pfeiffer Grant not to question him. "So what does this mean?" she asked, putting her hand on his arm, but not looking at him when she did. "What do you think?"

"I think this whole weekend has been a wild-goose chase. Roger Hart is not my father."

"Then why did Amber tell you he was?"

He stopped and she was forced to stop, too.

"She probably picked him out on the internet, a man who died right after she got pregnant. She chose Roger Hart so I could have a hero for a father. That seems obvious, doesn't it? She wanted me to be proud, and she hoped I wouldn't look into her story. She asked me not to. Now I know why."

"But why would she do that?"

"Why do you think?"

She was afraid to say it, so finally, *he* did. "Because my real father is not a hero."

"We don't know that. Maybe she did it because—" She stopped just in time.

"Go ahead."

She shook her head.

Again he was the one to finish. "Maybe she did it because my real dad's out there somewhere looking for me, and she knows it. Or maybe...she's not much of a hero, either."

She felt so bad she wanted to throw her arms around him for a hug. But she knew that wouldn't be welcome. "You don't know any of that, Will. You have to confront her and tell her you know her story was a lie and you want the real one."

They stood that way for a long time, and finally he shook his head. "Or I can do what I've always done. I can assume that my mother knows what to tell me and what not to. I forced her into the whole Roger Hart thing, and this is the result. Maybe instead of confronting her, I should just keep my mouth shut."

"I don't—"

He cut her off with a wave of his hand. "Not your decision." He turned and started back to the car.

"I'm sorry," she called after him. "About everything."

Will kept walking.

30

BY FRIDAY AFTERNOON, AS MUCH AS SHE DIDN'T
want to be, Cassie was hard at work at the dining table on
the fifth box of financial documents from the garage. She was
afraid there were at least a dozen more to go.

On Thursday her search had begun with the packet she had
gotten from Fletcher with details about Mark's departure from
Church Street. She was no expert, but to her it looked as if
Mark had gotten a fair shake. Just to be sure, she'd sent everything to her attorney. She was waiting for him to respond.

The first four boxes had been filled with neatly organized
records and receipts that stretched further back than the three
years the IRS recommended. Seven years of records were
necessary if certain losses were claimed, but even if that were
the case, she doubted old records would help her understand
why their nest egg had disappeared. Unfortunately, since she
couldn't be sure, she was painstakingly working her way toward the present.

Mark had believed that hoarding receipts, bills and bank
statements was a positive trait. Since she was a graduate of the

"you-can-get-a-copy-if-you-need-it" school of thought, she had probably driven him crazy. She wondered in what other ways she and her husband had been miles apart.

By the time Amber arrived home, she'd been working for two hours. Amber was carrying a shopping bag and her dress on a hanger. She wore a man's flannel shirt over athletic shorts that fell almost to her knees. The shorts had an elastic waist, but she'd tied the shirt tight around it, probably to keep them from making a quick exit. She was barefoot.

"A very striking outfit," Cassie said. "You look good in anything."

"No comment."

Cassie couldn't help a grin. "I won't ask if you had fun. Do you like his house?"

"If I was going to design a house, it would look like that one." Amber disappeared, and when she returned about half an hour later she was wearing jeans and a knit shirt. She plunked down beside Cassie and picked up the closest paper.

"Have you been working on this since I left?"

Cassie hadn't shared what she was doing with Amber. Rox knew a little about her situation, but only Nick knew all the basics, and he had been kind enough to check in with her twice in the previous weeks. She told him about her phone call with Sim, and he encouraged her to hire professional help to go through her files, but she still wasn't ready to expose her problems to a stranger.

"I'll be working on these for weeks," Cassie said.

"It must be important."

Cassie wasn't sure how to answer. "Unfortunately, yes. In a nutshell, I should have a lot more money than I do."

"Shouldn't we all." Amber smiled to encourage her. "Except I sense you mean something has happened to yours? Or don't you want to talk about it? Because I'm good at not talking about things."

That was an understatement. "It's a long story. Are you sure you want to hear it?"

Amber sat back and folded her arms. "Try me."

Cassie launched in, starting with the day Mark died and the fight they'd had. She ended with her telephone call with Sim.

"In a nutshell Mark lied to everyone, including our financial advisor, about where and how his retirement funds disappeared. He used Sim Barcroft as a scapegoat, most likely because he's living in Hong Kong, and Mark figured he was too far away to blow his cover."

"And you sank most of what was left into this house?"

"That's nobody's fault but mine."

"Um, doesn't your husband get a lot of it?"

"I can't do anything about Mark, but I should have been absolutely sure his retirement fund was still healthy before I spent so much money. I was a new widow, and I'd been kept so far away from our finances, I was out of the habit of asking questions."

"I bet that won't happen again."

Cassie gave a tired smile. "Not about anything. But you can see why I'm wondering if Yiayia needs a permanent hostess. You and I would work well together."

"You'd be on your feet for hours at a time for very little money. You can do better." Amber drummed her fingers on the table. "Have you found anything in the records?"

"I started with the earliest ones. I don't know what I'm looking for, but I don't think it was there. Back then, our financial situation was the way I remember it. Healthy."

"It sounds to me like you need some help."

"I've been talking to an old friend, Nick Andino. He's on

the police force here. He thought I ought to get some professional help, too, but I hate turning this over to strangers."

"I know Nick. Remember, he stops by a couple of evenings every week after we close and takes the receipts from our safe to the bank for deposit. Yiayia invites him into the kitchen after we close on Saturday nights for our weekly feast, but it's obvious he's doing the run because he's fond of her."

In theory the Kouzina closed at nine o'clock on Saturdays, but Yiayia made a point of never asking anyone who was already seated to leave. Sometimes it was ten or later by the time the dining room was empty, and the staff was finished. Then they partied.

Saturday night kitchen feasts were a tradition and a bonus. Food that wouldn't keep was brought out to heat and serve, wine was poured. Sometimes Roxanne, Buck or even Yiayia herself created new specialties for staff to sample while they laughed and gradually wound down after the long week. The parties often ran until midnight. Cassie stopped in occasionally, but she'd never seen Nick there.

"It's hard not to be fond of Yiayia," she said.

"And any man kind enough to help out just because he can." Amber was quiet a long moment. "Did I ever tell you at one point I planned to become a certified bookkeeper? I took classes for a while and earned credits then…" She shrugged.

Cassie was too interested to let the conversation lapse. She heard an offer being explored. "What happened?"

"We had to move before I was able to finish. But by then I realized I could make more money waiting tables than reconciling bank accounts or preparing payroll with just an associate's degree. When we settled somewhere else, I looked into finishing coursework, but much of what I'd done wouldn't transfer."

By now Cassie was good at guessing the things Amber

didn't say. Her friend had probably been afraid another move was on the horizon anyway. Since one always seemed to be.

"How far did you get?" Cassie asked.

"I'm not a forensics accountant or any kind of accountant. But between the classes I took, a few workshops and job experience, I think I could spot discrepancies if I came across them. Better than somebody without my background, but not as good as somebody you would pay two hundred dollars an hour."

"Will you let me pay you?"

"Of course not."

"Sorry then. You can't have the job."

Amber rested her fingers on Cassie's arm. "You've done more than enough to make up for Savannah's mistake. From this point on, if you won't just accept my offer as one friend helping another, you can put the hours I spend toward rent."

Cassie wanted to say no. After stupidly turning their finances over to Mark for years, she was reluctant to let go of anything financial again.

"It will go faster with both of us working on this," Amber said. "And the sooner you find out what happened, the better your chances of being able to do something about it."

"I think I gave up hope on that score. At this point I just want to know."

"I wouldn't assume you're powerless. If a crime has been committed..." Amber sat back.

In her recitation, Cassie hadn't reported the letters she'd received. She debated now, but Amber already suspected something more than fiscal irresponsibility. She made a decision and told her about them.

Amber listened carefully until she was done. "And Nick says there's nothing you can do to track down the sender?"

She followed with a cynical laugh. "Of course there's not. What was I thinking?"

"He says since nothing's been asked, the police can't treat it as extortion."

"And even if they could, it wouldn't be a priority."

"You don't like authorities, do you?"

"I don't see them as particularly helpful. I've had very little personal experience, but what I've had tells me some people wearing a uniform should be wearing an orange jumpsuit instead."

Cassie digested that.

"You think it over. I'm going to make us tea." Amber got up and started toward the kitchen. "Travis and I went to a funny little sandwich shop on the way home. Savannah's friend Helia was there with a couple of younger girls. It was fun to see her with them. She was very maternal, not the image she projects. And her hair's growing in."

"Savannah told me Helia's foster parents want to adopt her." Cassie thought about her daughter, who so rarely shared anything about herself or her friends. She'd seen this revelation as a step in the right direction.

"Maybe the girls were her foster sisters."

Cassie sat up straighter. "Wait a minute. Savannah and Helia are tent mates on the field trip this weekend. They aren't supposed to be home until tomorrow."

"Maybe she got sick and couldn't go. Or she was grounded. Why? Is that a problem?"

Cassie hated to hope that either of those things were the reason Helia was home. But she knew she couldn't assume anything about Savannah these days. Things were better, but Savannah was still a law unto herself.

"It is and it isn't, depending on what I find out. Do we know where Helia lives?" Cassie tried to remember if she still had the girl's address. She'd taken Savannah there and brought her home a couple of times. She remembered the general area.

"Did you use your GPS?"

Amber was right. She had it plugged in. She got to her feet. "Hold my tea. I'm going for a little ride."

"Will is on the trip with Savannah, you know."

Cassie thought that over. "No, yesterday morning she and Will went to the school together to wait for the buses. I dropped them off, but I knew they didn't want me to stick around. They're teenagers. So we don't know what happened after that or who got on the bus."

"Want me to come along?"

Cassie hesitated. "No. Why don't you start looking through the box on the table. Maybe you can figure a better way to make heads or tails of what's in there."

"Will do."

Out in the car Cassie scrolled backward through the GPS record of previous destinations and recognized Helia's address when she got to it. She followed the instructions, and after a few minutes she parked in front of a ramshackle two-story house with a wide front porch and almost no front yard. The sides and back were surrounded by chain-link fencing, and a swing set and aboveground swimming pool were visible in the back.

On the front porch, she knocked. The day was warm enough that only a screen door stood between her and the hall by the front stairs.

A girl of about ten with multiple rows of braids adorned by colorful barrettes came to the door, but she didn't open it. "Can I help you?"

Cassie introduced herself. "Helia is a friend of my daughter, Savannah. I was hoping I could talk to her for a minute."

"I'll get her."

Cassie heard adult voices coming from the back of the house or possibly from the yard, followed by the laughter of children. She was relieved the girl wasn't alone.

She waited so long she wasn't sure Helia was going to join her, but finally she came down the stairs. Cassie knew, from her expression, that this was not where she wanted to be.

"Shall we talk out here?" Cassie asked. When Helia didn't respond, she added another suggestion. "Or would it be better to go around back and have this conversation with your foster parents?"

Helia flipped a lock and came out, closing the screen door behind her. Her expression was as shuttered as a summer cottage in February. "Is there something I can do for you, Ms. Costas?"

"Want to tell me why you're not on the field trip with Savannah and Will? Because she told me you'd planned this whole weekend together. Yet here you are."

"I decided not to go."

It was a reasonable answer, and very possibly true. Except that Helia was shifting from foot to foot. Oddly enough, Cassie liked the girl better because she wasn't a good liar. Despite the way they'd been introduced, the purse and the party, Cassie thought that in the long run, Helia was a better person than she wanted anyone to believe. Which was at least part of the reason Cassie had given Savannah permission for the field trip.

"Please tell me the truth, Helia. Because it's going to come out sooner or later. *When* did you decide not to go?"

Helia didn't answer.

"Okay. I guess Savannah decided that if I thought you were going to be there, it made sense she would want to go, too."

"I wanted to go, but I couldn't. We were going to SeaWorld, only one of the kids got sick, so we didn't."

"Where is Savannah?"

"For all I know, she's on the field trip. She didn't tell me anything different, and I don't keep track of her." She looked right at Cassie. "That's the truth. She just told me that you thought I was going to be there, too."

"That didn't seem odd to you, Helia?"

She didn't answer. Clearly it had.

"Did she tell you if she planned to come back?"

Now she looked surprised. "Do you think she ran away?"

"I don't know what to think, but I know how worried I am all of a sudden."

"Well, yeah, I'm sure she's coming back. We made plans for next weekend, and she said this was no big deal, okay? That she just really wanted to go and you might not let her if you thought going seemed strange. She said everything would be fine."

"What about Will? Is he in on this?"

"Will Blair?" Helia clearly thought Cassie was missing crucial brain cells.

"How about Madeline? Is she involved somehow?"

"Madeline Ritter? Not likely. They're not friends. Not after the fish thing."

"Minh?"

"Miss Follow the Rules? She and her family went to the East Coast this weekend."

"None of this is making sense, Helia."

"I don't know what else to tell you. I'm sorry you're worried. But she's smart. She can take care of herself."

"She's fifteen." Cassie realized there was nothing else to learn. "Thanks for talking to me." She started to turn away, but Helia stopped her.

"Did you see her get on the bus?"

Cassie had already decided that if this turned out okay, and Savannah came home unscathed, she would never turn her back on her daughter again. Not until Savannah was at least fifty. "I guess I thought I could trust her. But she seems determined to prove how little she cares if I do or not."

"If she did run away, she would go to California to be with her real mother."

Cassie didn't flinch. She hadn't felt like Savannah's real mother in a long time, so why would anybody else see her that way?

"Maybe it's time she did," she said.

This time when she turned away, Helia let her go.

31

IN SAVANNAH'S OPINION THE TRIP BACK TO TARPON
Springs was even worse than the trip to Blayney. They hadn't
been lucky enough to score a real motel. Savannah had forced
Will to try one about forty miles north of home, but they
had been turned away. Pelican Paradise, which looked like
a haven for drug dealers, hadn't believed she and Will were
brother and sister.

Instead they had spent the night in something called a Wil-
derness Preserve. Will had known exactly what to look for.
After a fast-food dinner when conversation had consisted of
"Do you want my ketchup?" and "These fries have been sitting out all day," they had set up in a wooded area not far
from the restrooms, which only had pit toilets and cold water
faucets. Will had put the Mustang seats down making something that vaguely resembled a flat surface for her, and padded it with one of the two sleeping bags. He had slept on the
ground beside the car.

No s'mores. No Kumbaya. No sneaking out of camp to re-
connoiter with the boys in a different campground. Instead

they had silently settled in after the sun went down and the crickets and frogs began their serenade. She had never slept that badly in her entire life, not even when she'd been sick with the flu.

By the time they pulled into Roxanne's garage, she felt filthy, and she was pretty sure she smelled. After a good wipe down, the Mustang was safely parked. There were no notes on the garage door from Cassie or Amber, a hopeful sign they hadn't figured out what their children were up to.

"I can't go anywhere like this," Savannah said, once they left the garage for the house. "I have to take a shower."

"The buses are going to start arriving pretty soon."

"I'll be done in time. And it's better if we don't arrive at school together anyway. Cassie knows how much I hate being dirty, and I don't want her to suspect anything. I'm sure they had real showers on the field trip."

Will headed toward the front door. "You need to haul your own stuff to school. And you need to get there in time to merge into the crowd."

She hoped none of the kids she had to "merge" with would ask where she'd been all weekend. Certainly not in front of Cassie.

She'd had hours to ask Will how he felt about everything, but somehow she hadn't. Now she saw her last chance escaping. "Are you angry because I thought going to Georgia would be a good idea?"

"I'm not angry at you, if that's what you mean. I just don't want to talk about it."

"Are you going to tell your mother you know Roger Hart isn't your father?"

Like her, Will had turned off his phone as they left Blayney, just in case one of their mothers called to chat and figured out something was up. Last night, though, she'd half expected him to turn it back on and call Amber from their campground to confess. Now, though, he shook his head, then without another word he left, his bedroll neatly tied and his gear in a backpack.

Savannah made careful note of everything in the bathroom before she got into the shower. When she finished, she put everything back the way she'd found it, made sure the house showed no signs anyone had been there and locked up behind her, hoping no neighbors were gawking.

By the time she got halfway to school, she felt hot and dirty all over again. As she made the last part of the hike, she faced a few questions about her motivation. It was only right that Will learn more about his history. That part was true. Amber's silence wasn't fair to him—nor were the lies they had discovered. But on top of that, Savannah had to admit she had also liked orchestrating a secret trip behind her stepmother's back.

She and Cassie hadn't been fighting as much since Christmas. Sometimes Savannah even wished they could go somewhere fun together, the way they used to. But every time that happened, she imagined Mark Westmore watching and wondering how she could abide the same woman who had made him so angry that awful afternoon that he had gone sailing when he never should have.

The trip pointed out something she hadn't expected. When faced with Amber's lies about Roger Hart, Will hadn't gotten angry or vowed to get even. He was wrestling with what he'd learned, but one thing was clear. He still loved his mother, and he realized his questions had forced her into a lie. He believed she had a reason for what she had told him. Will knew how to forgive.

Savannah's takeaway? She did not. Which of them was wrong?

As she rounded the corner to head to the back of the school

building, where she intended to hang out until the buses arrived, she saw she was too late. One of the buses was already parked in front, and parents and students were greeting each other. She looked for a way to cut across yards and go in from a less conspicuous side road, but no options presented themselves. She hoped everyone would be too busy to notice her approach.

Closer to the school she saw that Will had already merged into the first group fresh off the bus. Another bus turned the corner and pulled in behind it, and Savannah sped up, hoping that with that arrival, no one would notice her.

Quite possibly nobody would have, except the dark-haired woman standing to one side, motioning to Will.

Cassie.

Savannah sped up, sure she could still pull this off. There was no reason to assume she and Will would have ridden in the same bus. If she could just skirt the school and come in from the other side, she could blend in. Or she could wait for the third bus. She was sure if she just made it around the school.

Cassie turned and looked directly at her.

Savannah froze, at least her body froze, but her mind continued whirling. With no better choice, she walked toward her stepmother, trying not to look guilty. As she closed the distance, she composed a story. When she was standing almost in front of Cassie, she managed a smile, hoping it looked as casual as needed.

"Hey. I was just heading over to Roxanne's to call you. My phone's been out of juice all weekend, and I didn't see you or Amber waiting."

Cassie didn't say anything.

Amber arrived just then in her own car, pulling up on the other side of the street, and Will, who had been walking slowly toward them, saw his mother, waved and took off, like he'd just got a stay of execution.

Savannah forced another smile. "I guess Will's going home with Amber."

Cassie looked as if she hadn't slept any better than Savannah. "I know you weren't on the trip."

"What are you talking about? Of course—"

"I asked a chaperone on the first bus to check the girl's roster. You aren't on it."

"That's weird. I guess they left me off for some reason. But I—"

Cassie raised a hand to stop her. "Shall we talk to the kids from the second bus? Who did you sit with? I'm sure whoever it is will back you up."

Savannah didn't answer.

Cassie waited, and when it was clear nothing was forthcoming, she stepped closer. "I tried repeatedly to reach you or Will on your phones, but I didn't get an answer. I spent last night terrified something awful had happened to you, Savannah, that you had made a terrible decision that might haunt you for the rest of your life. So right now I'm furious, and at the same time so relieved you're here and okay, I want to shake you and kiss you and I don't know which to do first."

Savannah tried to ignore a rush of guilt. "Look, I just spent the weekend alone at Roxanne's, okay? I needed time by myself to think about everything. And I knew you wouldn't give it to me. You treat me like I'm a baby."

Cassie just stared at her.

"So?" Savannah said.

"No fifteen-year-old girl wants or needs three days alone in an empty house. I wasn't born yesterday. We're going home for a good conversation. And on the way, I'd like you to consider telling me the truth about where you've been. The truth will get you a lot further than another lie. You have that long to decide."

"Or what?"

"I don't know."

"Then that's how you can spend *your* time. You can come up with some stupid punishment. Won't that be productive?"

Rage sparked in Cassie's eyes. Rage that Savannah had never seen before. Cassie moved closer, and for a moment Savannah thought she was actually going to slap her. Some part of her thought that it might be better for both of them if she did.

Then Cassie started toward her car. Savannah considered whether to follow, but she knew she had to see this through.

The drive home was absolutely silent. Cassie parked in the garage. Amber's car wasn't there, and Savannah wondered if she had taken Will out for lunch to give Cassie time alone with her. Her own stomach grumbled, which was particularly humiliating under the circumstances.

Inside Cassie gestured to the sofa. "Have a seat."

Savannah sat reluctantly. "I'm sorry you were worried. But nothing bad happened. That's the truth."

Cassie perched on the sofa edge, but not within touching distance. Savannah wondered if she didn't trust herself. "Let's hear a little more. Truth, I mean."

Savannah had made her decision on the trip. This was not Will's fault, and it looked as if *his* absence from the field trip might not have been discovered. She wasn't going to spoil that. If she did, then he would have to tell his mother where he'd been. That story wasn't hers to expose.

"I'm finished explaining," she told Cassie. "That's all I'm going to say. I promise it wasn't anything you need to worry about. I was safe. I didn't take any stupid risks."

"Where were you?"

Savannah shook her head.

"If you were safe, and everything was fine, then why not explain why you set up such an elaborate lie ahead of time? Because you pulled poor Helia into it. I know that much. And Will? Did you pull him in, too?"

"Will doesn't know anything about anything. There were a lot of kids there. I knew he wouldn't be worried if he didn't see me."

"So why won't you tell me?"

Savannah leaned forward. Turning this back on Cassie was the only way to escape. "I told you the truth about what happened at Pfeiffer Grant, and you couldn't care less. You thought I was lying. So what's the point of trying to explain?"

Cassie's cheeks had turned pink, as if an explosion was near. "I was not alone, Savannah. Your father didn't believe you, either."

"I think you convinced Daddy I was lying. I think if you'd left him alone, he would have believed me. He would have taken my side. He always did!"

"That's the first truthful thing you've said, because yes, most of the time your father did take your side. He couldn't say no to you. He left that up to me."

"And aren't you good at it?"

"Apparently I should have said it a lot more often. Every time you've been rude to me, which is almost all the time these days, I should have told you that you had to stop. Every time you refused to do homework, or do anything constructive with your time after you left Pfeiffer, I should have told you no. I gave you space. I gave you time. I know your dad's death was terrible, and it affected—"

"You killed him!" Savannah stood and began to pace. "Do you think I don't know? You two were fighting right before he left to sail. Daddy was a great sailor, and yet he missed the changes in the weather? You think that ever happened before? He didn't go back to port, because he was upset when he left. Because of you."

Cassie took a long time to answer. "There are fights in every marriage. That was not our first and I had a good reason for it. And yes, your father was upset. I'm beginning to learn just how upset. But not at me. And nothing I said drove him to ignore a squall. It appalls me that after years of being your mother—"

"You are my *step*mother! And I wish to God you weren't! I wish Gen had raised me. I wish my parents had never split up. I wish you'd married somebody else and had your own children! I am not your daughter. I have a mother! A real mother. And it's not you."

Spent, she stopped, shaken at everything she had said.

Cassie's eyes were closed, but her fists were clenched. Finally, eyes open again, she stood, too. "Is that what you really think, Savannah? That all the years I've spent loving you mean nothing? That baking birthday cakes and going to ballet recitals and reading you a million bedtime stories meant nothing?"

"Anybody can do those things."

"But I was the one who did them."

"I needed my real mother! Somebody who loved me just because I'm hers."

Cassie nodded. "I see."

"You probably don't!"

"I do. And, you know, there's still time."

Savannah's heart was pounding so hard she could hardly hear her own words. "What's that supposed to mean?"

"Your father and mother worked out a custody agreement when you were a baby. Now your father is gone, but nobody has worked out a new one. I love you, so I did what I thought was best for you. I kept you with me, even though it meant moving for both of us."

"Like that was a good idea!"

"Your mother, you know, your *real* mother, was in Africa. I didn't think you wanted to go to high school in Kenya. Maybe I was wrong. But whether I was or not..." She swallowed hard. Savannah could see the muscles in her throat constrict. "Whether I was or not, your mother is now back in California."

"Then maybe I ought to go live with her!"

Cassie looked at her for a long time before she spoke. "Maybe you should."

For a moment Savannah wasn't sure she'd heard her stepmother right. She and Cassie had fought before, and she'd threatened to live with Gen more than once. But Cassie had always convinced her to calm down and stay. This was different.

"So, you're kicking me out?"

"No, I'm finally giving you what you say you most desire. I'm handing you over to your real mom, who will automatically understand every need and thought you have because she shares your genes, while I only shared your life."

"Handing me over?"

Cassie didn't hesitate. "And Savannah, if Gen agrees to have you there, I think you should go right away. Because, and this is only the woman who raised you talking, but it would be best for you to enter a new school when their spring break is over. I suspect that the schedule in California is similar to the one here, and it won't seem as strange to the other students if you show up after they've been away on vacation."

"This sounds like you've given it a lot of thought. How long have you wanted me out of the house?"

"I can call Gen or you can. Which will it be?"

"I'll call her!"

"Pack enough to hold you over. If everything goes as planned, I'll have all your other things shipped."

Cassie paused, then she rubbed her forehead, as if she had a headache. "I'm sorry I've failed you so terribly. I tried to be everything you need. I know that's impossible, but all I ever wanted was for you to be my daughter, too. Mine, Gen's, Mark's. All of ours. I just wanted to be part of that. I'm sorry it didn't work that way for you. Maybe it's impossible... I don't know. But I'm still glad I tried. Because when it did work, those were the best moments of my life."

She turned and walked away, leaving Savannah to stare after her and wonder exactly what she had done.

32

ON WEDNESDAY AMBER STAYED IN HER SUITE UNTIL she heard Cassie's car pull out and the garage door close for the second time. The second thunderous bang meant that Cassie and Savannah were on their way to the airport.

She'd said goodbye to Savannah last night when she'd given her a denim travel wallet she'd made as a goodbye gift—a zip pouch would have been a slap in the face. She hadn't expected or gotten much of a response beyond thank you, nor had she been able to gauge the girl's feelings. Will claimed Savannah was glad she was going to live with her mother, but Amber hadn't noted excitement. She had taken a chance and suggested that if Savannah had anything to say to her stepmother, the ride to the airport would be a good time. That, too, had fallen flat.

Cassie had been resolved but fragile. In Amber's presence she told Savannah when they needed to leave for the airport and how many bags she was allowed to take. She asked if Savannah needed help washing her laundry or packing snacks. The girl had refused with one shake of her head. Now they were gone. Amber hoped that if they did hold a conversation, Cassie could stay on the road.

On the drive to school that morning, Amber had asked Will how he felt about everything. "I'm staying out of it," he'd said.

"Because you think that's a good idea? Or because Savannah asked you to?"

"Both."

Her son hadn't been chatty since returning from the field trip. When she'd picked him up on Monday, she explained how worried she and Cassie had been. Had he noticed that Savannah was missing? Will had replied that the groups, divided by gender and class, had been mostly separate, and he hadn't been looking for her.

She had hoped for more. "Minh wasn't there?"

"Her family's visiting relatives in Titusville this weekend."

In the end she hadn't discussed the situation any further. Will's loyalty might be divided, and she didn't want to make his struggle worse.

Now, with the house to herself, she went to the dining table, which had become financial records central, and prepared the next stack of documents she planned to look over. At lunchtime she was going to visit a local campground not far from the Sponge Docks. She had a pocketful of change and a telephone date with an old friend, and the campground had a pay phone. Most important, she wanted to be out of the house when Cassie came home from the airport. Her friend deserved a place where she could grieve without witnesses.

Her cell phone rang just as she sat down to begin. She answered with a smile. "Dining somewhere odd and unusual for lunch?"

Travis laughed. "If my kitchen counter is odd and unusual. I'm stuck inside all afternoon working on my review for Havana Seafood."

The owners would be pleased. Travis really liked the place.

She told him about Savannah and Cassie leaving for the airport. Travis already knew about Savannah's disappearance, because, with Cassie's permission, Amber had asked for his advice. Since they didn't know for sure Savannah wasn't on the trip, and since they had not been able to reach the chaperones or either teen at the campground, where cell phone service was nonexistent, he had counseled Cassie to wait until the buses returned before calling the authorities. At fifteen, Savannah wasn't eligible for what was known as the critical missing persons list, and while the police would take a report, they were not required to begin a search right away. Usually teenagers turned up after a brief absence.

Worse, if the authorities did locate Savannah, she would be taken to a juvenile detention facility, with all the attendant intervention and paperwork. If she was on her way to California, that state would have to become involved, too.

"I'm glad she's safe," Travis said now. "Does her California mother know everything that transpired?"

"Cassie said she sounded more resigned than enthusiastic about Savannah moving in with her. It has to be a shock. Single woman with an occasional short-term daughter suddenly becomes a full-time mom."

"She has to be at least marginally prepared."

"We'll see, or maybe we won't. Who knows when Cassie will hear a report from either of them."

"This has probably been stressful for you, too. You could come and enjoy a bologna sandwich at my kitchen counter."

Amber wondered what else Travis wanted her to enjoy, and the invitation was tempting. He was a surprise and a worry, and she was still mulling over the consequences of getting involved with a man who would be hard to leave. But they had already planned another dinner for the end of the week, and she couldn't delay her afternoon phone call.

After she hung up, she tackled the papers. At noon she stacked everything into neat piles, one to discuss with Cassie, another to refile and a third to finish later. Then she changed for work and left the house.

The RV park near the Sponge Docks was one of the dozen or so places in and around the city that still had pay phones. She'd found a list online and checked each one.

She tried not to use the same phone twice. She had no reason to suspect that the number she called was being monitored, but she was dealing with a sociopath with both resources and animal cunning.

To stay safe, Amber rarely called Betsy Garland directly, but every few months it was important to check in. Although she was retired, Betsy still lived in Chaslan and kept her ear to the ground. She was no longer a 4-H leader but she helped with the sewing curriculum when her arthritis wasn't acting up.

Betsy's interest in quilting had helped them create a signal so that Betsy would be waiting by a friend's phone and ready to take a call when Amber wanted to talk. To alert her, Amber left a message on a quilting bulletin board that Betsy had created, using the name Sue Simpson. Amber always inquired about a project she was working on and asked Betsy if her measurements seemed correct. From those, Betsy could figure out what day and what time in the afternoon Amber would call the following week. Usually Betsy replied, and if necessary, "corrected" her description if the time was inconvenient.

The day was expressed in yards. One yard was Monday, two was Tuesday and the time of day was expressed in measurements for cutting. So two yards, with a strip cut four and a half inches wide meant Amber would call on the following Tuesday at four thirty. Last week's message had followed their usual pattern. Amber hadn't received a response, but that had happened before, so she wasn't worried.

So far Betsy had always been waiting for the calls. Betsy's friend, Tammy, had no idea why Betsy needed to sit by Tammy's phone from time to time, but the two women had known each other since sixth grade, and Tammy was sworn to silence. Betsy had promised Tammy that when she could reveal what the calls were about, she would.

At the RV park, Amber pulled curbside near the recreation pavilion. The park was only ten minutes from the Kouzina, nicer than the one Amber and Will had stayed in before moving to Cassie's, with waterfront sites complete with docks and surfaced RV sites. Beaches were close by, and the big-city pleasures of Tampa were only a short drive away.

She found the pay phone with no trouble, smiled at the people taking their children to the playground and then turned her back, checking the posted rates before she slipped in change and waited for her call to go through.

Betsy always answered after the first ring, but today the phone rang ten times before Amber hung up. Afraid she'd dialed incorrectly or that Betsy hadn't yet arrived, she waited five minutes, then she reinserted the change that had been returned and tried again. The result was the same.

When a third try was no more successful, she considered possibilities. Her friend might be sick. Or maybe Betsy hadn't seen the message on the bulletin board or confused the time and thought Amber was calling on a different day.

But the worst possibility? Betsy had been ill with a chest cold the previous year, and a routine doctor's visit had turned up a stage one melanoma. She'd had outpatient surgery and appropriate tests afterward, and she'd been released from any further treatment. But had cancer recurred? Was Betsy in a hospital and Tammy unaware of a planned phone call?

Or worse?

Amber had just enough time for a quick stop at the library before her shift began. She settled in at one of the computers and went immediately to the website for the *Croville Chronicle* and ran a search for Betsy Garland, praying she wouldn't see an obituary.

When nothing turned up, she blinked away tears. Her best choice now was to go back to the quilter's bulletin board and insert another coded message.

As she walked back to her car, her thoughts turned darker. Was it possible Darryl Hawken was responsible for Betsy's disappearance? Betsy had a son who lived out of town, and it would be so easy to spread the word she was visiting him and wouldn't be home for the foreseeable future.

If somehow Darryl had learned that Amber and Betsy were still in touch, was it possible that he'd gotten her address from Betsy, too? What if he had also learned about Will? Were their lives in danger? And what about Cassie, who had taken them both in? It was too early to panic, but Amber realized she had to be on a state of high alert in the weeks to come.

The day had been fraught with drama, and she hoped the rest of it went better. Roxanne was returning to work that afternoon after her trip to Paris. Amber hoped that she and Yiayia would be so happy to see each other that the atmosphere at the Kouzina would be cheerful and carefree.

Her father had always said that trouble came in threes, and that was just for starters. Optimism had never been Ray Parsons's strong point. Today she was afraid she might have inherited more from the man who had sired her than her green eyes.

33

"YOU MUST BE SAVANNAH."

Just past airport security, Savannah stopped searching for her mother and turned toward the older woman standing six feet away. She had close-cropped gray hair and assessing pale blue eyes, and she was offering Savannah her hand.

"I'm Pauline, your mother's housekeeper. Your mother sent me. She's at the office and won't be home until late afternoon. I'm to get you settled."

Savannah shook her hand, although she was sure her own was limp and sweaty. Both flights, with a short layover in Phoenix, had seemed a hundred years long, and she was beyond exhausted. A baby behind her had screamed for the entire first leg, and a man who probably hadn't bathed that morning had squeezed in beside her for the second.

She said the only thing that came to mind. "I didn't know Gen had a housekeeper."

"I've always worked part-time for your mother, so I agreed to work longer hours now that you're here. I assume you have baggage on the carousel?" Without waiting for an answer, Pauline started toward baggage claim, which was housed in the north wing. Savannah barely managed to keep up with her.

The Palm Springs Airport was airy and attractive, with open spaces and tall windows that faced Mount San Jacinto. Desert mountains were made entirely of folds and shadows, and the way the sun illuminated them fascinated Savannah. But there was no time for sightseeing.

At the carousel Pauline checked her phone. "Have you texted your stepmother to tell her you arrived?"

Savannah wondered exactly how she could have texted anyone while they sprinted across the airport. "Not yet."

"I'm sure she'll want to know." Pauline went back to her phone.

Instead, Savannah texted Will.

Tell Cassie I made it to Palm Springs.

She debated, then added:

Hope you told Helia and Minh I said goodbye.

She slipped her phone back in the pocket of her jeans. By the time they were in Pauline's little Mazda heading toward Gen's condo, she was struggling to keep her eyes open.

"Gen said to tell you that she'll move her desk out of the study this weekend and put in a real bed. For now you'll have to sleep on the sofa."

The news wasn't surprising. Savannah always slept on the pullout sofa bed when she visited Gen. The study did have a small closet, but Gen had added shelves and stored her books and a wireless printer there. She wondered if she would also remove the shelves so she could hang up a few clothes.

For a while now she'd wondered why Gen had chosen such

a small condo when she knew Savannah would be visiting. But, of course, Gen was frequently out of the country, and until now, Savannah's visits to Palm Springs had been short. Gen must have assumed that would never change.

"Are you hungry?" Pauline asked.

"Starving." Savannah hoped the question meant they were going to stop for tacos or a burger.

"I made salads for dinner. There's enough for you to have a serving when we get to Gen's."

"I think I'll need more than a salad. I haven't eaten anything but snacks since I left Florida."

"There are plenty of crackers and cheese to go with it."

Savannah could hardly wait.

The drive was blessedly short. The condo complex was small, overlooking mountains and desert dotted by palm trees. The view was its best selling point. The buildings themselves were rectangular stucco with flat roofs and limestone walls that surrounded entryways and what passed for yards. Gen's unit had a tiny bisected pool with one narrow lane for laps and the rest for splashing. The complex had a larger pool with a handful of shaded cabanas, but Savannah had never seen anyone there who was close to her age.

"We'll take in your bags and then get your lunch."

Pauline was too old to have teenagers herself but too young to have teenage grandchildren, so it was no surprise that she didn't understand that a salad, after a day of pretzels and peanuts, was a bad idea. Savannah wondered how often she would be around. Her father had always told her to follow her instincts about the people she met, but not to make a final judgment too early. So she was trying not to go with her initial impression, that Pauline got an A on details and a D on empathy.

They parked in the utilitarian garage with a washer and dryer shoved against one wall, and entered through the condo kitchen. Most of the condo was laid out on one floor, a stone floor at that, and the kitchen was a smattering of additional hard surfaces. One flight of stairs led to the study upstairs and a small bathroom.

The downstairs had been newly painted a peachy beige, and the wall that surrounded the fireplace in the great room was the same color but many shades darker. New leather couches flanked the fireplace, and a flat-screen television loomed on the wall above it.

Pauline uttered one of her rare sentences. "Your mother has done a fair bit of decorating since you were here, I suspect."

Savannah took in the African masks on the wall and the brightly patterned pillows. A three-paneled photo of an elephant stared at her from the wall opposite the fireplace. She felt more like a stranger. "I like it."

"She redecorated the study, too, where you'll be sleeping now."

The stairs leading to the study were open, with a metal railing and empty space between treads, a style Gen had referred to as floating stairs. The openings always made Savannah dizzy as she climbed, even if she knew she wasn't going to slip through them. Now she followed Pauline to the top, carrying her backpack and the suitcase she had brought along. She wished she had a hand for the railing.

The room was smaller than she remembered. She tried to imagine it without the desk and sofa. There would be room for a double bed, but only just, and perhaps a small dresser.

"Gen thinks we can fit this desk in the hallway by the door." Pauline parked the larger rolling suitcase beside the sofa. "You can freshen up. I'll have everything ready when you come down."

The designer hadn't worked any magic here. There was some unfamiliar abstract art on the glistening white walls—

blotches and stripes and what looked like people peeking out of shadows—and the desk was new, contemporary in style with no pulls on the drawers and a glass top. On the back edge against the wall Savannah saw a framed photo of herself, the last school picture she'd posed for at Pfeiffer Grant. She wondered if Gen had added it as an afterthought, and she immediately felt disloyal. She took a clean shirt from her suitcase, washed up in the bathroom and then slipped on sandals to go downstairs to eat.

In the kitchen she watched as Pauline carefully folded a cloth napkin beside a small bowl filled with something green. "When will Gen be back?"

"I don't know. I'll stay until she gets here."

"It's okay if you need to leave. I'll be fine."

"No, I'll stay."

Arguing with Pauline wasn't going to get her anywhere. She sat and looked at the salad, thinly sliced cabbage, wontons, a few cherry tomatoes. She'd hoped for chicken at the very least, but the white cubes scattered here and there looked like tofu.

"Your mom's a vegetarian now," Pauline said. "But I'm sure she'll let you eat meat now and then if that's your choice."

Savannah wanted to start immediately with a burger and maybe some fries, or better yet, one of Yiayia's gyros. "It's very pretty the way you arranged everything." She picked up her fork and took a mouthful. There was a faint hint of peanuts in the minimal dressing.

"We have herbal tea and sparkling water."

"Water, thanks." Savannah took it and thanked her again. Obviously the offer of cheese and crackers had been forgotten.

"I'll be out sweeping the patio." Pauline retreated without another word.

Savannah told herself to eat the salad whether she liked it or not, because it was clear nothing else was forthcoming. Cassie always said gather the harvest while you can because it won't always be summer. It was one of Yiayia's expressions. Savannah wondered how long it would be before Cassie and all her Greek relatives were out of her head.

So she didn't really like Pauline, and the study was going to take some getting used to. At least she would be with her real mother.

After she finished the salad, she went upstairs to investigate how comfortable the sofa was. The next thing she knew the door to the study swung open, and Gen was staring down at her.

"Vanna!" Gen dropped to the edge of the sofa. "Poor baby. You look tired. That's some trip, isn't it?"

Savannah sat up and stretched. "Hey, Gen. I guess I fell asleep. When did you get home?" She could see through the lone window that the sky was already growing dark outside.

"Not soon enough." Gen reached over and stroked her hair. "I got stuck in a meeting. But Pauline took good care of you?"

Savannah wasn't sure what to say. "She gave me some of tonight's salad and helped me get settled up here."

"She's a treasure. She's going to be staying here in the afternoons while I'm at work, so you'll have company. And whenever I'm out of town, too."

Savannah drank in the sight of the woman who had given birth to her. Gen's eyes were more brown than hazel, and her hair was a lighter brown than Savannah's. These days she wore it in a glistening chin-length bob pushed back over ears sporting delicate gold hoops. Savannah's features were tidy and symmetrical like her father's, while her mother's nose was narrow but her lips were full, sheltering large perfect teeth. Gen didn't look like a sixties high school cheerleader. She looked like everyone's favorite teacher, the one who staged high school musicals, who smoked in the teacher's lounge when nobody was looking and encouraged, prompted and scolded—but only if absolutely necessary.

Savannah put her arms around her mother and they embraced.

Gen finally sat back. "Think we can make this room work? We can shop for a bed, maybe a little dresser. Pauline's husband is handy with tools, and he says he'll turn the bookcase back into a closet. If you can't live with the art—it's a little intense—we can store it."

"The room's fine. Maybe I can paint the walls something brighter, more like a bedroom."

Gen's eyes widened. "Really? I just had the whole house painted. The decorator chose a very pricey pearl white for these walls. Specially mixed. See that pretty lustrous undertone?"

Savannah thought white was white, and the walls looked more like icebergs than pearls.

Gen was nodding now, as if she wanted to compromise. "Maybe the room could use some color on the little wall around the window to frame the view. I can call my decorator for a suggestion." She changed the subject. "So you were having a tough time in Florida?"

Savannah shrugged. She knew better than to criticize Cassie. While Cassie and Gen didn't know each other well, they had banded together to raise her.

"Florida's not my home." She managed a brave smile. "And Cassie's not my mother."

Gen frowned. "She's been very good to you. She's done a great job."

Savannah just smiled again. "I can't wait to hear all about Africa."

"We'll do that over dinner. It's all ready."

"I know. I can tell you everything that's in the salad."

Gen laughed. "Come on down when you're ready."

Savannah joined her a few minutes later. Gen was sipping a glass of wine, and she'd poured a glass of some kind of juice for Savannah into an identical wineglass.

"Here's to us," Gen said.

Savannah raised her glass. "To us."

Gen had put out cheese and crackers, and now Savannah slapped together three and ate them quickly.

"Wow, you were hungry."

Savannah made another. "I didn't have time to grab anything in Phoenix between flights."

"You should have told Pauline to stop on the way home to get takeout."

"She thought salad would be enough."

"She's never had children. We'll have to educate her."

Savannah had her second disloyal thought. Gen did have a child, but she and Savannah had spent so little time together that now she wondered who was going to educate her mother?

"Did she tell you I'm a vegetarian now?" Gen asked. "But whenever we eat out, please feel free to order meat if you prefer it."

Savannah hoped they ate out often. "Why'd you become a vegetarian?"

As they divided the remaining salad and took it to the table, Gen told the whole story in detail. When she was out in the field with doctors on her team, she had gotten used to eating something called *ugali*, a boiled dough made from cornmeal served with cooked vegetables. The goat or mutton that was also served hadn't appealed to her, and eventually, she'd decided not to eat meat anymore.

"And there you have it," Gen said. "Vegetarian by degrees."

Savannah had been relieved to see there were rolls and butter on the table. Now she reached for her third one and used it to scoop up the dribbles of what was left of the salad dressing in her otherwise empty bowl.

"I guess I'm lucky vegetarian is my preference now," Gen said, "because Pauline's not much of a cook. But she did buy a Kenyan cookbook this week, so I guess we'll see how easy it is to translate what I ate every day into an American meal you can enjoy."

"That will be interesting." Eating vegetarian food cooked by a reluctant Pauline would be interesting in the same way that being forced to run around the Coastal Winds track by her sadistic physical education teacher had been.

"So, tell me what was the final straw for you and Cassie, Vanna? Why did you decide you'd rather live here?"

"It's not as sudden as you're making it sound. I would have come months ago, but after Dad died you were in Africa."

"Should I have come back then? You never told me you wanted to live with me. You could have asked."

Savannah supposed she could have. But if she had, what kind of repercussions might there have been? Would Gen have been angry about leaving Africa early? Would she have blamed her daughter for changing her life so drastically?

"The problems with Cassie just built up over the months," she said.

"So what was the latest problem?"

"What did Cassie tell you?"

"That you were gone this past weekend and lied about where you were. When you came back, you refused to tell her the truth."

Silently Savannah tried to pick the story apart, but it wasn't going to be easy. "I promise I didn't do anything wrong, nothing Cassie needed to worry about, although I couldn't tell her where I'd been, which infuriated her. Honestly? I was helping a friend, and I can't say who. But I wasn't in danger, and I wasn't drinking or doing drugs or having sex."

"Did you tell her that much?"

"Not exactly. I try not to talk to Cassie any more than I have to."

"Why is that?"

"What's the point? She doesn't believe me anyway. And besides..."

Gen sipped her wine and waited. She wasn't a particularly good listener, but today she was trying.

"The day Dad drowned? He and Cassie had a big fight first. He stormed out, and I'm pretty sure if that hadn't happened, then he would have paid more attention to the storm heading his direction."

Gen was frowning now. "I'm sorry, but are you saying your father's death was Cassie's fault?"

Savannah wished Gen hadn't stated it so directly. "Maybe not entirely, but some, yeah."

"Vanna, people fight. Your father and I fought when we were married. And despite that, he still lived to raise you and marry Cassie and join a flourishing medical practice."

"You don't understand. Things were tense before that. The atmosphere around our house was as thick...as thick as a tree trunk. His mind wasn't on sailing." She didn't know what else to say.

"It seems to me you have forgotten that Mark knew better than to sail when he was upset, especially alone. I'm guessing whatever happened on the water that day had absolutely nothing to do with Cassie and absolutely everything to do with bad weather and a race for shore that just ended badly, as sailing sometimes does."

Savannah was angry. She wanted to rail at Gen for taking such a ridiculous stance, but she was also aware that while living with Gen had always been her fallback position, now she *had* no fallback position. This crowded little condo was Savannah's last stand, and from here, there was no other place to go. She and Gen had to get along. She and Pauline had to get along. She had to get along with whatever idiots she ran into at whatever Palm Springs high school she attended.

She was fifteen, and she had three years until she could strike out on her own. She took a deep breath and hoped that giving in and giving up weren't all it took to be an adult. "Can we talk about something else?"

Gen got up to take their bowls to the sink. "What do you say we go out for ice cream? I'll get my keys." She left for her bedroom.

Savannah wasn't surprised Gen had decided on ice cream without consulting her. She rarely asked Savannah for suggestions. She wasn't selfish, witness the many hours she gave to charitable causes when she could have been raking in big bucks. Gen just wasn't used to thinking of anyone but herself. Taking suggestions wasn't on her radar, particularly from a daughter she really didn't know.

Tonight, if given the choice, rather than ice cream, Savannah would have chosen to go somewhere for pizza to fill the hole inside her that the salad hadn't touched.

Although as she considered that third disloyal thought of the day, she wondered if the hole inside her had anything to do with food at all.

34

CASSIE HAD NEVER FELT AT LOOSE ENDS IN NEW York. Between volunteer work, friends and Savannah's busy schedule, her days had been happily filled. Now with Savannah already gone for a week and no job or worthwhile interviews to fill the hours, she had organized and scoured the house, shopped garage sales for containers for the patio and carefully pampered half a dozen plants from her local home improvement store's bargain table. Travis had given her a tray of cuttings to root, which she tended every day, but once she'd settled everything into its appropriate place and routine, boredom had set in again.

On a Friday morning Amber watched her staring at a spoonful of scrambled eggs and took matters into her own hands. Literally. She waved them in Cassie's face until her friend looked up.

"I know what you're doing. No more kicking yourself. You made the best decision you could when you allowed Savannah to leave. She pushed you to the wall."

Cassie was too depressed to pretend otherwise. "I keep asking myself where I went wrong raising her. I've gotten all the way back to the year she was five and wanted to take horseback riding lessons, and I told her she had to wait. By the time she turned six, she was afraid of horses. Now it's my fault she'll never be on the Olympic Equestrian Team."

"You're kidding, right?"

Cassie tried to smile. "Am I funny yet?"

Amber got up to fill both their coffee mugs, bringing the pot to the table. "You're coming with me to the Kouzina today. Yiayia gave me the go-ahead to sort and organize the supply room. I had to pick Roxanne up off the floor when I told her."

Cassie knew exactly what was happening. She wasn't needed. Amber was trying to entertain her. "You'll do fine without me."

"We'll never know." Amber set the pot on the table and herself in the chair across from Cassie. "Listen, between the two of us, we can make the Kouzina twice as efficient. Yiayia seems to be pulling back a little, and this is exactly the right moment to get in and do what we can before she changes her mind."

"Pulling back?"

"You want proof? She let Rox choose the specials on Wednesday night and yesterday at lunch."

Now Cassie looked up. "You're kidding."

"We sold out of both just an hour after they went into the menus. Even Yiayia seemed impressed. Roxanne was the chef in charge."

"Where's Buck?"

"He's been away. Roxanne thinks he's getting ready for a trip to see his family in Greece."

"Is Rox going to pack Yiayia in his suitcase?"

"If she can get away with it."

"Yiayia and Rox love each other. They fight, but the love is always obvious."

Apparently Amber could tell who Cassie was really talking about. "You and Savannah will settle this eventually. But for now? You're coming with me. I really need your help."

Forty minutes later they were inside the Kouzina's storage area, looking at the mess they had to deal with. Roxanne in her chef's coat had joined them, eager to put in her own two cents on how to organize supplies.

"I can see this space being so useful." Cassie wandered as much as she could, taking care not to trip over jugs and boxes. "In fact I can see it adding a lot of value."

Roxanne lowered herself to a stack of crates. "What would you do with it?"

"Well, if you're really going to waste this valuable space and continue to use it as a storeroom, you need to do an inventory, then have a handyman—or woman—come and build shelves, or buy ready-made units to add to what you already have. You'll want to figure out what you use most often, and where it should be stored, here or in the kitchen, which frankly needs a major renovation."

Roxanne was nodding along. "My dream is to gut the kitchen and open it to the restaurant. Have everything in sight, stainless steel and sparkling. There are all kinds of ways to manage storage in there, but best yet, I think we could close in the little porch overlooking the parking lot for that purpose."

"That would be perfect. I'm sure you've told Yiayia?"

"Mama sees every change as a criticism of what she's done or not done since taking over the restaurant after my father died."

"If you added to the kitchen and didn't need this space for storage? I would follow your father's original instincts. You said Pappou hoped to add to the Kouzina when he bought it?"

Cassie waited for Roxanne to nod. "So first, open it up to the restaurant. Then put a bakery display case along this wall and fill it with baklava and the other dessert goodies on the menu. Not everything would have to be baked here. There are plenty of talented local bakers who can't afford their own storefront." Cassie pointed. "And on this wall? I'd put in a good quality refrigerated display case that had an area for frozen food, too. And I'd fill the freezer with specialties the Kouzina's known for. Yiayia's moussaka. Pastitsio. Tiropita and spanikopita for parties. Diners would be delighted to bring home something for later in the week. The refrigerated area could feature Greek salads, stuffed grape leaves, hummus and tzatziki. You get the idea. You'd put a note on the menus making customers feel you're doing this as a favor because you want them to eat well all week." Cassie could have gone on, but she didn't.

"All those ideas without even a few minutes to think about it?"

Amber advanced the fantasy. "Tables in the center. No. Make that one long narrow table, a high top with room for maybe ten or even twelve people for sharing special menus family style. I think that would fit, and people could still shop along the edges. We could also use the room for small dinners or parties if we could rearrange things. Maybe build the table in pieces so the configuration could be changed. Add a wine display if licensing allows us to sell wine by the bottle."

Cassie was making additions in her imagination. "Soft lighting and music. You might be able to get local artists to display and sell their work here. Have a revolving show. Great publicity."

Roxanne looked as if she could envision it. "Move into the twenty-first century with a real point-of-sale system, and no more time trying to use nineteenth-century accounting systems. So how about this? Cassie, you be our marketing manager, in charge of renovating and stocking this area. You can oversee the project, plus market the restaurant in new and better ways. Amber, you be the general manager, keeping back and front of house on track. We'd work together on improving the ambience with new tables and chairs, paint, more local art."

"What about you?" Cassie asked, although she knew the answer.

"Executive chef."

"Nouveau Greek cuisine," Amber said. "Old favorites both the traditional way and newly updated. Customers could choose. Greek but not kitschy. Everything as fresh as Yiayia insists on it now."

They all fell silent, thinking about how much fun that would be and, at the moment, how impossible. Finally Roxanne got up. "I have things to do before the lunch rush. You two let me know if there's anything you need from me."

"Quite a fantasy, huh?" Cassie said when Roxanne was gone.

Amber nodded. "Back to reality."

Two hours later the shelves had been cleared and cleaned, and ingredients sorted by types of packaging and how often items were used. They had heaved everything useless or outdated into a corner to be removed for good and moved shelves to open up wider walkways. Cassie had created a list of what was where and why, and she had promised to print and laminate it and come back tomorrow to label each shelf.

"That's all we can do today," Amber said. "I have to wash up and change to work out front. Go ahead and drive home, and I'll get a ride tonight."

"I thought I'd scrub the shelves we didn't get to."

"You already did plenty."

"I like being here."

After Amber left, Cassie thought about those words. Today, as during her childhood, the sounds and smells of the Kouzina soothed her. Some of the best moments of her childhood had been spent under this roof. Here with her grandparents and Roxanne, she could be the child she couldn't be at home, where too often she had been the most adult person on the premises.

In New York, away from both good and bad memories of life in Tarpon Springs, she had fallen in love with a man whose career was already assured, and later with his tiny daughter who had needed and wanted her love. Married to him, she could devote herself to creating the happy home she'd been denied.

Had Mark demanded that of her? Or had she snuggled into his life, like a warm blanket, because her own insecurities had made it difficult to ask for more? If she had asked, would they have been able to solve their problems?

She was still thinking, still scrubbing, when her cell phone buzzed. While Cassie knew better than to expect a call from Savannah, she still fished the phone from her pocket and answered without checking ID.

"Miss Costas? Will you hold for Dr. Farthington?"

For a moment she was disoriented. Diane Farthington was the headmistress of the Pfeiffer Grant upper school, as well as the woman who had kicked Savannah to the curb. The last time they'd spoken was almost a year ago.

She waited until Dr. Farthington said hello. Then some of the pent-up anger that had festered over the year seeped out. "I hope this isn't a fundraising phone call. I'm not inclined to contribute this year, Diane."

"How are you, Cassie?"

"Curious."

"I was so sorry to hear about Mark. He was always such a wise presence in parent meetings."

"Yes, I think the school sent a sympathy card."

"I can understand why you're angry."

"I'm not angry so much as mystified. I'm living in Florida now. If you've changed your mind about Savannah's expulsion, you're a bit late."

"Here's the reason I'm calling," Diane said. "Our honor code says that students must uphold standards of truth, honor and integrity. The faculty and administration have to be held to the same standards. And this week I've learned that despite looking into the fight between Savannah and Gillie Robinson myself, despite separating the girls who were there and insisting each one tell me exactly what happened, I didn't dig deeply enough."

Cassie found an overturned storage bucket and lowered herself to it. "Go on."

"Savannah said that Gillie had been persecuting a younger girl—"

"Liza."

"Yes. Liza Jenkins. At the time I questioned her myself. She was emotionally overwrought, and I sympathized. But when she told me that Gillie hadn't bothered her, that Savannah attacked Gillie for something else, I felt I had no choice but to believe her. Liza was supposed to be the victim, and she claimed she wasn't."

"For the record, I remember the story. For us, after all, it was life altering."

Diane sighed. "I demanded Savannah tell me the real truth. I don't know if you know this part, Cassie, but the last time I met with her alone, I told her if she would just admit what she'd done, I would find a way to keep her at the academy, even though Gillie claimed she'd been injured and her parents were furious."

Cassie could envision her daughter in front of the headmistress, head high, shoulders back, eyes shooting fire. "She said no, right? She refused to tell you the version of the events that you wanted to hear. She repeated what she'd already told you."

"And because she refused to budge, I had no choice but to expel her from the school."

"Which you did quickly and efficiently."

"Yes." Diane paused. "And incorrectly as it turns out. Savannah should never have laid a hand on Gillie, but she told the truth. This week Liza made a suicide attempt—"

Cassie clutched the phone harder. "No—"

"Don't worry. She's fine. It was a small cut on her wrist, a plea for help. She's in counseling, and she's getting the help she needed. But afterward she confessed that Gillie has been harassing her for more than a year, and she was terrified to admit it. Gillie told her that her family gave a lot of money to the academy, and we would never send her away, no matter what she did. Liza was desperate. She thought if she supported Savannah's story, Gillie would hurt her even more seriously. By the same token, she thought if she agreed that Gillie's version was true, Gillie might finally leave her alone. Fortunately for us, we installed better video after the incident with Savannah—wider coverage, clearer images. After Liza was hospitalized we reviewed several days of footage and caught Gillie shoving her and calling her horrible names."

Cassie couldn't help herself. "So tell me, was Liza right? Was Gillie's family too important to expel her? Did you make her stay late one afternoon and write a paper on bullying?"

"Gillie's gone. Forever. And now that she is, the other girls who were there when Savannah defended Liza have come forward to admit they were afraid of Gillie, too, and didn't tell the truth."

Cassie had discharged enough anger that now she just felt sad and tired. "Do you have any idea how this affected our family? Mark believed you, even when I didn't at first. He convinced me I was twisting facts to match my idealized version of our daughter. And Savannah? She came away convinced that telling the truth and protecting the weak aren't all they're cracked up to be. Pfeiffer removed a barrier in her mind between doing what's right and doing whatever she wants, because nobody will see the difference anyway."

Diane sounded sad, too. "I can't tell you how sorry I am. I promise I did investigate thoroughly, that I never believed Gillie over Savannah just because Gillie's family were generous donors. You were donors, too, and it wasn't about money anyway, although too many things at the academy are. In the long run it was four girls against Savannah, and even the so-called victim sided with the others."

Cassie didn't want to see Diane's side, but she could. The headmistress had always tried to be fair, and Cassie had seen tears in her eyes the day she told Savannah she had to leave that afternoon for good.

"All right," she said after a long moment. "Thank you. Calling me can't have been easy."

"Would you like me to talk to Savannah? Or would you like to talk to her first and prepare her? Either way I need to apologize directly."

Cassie didn't want to explain that Savannah was no longer living with her. Diane felt enough guilt without knowing that.

"I'll talk to her," she said. "And I'll let you know if she wants to talk to you."

"I would appreciate that. Are you both doing okay? Under the circumstances?"

"We've been better," Cassie said.

"Please know I'll be thinking about this for a very long time."

Cassie hung up. For the first time since Savannah had disappeared into the bowels of the airport without her, Cassie was glad her daughter was gone. Now she had time to consider what to say and how to say it.

She was afraid no words had been invented to convey what she was feeling.

35

SAVANNAH HOPED THAT WHEN SHE WAS FINALLY back in school, life in Palm Springs wouldn't be as boring or lonely as it was now. Pauline rarely spoke, except to tell her what to do, and when Gen was home, which was rare enough, she didn't consult Savannah about things they could do together. Instead she entertained her daughter with stories about her day.

The pattern was familiar. Their week in Paris when Savannah turned thirteen was an example. Gen had been so excited to plan a trip to celebrate Savannah's first teenage birthday. Savannah, who had been studying Spanish for two years, had really wanted to go to Barcelona. She'd studied the city and written a paper about Antoni Gaudi, and she was excited to see his flamboyant architecture up close. She'd mentioned Barcelona as an alternative, but Gen had run right over her. Every girl needed to see Paris. All the designer boutiques, the shopping, the Louvre.

Savannah liked to shop for maybe an hour. After that she was bored. She wasn't crazy about French food, and while she liked art and museums, countless hours at the Louvre hadn't sounded like fun, especially with no chance to try out her language skills.

Of course the trip had been incredible—being with Gen always was—but the entire time, a part of her had still wished they were in Spain.

Afterward when Savannah had mentioned her feelings to her father, he had pointed out that Gen lived alone, so she wasn't used to consulting anyone. And Gen had to make decisions quickly. She had to rely on herself without worrying about the opinions of others.

Savannah heard the message. Gen wasn't going to change, so Savannah needed to adjust. At the time she had wondered if her father had married Cassie at least partly because she was a team player.

"It's not that Gen doesn't listen," she told Will on the telephone that evening. She'd been in Palm Springs for four days, and while Gen had taken her hiking in the Indian Canyons early one morning and had promised to take her out to dinner tomorrow, mostly Savannah had been at home with Pauline. She didn't hate the housekeeper, but she disliked being forced to listen to her expound about not wearing shoes inside or why Savannah should wipe down the sink every time she used it. Savannah was just one rule away from telling Pauline to post a list, since nobody could keep that many edicts in their head. She could imagine how that would go over.

"Then what is it?" Will sounded tired. School was still in session in Tarpon Springs, and he was working the maximum hours allowed at the Kouzina, which remained in the throes of tourist season.

They had talked or at least texted almost every night since she left. Savannah was hungry to know what was happening at school and with her friends.

"She listens if I can get her attention. It's just that..." Savannah tried to find the best way to say it. "It's like I'm an afterthought. And I don't mean that in a spoiled brat kind of way, you know? I don't expect her to be dancing around, waiting on my every whim. I just think that most of the time she's only listening when she realizes she's supposed to be. Then she rivets attention on me, and it's almost scary. Like she's trying to suck everything out of the conversation."

"Does she have friends?"

"She talks to some guy every night, somebody she met in Africa last year. He lives in Oregon. I get the feeling she had to cancel some kind of trip they were going to take together, or a week shacked up in some lodge."

"Because of you?"

"That's my guess. She doesn't complain or anything."

"Makes sense she had a life before you got there."

"My dad had a life, too, but he was still there for me. Like Amber is for you."

"She probably has to get used to having you around."

"If she can."

"Cassie was like that for you, too. The way my mom is for me, I mean."

She started to protest, then she fell silent.

"She misses you," he said.

Cassie had left several voice mail messages, but Savannah hadn't responded. "She called and said she needs to talk to me about something. Do you know what?"

"Why don't you call her and see?"

"I don't think so." Savannah wasn't even sure why she didn't want to talk to Cassie. Of course, she was still angry. Yes, she wanted a clean break with her stepmother, or thought she did. But there was more, and she couldn't shove it away.

No matter how she felt about Cassie now, Will was right.

Cassie had been there for her. Even when Savannah was kicked out of Pfeiffer Grant, Cassie had tried to get her to open up, to talk about what had happened and what to do next. Her father had simply walked away.

"If you won't talk to her," Will said, "I'm going to. I'm going to tell her where we were the weekend of the field trip. I guess I'll just have to deal with my mother knowing the truth, too. But Cassie needs to know you did it for me, to help me."

"It's way late for that, and it's not a good idea anyway." Savannah looked at the clock on Gen's desk, which remained across from the sofa—which also remained where it had always been. Gen had promised they would shop for bedroom furniture over the weekend, but Savannah wondered if she would be consulted about those choices.

"Look, I have to go," she said. "I know it's past eleven there. I'm an hour early, but—" She launched into a chorus of "Happy Birthday."

Will laughed when she'd finished. "You can't sing."

"It's the thought that counts."

"Thank you for remembering."

"What are you planning to do?"

"Mom and Cassie are taking me to Rusty Bellies for dinner. I already know what Mom got me. An iPad so I don't hog our computer all the time. Cassie's getting me a keyboard case to go with it."

"That's cool. I got you something, too."

"More cool. Where and what?"

Savannah hoped she hadn't made another mistake. "I feel bad that the trip to Georgia was such a bummer. And I know you don't want to tell your mom what we learned. So I thought of a way for you to maybe get a little information on your own."

"I'm not driving anywhere again."

"Wimp. This is much easier. I bought you a 23andMe test kit." He was silent so long, she thought she had to explain. "You spit in a tube, and then they find your biological relatives, but you don't have to tell anybody, not even the people they match you with. You can bypass Amber entirely. She never has to know."

"Are you crazy?"

"No! Look, it's already on the way to you. I made up a name for your registration. Jake Green. So it's coming to Jake Green at our house, and I created an email address at Yahoo for all their correspondence. I'll text it to you with the password, and you can change it to keep the account private. You usually get the mail anyway. Just grab the package from the mailbox. I had to kinda lie, you know. Not just about your name and address, but your age, too. You're supposed to be eighteen, but that doesn't matter because it's all about your spit. And nobody's allowed to get in touch with you unless you want them to. It's like foolproof!"

He was silent so long again, she gave up. "Okay, you don't have to do it. They don't care if you never send it in. They got their money. But if you're going to, the sooner you do, the sooner you hear back. Maybe the kit will turn up something, and maybe it won't, but how can it hurt?" She paused for just a moment to let that sink in. "And you know, your father might be registered. Maybe he's still alive."

"I don't know…"

She was glad he was still there. "I just wanted to make something good out of something bad."

"I'll think about it."

"At least it's an interesting birthday present, right?"

"Interesting. Thank you, I think."

"Have a good one, Will."

"Call Cassie, Savannah."

She disconnected. She missed Will. She'd really only been gone a few days, so it seemed weird to miss him already, but she missed her whole life in Florida. She missed the way Cassie and Amber always made sure there was lots of food to choose from at meals, and the goodies Cassie baked for their morning rush out the door. She missed Yiayia's Kouzina and Greek food that made her stomach happy in a way that Pauline's spartan salads never did. She'd spoken to both Helia and Minh, but phone calls weren't very satisfying. With Helia, interpreting subtle changes in facial expression was the key to figuring out what she really thought. And Minh was so busy worrying about Savannah's sudden departure that she couldn't talk about anything else.

She even missed her History class. That was unexpected.

She wondered what might have happened if she'd taken Cassie aside to tell her where she'd really been that weekend and asked her not to tell Amber. Cassie wouldn't have been happy. She would have been furious that Savannah had ranged so far on a wild-goose chase that was none of her business to start with. But would she have gone to Amber and caused a problem for Will? Will's father was a delicate matter, and Savannah had tried to protect both Blairs.

Now, just thinking about it, she realized she probably should have trusted her.

And if she had? Would she still be living in Tarpon Springs?

It didn't matter. Once she was enrolled in school here, once she didn't have to hang around Pauline all day, and maybe once she had fun things to relate to Gen at day's end, maybe then, everything would be better than okay. She would be fine.

She tried not to think about how Cassie would be.

The next evening when Gen said she was taking Savannah to a popular vegetarian café, Savannah knew it was time to assert herself. "I was hoping for a burger, Gen. I've pretty well reached my limit on salads."

"I promise you'll love this place. They have all kinds of plant-based burgers. You won't be able to tell the difference."

Savannah was pretty sure she would. She suggested pizza, but Gen told her they were ordering pizza on Sunday night because that was Pauline's day off.

"Trust me on this," Gen said.

Savannah thought she ought to embroider the phrase on a pillow to give Gen for Christmas.

The café was only a short drive away, cute and informal, wooden benches and tables, cartoonish art on walls of more wood, which took some of the sting out of being there for Savannah. As they walked past other tables, the food made her mouth water.

"I've had the jalapeño burger," Gen said after they were seated. "It's scrumptious, and the nachos are amazing. We can share a plate."

Savannah was in the mood to protest, but she loved nachos, and a quick glance at the menu showed that the jalapeño burger really did look awesome—if it didn't taste like boiled peas.

Gen ordered the nachos to share, the jalapeño burger for Savannah, and a Nashville hot "chicken" sandwich for herself. When she suggested Savannah try the sweet potato fries as her side, Savannah asked for regular fries instead. A skirmish, not a battle, but she was glad to see Gen didn't care.

"I try to come here when I can," Gen said. "Whenever I'm here, I think how much I want to share it with you when you visit."

"I haven't been in Palm Springs all that much. We usually travel when we're together."

Gen had a lovely smile, sort of a Julia Roberts twinkle in

her eyes, and Savannah was always happy when it was aimed at her. "I'm more of a tour guide than a mother, aren't I?"

Savannah was thrown off guard. Of course, it was true, but she hadn't realized Gen knew it, too. "I guess… I guess being a mother takes a lot of practice."

"I know." Gen picked up her fork like she wanted to stab something, but nothing presented itself. She set it back down. "Savannah, did your dad or Cassie ever explain why he had you most of the year and I only had you for a few weeks?"

"You traveled a lot and he didn't. Then he married Cassie and I had two parents in New York." She leaned forward. "Was that true?"

"As far as it went, but there was a lot more."

"Maybe I ought to hear it?"

"Do you really want me to go into it? It's not a story to stop in the middle." When Savannah nodded, Gen started slowly. "You know I was raised in Nigeria? You only met your grandparents once when you were much younger, but they are rigid people, much more focused on hell than heaven, on what we do wrong rather than God's mercy. In fact they're so strict and unforgiving, a few years ago they were nudged into administration at the denominational office in South Africa. These days they're pushing paper around, not children."

Savannah was surprised at Gen's tone. She'd known that Gen and her parents weren't close, but she hadn't realized the depth of feeling.

"Are they unhappy about the change?"

"I see them so rarely it's hard to tell. Growing up as their daughter was tough. I lived exactly the way the children in the orphanage they'd built from the ground up lived. They didn't want me to feel privileged when so many others weren't. So I slept in dormitories with other girls, learned what they learned, ate what they ate and sat through religious services every night, where my father made sure we understood we were all sinners."

Savannah tried to imagine. "Your whole childhood?"

Gen took her time explaining, pausing from time to time as if she needed to figure out how to convey her history. "Luckily, later they sent me to a boarding school for the children of missionaries. More dorms. More lectures, but a better education and a real understanding of love and compassion. Anyway, the education was good enough that between the funds our church raised and scholarships, I was able to attend college in the U.S. But childhood marked me. First and always, Africa will always feel like home to me. Second, I vowed that someday I would go back and do real good for children there without breaking their spirits. Third, I vowed I would spend the rest of my life making my own decisions and enjoying peace and quiet and as much time alone as I wanted."

Their food arrived and it took a few minutes to settle it, order the drinks they'd forgotten and get extra napkins.

Savannah tried the nachos, which were absolutely delicious, before she spoke. "That explains why you became a doctor, and why you spend so much time in Africa."

This time Gen's smile lost its twinkle. "I'm afraid it also explains why, when you were born, you went to live with your dad."

"Why did you get married in the first place if you needed to be alone?"

"Your dad and I met when we were residents in the same hospital. I'd like to say we fell in love. Every child deserves parents who love each other, but we didn't. We were friends, then briefly we were lovers, and then, after we said goodbye and wished each other well, I discovered I was pregnant. I might not be religious in the standard sense of the word, but I did know I wanted to have the baby. And when I told your father, we decided it would be better for all of us if he and I married, even for a short time. Today we probably wouldn't have. But all those years ago, a child born out of wedlock would have been a bigger deal."

"Did you know you were going to divorce? Even when you got married?"

"No. We gave the marriage a try, Vanna. We really did. But after you were born, I suffered from postpartum depression that was so serious, I went into a hospital for a few weeks. And when I got out, it was clear to both your father and me that taking care of a baby was going to put me right back in. Please don't think I didn't love you. I did. Right from the first minute I saw you, I loved you. I just didn't know what to do with you. In the end it was clear I was the wrong person to raise you. I'd never had a mother. I didn't know how to be a mother."

"You didn't want to be a mother." Savannah could feel her eyes filling with tears.

"Maybe not, but I would have given anything to be a good one. I just didn't seem to have it in me."

"So you turned me over to my dad." Savannah wiped her cheeks.

"Not as bloodlessly as that sounds. We found a wonderful nanny. Your dad and I took care of you together in the evenings, but when he got the offer to join the practice in Manhattan and I got one here in California, we both knew where you belonged and with whom. Everything that was so hard for me was simple for your dad. He loved everything about being a father."

"Yeah, he did."

"I really envied him that. Anyway, we worked out the custody arrangement. I cheered you on from the sidelines. I believed that once you were older, and especially once you were an adult, I might have something to offer you. I still hope that's true."

Savannah thought that at this moment, Gen should be comforting her. That's what mothers did. Instead, she covered Gen's hand with her own. "I think I knew most of this, without the details. But thanks for the context."

Gen looked up, and her eyes were sparkling with tears. "*Context* is a pretty sophisticated word coming from a teenager. But yeah, that story is really the context for your life."

"I'm glad you had me, even if it wasn't what you planned. And I'm glad you knew my dad should raise me."

"He did a superior job. He and Cassie." She tilted her head, and then she threaded her fingers through Savannah's. "I wasn't jealous Cassie had you every day, that she dried your tears and went to your recitals and bought your Halloween costumes. But I was jealous I couldn't *be* Cassie. That none of my abilities and talents lent themselves to doing those things. You were lucky to have her. You know that, right?"

Savannah shrugged.

Gen's grip tightened. "And you know your father wasn't perfect, don't you? That Cassie sometimes had a lot to contend with? But as much as she loved Mark, and she really did, she would never have said or done anything that would endanger his life."

Savannah pulled her hand from Gen's. "Are you trying to convince me to go back?" She could hear her tone growing sharper, but she was powerless to change it. "Am I still that much of a problem for you, even at fifteen?"

Gen took her time answering. "I have never for one moment of your life thought of you as a problem. You are the daughter I love, the person I love most in the world. But I want things to be right for you. You can live with me as long as you want to. I'll do everything I can to make you happy. But honestly? I don't see it happening."

"It might if you fire Pauline."

Gen managed a smile. "Pauline may be a problem, but the big one? It's Savannah. Because Savannah needs her real mother, and that person is not me. If nothing else, Savannah needs to make peace with her mother, because she loves her, and this is tearing them both apart. Do that, and then decide where you really want to spend the rest of your school years. I'll support any decision made out of love, but not one from misplaced anger. Because I think that as you've grieved, you've wanted to blame somebody for your dad's death, so you chose the person who was safest."

"I don't see it that way."

"At least think about what I've said?"

Savannah shrugged.

Gen appeared to think that was good enough. "Whether you stay in California or not, I'm going to find us a better place to live when you're with me. A house or condo with a real bedroom for you, one with families nearby. I'll give up summers in Africa unless you'd like to go. But I can find a larger place and still take you to Africa, whether I'm your main address or not. Either way it's time for us to be together more. But without Cassie in your life?" She shook her head.

"I can really stay? It's my choice?"

"Nobody else's."

Savannah frowned. "Giving people choices isn't what you do best."

"I can learn. I will have to, one way or the other."

"I don't know what I could say to Cassie if I called her."

"You'll think of something."

"What are you hoping for?"

Gen considered. "Here's the honest to God truth. I'm hoping you do whatever will make you the happiest."

"I don't know what that is."

"You have time to decide. In the meantime I'll ask Pauline to leave every day after lunch. She'll be happier, you'll be happier, and we'll eat dinner every night at any restaurant you want. I might even try cooking. Deal?"

She raised her hand and Savannah slapped it, palms together. "Deal."

"I really do love you. I'll always be here for you, Vanna, no matter what."

"Can I ask a favor? Please don't call me Vanna. Whenever you call me Vanna, I think of *Wheel of Fortune*."

"What's that?"

This time Savannah smiled. "We'll watch it together."

Gen took her hand and raised it to her cheek. "You know what? You look like me when you smile, *Savannah*. You have my smile. It's so nice to see a little of me in you."

"I'm glad it's there, you're there."

"Me, too." Gen kissed Savannah's hand before she released it. "Me, too."

36

AMBER WONDERED HOW MANY PEOPLE ACTUALLY
kept financial records as carefully and meticulously as Mark
Westmore had. He must have been at least a little obsessive.
And maybe, when it came down to it, that was a good quality
in a physician. But every single bank statement? Every single
receipt? She couldn't imagine her own life if she'd kept that
much paper. She and Will wouldn't have had room in their
car for anything else, including them.

After hours of patiently going through multiple boxes, she
had finally caught up to the year right before Mark's death.
So far the most interesting thing she'd found was a detailed
log of every gift Mark had bought for Cassie and Savannah.
He'd been neither extravagant nor cheap, but he'd obviously
paid close attention to what he bought each year, as if he'd
worried about repetition. She'd had to smile. Mark didn't like
to make mistakes.

Now Cassie came into the dining area buttoning the cuff
on a long-sleeved shirt, tricky under any circumstances since
she was also clutching her cell phone. She had another job in-

terview, and while she wasn't excited, she was going anyway. Cassie wasn't excited by much right now. Savannah wasn't returning her phone calls, and her life was in limbo.

Amber used her arrival as an excuse to stand and stretch. "If they offer you the job, will you take it?"

"If it doesn't involve leaving flyers in the doors of strangers, I'll give it some thought. It's an entry-level position in a realty office with a salary that's just over minimum wage. But it will give me a peek at the field. I might want to get my license."

"Really? And for Pete's sake, let me button that!"

Cassie set the phone on the table and held out her arm so Amber could finish. "You have tiny hands," Amber said. "Next time button it before you put on the blouse and slide your hands through."

"Thanks, and no, I don't really want to sell houses, and I'd sure have to improve my driving skills. But at least it would be something." Cassie finished tucking the shirt into her skirt. "Find anything I should look at before I leave?"

Amber waved paper in her direction. "You don't have to look at these now. Luckily most of your bank transactions were done electronically, and the info is right on the statement, but not the checks. Things were easier when canceled checks were included. Now there's no information about what the checks were for or who they were made out to, just that they were written. So unless the amount and date jiggle a memory, you'll have to go online for details. The bank will have a photocopy."

Cassie took the statements. "Every check?"

"That seems pointless. I've just marked the ones that were sizable enough to make me wonder what they were for. And that brings up another issue. I checked to see if any of these amounts might be listed as deductions on your taxes for that year, if they were written to charities, etc. I looked through that file and didn't find the most recent. Would that 1040 be somewhere else? I'd like to have them all together so I can compare."

"I have mine somewhere. I don't know what happened to Mark's. We always filed jointly, but that time, we filed separately, and he gave me copies of mine. He claimed we would save money."

Amber wasn't an expert on the changing tax code, but filing separately surprised her. "He handled your taxes?"

"He always did them. He liked trying to make sense of all of it. If he ran into a problem, he had people he could call. I'll be using an accountant this year."

Amber could see how a man fascinated by record keeping might find taxes fun, even though the remainder of the planet despised it. "We can file for copies. I'll get the form for you to fill out. But you should have his, too."

"I have a little time before I have to leave." Cassie took the chair beside Amber and started riffling through the statements she had given her.

"There are just a couple of anomalies, but they were large enough to catch my eye. One in June that year for ten thousand dollars. Do you know what that might have been for?"

"No idea." Cassie leafed through some more. "Here's another you marked. Oh, I remember this one. Twenty-five hundred dollars. It was for a fundraising art auction at Savannah's school. I remember the date and the amount because I thought it was ridiculously expensive."

She handed that statement back to Amber and looked at the next one. "And I bet this one for forty-five hundred was a contribution to an upstate drug treatment program where he referred some of his patients. He said they ran the program on a shoestring but he thought they did a particularly good job. He even took some time off to volunteer there when their director passed away suddenly. He told me he was going to make a donation to help keep them up and running. It looks like he wrote the check when he got home."

"So both of these will probably show up on his 1040 when we get it. For what that's worth."

Cassie handed that statement back, too. "I'll go online later and get copies of the checks. Anything else?"

"There were two withdrawals. Ten thousand each, two months apart and the first was a month after the check you're going to look into."

"Just cash withdrawals?"

"That's all I see."

"I'll think about it, but as great as it would be to have that money in our hot little hands right now, it's a drop compared to what disappeared."

Amber considered her next words. "Cassie, is there any chance Mark had a gambling problem?"

Cassie pulled a long face that said the thought had occurred to her, as well. "I know that sounds like a good way to lose a lot of money fast. But Mark never so much as bought a lottery ticket, not even when the jackpots were astronomical. He treated a few gamblers who lost everything—houses, jobs, families—and he said it was one of the saddest addictions because it could be absolutely invisible until the person's whole life completely disintegrated."

"I'll keep looking."

"You've earned a year's worth of rent already."

"See? You may have trouble getting rid of me."

After Cassie left for her interview, Amber got up to make tea. She brought it back to the table and saw that Cassie had left her cell phone. With luck, Savannah wouldn't choose the next hour to call, because Cassie would be devastated if she missed her.

She picked up the phone to set it on a kitchen counter when she realized what she had. Cassie had kept her New York number. With no reason to change it, she hadn't bothered. Now, if Amber called someone using this phone, their display would show New York, if it showed anything at all. She was hoping she remembered the code to block the number entirely.

With a silent apology to her friend, Amber took the tea and phone to the closest sofa, then she keyed in the passcode to unlock the phone. She'd used Cassie's phone once before to order a pizza, and she knew the passcode was their address. Amber had cautioned her to change it to something less obvious, but apparently she hadn't bothered.

Staring at the screen now, she thought about Betsy Garland. The last message she'd left for Betsy on the bulletin board hadn't garnered a response, and when Amber had tried Tammy's number at the requested time anyway, the phone had rung without anyone answering. Something was very wrong.

Through the years she had so carefully avoided dialing Betsy directly, but she'd reached a point when she had to try. She only needed a few seconds to be sure Betsy was okay. She would try to block her number, then she could pretend she was calling about a quilt, use their method to tell her when to be at Tammy's for a real call and hang up. If Darryl was tracing Betsy's calls, a short one might not be logged.

Without overthinking the consequences, she punched in the blocking code, then Betsy Garland's phone number. The phone rang until Amber finally disconnected without even the opportunity to leave a message.

She debated, but not long. She tried Tammy's number again, using the blocking code, too. At the very least, if Tammy was there, she could tell her if Betsy was all right.

A woman answered on the first ring. Amber was so startled it took seconds to figure out what to say. "Hi, is this Tammy?"

"Who's calling? Why does my phone say unavailable? You're not one of those telemarketers, are you?"

For just a moment Amber bathed in the Appalachian twang of her hometown. "No, I'm sorry. I'm a friend of Betsy Garland's, Sue Simpson, one of Betsy's 4-H girls. I've been trying to get hold of her. We...we like to chat. In fact I think I've called her at your house a few times."

A pause ensued. Then a friendlier Tammy answered. "I see. Then I don't reckon you know."

Amber closed her eyes and waited.

"She's doing okay, so no need to fuss, but Betsy was in an automobile accident while she was visiting her son. You know she has a son?"

"Yes, I—"

"Good. Anyway, a car struck her while she was taking a walk. It was a hit-and-run, too. Nobody saw it, and by the time someone found her, Betsy was almost a goner. But she pulled through. Our Betsy's a fighter."

"Always. I—"

"She's out of the hospital now. Finally. It took them long enough. Anyway, as they say, she's being rehabilitated. Like as not they've got her doing physical therapy, occupational therapy, you name it."

Amber spoke quickly before she was cut off again. "Does she remember the accident?"

"Blessedly no. I'm going to see her this weekend. Want me to tell her you called?"

Amber thought fast. "Please. Tell her I'm still working on that baby quilt we discussed online."

"She's always glad to know some of her 4-H girls kept on sewing."

Amber didn't know where Betsy's son was living now. Karl, her only child, was just out of graduate school and had a job that required frequent moves, so he might even be out of state. But Tammy was going to see Betsy this weekend. Hopefully that meant Karl wasn't too far away.

She spoke while she had the chance. "Would you mind telling me how to get in touch with her? I bet she has a phone by her bed."

"She's not up to talking on the phone to anybody yet. Not even me. Too hard to hold. Her hand's a mess. I'll pop in and see her in person, but not for long. No, better wait for an all clear before you call."

"I'd like to send—"

"Sorry, hon, I'd like to keep talking, but I was on my way out the door. You call back in a week or so, and I'll catch you up on how she's doing. Nice talking to you."

Amber was left clutching Cassie's phone with nobody on the other end.

Betsy had been in an accident, a hit-and-run out of town, at that, which is why it hadn't showed up in the *Croville Chronicle.* If Betsy had seen the driver, she couldn't remember.

Had Darryl tracked Betsy to her son's, where getting rid of her would draw less notice? Her friends knew she always walked early in the mornings, before most people stirred. Betsy liked to hear the birds waking up. If she was walking along a road, it would be so easy to swerve, send her sprawling on the grass and continue on. No one would be around to note the license plate or rescue a dying woman.

The good news was that somehow Betsy had survived. The bad news was that she might have been targeted because she had helped Amber through the years. But why now, and how would Darryl know? Amber couldn't even guess. She only knew she had to talk to Betsy as soon as possible. It was unlikely that even if she called Tammy again, the woman would volunteer any information about Betsy's whereabouts. Amber had to locate Karl Garland so she could call every rehab center near where he was living.

Tonight, once she got home from work, she would search the internet.

In the kitchen, leaning against the counter, she went into Cassie's phone settings and deleted all record of the calls she had made. Then she left the phone on the counter and went to get ready for work.

37

ALTHOUGH IT HAD ALMOST TWICE AS MUCH SQUARE footage as the condo in Battery Park City, the house in Sunset Vista wasn't large. But when Cassie was by herself, like she was right now, the house felt like the White House or Buckingham Palace. Without other people underfoot, she almost needed a map to find her way from one end to the other.

Alone, too, the relative silence of the middle-class subdivision made her uneasy. With its constant drumbeat of cars, jackhammers and sirens, New York was never silent. Here, outside noise was rare and didn't drown each creak of concrete and wood as the house settled. Every time she heard a sound, she imagined sinkholes swallowing the whole block, like the snapping jaws of a horror movie monster.

She considered turning on loud music, even if it would mask the sound of a break-in or the house collapsing around her. Instead, she settled for a mug of herbal tea and took the bank statements Amber had left for her back to her suite, settling at the computer to call up her online banking website.

Once she was there, she searched for the checks Amber had

marked. As she'd guessed, one was made out to Pfeiffer Grant
and the second was made out to the Grandy Rayburn Drug
Treatment Center. The date was around the time Mark had
filled in there. Mark had been something of a pushover for
good causes, and she had loved his generosity. Now she wondered if good causes had anything to do with the disappearance of their financial safety net. Nothing could be discounted.

The third check was the one for ten thousand dollars, and
looking at the statement she remembered that Amber had
pointed out two cash withdrawals, one a month later, the next
a month after that, for the same amount.

She located the check and pulled up a copy. It was made out
to Rinkel Medical Supplies. She moused over the flip side,
which was signed with a scrawl she couldn't read.

Cassie leaned back in her desk chair. The company was unfamiliar, although somewhere in her memory she felt a faint
tug. She squinted at the signature again, but it was illegible.
She doubted the original existed. Unlike Mark, banks probably got rid of paper immediately.

Could Mark have purchased something for Church Street,
instruments or furnishings, using his own money and later filing for reimbursement? She could imagine scenarios. Maybe
Mark had needed something right away, but the office had
been closed. Maybe he wanted whatever it was to be shipped
that day.

She scanned the statement for a deposit of roughly the same
amount in the following week, but nothing showed up. It
was possible reimbursement paperwork had taken longer. She
didn't have the next month's paper statement, but she found
the next two online statements and searched. Nothing showed
up except the two withdrawals Amber had noted.

If it hadn't been for those, she might have sloughed off the
check. Mark was a doctor, and the check was for medical sup-

plies. But the two withdrawals worried her. A total of thirty thousand dollars unaccounted for was too much. And Rinkel Medical Supplies still tugged at her memory.

She tried once more to read the signature. Finally, with nothing to lose, she downloaded the check to her computer and clicked on the file.

"Perfect!" The downloaded file could be magnified to almost any size. She slid her cursor to the right until the signature was legible. "Ilsa...Victoria Rinkel."

Something in her memory tugged harder now. She closed her eyes and repeated the name silently. Ilsa Victoria Rinkel. IVR, like IVF, which brought back unhappy memories.

She and Mark had not been able to conceive a child together, which had made Savannah even more precious to both of them. Mark's sperm count was low, and Cassie's periods irregular. They had tried IVF when nothing else had worked.

They had tried three times, and Cassie had been the one to decide not to try a fourth. None of their attempts had resulted in a positive pregnancy test, much less a baby. She hadn't been willing to continue the onslaught of hormones, the waiting, the hopes that this time, this time...

IVF. IVR. Ilsa Victoria. IV.

And then, she knew.

"Ivy." She opened her eyes and stared at the screen, but now she was seeing something else entirely.

The first time she'd met Ivy Todsen, the nurse had been celebrating with other hospital staff at a Christmas party. For some reason she and Ivy had ended up in a corner together, over a plate of crackers and green cheese laden with flecks of pimento for the season. Ivy had been wearing a tight, spangled dress and too much makeup. She had made a point of introducing herself, as if she thought that Cassie, as Mark's wife, might be important to know.

"Ivy, that's a lovely name," Cassie remembered saying.

"Is Cassie short for something?"

"Cassandra. I guess Ivy can't be short for anything, can it?"

Ivy laughed too loudly. Without a doubt she'd spent too much time chatting up the bartender who was mixing drinks in the corner. "It sort of is," she said. "It's actually my initials. IV. Ivy. My given name sounded like I was born somewhere else instead of right here. So I go by my initials."

Cassie had been surprised, as well as mildly offended, that anybody would worry their name sounded foreign. She had insisted on keeping Costas when she married Mark, because she was proud of her Greek heritage, and she had stood firm.

Now Ivy was divorced and had probably taken back her maiden name. But did her ex-husband own Rinkel Medical Supplies? And if he did, why was Ivy's name on the back of the check?

She went to her search engine and typed in Rinkel Medical Supplies with no success. She looked a little closer at the endorsement and noted that the check had been deposited in a New Jersey bank.

Hours later, after chasing websites and frequently-asked-questions on how to proceed, she knew that the registered agent for Rinkel Medical Supplies, LLC, in North Bergen, New Jersey was Ilsa Victoria Rinkel. Nothing else about the company appeared online, and no one else was listed. For all practical purposes, there was nothing except an address.

"And a bank account."

She heard a light rapping and then Amber's voice. "You're talking to yourself."

Cassie hadn't realized so much time had passed. She had been at her computer for hours chasing a shadow. She faced her friend. "I didn't hear you come in."

"I could have dropped a bomb on your head and you'd have

been slow to react. I didn't see any dishes in the kitchen. Did you eat dinner?"

"I got...busy."

"Sure seems like you did. Luckily I brought home half a pan of kolokithopita. Roxanne got a deal on fresh zucchini. It's out of this world."

Cassie remembered eating the zucchini and feta dish sandwiched between buttery sheets of phyllo dough at her grandmother's house. She realized how hungry she was.

"And I have chicken souvlaki, too," Amber added. "But we need to beat Will to the kitchen. He's out in the garage checking our tires."

"I don't want to eat Will's dinner."

"Are you kidding? Between tables tonight he ate his weight in both dishes. You'll be doing him a favor if you get to the leftovers before he does."

Cassie followed Amber to the kitchen, where she dished up a plate for each of them. "Unlike my son, I did not have a break tonight," Amber said. "It's still warm."

Cassie pushed paperwork to the side and they took seats. She was too hungry to speak for a few minutes, and they sat across from each other and shoveled in the food. Will came through and greeted them, but he must have been full, because he went to his room to study and left them alone.

"What kept you so busy? How did the interview go?" Amber asked.

Cassie swallowed more than kolokithopita. She suddenly missed Mark the way she might miss a limb. Grief swept over her in a wave. He had always asked about her day and listened with interest while she recited where she'd gone and why, who she'd run into, what she'd planned for dinner. Those were the little things about a marriage that went unnoticed until they disappeared.

Now, in addition to missing Mark, she was ridiculously grateful that Amber was there to listen. But she was feeling much more, too. Because as she pondered her reaction, she realized that Mark had *stopped* listening by the end of their marriage. When he had forced himself to make the effort, he'd seemed annoyed, as if the small details of her life were deflections from the weightier details of his own.

In those final months together, she had stopped recounting her days. She had asked about his, listened to his brusque replies, and then watched as he turned on the television, to drown out the thoughts they were no longer voicing.

"Cassie?"

She'd left Amber's question hanging. "I'm sorry. It's been some night."

"The interview didn't go well?"

"It might lead to something better if they offer it to me." She asked about Amber's evening, but Amber cut her off.

"Look, what's up? You were pretty engrossed in whatever you were doing on the computer. I'm listening if you want to talk."

Cassie pushed her plate away. "That ten-thousand-dollar check you found? It was made out to a medical supply company."

She explained how she had figured out the details, summing it up at the end. "Ivy, the nurse on the behavioral health unit? The one who's been calling me to chat? She signed the check. She's the agent for the LLC. I think she's the only person connected to it. Her married name must have been Rinkel."

Amber didn't say anything, as if she was waiting for Cassie's interpretation.

Cassie went on. "It's pretty obvious that Mark paid her ten thousand dollars that month. And then maybe by the next month, he worried a check might draw my attention if I ever looked at our account, so he withdrew the next ten thousand in cash, and then another ten the next month. I don't know how anybody takes out that much cash at one time. But he obviously managed it."

"You can't say for sure the money went to Ivy."

"The check and then the withdrawals are exactly a month apart. Three months, thirty thousand dollars. Ivy's name is on the check."

Amber spoke with such care Cassie knew she was trying to be a sounding board. "I suspect you've been coming up with possible reasons Mark would give Ivy thirty thousand dollars."

"You come up with them first. You're not emotionally involved, so you'll be more logical."

Amber ate the rest of her dinner, then she, too, pushed her plate away. "Most of my logical reasons are not flattering to your husband."

"I figured."

"You won't shoot the messenger?"

Cassie shook her head. "Can I cry?"

"Be my guest. One, he was having an affair with Ivy and helping her financially. Maybe she needed a nicer apartment for their trysts." She looked up to see how Cassie had taken that one.

Unfortunately for Cassie, the thought wasn't new. "Go on."

"Two, Ivy knew something about him. A mistake he'd made with a patient, maybe? Mistakes are inevitable. It might have been a bad one, though, bad enough that he paid her to keep quiet."

"So...blackmail."

Amber nodded. "Three. She was in a jam, and he just agreed to help her. You said she's divorced. Maybe her ex was up to something? Or maybe Ivy was the one with a gambling problem, or she needed medical help or a procedure her insurance wouldn't cover."

"Mark was generous, but I think he would have told me."

Amber's expression said she agreed. "She was fired from the unit recently?"

"That's right. She implied she was fired because she was asking around about why Mark left the practice. She said Fletcher was responsible."

"That explanation is grist for the mill, as they say, Cassie. She was fired. It's not easy to fire anybody these days without risking a lawsuit. So a hospital would be very careful. They would need plenty of evidence she wasn't doing her job well. Or…"

"Or?"

"Or they would need something to hold over her, so they could be sure she wouldn't come after them later."

Cassie's head was swimming now. "How on earth do I find out what this was about? And do I need to know? A lot more than thirty thousand dollars is missing. That's a drop comparatively."

"I hate to say it, but what we've found might be just the first drop. The one that leads you to the rest of the missing money. Is there anybody who might know more about this? Anybody in New York?"

Cassie had already asked herself the same question, and she didn't like the answer. "Valerie."

"The old friend who went missing?"

"Maybe I finally understand why she did. She knew something and she didn't want me to know it." She made a decision. "I'm going to New York and I'm going to confront her, no matter what. And then, I'm going to see Ivy."

"By yourself?"

Cassie remembered how uneasy she'd been alone in her

own house at the beginning of that evening, but she knew she was stronger and braver than she gave herself credit for. "By myself. Because I'm the one who has to find out the truth."

"I would come if I could."

Cassie never quite forgot what a chance she had taken by allowing a woman with so many secrets to live in her house. Some people might say she was a fool, but Amber and Will had proved themselves to be honest and hardworking while enriching her life and Savannah's, too. Amber was the best kind of friend, the kind she was going to need to get through this.

Cassie wasn't a fool—she was lucky.

She was just getting ready for bed when her cell phone rang. She checked the display and saw that Savannah was the caller. She clutched the phone a moment before she answered, praying she would handle whatever was to come with patience and love.

"Savannah," she said in greeting. "I'm glad you called."

"Cassie..." Savannah cleared her throat. "I know you've been calling."

"I have. First tell me how you're doing?"

"I'm okay. Spring's a good time to be here, before it gets too hot."

"Are you enjoying your new school?"

"Gen thought I ought to wait and register after spring vacation ends here. Their breaks and ours in Tarpon Springs are different."

Cassie wondered how much school Savannah could miss without serious repercussions, but the problem was no longer hers. Savannah was no longer hers.

A weight settled across her shoulders, and she felt them sag. "Are you doing some sightseeing?" she asked, hoping the question was neutral enough that her daughter wouldn't throw her phone across the room.

"We did a little hiking, and I've walked around some on my own. Gen has a little pool, nothing like ours, just kind of a place to sit and soak. I've done that a few times."

Cassie told herself that "ours" was just a figure of speech and meant nothing. "A good way to beat the heat."

"How are you? How are things there?"

Cassie was warmed by the question. She knew every nuance of her daughter's voice, and Savannah sounded tentative, as if she didn't know what note to strike.

"We're okay," she said. "Amber and Will are working a lot. I had another job interview today."

"Doing what?"

"A receptionist. It's at a realty, and I'd do whatever they needed."

"Did they hire you?"

"They have two more days of interviews lined up. Jobs are hard to find right now, and a lot of people are looking."

"They ought to hire you."

Cassie wasn't sure that was a compliment, but she decided to take it as one. "Savannah, I've been calling for a reason." She launched in, afraid Savannah would end the call before Cassie could apologize. "I called to apologize—"

"No, you were right. I shouldn't have lied to you."

For a moment, Cassie didn't know what to say. An apology? Her stubborn daughter was always determined to prove she was right, even when she knew she was absolutely wrong.

"You're talking about the weekend of the field trip?" Cassie asked.

"I still can't tell you where I was, because it involves somebody else. But I should never have pretended I was going on the school thing. And…I shouldn't have gone anywhere. It was a mistake."

Cassie was alarmed. All the traps a teenage girl could fall prey to ran through her mind. "Are you all right? Did something happen while you were gone?"

"No, no, nothing like that. I promise. It was just that I went to help somebody, and, well, it didn't help. The mistake was that I didn't think it through the way I should have. I just…did what I thought was right. And I'm not always, you know, right."

Cassie dropped to the bed. "Well, none of us are. That's why it's good to have other people to talk to."

"You wouldn't have let me go."

Cassie was almost certain Savannah was right. "Would that have been worse?"

"I don't know. Maybe not."

"I was angry at you because I was worried." She decided to be totally honest. "And also because I just felt like you stopped listening, and I hated that you'd lied. Because I've always trusted you."

"Not always."

And there it was. Cassie closed her eyes. "Savannah, your dad and I were a hundred percent wrong not to trust you when you told us what happened at Pfeiffer Grant. Dr. Farthington called last week. The girls who were there that day, including Liza, came forward to say that Gillie had been bullying her. And afterward the administration went back and caught Gillie on video doing just that. They realized how wrong they'd been and how unfair to you. Everyone was scared of Gillie. Liza thought if she lied and didn't stand up for you, Gillie would leave her alone."

There was such a long silence that Cassie was afraid Savannah had hung up. Maybe forever.

"Gillie didn't leave her alone, though, did she?" she said at last. "She wouldn't have. She's one of those people, like Madeline, who thinks she's charmed or something."

"No, Gillie didn't leave Liza alone." She decided to tell the whole truth, because it was possible Savannah would find out anyway. "Liza made a suicide attempt, not a serious one, fortunately. She's fine, but she's finally getting help to work through this."

"She was scared. And she wanted to fit in. Gillie was like the keeper of the golden gate to popularity at Pfeiffer."

Cassie could visualize that.

"What did they do to her?" Savannah asked. "To Gillie, I mean."

"She's out."

"Boy, Dr. Farthington's going to miss the Robinsons' donations. I guess it says something good about Pfeiffer that they sent her packing anyway."

Cassie was surprised at how maturely her daughter was handling the revelations. "The thing is, it's nice that it's been resolved. I'm sure anything negative that appeared on your school record there will be expunged forever. But I wasn't calling just to tell you about the phone call. I wanted you to know just how bad I feel that I believed the school and not you."

Again, a long silence. Finally Savannah cleared her throat. "You wanted to be on my side, didn't you? But Dad was sure I was lying."

Cassie thought about Mark's final months on earth, and how the huge store of patience he'd had as a husband, father and probably a doctor, had just disintegrated.

"Your dad was going through a bad patch when that happened, sweetheart." She used the endearment without thinking. She wished she hadn't, but Savannah didn't protest. "I think the way he was feeling, as much as what happened, made it hard for him to look beyond the surface."

"What was wrong with him, do you know?"

"I honestly don't. I'm trying to figure it out. The fight you heard wasn't the only one we had. Still, I should have stood up for you. I should have followed my own instincts."

"Dad was always sure he was right, and even when he wasn't, he had a way of making you think his mistake was your fault. So it was hard to take a chance on being wrong."

Cassie was surprised. She filed that away to consider later. "I am so happy you're not furious with me about this, about the whole thing," Cassie said.

"I'm not furious. Not at anybody. I'm sorry I've been… who I've been."

"Family makes allowances for mistakes. Sometimes huge mistakes." She thought about what she'd said. "I mean, I'm kind of family—"

"Cassie… You are my family." Savannah sniffed. "I miss you."

"Oh, sweetheart, I miss you back. So much!"

"Can I come home? And it's not because it's bad here. Gen and I are getting along and really learning about each other. It's good I came—it really is. But I don't want to stay, and she knows it. I think that's why she didn't register me for school. She knew I'd go back to Florida if you'd have me. She knows I need to be with you."

Cassie was crying now. "Are you sure? I don't want Gen to be angry."

"No, no, she won't be. We're going to spend more time together from now on. She's taking me to Africa this summer. But Gen's like a big sister or a BFF. And you're, like, my mom. Can I be your daughter again?"

Cassie could hardly talk. "That never changed. You've got two women who adore you."

"Kind of like having a spare, huh?" Savannah was sniffing now and talking through tears.

"Exactly like that."

"I'd like to come home in a week or maybe a little longer. I'd like some more time here. Gen's taking some days off. We're driving over to Joshua Tree to do some hiking, but I want to be home to start school again after spring break. I'm going to email my teachers and see if they'll send work for me to do so I won't be too far behind. Will that be okay?"

"Better than okay."

"You're sure?"

"I couldn't be more sure."

"I guess I'd better go. I know it's late there." She paused. "Can I call again?"

"Every single day."

"I love you."

Cassie remembered their parting phrase at night through all Savannah's childhood. "I love you right back."

"Tell Will and Amber I'm looking forward to seeing them, *Mom*." Savannah disconnected.

Cassie held out her phone and stared at it. Then she clutched it to her chest and began to cry.

38

FLETCHER AND VALERIE DORMAN LIVED IN A CO-OP
in a former coconut processing plant in Tribeca, just across
from a cozy triangular park. The Dormans' building had the
usual charming eccentricities of any industrial structure con-
verted to living space, and Duane Park had earned its place in
history as the first land purchased for a public park in the city.

The park was familiar to Cassie, as was the entire geograph-
ical area close to the Church Street office. She and Valerie had
often perched on a bench there, chatting and eating Nutella
croissants from a nearby bakery. Today Cassie had settled for
a lemon tart. Nostalgia was best in small doses.

When she arrived from the airport that morning, she carefully chose this bench, not because trees blocked the cold
spring breeze, but because it gave her the best—if not perfect—
view of the Dormans' building. She wanted to start her stake-
out early, and despite rush hour traffic, she had still made good
time into Manhattan. She hoped Valerie, usually a late riser,
hadn't left for the day.

If she missed her, Cassie planned to catch Valerie coming

back in the afternoon. Ten days had passed since she had decided to make this trip. Now she was hopeful she wouldn't have to renegotiate tomorrow's flight back to Tampa. But no matter what, she was prepared to wait. She hoped that after today, she would be finished ambushing the Dormans once and for all.

She finished the tart and licked her fingers. Just as she was considering a quick walk around the perimeter, she saw a small group of people exiting the building. The last out the door, not traveling south with the others, was Valerie.

She started toward her. Luckily Valerie stopped and lifted her phone to her ear, stepping out of foot traffic for a conversation. Cassie could imagine her talking to one of her daughters, both adults now and living in different parts of New England.

Like Cassie, after marriage, Valerie's career had disappeared into permanent storage, and she had devoted her life to her family. As Cassie crossed the street, she wondered why both of them had so easily dismissed their educations. Had the women's movement sprinted right past them while they lounged over coffee at a Manhattan sidewalk café, discussing which Pfeiffer committee to volunteer for and who was doing what at their husbands' workplace?

By the time Cassie was almost in front of her, Valerie was slipping her phone back into her pocket. Cassie waited silently until she looked up. To her credit Valerie didn't try to escape. She didn't even glance from side to side to see if she could.

"Cassie," she said, when Cassie stopped just an arm's length away. "I'd say this is a surprise, only I can tell it's not a surprise for you."

"When you didn't answer my calls, I realized I was never going to have a conversation with you unless I showed up on your doorstep."

"There was a message there."

Valerie was an attractive woman, who balanced nature with medical science. Her blond pixie cut was liberally dusted with silver, somewhat prematurely but attractive. With a little help from the cosmetic surgeon she visited regularly, time would be kind to her.

"I got the message," Cassie said. "You just underestimated my determination."

"I'm on my way somewhere."

"Aren't we all? I'll walk with you."

"I'm not much in the mood for company."

"And I'm definitely not in the mood to be pushed aside again."

"Cassie, you don't want to do this."

"But here I am anyway."

Valerie looked uncertain. She had a leather gym bag slung over one shoulder, and she was dressed for Spin Cycle or Pilates in black yoga pants and a dark red cardigan. Her expression said she'd prefer boot camp to this.

"I think we can take care of this pretty quickly," Cassie said, since Valerie didn't move. "It's not like either of us wants to catch up on what our kids are doing or the movies we've seen. I need to ask you some hard questions about Mark, and you need to answer them as honestly as you're capable of. You probably already know everything Fletcher told me back in November. I just need you to tell me what he didn't say."

Valerie slumped a little—and not from the weight of the bag. "Did it ever occur to you that we've been trying to protect you?"

"That flashed through my mind early on, but lately I've been more inclined to think Church Street is protecting itself."

"Truthfully, it's both."

Cassie was encouraged Valerie had admitted that much. "You need to explain how."

"You can't just leave everything the way it is? Is it really helpful to dig up the dead?"

Cassie winced.

Valerie winced, too. "It's an awful expression, isn't it? I just meant—"

"I know what you meant."

Valerie appeared to weigh her options. "Let's sit in the park," she said. "We can grab sandwiches on the way."

They walked half a block to a deli, and Cassie grabbed turkey and Brie on a hard roll and a bottle of tropical fruit juice. She shook her head when Valerie tried to pay for her food. Instead she inserted her credit card, then followed Valerie out the door to the park. They took the first available bench.

"Let's start with what you know about why Mark left Church Street." Cassie twisted the cap off her juice and took a swallow. "I heard Fletcher's version. Let's hear yours."

Valerie answered so quickly Cassie wondered if she had decided to be honest and end this now. "Mark went from being an affable, caring psychiatrist who everybody liked, to one who jumped down throats indiscriminately."

"That's what Fletcher said, too." Cassie decided to take a side trip. "I've heard from other people associated with the practice that Fletcher was the problem, that he was angry at Mark for challenging him. Mark thought Fletch needed to improve his skills and take advantage of advances in the field instead of lagging behind."

Valerie looked perplexed, which was not what Cassie had expected. "You know how well thought of Fletcher is professionally. How can you believe that kind of garbage?"

"What else can I believe or not believe? I've been kept in the dark."

"Who told you that?"

"Somebody who asked to remain anonymous."

"Well, it's crazy. Ask any of the other doctors."

Cassie thought about the girls at Pfeiffer who had sided with a bully against Savannah. "Dr. Farthington called me about ten days ago. She wanted me to know that Savannah was telling the truth about the fight at Pfeiffer last year. The other girls who witnessed it lied because they were afraid to defy Gillie Robinson. They thought she was too powerful and might find a way to hurt them."

"You're trying to draw a parallel between a fight with schoolgirls and what happened at Church Street with Mark?"

Cassie shrugged. "If the parallel fits..."

"Let's go at this a different way." Valerie opened her sandwich and took a large bite. She had always been a stress eater, and the size of the bite said a lot about their conversation. Cassie waited for her to swallow and continue, but Valerie ate half the sandwich before she wrapped up what was left and dusted crumbs off her yoga pants. "Have you considered why Mark changed so much before he died? Don't pretend you didn't notice."

"When things aren't going well at work, even well-adjusted people bring their problems home."

"Try to divorce yourself from your theories. How was Mark when he was with you? Because at work he was angry, jumpy, thoughtless, and he was making mistakes."

"What kind?"

"One that would have been tragic if Tom Wallings hadn't intercepted it before a patient died. Tom was covering for Mark at Riverbend on one of the nights Mark was supposed to stop in to check on a patient and didn't show up."

Cassie stopped her. "You're saying Mark was missing appointments?"

"Maybe not an appointment so much as a promise he'd swing by and see how the guy was doing. And he should have, because then he would have realized the new medication he ordered that morning was part of a family of meds that had been abandoned because of the man's allergic reaction."

"Aren't there safeguards to make sure that doesn't happen? Notes in a patient's records? A nurse or the pharmacist would have seen it."

"They should have, but mistakes happen, especially on a busy night, which that one was. When it comes right down to it, Mark, more than anybody, should have known better. He should have looked closer, paged back further. And he didn't. Because he was preoccupied."

Cassie had never heard this story, but who would have recounted it except Mark himself? And by then, Mark wasn't talking about work.

Valerie went on. "I don't think anybody at the hospital ever realized how bad that situation might have been, because Tom did a good job of hiding it. But afterward he went to Fletcher and the others and asked what he should do if anything like that happened again. And that was when people began to talk about what they'd seen and their own concerns about Mark's behavior."

Cassie wished she could push Valerie's words aside, that she could pretend the story was a carefully considered excuse for the way the other doctors in the practice had treated him. Unfortunately, she believed it. The story fit too well with what she had seen herself.

"When they discussed this," she said slowly, carefully, trying to phrase her thoughts in a way that didn't imply either belief or disbelief, "what was the consensus?"

When Valerie didn't answer, Cassie assumed she wasn't going to. But finally she turned and her eyes met Cassie's. "There was no consensus, at least that's not the word Fletcher used. But there was a very real concern that Mark's weeks in drug treatment hadn't worked."

Cassie stared at her, the way she would have stared at someone who was speaking another language, someone who expected her to answer in the same. "Drug treatment?" she asked at last.

Valerie closed her eyes a moment. They were filled with unshed tears when she opened them again. "You didn't know, did you? I told Fletcher you didn't, but he couldn't believe it."

"Know? Know what? What are you saying?"

"Apparently Mark was better at covering his problems than any of his colleagues guessed. But after you cornered Fletcher in Orlando, he began to wonder because of the questions you didn't ask. Did Mark manage to keep you in the dark? It seemed impossible. But now, I guess we know."

Valerie stretched out her hand, as if to lay it on Cassie's shoulder, but then she pulled it back, guessing, accurately, that it wouldn't be welcome. "After he injured his back, Mark's doctor prescribed opioids, Cassie. I don't remember which ones. But surely you knew?"

"Of course. That was the only thing that helped."

"Overuse of oxycodone and its little pals were more common then than they are now. For a while, the medical establishment believed they were absolutely safe. Now, there are new safeguards, but back then they were just beginning to come to terms with addiction problems nationwide. Do you remember how much pain Mark was in?"

"He couldn't get relief any other way, and the prescription only had so many refills," Cassie said. "After he started the drugs, he could finally sleep, get out of bed, do some moderate exercises. Everything seemed to come together again."

"Only it didn't, not really. I don't know all the details. Nobody does, but it seems clear he was getting drugs a number of ways. We do know that early on he finished his first round and needed refills, so Fletcher wrote him a prescription. Easy enough to do. Apparently, then Mark asked his own internist for more and got another refill, but he was advised to start tapering off. Instead, he started going to a pain relief practice across town, which, in itself, should have been a clue. Unfortunately, the only thing Fletcher saw? Mark was back at work and functioning. Everybody assumed for a while that any behavior out of the norm was because he wasn't fully recovered."

Cassie was trying to listen through a wall of denial. But too much of what Valerie was saying seeped through. "After those first few weeks I never saw him take a pill."

"Addicts are good at hiding problems, but eventually the addiction took over. Meds began to disappear from the supply closet, and then Fletcher got a call from a pharmacist in Brooklyn asking about a prescription he'd called in for Mark that the pharmacist was concerned about."

"Had he called it in?"

Valerie shook her head. "At that point Fletcher took Mark out to dinner and told him what he suspected and what he had to do. Fletcher didn't have hard proof, and frankly he wanted to keep it that way. So he told Mark he wasn't going to report him. But he wanted him to check himself into the Grandy Rayburn—"

"Drug Treatment Center," Cassie finished.

"You know about that?"

Cassie saw no reason to lie. "Mark told me he was filling in there after their director passed away suddenly. He was gone for weeks, only coming home occasionally on weekends."

"The director is alive and well, and Mark was a patient, not a staff member, because Fletcher told him if he didn't check himself in, he would report him for substance abuse and his license could be taken away. They have special programs that shield physicians from disciplinary actions and make sure treatment remains anonymous. If he'd gone to one, Mark would have been closely supervised and gotten the specialized therapy he needed. But Fletcher thought Grandy could turn him around, and then nobody would need to know about his problem. He thought he was looking out for Mark's future."

Valerie must have seen her confusion. "I know this is hard to accept, but addiction in the medical field is much more common than we think. Something like one in ten physicians are addicted to either drugs or alcohol at some point, and it's even higher for nurses. They have easy access to drugs, and their jobs are so stressful that getting away from them, zoning out for even a little while is too tempting. I'm guessing that a lot of physicians believe they can control their addiction, and then when drugs begin to control them, they don't know what to do. Their families, their jobs, their income, the profession they worked so hard to achieve? All of it teetering on the edge of oblivion."

"You seem to know a lot about it."

"I know a lot more than I used to."

"I can't believe this. If he had a headache, Mark usually toughed it out."

"But you do believe it. Because you lived with him."

Cassie knew that in the weeks ahead she would run through every moment of that last year of Mark's life, play back what she remembered through this new and horrifying filter. For now, though, she had to move on. At least a little.

"Grandy Rayburn didn't work the magic Fletcher thought it would?"

"For a while, things were promising. Mark seemed to be back in control. And there's a high rate of success when a physician is treated correctly, although those statistics come from the specialized programs I mentioned."

"If any of this is true, Fletcher has a lot to answer for."

Valerie didn't disagree. "He was trying to save Mark's career. They were friends. Good friends. You and I were friends. He didn't want to see your lives go up in flames."

Anger was beginning to outdistance disbelief. "I think Fletch didn't want to see Church Street go up in flames. That's it, isn't it? He didn't want the practice to suffer. He didn't want the publicity that might have come from this. He didn't want to lose credibility and income."

"Of course he didn't. Would you have wanted the publicity, Cassie? For your family? For Savannah? If Fletcher had known the way this would turn out, he would have done things differently. But he's not God. He took his best shot for everybody."

"And at the end?"

"After Tom Wallings brought his concerns to the other partners, Fletcher finally told them what had transpired. He was nearly asked to resign because he'd withheld the truth initially and helped Mark on his own."

"Apparently they thought better of it."

"I think everyone there could imagine themselves behaving the same way. They discussed what to do and shared suspicions about other incidents. At the end they decided to confront Mark, an intervention of sorts, and if they suspected he was still abusing drugs, they would give him a choice. Either he could resign, or they would report him. If he resigned on his own, they would all move on."

"They let him walk away, probably to get another job somewhere else and do the same things? They thought he was a drug addict, and as long as he wasn't *their* drug addict, everything was going to be fine?"

"Nobody had hard evidence. They only had suspicions."

Cassie's voice was rising, but she didn't care. "Nobody was

looking very hard, were they? They didn't want to know specifics, so they couldn't be held accountable."

"Trust me, I know the way the practice dealt with the problem was a cop-out and probably against the law. I've said as
much to Fletcher and some of the others. Even without details,
they should have reported him. But Mark was their friend,
and more important their reputations were on the line. They
backed away."

"When did you know all this?"

Valerie didn't whitewash the truth. "While it was happening."

"And yet, you were my friend, my closest friend, and you
never told me any of it? You never warned me. You never told
me so I could get help for Mark on my own."

Valerie looked away. "I had to choose, Cassie. I was told
not to warn you. The doctors themselves were of two minds.
Some thought you knew and didn't want the truth exposed.
Others were afraid when you found out, you wouldn't accept
their solution. If you exposed them, Fletcher and all his colleagues would have been in serious trouble."

Cassie was having problems fitting everything together,
but one piece of the puzzle was conspicuous in its absence.

"What did Ivy Todsen have to do with any of this?" she
asked.

Valerie looked as if she preferred not to answer. "What do
you mean?"

"I mean Ivy's insinuated herself into my life. How was she
involved?" When Valerie still didn't answer, she leaned closer.
"Were they having an affair?"

"An affair?" Valerie looked shocked. "Do you know her
well? She's a thoroughly unappealing woman. Arrogant, un-
friendly unless she wants something. Calculating. I would

stake my life on this. Mark was never interested in her in that way."

"Did she want something from Mark?"

"Her job."

"What do you mean?"

"A few months before he resigned, the hospital wanted to fire her. One of the other nurses suspected she was stealing meds from the drug rehab unit. Nobody had conclusive evidence, but other staff members were concerned about her, too, and they were planning to conduct an investigation. Instead Mark made sure she wasn't fired."

"Is she an addict herself? Is that why they thought she was stealing drugs?"

Valerie gave a small shrug. "On the street, opioids sell for something like ten dollars a milligram. So an eighty-milligram pill sells for maybe eighty dollars, and once someone is addicted, they can and do take many each day. Anyone who sells them has a ready market and steady income. Considering the way Mark protected Ivy, Fletcher and the others believe she helped him procure drugs. He may have been addicted until the day he died." She paused. "He may have been addicted *on* the day he died."

"He wasn't." That was something Cassie thought she knew for sure. "There was a routine autopsy. I'm sure they did a drug screen."

"Oxycodone is eliminated from the bloodstream quickly, as fast as twenty-four hours, or maybe he was attempting withdrawal by himself."

Cassie felt battered on all sides. She couldn't think about that day now, or the possibility that Mark's judgment had been altered by a struggle to stay clean. Instead she thought about the check to Ivy and the identical withdrawals the next two months. If one pill sold for eighty dollars, ten would sell for eight hundred dollars. She didn't need a calculator to know that even thirty thousand dollars would buy a limited number of pills, maybe just enough for a month or two, depending on his needs.

She wondered if there were other revelations to finish her off.

"They did fire Ivy as soon as Mark went on his way," Valerie said. "They got rid of her with a warning that if she protested, they would have her activities looked at more closely."

"So they did it again, only this time it was the hospital, not just Church Street. They got rid of her without reporting her, the way they got rid of Mark. What were they thinking? That with luck maybe her next employer, or her next, would finally stop her?"

"You can be sure Ivy didn't get a good recommendation."

"I'm guessing the possibility of drug theft wasn't mentioned."

When Valerie didn't answer, Cassie went on. "Ivy can go to any poorly served hospital, and they'll snap her up."

"Do you want this made public, Cassie? If the authorities can dig up enough proof Ivy was stealing and selling drugs, don't you think she'll name names? Mark will be exposed. Do you want Savannah to know what her father was doing and why he really left Church Street? I wouldn't, not in your place."

"Is there anything else?"

Valerie shook her head.

Cassie got to her feet. "Then we're done."

Valerie got up, too. "I never wanted it to be this way. But I had to protect Fletcher. And in my own way I was trying to protect you."

"That was thoughtful."

Valerie looked hurt. "You never used to be sarcastic."

"I never used to be a lot of things."

"Are you heading back to Florida?"

Cassie glanced at her watch. "No, I'm heading to New Jersey. Where Ivy lives."

"Do you really think—"

"You don't want to know what I really think. As for what I intend to do? I think I'll keep you in the dark to protect you. Have a good life, Valerie." She pivoted and started across the park. She thought Valerie called her name, but she kept walking.

39

SAVANNAH HAD GEN'S CONDO TO HERSELF. AFTER work Gen had brought home takeout Chinese food, and they'd chatted over dinner, checking in on each other's days. Savannah had actually had something to report. She'd hung out with the granddaughter of a doctor in Gen's practice, and it hadn't been the disaster she had anticipated. Pauline had driven them to an ice rink, which seemed like odd entertainment in a desert community, but Savannah had been glad just to go somewhere with somebody her own age.

Tonight Gen was speaking at an information session for a local country club, and Savannah turned down the chance to join her for slideshows about breast augmentation and liposuction. She liked that Gen helped people who needed reconstructive surgery, but the cosmetic part made her wonder what Gen would change about her daughter's face or body if Savannah asked her to.

Good news for Gen's budget. She wouldn't be asking anytime soon.

Unfortunately, while being alone meant she could lounge

or wander unobserved, it also meant she was bored. Gen was home so seldom that she only subscribed to the most basic cable package, and network television was so yesterday. Savannah had signed up for a trial app for her tablet, which was supposed to be perfect for teens, and deleted it half an hour later.

Upstairs in the-study-that-passed-for-a-bedroom, she was thinking about making the sofa into a bed when her cell phone rang. She was so bored, even if the call was a telemarketer, she might buy what they were selling, just to have somebody to talk to.

"Savannah?"

She fell to the sofa and stretched out her legs, flooded with gratitude. She hadn't heard from Will in days, since he was still in school and working late. "What's up? Everything okay there?"

"Yeah. I've got the house to myself."

"Me, too. Are you as bored as I am? And where's your mom?" Savannah knew Cassie was back in New York taking care of what seemed like interminable business related to Savannah's father's death.

"She and Travis are out to dinner with some friends of his. And no, I'm not bored. Not a bit. Because I got my 23andMe results today."

Savannah sat up. "Really? Already?"

"Pretty neat, huh?"

"I thought it would be weeks."

"It probably depends on how many people are submitting samples at one time."

"Maybe nobody's in the mood to spit right now. What'd you find out?"

"I'm like all European from places like Scotland and England, with some French and German thrown in. Boring."

"I could have told you that, but at least you know, huh? Your father wasn't a Martian. That was a possibility."

"I don't have any big family health issues, either."

Savannah listened as he talked about traits, health and wellness, along with carrier status. As far as she could tell, Will was a walking, talking all-American boy.

"Good job talking about all the stuff that doesn't matter," she said once he finished. "What about family?"

He hesitated, and she wasn't sure why. Then when he spoke, she realized the silence had come from being almost too excited to tell her.

"I have an uncle. A real uncle. Not like four generations away. I've got some of those, too. But a regular uncle."

"Is he your mother's or father's brother?"

"I don't know. The thing is, my mother and/or my father would have to be tested, too, to line that up."

"I'm thinking Amber's not going to be excited if you ask her. She could just tell you what she knows and save everybody money."

Savannah hadn't been able to check for emails herself. Will had changed the password for the email address she'd set up for his fake identity, which was wise but annoying. She wished in some of her spare hours she'd done more research on DNA results.

"So, what are you going to do?" she asked. "What can you do?"

"I looked him up online."

"How?"

"I have his name. You don't have to put your name in your profile, but he did. Some people use initials. That's what I did. His name is Darryl Hawken."

"So what do you know about him?"

"I checked him out on Google. If it's the same man, he's

a sheriff. He's about the right age. Older than my mom, but not a lot. A year, maybe two."

"Nobody else with that name?"

"A few, but no one else who seems right. A cricket player in Manchester, England. A couple of obituaries of old men with big, loving families."

"What did you find out?"

"The sheriff lives in West Virginia. Mom and I never lived there that I remember."

Savannah had never considered that Will could move from simple DNA results to getting details about somebody on his profile. "Are you happy enough now to know that much and no more?"

"Savannah... I saw his photo. I know he's the right man. He looks like me. I'm sure he's my uncle. Same color hair. Same long nose. Same chin."

"He's that ugly, huh?"

"What should I do? You always have ideas."

Savannah thought about the trip to Georgia. "Not necessarily good ones."

"Cassie says you're coming back this weekend."

"Yeah. She and I are okay. Gen and I are okay, too. We're going house shopping tomorrow so I'll have more room when I visit. It's all good. But I'm ready to come home."

"The Croville County website can't say enough good things about Sheriff Hawken. They also didn't mention anything about a family. Maybe he's as alone as Mom and I are."

"The thing is, your mom's not in touch with him, right? Let's assume she knows who he is and where he lives. Maybe she grew up in West Virginia, too, but she's not the kind of person who just goes off on somebody for decades for no good reason. She wasn't truthful about that family feud thing in

Georgia, but what if it was basically true, only in West Virginia?"

"Then isn't it time to end it?"

"How would we know? We don't know what caused it. Maybe somebody shot somebody's dog, or maybe somebody shot somebody's wife? Bad feelings can go on and on, and sometimes they just get worse."

"You don't think I should go any further, do you?"

Savannah didn't know what she thought. She wished she'd considered this more carefully, too. Just like Georgia.

"I have an idea," Will said, when she didn't answer. "I can contact him through the site, using the Jake Green name. I don't have to tell him anything about myself. But I thought maybe I'd tell him I'm a foster child somewhere like Georgia, where Roger Hart was from, checking to see if I have family. That would be safe, wouldn't it? He could never trace me to Florida."

"What would that accomplish?"

Will stumbled over his words. "He's the first blood relative other than my mom that I've ever even heard of. At least I can find out a little more. Maybe someday when I'm an adult on my own, I could meet him and get to know him. Not now, but later. At least I'd know he was out there."

"What about the rest of your profile? Other people?"

"Distant cousins and stuff. Way distant."

"Maybe you'd better sleep on this. Think about all the things that could happen."

Will cleared his throat. "I already contacted him. I don't know if he'll even get back to me or want to. But I didn't want to waste time."

Savannah had a bad feeling about this. She promised herself and God above that if this just turned out okay for Will, she would stop interfering in other people's lives. "You'll be careful, right? You won't tell him anything about who you really are or where you live?"

"Of course not."

She felt marginally better. "When I get back, we can talk about this some more, okay? See what you can do that will help you feel better without giving anything away?"

"It's going to be okay. It's just exciting, that's all."

Savannah wondered what she would find if she spit in a tube. After what Gen had told her about her maternal grandparents, and after what she knew firsthand about her other ones, she decided she would be content to just pass through life with two mothers, a father who had given so much when he was alive—and nobody else.

"Just take care," she said.

"I gotta go. Some of us still have school."

"Hey, I'll be doing schoolwork for the whole spring break. I emailed all my teachers. You ought to see the list of stuff I have to make up."

"It'll keep you out of trouble."

They said goodbye. She realized that when she'd silently listed her family, she'd forgotten to add Will, who was the closest thing to a brother she'd ever have.

Now that she thought about it, there were more, too. Yiayia. Roxanne. Amber. Travis. She almost called Will back to point out that family wasn't about blood in your veins, Cassie being a case in point. But that was so sappy she couldn't say it out loud.

She got out her tablet and looked up Darryl Hawken, West Virginia sheriff. He wasn't hard to find. She found a good close-up of him lecturing other law enforcement officers. He was a man who looked relaxed and in command, dark-haired, with the long nose Will had mentioned and a square jaw.

Sheriff Darryl Hawken really did look like Will. Could that be a coincidence? With everything else, it seemed unlikely.

The whole situation was mysterious. She just hoped it was mysterious in a good way.

40

AFTER YEARS OF KEEPING TRACK OF DARRYL, AMBER
knew how to search for Betsy's son. Five minutes after everyone left on Monday morning, she discovered that a Karl Garland had been hired by the West Virginia Aeronautics Commission in Charleston to assist the director. She knew that Karl had a pilot's license and a degree in aerospace engineering. This was the right man.

After determining that Karl was living in Charleston, she made a list of care centers, hospitals and rehab facilities in the general vicinity. She listed dozens that might treat patients with the kind of injuries Betsy had sustained, especially when Amber expanded the search to all of Kanawha County. Finding phone numbers, getting connected to someone who could tell her if Betsy was a patient, convincing that person she had a right to know? All of it took time. By Tuesday morning she'd managed to work her way through the first dozen listings. She had dropped Will at school, picked up a few groceries, and then hurried home to make more calls. Cassie had texted earlier to say she was delayed in New York and would call that evening to explain. In the meantime, Amber hoped to find Betsy.

The next facility on her list was the West Virginia Center for Successful Rehabilitation in Elkview, northeast of Charleston. She saw the rating was high and patients and families were as satisfied as they ever were. Nobody liked the food, but that was to be expected. If Betsy was there, she'd whip the nutrition staff into shape.

She took a deep breath and donned her Sue Simpson persona, Betsy's fictional cousin. Some facilities were more amenable to putting family through than friends.

The staff member who answered was brusque and professional, immediately inquiring who Amber wanted to speak with.

"My cousin Betsy Garland is a patient there. I just got your number. I am so relieved. May I speak with her, please?"

The woman hesitated, and Amber thought she heard papers being shuffled. "She may not be back from breakfast yet."

Her heart sped up. She struggled to sound casual. "Betsy always likes a good breakfast. So she's doing well enough to go to the dining room on her own?"

"I believe it's part of her therapy. Of course she has help." The last was said as if the woman was making sure Amber knew no one was forcing poor starving Betsy to crawl on hands and knees to the dining room.

Amber infused warmth into her voice. "I've seen your reviews. I know how lucky she is to be in a facility like yours."

"Well, I'll put you through to her room, but if she doesn't answer, please call back in about thirty minutes."

"I'll make sure to do that." She hadn't realized how tense she'd been until relief worked its magic. Not only had she found Betsy, but her old friend was well enough to go back and forth to the dining room.

The phone rang and rang, and just as Amber thought she needed to try again later, someone picked up.

"Hello…" The voice quavered, and the woman cleared her throat immediately after that one word, as if she was afraid more might not emerge.

Quaver or not, Amber recognized the voice. "Betsy!" She lowered her voice. "Betsy, are you alone?"

"Heather?"

"Amber now."

"Of course. Neither of my roommates is here at the moment. Darling, how are you?"

"I've been worried sick about *you*. I finally called Tammy and told her I was a former student named Sue Simpson—"

"She told me. Did she tell you what happened?"

"Do you feel well enough to give me details?"

"Let me get comfortable. I'll be alone for a while. I'm supposed to practice holding a pen and writing my name. My hand got pretty smashed up."

"Tammy told me you were visiting Karl and taking a morning walk. She said a driver hit you and then drove off and left you. Is that true?"

"That's what they tell me."

She wasn't surprised that the shock of a nearly fatal accident had wiped away memories of it. "So you don't remember?"

"I remember leaving the house." Betsy paused as if to rest, and her words came slowly. "I remember where I was walking, too—a road not far from Karl's new condo. I think I remember stopping because I heard an indigo bunting. It was a little early in the season to hear one."

"You taught me so many birdcalls."

"You're like a daughter to me."

A tear spilled down Amber's cheek. "Do you remember anything else?"

"Waking up in the hospital. Karl was sitting next to my bed. He told me I'd been unconscious for three days."

"It's a nightmare. I've been so worried."

"Don't be. I'm getting better. Steadily better. Once I'm released, I'll stay with Karl another week, then I can go home. I'll need a little household help, but they tell me eventually I'll make a full recovery. But why were you calling? Originally, I mean? Did you leave a message online?"

"I did. I was just checking to see if you had heard anything new." She was sure Betsy understood exactly what she meant.

"My memory's not what it was. But I think I remember… I do remember. I needed to talk to you. Then this…"

"Do you remember why?"

"Give me a moment."

Amber waited, trying not to picture her friend alone on the roadside bleeding and unconscious, while Betsy formed a halting reply.

"He was harassing one of my sewing girls, flirting with her and making suggestive remarks at a little fashion show we did. One of his deputies has a daughter who modeled her dress, and he tagged along. I confronted him and put a stop to it. He… He was unhappy I intervened. The argument escalated. I lost my temper. I said he didn't deserve…to wear a badge."

Amber felt vaguely sick, as if the worst was yet to come. "He didn't like that, I'm sure."

"He asked how I would know… And, I made a mistake. I said…" Betsy paused a long time, but Amber didn't interrupt. "I said he should be in jail, not running it."

"Oh, Betsy…"

"I know, I know. I've been so careful, Heath—Amber. I lost my temper."

"Was that all that happened?"

A long pause. "Maybe."

Amber couldn't let that pass. "Something else?"

"I don't know. But…I came home from the store a few days before I went to Karl's. There were no obvious signs someone had been there, but…" She sighed. "It felt like it. Do you know what I mean? A few things had been rearranged… Like mail on my desk, books out of place on my shelf."

Betsy was a cheerfully meticulous housekeeper, and in her house, every book was perfectly lined up with every other in alphabetical order.

The next question was hard to ask. "Was anything missing?"

"Something might have been. I…I just don't know if somebody took it, or maybe I put it somewhere else and can't remember." She paused, as if she didn't want to go on, but she did. "The photo of you and Will in North Carolina. The one at the overlook? Mountains behind you?"

"You kept it?" Amber had expected Betsy to destroy the photo, the way she'd destroyed the others she'd sent.

"I know. I shouldn't have. But I miss you, and I loved seeing that boy growing up. And I…I thought it would be safe… if I put it in my Bible."

Amber closed her eyes.

Betsy sounded like she was going to cry. "I thought a Bible was the last place a man like that would ever look!"

"Don't worry. Please don't worry. If it was him, maybe he won't recognize me. And even if he does, he won't know where we are. I am so, so sorry to involve you in this."

"No, I'm the one who's sorry. I hope… I hope I just put it somewhere else. But I think, I remember… I tried to find it before I went to Karl's and couldn't. Maybe I was smart and threw it away."

"I'm sure you did." Amber wasn't sure at all. She'd never tell Betsy, but if Darryl really had broken into her home and taken the photo, the worst part wasn't the theft. Now Darryl knew she had a son, and one who looked like him. Will's resemblance to the Hawken family was unmistakable.

Almost as bad, Darryl knew what she looked like, or had looked like when the photo was taken two years ago. Her hair had been blonder and shorter. She thought she'd been wearing a cap in the photo, and maybe, with luck, sunglasses. But no matter how she was dressed, it was clear she no longer looked like the Goth girl Billy had fallen in love with.

Betsy couldn't be fooled. She began to cry, small tidy sobs that still broke Amber's heart. "Do you think… Do you think Darryl was driving the car that hit me?"

Amber swallowed her own sobs, determined not to upset Betsy even more. "Do you?"

"Why would he attack me? Wouldn't…wouldn't he want to know what I know?"

Amber tried to imagine the scenario. Now that Darryl knew Amber and Betsy were in touch, he would be sure of two things. One, if Betsy knew Amber's whereabouts, she would never reveal them, no matter how much pressure he applied. And two, if he managed to find and dispose of Amber and her son, eventually Betsy would contact someone in authority, a sheriff in another county or the FBI, and tell what she knew. Most likely no one would believe her, not unless bodies were discovered, but why would Darryl take that chance?

A better strategy? Get rid of Betsy first, preferably outside Croville County. Betsy was a fixture in Chaslan with dozens of friends, and if she disappeared mysteriously while she was there, the whole town would search.

Amber had to alert her friend without scaring her to death.

"It's hard for a normal person to think the way he does. But since we don't know? Please don't go home, okay? Stay with Karl or stay with friends, preferably somewhere outside West Virginia at least for a little while."

"I can't impose on people that way."

"How many have imposed on you? Time to ask your friends for help. Isn't there somebody who's been begging you to visit?"

"Well, but—"

"Stay with Karl until the doctor gives you the okay to leave town. Then visit the friend who lives farthest away. Tell them you're still a little unsteady on your feet and you need people around. They'll be delighted to have your company. Later we can figure out what should come next."

"You really think it was him, don't you?"

"Paranoia is a normal state of mind for me, but we can't take chances. I think we need to assume he has the photo and probably figures you know what happened all those years ago." She steeled herself to say what had to be said. "If that's true, then he's going to feel a lot safer if you're out of the picture. And I don't mean visiting friends. I mean permanently."

"I hope you're wrong."

"Will you do it anyway? Will you get out of town and not tell anyone where you are except Karl? And tell him not to tell anyone, either?"

"He'll want to know why."

"Tell him you need time and space to recover and don't want people fussing over you. That sounds like you."

Betsy didn't sound happy, but she didn't argue. "I have a new cell phone. Karl bought it for me after the accident. Mine was...destroyed. He changed my number because I was getting so much spam at the old one. I have it somewhere." The call went silent a minute, and then she returned and dictated the new number to Amber.

"You'll stay in touch?" Betsy asked after she'd finished. "He won't have that number. He couldn't."

Something as minor as privacy laws would never stop Darryl Hawken, but Betsy already had enough to worry about. Amber just hoped she followed her advice. "I'll call. Or a friend of mine will call you. I'll be Sue Simpson."

"You're not a Sue. Amber suits you."

Amber thought it did, too. She hoped she didn't have to change it again in the future. "I'm going to let you rest now. Don't work so hard in physical therapy that they let you leave too soon. You said you have roommates?"

"There's always somebody around. It's annoying."

"It's safer that way. Try to stay as long as you can."

"You stay safe, too."

"Sending my love." Amber disconnected and rested her head on the back of the sofa.

She wondered what she should do next. She had the same internal conversation she'd been having with herself for years. She could run. Again. Still. But would running accomplish anything except more disruption in Will's life? Darryl had a photo, but hopefully he didn't know more. Maybe, if she was lucky, he thought she was living in the mountains.

What did he know that really mattered? Amber had a son, and judging by Will's features and general age, Darryl would know he was family.

Darryl wouldn't care that Will was related. Darryl would see him as a threat, a boy, almost a man, who might stalk him in the future and right the wrongs of history. Darryl wouldn't tolerate that possibility.

Wasn't she safer right where she was? At least until Will finished school? Surely she wasn't putting anybody else in danger the way she'd put Betsy in danger by sending her the photo.

She wished she could tell Travis or Cassie, ask for their advice and follow it. She wished that just once, she could share this awful burden.

41

AFTER LEAVING MANHATTAN ON MONDAY, CASSIE took the subway, then a bus to New Jersey to confront Ivy. While she felt shaky and disoriented after everything she'd learned, the trip gave her time to begin making sense of it. Cassie finally understood why no one from Church Street had offered comfort after Mark's death. The problem of what to do about an addicted colleague was solved. They no longer had to second-guess their actions. They could bury what they had done—along with Mark—and move on.

While she finally had closure with Valerie, their conversation had opened deeper wounds. She would have to come to terms with the way she had allowed Mark to set the rules in their marriage. Maybe if she'd been accustomed to standing up for herself, she would have discovered the truth. Mark had struggled with an addiction serious enough to ruin his life, and she, like too many other people in the same situation, had closed her eyes to the signs.

Once off the bus, she took a moment to get her bearings. Finding Ivy's address wasn't difficult. She had phoned Riverbend's behavioral health unit and explained she'd discovered paperwork Mark had completed for Ivy before his death. She already assumed that Ivy's home address was also the so-called business address of Rinkel Medical Supplies, and with no surprise, she learned that Ivy lived in an apartment building in North Bergen.

She hadn't guessed what a nice building it would be.

The complex on the Hudson River had a priceless view of Manhattan. A stroll through the beautifully landscaped grounds turned up expensive amenities like a pool, a dog park, a patio with grills and firepits.

After more investigation, including a visit to the sales office, she found a concierge in the main building, and with her warmest smile asked to be directed to Ivy's apartment. On the fifth floor—and on the side of the building facing the river—she found the apartment and knocked. When nothing happened and after she tried again, she headed back to the lobby to watch.

By dinnertime she knew she had to find a hotel room and try again tomorrow. She reserved a room in a so-called budget hotel, and once there changed her airline reservation. She spent what amounted to a sleepless night going over the final months of her marriage, hoping unsuccessfully to find some clue that Valerie had been lying.

Tuesday morning she was back at Ivy's apartment wearing the emergency change of shirt and underwear she'd packed in her oversize purse, along with toiletries.

Now she took a deep breath to prepare for the next round of unwelcome revelations and knocked, the sound echoing through an empty hallway. She was lifting her fist for a second volley when the door swung open. Ivy, in garnet-colored satin pajamas, gaped at her from the doorway.

"Cassie?" she said at last.

"I thought I'd surprise you."

"You certainly managed that."

Cassie waited, and Ivy finally stepped back and left a path. "Come in. I'm sorry. I'm not awake yet."

Inside, the view of the river was as magnificent as she'd guessed. "What a place. And on a nurse's salary, too. You must have a ton of roommates." She managed a smile. "I hope I didn't wake them up, too."

"There's no one here but me."

Ivy had carefully sidestepped the question of whether she shared the apartment, but a quick glance at the antique mahogany furniture with its sleek surfaces and carefully arranged tableaux of books and sculptures was evidence Ivy lived alone.

Yesterday Cassie had talked to the sales manager, pretending interest in renting and taking brochures and price lists back to her hotel. A one-bedroom apartment looking over the river would eat up every cent an RN could earn. But by now Cassie was sure that Ivy had other sources of income.

"You were lucky to land this," Cassie said. "And am I right? They actually have a shuttle here that takes you to the ferry into the city? I mean, how perfect is that. Back when you had a job, that must have been a help."

"It's awfully early, Cassie. You never told me you were coming."

Cassie faced her, and without answering, did a full appraisal. Ivy was much as she remembered, but if anything, thinner and more haggard. The pajamas hung from her shoulders without hinting at a single feminine curve. Her overly bleached hair stuck out like straw.

Ivy moved toward the kitchen, which was off the entry hallway. "Since I'm up, I'll make us a pot of coffee."

Without waiting for an invitation, Cassie followed behind.

The kitchen was small but gleaming, with stainless steel top-of-the-line appliances and dark granite counters.

"I'm afraid I drink my coffee black," Ivy said. "I don't have milk or cream."

"I had coffee with breakfast. I'm good." Cassie leaned against the counter by the doorway. She guessed Ivy was trying to decide whether to continue the pretense she was Cassie's friend, her eyes and ears in New York.

Cassie put an end to speculation. "I had a good chat with Valerie yesterday. Your name came up. Actually, I brought it up. I asked if she thought you and Mark were having an affair."

"What?" Ivy slammed down a bag of coffee she'd just removed from the refrigerator.

Cassie held up her hands. "Don't worry. She said of course not."

Ivy narrowed her eyes. "What do you want here, Cassie? Apparently not to strengthen our friendship."

"You see? Right off the bat you've started with a mistake. We've never been friends. It's more like you were a spider, hoping to trap me in your web. I was just somebody else you were hoping to use and abuse."

"You need to leave."

"I don't think you'll call anybody to have me escorted out. Because they won't like knowing the apartment belongs to a drug dealer."

"You're crazy."

Cassie made a show of ticking off her most important points on the fingers of one hand as she spoke. "Crazy not to see that my husband was addicted to painkillers and couldn't wean himself away from them. Then crazy to think that you really wanted to help figure out what was going on at the end. Last of all, crazy to feel sorry you were fired, when all along you were probably feeding my husband's dependence on drugs."

Ivy reached for the coffee maker's filter basket and dumped coffee into it without measuring. She didn't say anything until she'd filled the reservoir and flipped the switch to begin brewing.

"You can't prove a thing," she said. "Nobody's going to believe you."

"And…?"

"What do you mean *and*?"

"And if I try, you'll tell the world my husband was addicted to drugs, and you were just trying to help him kick his habit."

"Well? So what! Because it's true. Yes, I knew. He trusted me to help him. I guess he didn't trust you."

Cassie stepped a little closer. "I guess he didn't. On the other hand he didn't pay me thirty thousand dollars to help him, either."

"I don't know what you're talking about."

"Rinkel Medical Supply and a ten-thousand-dollar check I found. I can prove Rinkel Medical Supply is housed right here in this lovely apartment. You're listed as Rinkel's contact, and I doubt Mark was buying bargain stethoscopes. Then there were two similar cash withdrawals, exactly one and two months later. It all leads back to you. I bet we can check your bank account to see if you deposited the same amount on those dates or right after."

"I was helping him."

"Stealing money more likely."

"That's ridiculous. Mark trusted me. I found help for him, an excellent doctor who agreed to work off the record. I helped get the medications he prescribed for Mark to ease withdrawal. Mark didn't want anything on his record, so he couldn't use insurance to buy them. Drugs are costly. So I had to open a few doors that weren't absolutely legal."

Cassie didn't buy a word of it. "Like the doors to the drug

supply closet at Riverbend? Because that's at least part of the reason you were fired. They suspected you of stealing."

"That was Fletcher Dorman's fault! He knew I wasn't stealing, but he used it as a—"

Cassie took another step closer, anger bubbling over. "You got off so easy. They didn't turn you in. They were so concerned about appearances that they let Mark resign without offering help, and then they sent you away with nothing but a mediocre reference. And look at this apartment! I know what you pay to live here. I can make a good guess about what you earned at the hospital. Anybody can tell you're making money on the side, Ivy. And I don't think you're doing private nursing at night."

"You're wrong." She cocked her head as if to see Cassie in another light. "But let's just say you aren't. What would you do about it? Because you don't have enough proof to have me arrested."

"Riverbend probably does. I could go to Mark's colleagues at Church Street and insist. And if they refuse to cooperate, I could explain that when I report you, I will also tell the authorities they knew the truth about you and Mark and didn't do a thing."

"You won't."

"You don't think so?"

Ivy gave a small satisfied smile. "Sa—van—nah. Do you want Mark's little princess to know her father was a junkie? That even with help, he couldn't kick his addiction? That he put people in harm's way because he wasn't thinking clearly? That at one point, his addiction got so out of hand he was stealing meds prescribed for his patients, even injecting himself with drugs meant for them and leaving them confused and in pain?"

Cassie schooled herself not to show her horror. "So that's what you think you can hold over me?"

"Did I say that? I just asked if you were ready for the hornet's nest you're threatening to stir up."

"I might be. Maybe it's time to clean out and exterminate every single hornet and start fresh."

"You can't exactly start fresh with your husband, can you? Because Mark's dead, maybe by his own hand, but almost certainly because he didn't want you to think less of him. He struggled and suffered because he didn't want you to know he was human. He didn't want you to look down on him, to think he was less than he was."

They were the same words Cassie had repeated in her head all night. In the future when she was feeling most shaky, she would probably repeat them again, no matter how hard she tried not to. But she knew better than to let Ivy think she had hit home.

She shook her head slowly. "Nice try, but I never expected him to be perfect. Mark expected perfection of himself. He was willing to pay you that money and whatever else you stole from him because he couldn't admit he wasn't."

"I earned the pittance Mark paid me. And now I'm out of a job. I helped him live his lie, because sometimes lies are the only merciful solution."

"Lied and stole to be charitable, huh? Was that why you've been sending me anonymous letters, hoping either I would come crying to you and you could find out how much I knew about Mark's problem—"

Ivy looked away. "Ridiculous."

Cassie went on. "Or else you were prepping me for blackmail, using our daughter's love for her father as bait. Of course the thing you got wrong there? You can blackmail me until Armageddon, but I have almost nothing left to give you."

Oddly, Ivy didn't look doubtful or even surprised. One thin eyebrow shot up, and for a moment, she almost looked as if she wanted to smile. "I wondered about that. All your talk of looking for a job. He didn't leave you much of anything. It figures. But if you're still looking for more connections to me? You won't find them. You can search all you want. I don't care."

"Maybe I'll have the authorities do it."

"You may find a few things about your husband worse than addiction. Do you really want to take that chance? Addiction is a medical problem, but there are things you don't know that aren't medical. And they will affect Savannah directly for the rest of her life."

The air in the apartment suddenly seemed foul and dangerous. "You're bluffing." Cassie slid her handbag farther up her shoulder in preparation to leave.

"Think so? Do a little more sleuthing, but do it before you start trying to be a hero. Savannah's one thing. But you'll always be Mark's widow. For the rest of your life, do you want people whispering behind your back? Wondering how you could have been so gullible, and how you could have known so little about your husband?" Ivy gave a sharp, humorless laugh. "Anything I did to help Mark—"

"You sold him drugs!"

Ivy took a step closer, smirking. "I'd be so careful if I were you. For old time's sake I'll give you a little hint." She leaned forward and whispered the next sentence. "There's more to find."

Cassie couldn't counter innuendoes, and it was clear that was all Ivy was going to offer. She walked through the apartment and let herself out, moving so fast that outside she nearly mowed down an elderly couple exercising a yapping poodle.

She didn't slow down until she was away from the grounds. She knew she could call a cab, but since her flight wasn't until that evening, she took public transportation to the airport. Three buses and one subway ride later she stood in a line at La-Guardia to see if she could find an earlier flight, although the real truth was that she was standing there for something to do. She was afraid if she didn't continue putting one foot in front of another, her anger and anguish would erupt and destroy her.

During the trip, as she'd gotten off and on buses and descended to the subway, she'd thought about Mark's deceptions and grown more furious. But if she didn't turn Ivy in to the authorities, wasn't she just as bad? Mark had lied to protect his career, his family and image of himself, in addition to his addiction. If Cassie pretended her silence was just for Savannah's sake, that would be a lie, as well, because silence would also preserve the fable of her perfect husband and marriage. At least at the end, they had been anything but.

There was no chance Ivy would blackmail her now, and the nurse was almost certainly not going public about Mark's addiction. For Ivy, this story was finished. She would find another job, find more ways to sell drugs to addicts who desperately needed them, and then when they were under her control, find ways to extract more money. Ivy would continue to leave a trail of broken souls behind her.

If Cassie didn't speak up, she was allowing that to continue.

Were there really more grim revelations in her future? Maybe Ivy's threat was just one more manipulation, but the money Mark had paid her was still only a small percentage of what had disappeared.

Mark had been an addict. It was entirely possible whatever

was missing had been spent on drugs. Did she need to continue the search? The money was well and truly gone.

Mark was gone, too. She and Savannah had the rest of their lives ahead of them.

How were they going to live them?

42

ON FRIDAY AFTERNOON SAVANNAH EXPECTED TO find Cassie waiting beyond security at the Tampa airport, but Will stepped out of the crowd to greet her instead.

"Hey!" She threw her arms around his neck for a hug, then stepped back. "Where, Mom?"

For a moment he looked confused, then he got it. "Cassie and *my* mom are at home cooking a welcome dinner. They sent me."

"What is this? Like a rite of passage or something? Will goes to the airport? Do you need a photo for your scrapbook?"

"I forgot what a pain in the neck you are."

"Only you would say *neck*."

They chatted as they headed to baggage claim. Will told her how lucky she'd been to miss the past week at school, when the upcoming spring break was the only thing anyone could think about.

"They're all going somewhere," he said as they waited for

Savannah's bags. "Beaches, family vacations, sneaking off with their boyfriends."

"They can have it. Flying is brutal. It's like a mosh pit. I don't want to go anywhere again." She paused for effect. "Not until summer." She told him about the trip she and Gen were planning to Kenya and how Gen was going to teach her to do some basic procedures to help. "And you know what?" She looked sideways to be sure Will was listening. "I can bring a friend."

He was listening. "To Africa?"

"Do you know how great that would look on a college application?"

"I can guess."

"Maybe you'd like to be my friend?"

Will turned. "Me?"

"Gen will pay our way. We have to work while we're there to earn it back. She trains local doctors. That's her main thing, and she said sometimes they work twelve-hour days so we would, too. But I told her you'd think that was a vacation."

"I don't know. My mom—"

"Amber will know right away what a great opportunity this is."

His eyes were shining. "It's something to think about."

Savannah knew she could convince Cassie to talk to Amber if there were any issues.

They were out of the parking garage and on the highway before they talked about anything other than Africa.

"You do have some good ideas," Will said. He was driving Cassie's car. She was sorry it wasn't the Mustang, but he did seem more comfortable behind the wheel of a basic Toyota, as if he were no longer calculating the cost of repairs every time he switched lanes.

"It's nice of you to say so." Savannah was about to pull out her phone to check for texts from Helia or Minh when he spoke again.

"You had a good one about 23andMe."

She was surprised at the compliment, then she remembered that the last time they'd talked, he'd told her he had contacted his uncle. "Have you heard anything?"

"He got back to me! We've been emailing. He wants to meet me. He's so excited. He says I must be his brother Billy's son."

"Wow." Savannah didn't know what else to say. She knew she was supposed to be excited, and she was. Kind of. She was also worried.

"I know my father's name! I must be named after him. That has to mean Mom loved him."

"Slow down, okay? You didn't tell him where you live or anything revealing? I mean, all these years Amber's kept your dad's identity secret and—"

He interrupted, clearly frustrated. "I know I can't. And I lied about Mom in case, well, telling him could cause trouble for her or somebody. I told him she died and I'm a foster child, you know, like Helia. I've talked to Helia enough to know what it's like, sort of. He believes me."

"Okay…" She was trying to think ahead. "So he thinks you're a foster kid named Jake Green. And he doesn't know from where? I mean, what did you tell him when he asked?"

"I said Georgia."

"Okay…" She remembered he had thought Georgia was a good idea when they'd talked before. She hoped she was worrying for nothing. "And you didn't send him a photo or anything, did you?"

Will was silent.

"Will!"

"I sent him the one you took of me in front of the library

in Blayney. He says I look like my dad." Will cleared his throat. "Now I know my dad's name, and I know I look like him."

"You shouldn't have sent a photo."

"Why not? It was taken in another state, so he won't know where I really live. I didn't have a lot of photos to choose from. My mom doesn't keep any."

Amber didn't keep photos? Something felt wrong. Savannah just couldn't put her finger on what.

"He wants me to visit," Will said. "He wants me to go to West Virginia and meet him."

She began to worry. Spring break had just started in Tarpon Springs. Theoretically this would be a good time to leave. "You're not going, right?"

"Of course not. I told him that I have school and my foster parents are strict and wouldn't let me. He said he could talk to them, but I told him it would be better to wait until I'm eighteen."

"What else have you told him about your life?"

"I hate lying. So I've told him some true stuff. Like what I'm studying in school, and what I like to do. But, you know, I keep wondering why I have to lie in the first place? What's the problem with just telling him who I really am and having him talk to Mom? Maybe they could work things out."

"You don't know what *things*, Will. She's not being honest, and now neither are you."

"I've been thinking, maybe I could meet him somewhere else. Like back in Blayney. On neutral ground. Mom would never have to know."

"There are five million things wrong with that. All he has to do is ask around once he's there, and when nobody's ever heard your name, he'd know you were lying."

Will was sucking on his bottom lip. "I want to know about my dad. I'm never going to learn anything from Mom."

From the beginning, the search for Will's family had been academic for Savannah, a puzzle to solve, like a murder in a juicy novel. The reader worked out the solution right along with the police detective, like partners. Case closed at the end after hours spent together.

She had expected Will to maybe get a few answers and then move on. She had never realized that straight-arrow Will would be willing to lie to the mother he adored in order to meet the uncle he never even knew he had.

"This might be getting out of hand," she said, after thinking it over. "The sheriff's not going away anytime soon. He'll be there in West Virginia when you're older, right? Maybe you ought to just put this on hold."

"And maybe I don't want to."

"I'm starting to get worried."

"Don't. But when it comes down to it? This is my decision, and from this point on, you can step out of it. You don't have to think about it. I'm grateful to you for getting the ball rolling, but I can handle things from here on out."

Savannah wasn't sure that was true. After all, she knew from experience that families could do terrible things to your head. She thought about the way she'd blamed her father's death on Cassie and almost pushed her away forever. Love, loyalty, lies. They were all mixed up somehow, and she hoped when she was older, she'd be able to separate them. Getting older had to be good for something other than drinking and voting.

"I just want the best for you," she said.

"I want the best for me, too. So don't worry."

But she was worried. "Don't shut me out, okay?"

"Tell me about California."

She hoped they could come back to this later. Will might

not want her involved now, but she had to find a way to make sure he stayed safe.

As they finished the drive to Tarpon Springs, Will's uncle wasn't mentioned again. But Savannah didn't stop thinking about him.

43

SAVANNAH HAD ALWAYS LOVED SEAFOOD SO MUCH
that even the dead fish prank hadn't ruined it for her. Cassie
knew she would want it for her homecoming dinner, or maybe
one of the Greek meals she'd grown up with. To cover both,
she bought plump fresh shrimp right off the boat to bake in the
homemade tomato sauce she was preparing now. She would
top the dish with feta and mint and serve with crusty bread
she'd bought at a Dodecanese Avenue bakery. She'd learned
the recipe at Yiayia's knee, helping to make it on weekends
when she hid out at her grandparents' house.

She'd grown up with addiction. How could she have been
so blind to signs of it in her own husband?

Amber had offered to help with dinner, and now she was at
the refrigerator pulling out ingredients to make a Greek salad.
Baklava was already finished and resting on the counter. For
the last few minutes she and Amber had been working side
by side but staying out of each other's way, because by now
they knew each other's movements.

Amber joined her at the counter with fresh cucumbers and

tomatoes. "Eventually you're going to tell me what happened in New York. Will's not going to be home with Savannah for at least another hour. We have time."

Cassie had spent the past two days absorbing what she'd learned, and Amber had been slammed at work. This moment felt as right as it could.

As Amber listened, she told her about each step of the trip, ending with the confrontation at Ivy's apartment. She didn't add Ivy's parting comment, that there were things Cassie still didn't know. Until she knew what Ivy had been referring to, she wasn't ready to share.

"You should have seen her apartment," she finished. "It's obvious she was raking in money from somewhere other than Riverbend."

"Do you think she's behind your financial problems? The thousands we know Mark paid her are only a small part of what's missing, right?"

While Cassie was gone, Amber hadn't found anything else incriminating in the bank statements, although she hadn't had much time to dig.

"Ivy claimed I won't find anything else that I can trace to her. She was so smug about it."

"This has to come as a huge shock."

"That my husband was a drug addict? That my best friend was hiding it? That my new friend was setting me up for blackmail?" She tried a smile and failed. "I'm not just feeling sorry for myself?"

"Mark was one of thousands of people who get addicted from perfectly legitimate pain prescriptions. It happens a lot more than people know. It must have been so hard for him."

Cassie hadn't graduated to sympathy yet. She was still grappling with the lives he had destroyed. "He was stealing drugs from patients, Amber, leaving them in pain. How despicable is that?"

"You don't know that part's true. Ivy's an untrustworthy source. But even so? Addiction can rob people of everything good and virtuous."

"How do you know so much?"

"There's a lot of it in the restaurant industry. Late and long hours, low pay so people have to work more than one job. Easy access to alcohol and drugs, and partying in the kitchen to pass the time. I've seen my share up close. Maybe I was lucky I had Will waiting at home every night, because I was never tempted. But sometimes I felt like the only person on the floor who wasn't having fun."

"Tell me that's not true at the Kouzina."

"Not with Roxanne around. She ran into it in her restaurant in Virginia, so she knows what to watch for."

"Why didn't I know what was going on? Why didn't I see it?"

Amber considered. "I didn't know Mark, but I know what you've said about him. For all the good they do, a psychiatrist knows how to manipulate people. Who better than somebody who's paid to get inside your head?"

Cassie was afraid Amber was on target. "Whenever I tried to express concerns, somehow the problem always became about me. If I got upset at being analyzed, that became his next target. Eventually I doubted myself instead of him."

"The curse of the helping professions. But by the same token that must have made it hard for Mark to get the help he needed. Because he knew how to fool people who were just like him."

"They have programs designed to help medical professionals, but Fletcher, and whoever else was in on this, didn't want him under scrutiny. They didn't want bad publicity."

"Can you really say for sure that Fletcher was at fault? Because in the end, isn't it the addict who has to commit to change and find the best way to make it happen?"

"I'm just so furious right now at everybody, I don't know. And, you know what? Everybody's getting off scot-free."

Beside her Amber finished peeling the cucumbers. "Is that how it's going to be? If nothing else, isn't Ivy going to sell whatever drugs she steals from her next place of employment? She has a beautiful apartment to keep up, and you said it yourself. She'll get another job when she wants one, maybe in a setting where she's surrounded by people even more desperate."

"Remember the story of Pandora's box?"

"You're afraid if you report her, everything will come back to haunt you and Savannah."

"It could."

"Is keeping everything a secret to protect a dead man's legacy worth it?"

Cassie had asked herself the same thing, but hearing it asked by someone else was worse. She felt a stab of anger. "Do you want to talk about secrets and lies? Because I've told you mine. I'm struggling with this, but how about you? You're keeping your own Pandora's box locked tight. You think I haven't figured that out?"

"Of course you have."

Cassie's anger slipped away as quickly as it appeared. "It's clear you're afraid. You know what else is clear? Every day I expect to wake up and find you gone." She hesitated before she plowed ahead. "I'm so tired of secrets, Amber. Did you do something in your past and you're afraid it'll come back to haunt you? That you'll end up in jail?"

"Are we going to play Twenty Questions? Because that would be my first no."

Cassie heard a way into Amber's story. "Okay, then you're running from someone in your past. A man."

"And that would be my first yes."

"Will's father?"

Amber was silent. Cassie thought the game had to end right there. "We've done enough prep. Let's take iced tea out to the lanai. I'm sorry I pushed."

"Anybody with an ounce of self-preservation would have done it a long time ago."

"I didn't want to scare you away." She glanced at her friend and saw she was on the verge of tears.

Amber spoke before Cassie could apologize again. "I don't want to talk about this, but things have reached a point where I have to stop making choices for you."

Cassie was more worried than mystified, but she left the sauce to simmer and went to the refrigerator to get the tea. A few minutes later they were sitting by the pool. Neither had taken a sip. Instead Cassie held the glass against her cheek. The temperature was in the low eighties, but luckily the humidity was comfortably low.

"I don't even know where to start," Amber said at last.

"As early as you have to and late enough that you won't still be explaining when Savannah and Will arrive."

Amber put her head down, as if she was too tired to hold it erect. Or too ashamed. "I haven't had much experience doing this."

"Travis doesn't know?"

"Only one other person knows, and it's not Will."

"I'm not going to ask you to move out once you tell me. You already said you aren't running from the police. That would be hard."

"I didn't say I wasn't running from the police. I said I didn't do anything in my past that would land me in jail. But a sheriff is pursuing me. Darryl Hawken, the sheriff of Croville County, West Virginia, where I grew up. He's been hunting me since high school."

Cassie gave a soft whistle. "Not Kentucky. Not Arkansas."

"I've never lived in either place. I just sound like I might have. Darryl couldn't put me in jail, but he would love to put me under it."

Cassie knew Amber was feeling her way, so she saved the rest of her many questions. "Go on."

Amber stared over the pool to the yard beyond. The lanai was backed by a wide retention pond and a snowy egret with dinner on its mind was at the edge searching for a likely candidate. Amber watched in silence until the egret launched itself at the water and then retreated to fly away.

"From what you've told me," she said, "our childhoods weren't terribly different, although my parents neglected me mostly from inertia. I had a roof over my head and food to eat, and sometimes my mother was home in the evenings, but she rarely talked. The thing that saved me? I loved school. And I joined 4-H, more to have someplace to go, but later because there were adults in both places who paid attention to me."

She angled her body so she could see Cassie. "I hated being a teenager. I hated everything about myself. So I tried to be somebody else. You know Helia, Savannah's friend? That's who I was. I dyed my hair black, wore Goth clothes and heavy makeup. It was a disguise. I wanted people to leave me alone."

"Did it help?"

"I guess not, because eventually this boy I'd known forever started paying attention anyway. He was Darryl's younger brother. Every town has its criminal elements, and Chaslan is quiet and ordinary, but it wasn't immune. His family lived just outside town on acres they owned for generations. His cousin cooked meth in a shack in the woods with a loaded shotgun pointed out the window. His father was a handyman and preyed on people too old to know they'd been fleeced. My own father was no saint, but he used to talk about Billy's family."

"Billy?"

"Will is named after Billy."

"I'm glad Darryl wasn't his father."

Amber looked away before she began again. "My father warned me to steer clear of any Hawkens. They were all black sheep, but none worse than Billy's uncle. And the thing is?" She gave a humorless laugh. "Back then Billy's uncle was the sheriff, corrupt as all get-out but electable because he gave the people who controlled the town whatever they wanted. That's how his family members got away with everything they did."

Cassie realized she was shaking her head.

"Apparently it's a family dynasty," Amber said, "because Darryl Hawken is the present-day sheriff."

"Do they elect sheriffs in West Virginia?"

"Yes, with term limits. In this case Darryl is hoping to move on to the House of Delegates. From what I can tell from the internet, he might succeed."

"I'm assuming Billy was different."

"Night and day. Billy told me once that he learned how to be a good person by doing the opposite of everything his father and uncle did. And his mother was a good woman, just married to the wrong man. She was good to Billy. He took after her side of the family, slighter in stature, gentler, and he loved books. His father thought Billy was worthless, but Darryl? Darryl was his personal creation. He absorbed everything his father taught him. He bullied Billy when nobody better was around. Billy learned to stay out of his way and how to placate him if necessary."

Cassie wanted to know where Billy was now, but she knew that would come when Amber was ready.

"I'll spare you the love story." Amber's eyes filled with tears, and she swallowed hard. "It wasn't a simple high school romance. We saw everything that was missing from the rest of our lives in each other. We could talk about everything and did. With Billy I could dream about a real future, and so could he. We were good students. We saw college scholarships on the horizon, maybe not to top-tier universities, but somewhere away from our families. We were going to head there together, marry, earn whatever extra money we needed and then settle far away."

Obviously, nothing had worked out that way. Cassie lay her hand over Amber's and squeezed without saying anything.

Amber managed the ghost of a smile, and she didn't remove her hand. "One evening in the fall of our senior year, Darryl talked Billy into going to a convenience store where he claimed he was meeting a friend who could buy beer for them. Darryl graduated the year before, and he was working for his uncle doing nothing good. Billy called me. He said not giving Darryl a chance to pick a fight was his best choice. I was supposed to meet him for a late-night picnic so we worked out details. He promised he'd buy soft drinks and chips. The rest of what happened I've put together myself. When they got there, Darryl told Billy to wait in the car. Then he went inside and robbed the store. When the clerk resisted, he shot him."

She closed her eyes. "I don't know why he did it. Maybe he was bored. Maybe he was trying to prove something, or get Billy involved so he could hold it over him. Because instead of following Darryl's instructions, Billy went into the store to buy what we needed. He got there just in time to see Darryl in a ski mask holding a gun on the clerk. The clerk struggled and pulled off the mask, and Darryl killed him."

Cassie squeezed Amber's hand even harder.

"Darryl ran out and drove off without Billy. Billy didn't know what to do. He knew he couldn't go to his uncle. Either he wouldn't believe him or he'd bury the evidence. And Darryl was his brother. I've thought about this for so many years, Cassie. Why did he go home, knowing what he did, knowing what kind of man Darryl was? My best guess is that he was afraid I would show up at the house for the picnic, and Darryl might be there packing a bag. He didn't know where Darryl had gone, but I do know he thought Darryl would get out of town, and that would be the last anybody would ever see of him in Croville County."

Amber rose and began to pace along the front of the pool. "Billy got there and found Darryl on the porch, as if nothing had ever happened. Nobody else had witnessed the shooting or the robbery attempt. Darryl thought it was likely nobody would find the clerk until the shift changed in the early morning, and nothing would tie Darryl to his death."

She stopped in front of Cassie, arms folded. "And then Billy made his worst mistake. He was so shaken, and furious that Darryl had killed the clerk, he threatened him. He told Darryl he was going to turn him in and tell the sheriff in the next county what he'd seen. He knew his father and uncle would cover up the crime, and he had to report it somewhere else. When he turned away, Darryl shot him in the back. Then he dragged his body toward the woods beside their house."

"How do you know this? Billy didn't live to tell any of it."

"Billy was supposed to meet me at the creek where we were going to have our picnic. When he didn't show up, I walked to his house. I stayed out of sight in the woods, hoping to avoid anybody from his family. I heard the entire argument in enough detail I could piece together what had happened, and then I saw Darryl shoot him and start to drag his body away."

"Oh, Amber..." Cassie couldn't imagine.

"When I saw Darryl heading in my direction, I ran. He heard me, then I guess he saw me, because he started after me."

"He didn't catch you?"

She took a deep breath before she answered. "I managed to get away."

"You never told anybody what happened? What you saw?"

"My 4-H advisor, Betsy Garland, was like a mother to me. By then my own mother..." She shook her head. "Mom had moved in with some man from Morgantown, so Dad came back to take care of me. He came home some nights, left me cash for food. But that night he was out of town hauling logs. I knew our house was the first place Darryl would look for me. So I went to Betsy's. She was horrified, but she believed me. Right from the first word. She knew about Darryl, and she knew about me and Billy. She wanted me to go to the sheriff in the next county and tell him what I'd seen. I wanted to, but I didn't have proof. Not one bit. Somehow Billy's uncle would make Darryl's part in it go away, maybe pin the clerk's murder on Billy, maybe even Billy's murder on me. He'd call it a lover's quarrel. And I was a nobody. My own parents probably wouldn't stand up for me."

"She helped you leave town?"

"Betsy had friends all over. She called one in Northern Virginia and told her she needed a place for a young woman. That woman found me a job taking care of an older couple in her church. Betsy said I should stay there and think about what to do, that whatever I decided, she'd help. Then maybe with good legal representation, I could come back and safely tell what I knew. In the meantime, everyone thought that Billy and I had run off together to get married. Nobody was looking for us."

Amber sat again and leaned against the back of the love seat cushions.

Cassie faced her. "I'm guessing you didn't go back."

"A month later I realized I was pregnant. Billy was gone, but I was carrying a baby. I knew then that I would have to spend the rest of my days protecting my child from Darryl. It was no longer just about me. I knew what would happen if he found us. That's what I've done."

Cassie was still trying to absorb the story. "At the beginning you said the time had come for me to know so I could make a choice. Do you have reason to believe Darryl knows where you are now?"

She listened wide-eyed as Amber told her about Betsy's accident and the photo stolen from the Bible. She waited until Amber finished. "So you think he was the one who injured Betsy?"

"I think it's likely. If he didn't know I had a son before, now he does. And Darryl might assume, being the man he is, that my son will make it his mission to find and destroy him someday. So even if he'd more or less given up on finding me after all these years, now he'll double down. Starting with going after Betsy to keep her from telling anybody what she knows. She's promised to stay with friends out of town once she's out of rehab."

Cassie slipped her arm over Amber's shoulder and nudged her closer. "Try to make a guess, Amber. What are the chances this psychopath can track you down? What could he tell from the photo?"

"Billy and Darryl were only ten months apart, and except for size they could have been twins. Will looks like a Hawken through and through. If he ever finds him, Darryl will know who Will is, even if the photo is more than two years old."

"And you?"

"Darryl knew me as the Goth girl. In the stolen photo my hair was light, but most of it was covered by a ball cap. We were in the North Carolina mountains. I really don't know what he could figure out from that."

"So he knows you've changed the way you look, which I'm sure he figured you would do even without the photo, and he knows you and Billy had a son. Has anything happened here in town to make you suspicious he's closing in?"

"Not yet. I promise until now, I was as secure as I've ever been that Darryl wouldn't find us here in Florida. I've been planning to move on again, but Will's doing so well in school here. I didn't want to drag him away."

"Just Will? You're happy here, too."

"Don't make this harder."

"You've made a family for yourself. With me and Savannah, at Yiayia's and with Travis. You want to stay, and we want you to."

"I'm putting you in danger."

"Probably not. You've always managed to cover your tracks. Have you done anything you shouldn't have?"

"Other than trust Betsy to destroy that photo? No."

Cassie didn't have to think about what came next. "Isn't it time to end all this? Let's go to Nick and tell him what you've told me. He'll be sure you're protected, and he can look into all those events in the past without alerting Darryl. A man like that must have made a million enemies along the way. Nick can find out who they are—"

"You don't know Darryl! He'll find a way to hurt us, all of us now, including you and everyone else here. He'll blame me for Billy's disappearance and maybe even mysteriously discover Billy's body in the yard of my old house. Or down by the river where we used to meet. It's probably in one of those places, just waiting. There's no way to prove Darryl killed anybody, just like there's no way to prove he was be-hind Betsy's hit-and-run."

"But this guy's out there, and he must be hurting other people the way he hurt you. Look what he's done to your life. Don't you have to try to stop him?"

Amber pulled away and faced her. "The way you have to stop Ivy?"

Cassie had trapped herself. Both of them knew what needed to be done, and both of them had so many reasons not to do it. Starting with their children.

She heard the garage door lifting and the toot of a horn. Those same children had come home.

"Don't you dare pack and leave," Cassie said, getting up to greet them. "We'll figure this out together. Promise me."

Amber stood, too. "I can't promise."

"But you'll try?"

"I don't want to leave. Is that good enough?"

"Say you'll at least talk to Travis if you won't talk to Nick."

"No." She paused. "But I won't leave without telling you first."

"We'll be safe. We'll come up with some way to make sure of it."

"Let's go hug our kids." Amber started into the house, and Cassie followed. But even Savannah's hug, even hearing herself called Mom once again when Savannah greeted her, couldn't erase Amber's story.

Or the fear that she hadn't yet heard the ending.

44

ON SATURDAY AFTERNOON, HALFWAY DOWN A winding dirt road dotted with rusting mobile homes, vegetable stands and a wildflower nursery, Cassie wondered how many wrong turns she'd made. She was meeting Nick at a clearing by the river, and she thought she'd followed his instructions. Just as she was looking for a place to turn around, she spotted cars and an equipment trailer. She parked and walked down to the shore, where four men in red-and-black scuba dry suits were just coming out of the water as others in swim trunks and shirts watched.

One of the dry suited men was Nick.

He removed his other gear and mask, then lifted his hand in a wave when he saw her. She waited until he conferred with his colleagues. Then, as she watched, he stripped down and lay everything to one side on a tarp. She was used to divers. She'd grown up around them, but now the mystery of what was worn under a dry suit was answered.

Shorts and a T-shirt. She told herself she was not disappointed.

She found a fallen log with no visible insect life and perched there as he and the others cleaned and stored their equipment in the trailer. Finally Nick slipped on sandals and walked over to join her. His hair was barely damp, but his cheeks were flushed and his dark eyes shining. He obviously loved this part of his job.

"A training exercise?" she asked.

He hesitated, as if wondering how she would react. "Rescuing a dummy from a sunken car."

Cassie was glad there were people like Nick willing to take these risks. "A real car?"

"Some bozo drove a stolen jalopy into the water last year after a drunken joy ride. The owner gave it to us for training, since that was cheaper than having it hauled out and away. We use it a lot."

"What happened to the bozo?"

"Unfortunately he was the real-life dummy we had to pull out of the car more than an hour after he went down." He was silent a moment before he offered her a smile. "You doing okay? I couldn't tell from our phone call."

"I don't want to take you away. You're busy."

"Done for the day." He looked at his watch, and she thought it must be a good one since he'd worn it into the water. "There's a little bait shop just up the road."

She remembered passing it. "Are we going fishing?"

"They sell sandwiches and have tables under the trees. I'll meet you as soon as I wrap up here."

By the time he joined her, she'd already bought them both coffee and sandwiches and settled at the cleanest table of three. He thanked her and took the seat across from hers.

"So did you get there in time to save Mr. Dummy's life?" she asked.

"In real life it would depend on how fast we showed up and

air pockets in the car. But if we'd seen him go down, maybe. Rescue is the best part of the job when it goes well and the worst when it doesn't." He changed the subject. "How's your job search going?"

Cassie told him about the offer she'd received that morning from the real estate office. "Fetching coffee and answering phones isn't beneath me, but I realized the job wasn't going to lead anywhere. I might go back to school instead if I can afford to."

"Would you do that here?"

"They have classes locally that would help me update my skills. But right now…" She needed to end the small talk. She hoped someday she and Nick could sit somewhere nicer and just spend a whole evening talking about themselves and everything they'd been through. They were friends, old friends, who understood each other from the inside out, but now was not the time.

"So, what do you need from me?" he asked.

"Someday when I can put the past behind me, will you let me take you out to dinner? I need to thank you for being such a good friend."

"Well, yeah. I'm only doing this for future surf and turf."

"Were you this nice in high school?"

"Maturity works in both our favors."

She moved on. "Drink your coffee before it gets any colder, and I'll tell you what I've learned."

She told him what Amber had found and then about her trip to New York. She ended with the discovery of Mark's addiction.

"Opioids changed the world," he said, showing no surprise. "I'm sorry. I've seen more lives destroyed than there are hours to tell you about them. You're sure what you learned is true?"

Her cup was empty, but she wrapped her hands around it

anyway. "It's like I was handed a key and suddenly everything opened up. Before I left, I confronted Ivy, the nurse Mark paid off to the tune of thirty thousand dollars. Maybe for drugs? Maybe to keep her from telling me or his colleagues what was going on? I don't know which. Probably both. Ivy's the one who sent me the letters you have."

"Did you consider just turning her in and letting the guys with badges and guns do the questioning?"

"I needed to be sure. I went to her apartment and confronted her. The good news is that she's been fired. At least she lost her access to the supply closet."

"And you think that will stop her from doing the same thing somewhere else?"

"No, but she wasn't alone in enabling him. The doctors in Mark's practice let him resign without notifying the medical board. They really don't want anything to blow back on them."

Nick unwrapped his sandwich. "Did you call me just to let me know the upshot? Or is there more?"

"I honestly don't know."

He finished half the sandwich before he spoke again. "So do you think your husband was paying for that apartment? Is that where all your family's money went?"

She liked the way he hadn't called it "Mark's" money. "Family" went right to the heart of everything, because Mark's actions had affected all of them. "I wouldn't be surprised if more of our money went to Ivy, but I don't think she was the whole deal. The apartment? I'd guess Mark wasn't her first rodeo. She's probably been cashing in on the opioid epidemic for a while."

"And will continue. Why not?"

"I'd like to stop her."

Nick nodded but didn't say anything.

She was glad he was letting her feel her way through this. "I'd like to turn her in, but I want to do it without dragging Mark's name into it. Maybe report her anonymously? Get the ball rolling and then bow out."

"Why?"

That seemed obvious. "I don't want Savannah to know her father was addicted, that almost every cent we saved for retirement is gone. She doesn't need anything else weighing her down."

"Nothing heavier than secrets."

Cassie didn't know what to say. Nick finished his sandwich and then sat back with the rest of his coffee. "If you really want to know, I can probably tell you what an anonymous call will accomplish. Eventually somebody in authority might do a cursory check, if nothing else more important is happening— and something always is. But let's pretend somebody from the narcotics unit spends some time looking into the tip. Maybe they even drop by the hospital where Ivy worked. They ask around. Nobody wants to go on record, and Ivy's not employed there anymore. So everyone shrugs. And that's it. Because you haven't given them real evidence and leads. 'Ivy's been a bad girl' just isn't enough to help them move forward. They go back to their big drug busts, their tried-and-true informers, and somebody files your tip where it will never be seen again. You give them nothing to go on, you get nothing in return."

"Then there's no point?"

"I didn't say that. I said there's probably very little point in doing it the way you're thinking. There's a much better point in giving the NYPD and the medical board everything you know, including the names of the doctors in your husband's practice and the way they chose not to report what they didn't want to face. Will it result in arrests or citations?" He answered his own question with a lift of his shoulders. "It depends on how good or how busy the investigators are. But there's a much better chance that in the end, Ivy won't be hawking drugs to addicted patients or other medical personnel once the investigation concludes. And with really good luck, she'll face charges. I don't know what a medical board in New York might do to your husband's colleagues, but you can bet that at minimum, a few reputations will be damaged."

"I never wanted to be a crusader."

"I don't think anybody wakes up one morning and decides that crusading is what they want to do for a living, Cassie. They just decide they can't shut their eyes to whatever is all around them."

"I have a lot to think about, don't I?"

He reached across the table and covered her hand with his. "Only you know what you can do. You're the one to measure the consequences for everybody involved. Whatever you do, I won't think less of you."

She turned her hand palm up and threaded her fingers through his, just for a moment. It helped.

Amber and Will left early for the Kouzina. As she was following Will out the door, Amber spotted Cassie and turned back.

"I forgot to tell you, but I worked on the records while you were gone. I found something confusing, but it can wait. Just set some time aside tomorrow afternoon to help me figure it out. And you got something from the IRS. Probably Mark's tax returns."

"Planning to be back late?"

"I think we'll stay for the Saturday feast if Will wants to. Why don't you and Savannah join us?"

Cassie had less festive plans. "Thanks, we'll see."

Savannah had dragged herself back home after catching up with Helia and Minh, and now Cassie peeked in the den and found her sleeping off the time change in front of the television. When it was almost nine o'clock, she pulled leftovers from the fridge and warmed up some shrimp in the microwave before she woke her.

A few minutes later and midyawn Savannah flopped down at the table. "I'm surprised Will left any." She had brushed her hair and coiled it on top of her head with rhinestone hairpins. She looked fresh and pretty, more innocent than she would be at the end of their conversation.

"I made a ton, hoping he couldn't finish it," Cassie said.

"He was eyeing the leftovers earlier, but he said he was going to save his appetite for whatever they serve tonight after hours."

Cassie dished up her plate, although she wasn't sure she'd be able to eat anything with what lay ahead. "They've been doing Saturday-night feasts there for years. When I was a little girl, if I was staying with my grandparents for the weekend, Pappou would take me to the Kouzina on Saturday nights, and they'd have a plate ready for me in the kitchen. There was so much laughter. A lot of the conversation was in Greek—probably everything they didn't want me to know. Those were some of the best memories of my childhood."

"Your parents didn't mind?"

The question pointed out their new relationship. Savannah wanted to know more about "her" family now, as if she finally realized the way she fit. The question was also the perfect lead-in for what Cassie needed to tell her.

She scooped food on her plate and watched Savannah do the same. "Both my parents were alcoholics. Some of the time, to be honest, they didn't know where I was. But the larger family made sure I was taken care of. I owe them a lot."

"That's why you don't drink. Right?"

"It's probably an overreaction, but it's my way of establishing a boundary between who they were and who I am. And it's no sacrifice since I never began. But addiction is a terrible thing." She was feeling her way now. "When I was small, my parents, especially my mother, managed their lives most of the time. They were very young when I was born. I think my father hoped to travel and see the world, and instead he was saddled with a baby and a wife he probably wouldn't have married otherwise. Yiayia says he was a charming little boy who gradually changed into the bitter, angry man I remember."

"Do you blame yourself? I mean for being born?"

It was a surprisingly mature, insightful question. Savannah was definitely Mark's daughter.

"I probably did when I was too young to understand. Once I left home, I saw the way addiction latches on to someone and makes it impossible for their better nature to shine through. Which is not to say my father couldn't have changed. He could have. But for him, blaming others became a way of life. That would have been as hard to give up as alcohol."

"That's awful."

"It's not always like that, though. Some people struggle hard to overcome whatever has hold of them, and they still can't shake it loose. No matter how hard they try."

"You don't think they're just weak?"

"We can't know what it feels like to need something as badly as my dad and mom needed to drink."

"Helia's brother had to go into treatment. Drugs and alcohol. But he's out now. He has a job, and next year he's going to start taking college classes. Her foster parents are letting him fix up a little apartment over their garage, so he can move in and not pay rent while he goes to school."

Cassie was thankful for people like Helia's foster parents.

"I bet he'd be the first to tell you it's going to be a hard road back. The temptation is always there to relapse, because once you know something can take you away from your problems or pain, you always want to do it again. Whether it's alcohol, gambling, food...drugs."

"This is kind of a depressing subject."

Savannah was ready to move on and now Cassie had to. "I'm afraid we're talking about it for a reason."

Savannah looked up. "You don't have to worry about me. I've, you know, smoked weed. But I didn't like it."

"Savannah..."

"Mo-om." Savannah grinned. "Concentrate on my last sentence. I didn't like it."

"Don't develop a taste, okay?" Cassie had smiled, too, but now she sobered. "Look, I have something else to tell you, and it's not going to be easy. You and I have had some serious problems here, and I think they've been compounded by not coming clean with each other. We've talked about the Pfeiffer problem, and you've been up-front about why the weekend of the field trip is still off-limits. So I think we're squared up there. But I have something to tell you, and I know it will make you unhappy. If there was some good way to keep it from you, I probably would. Only it's time we faced things, head-on, and dealt with them. Together."

Savannah looked troubled. "Are we leaving Tarpon Springs?"

"No. We're here for the long haul."

Cassie took a deep breath, still wondering if she was making a mistake but unable to think of a way to stay silent. "Secrets in families almost always come out. That's one of the big dangers of keeping them. Even if they don't come out for a long time, they corrode relationships. And there was a secret in our family, one I've just learned. I should have known sooner, but I closed my eyes to it. It's about your dad."

Savannah pushed her plate away. "You're scaring me."

"I know. But I want to prepare you a little."

"Is this about the fight you had before Dad died?"

Cassie knew there was no going back now, that this conversation was inevitable. "The fight you overheard was about money. I had just discovered that your dad emptied and closed our savings account. He didn't expect me to find out because he handled our finances. That afternoon he was very upset that I wanted to know what happened to the money."

"Did he tell you?"

Cassie wondered again how she could have allowed Mark to walk out the door that day without giving her an answer. "It turned out to be worse than that." She explained about the investment account. "So far I don't know where all that money went, either. But I do know where some went. And that's the hard part, Savannah."

Savannah backed up. "Our money's all gone?"

"I still had his life insurance. That's how we bought this house."

"What about our condo? You sold that and made money, right?"

Cassie explained about the extra fees. "This is very hard to understand, I know. And it's hard to believe. But the next part is the worst."

Savannah looked as if she wanted to put her hands over her ears, but after a moment she sat up straighter. "Just tell me."

"I talked to Valerie in New York. She finally leveled about why your dad left the practice. Remember when he injured his back?" She waited for Savannah to nod, and then slowly she let the story of Mark's addiction unfold, trying to stress how hard it was to control and how easy to get his prescriptions refilled.

Because Savannah remained silent, her face growing pale, Cassie moved on to Mark's final days. "He went into rehab secretly for a while, but in the end, it didn't work. He was addicted, and a lot of what we saw at the end of his life, the irritation, the lack of interest in us and what we were doing? That's what caused it. He was making mistakes at work, and he was also paying a nurse at Riverbend to get drugs for him."

Savannah stared at her. "Drugs? He spent all our money on drugs?"

Cassie explained how she'd learned about Ivy's involvement. "Amber's helping me look through our financial records. But the money that went to Ivy was a small part of what's gone. I don't know if we'll ever know what happened to the rest of it." She didn't mention the possibility of blackmail, since Savannah already had enough to handle.

She waited for her daughter to speak, but when she didn't, she finished. "I'm telling you not just because I want you to know what your dad was going through, but because I need your permission for something. I want to report what happened to the New York police. There needs to be an investigation. Ivy has to be stopped because she's going to continue stealing drugs from hospitals and selling them. And I want to go to the medical board and report what went on at Church Street. Your dad's colleagues should have turned him over to people who could help. If they had, things might have turned out differently. I don't think they should get away with it, but I don't want the consequences for you to be so terrible you can't live with them."

Savannah rested her head in her hands. "I can't believe this. He was a doctor. He should have known!"

"As strong and smart as he was, the drugs got hold of him and wouldn't let go."

"You want me to decide what to do? Really?" Savannah lifted her head so she could see Cassie's expression. Her eyes filled with tears. "That's why you told me?"

"I want to go to the police, but I'm not going to do it if you don't want me to. I don't know what will come out if they start an investigation. It's possible nobody here will ever know. But you've been through enough, and I'm not going to add to it without your permission."

Savannah didn't answer.

"It's a lot to think about," Cassie said. "You don't have to decide right away. Let everything settle. But I wanted you to know that nothing you did caused the changes we saw. Your dad hid his addiction because he was trying to protect us."

"He shouldn't have hidden it."

"And that's why I decided I couldn't hide it. Because this secret has caused enough damage." Cassie wondered if she should get up and leave Savannah alone, but Savannah stretched out her hand and suddenly she was crying. Cassie circled the table to hold her close.

"If he'd just told us!" Savannah said at last. "Maybe he promised somebody he wouldn't tell."

That seemed odd to Cassie, but Savannah went on. "If he did, he shouldn't have."

"I'm not sure what you mean."

Savannah pulled away and grabbed a napkin from the holder on the table to wipe her eyes. "Sometimes people promise other people they'll keep a secret, even when they know it's a bad idea."

"I can't imagine who he would have promised."

"It works that way sometimes. You tell somebody you'll keep something to yourself, but you know you shouldn't."

Cassie sat back. Somehow, they were no longer talking about Mark, and whatever they *were* talking about was so important Savannah needed desperately to tell her, despite the revelations she'd just heard.

"You have something you want to tell me, don't you?"

Savannah looked miserable. She didn't move, didn't speak while Cassie waited. Finally she shook her head, but she met Cassie's eyes. "It's not about Dad. Not my dad. It's…"

"Not *your* dad?"

"Will's dad. And it's about lies, and not telling somebody who you love what's going on!"

For a moment Cassie couldn't breathe. When she could, her words came out in a rush. "I think you need to tell me anyway, sweetheart. Because now we both know how dangerous secrets can be." She decided to go on. "And this one could be very dangerous. I need to know."

Savannah began. "It's all my fault. I didn't think it was fair that Will didn't know who his father was."

Cassie listened as she told her story, but as Savannah explained about the trip to Georgia, and later the DNA test, and finally that Will's uncle Darryl had contacted him and Will was tempted to see him, Cassie felt like someone had slugged her in the chest.

"Has Will talked to him? Has he told this man where he lives?"

"He says he hasn't. He used a fake name, and he told his uncle he lives in Georgia, in Blayney where we went to look for Roger Hart. He figured that would be safe."

"This is not my secret to keep or tell. Amber will have to do that. But I can tell you that Will's uncle must never, *never* know where he lives."

"How was Will supposed to know that? Amber kept everything about his father a secret. Didn't she understand how messed up that was? That someday he would go looking on his own?"

"She was wrong, but she was protecting him."

"The way my father was protecting us?"

"Different story, same terrible mistake." Cassie got to her feet. "I have to tell Amber. She's got to know."

"Will's going to kill me for telling you."

"You did exactly the right thing. You may have averted a disaster. I have to go now, but you stay here. Lock every single door and don't answer if anybody knocks."

"But he doesn't know where Will lives!"

"Savannah, the man is a sheriff. He has untold access to information. We have to be sure Amber and Will are protected."

"They're going to leave, aren't they? Slip away and never come back."

"I don't know." But Cassie was afraid that slipping away might be the best solution. Because the alternative, that Darryl Hawken discovered where Amber and Will lived and came to find them, was terrifying to consider.

45

AMBER'S FATHER ALWAYS SAID CONFESSION WAS
good for the soul but bad for the reputation. He'd been wrong.
Tonight, after her talk with Cassie, her soul felt bruised, and
if she had a reputation, it was for being someone no one could
count on for the long haul. That wasn't going to change.

Recounting the horror of the night Billy was murdered
hadn't lessened her burden. She hadn't told the whole story,
and in addition confession hadn't made her feel safer. Darryl
Hawken was a county sheriff, and she was an itinerant wait-
ress. Which of them would anyone in authority believe?

Roxanne stepped into Amber's path and waved her hand
at the far wall of the dining room. "We're supposed to finish
adding up the night's totals, but you've been staring at that
mural like you're trying to transport yourself to Santorini."

Amber couldn't manage a smile. "I was connecting the
grease spots in my head to see if there was a hidden message."

"The only message you'll find is that we need new decor.
Tonight I'd be especially pleased with a real computer system
instead of these two antique registers we're tackling."

"At least we don't need a new cook. Tonight the food was perfect." Amber lowered her voice. "Buck was gone, and Yiayia left you alone in the kitchen for most of the evening?"

"She went off for a little while." Now Roxanne lowered her voice. "I think she was with Buck."

"So that's heating up?"

"Well, he hasn't left for Greece. He's dragging his feet. Mama said she's helping him shop for presents to take to his family."

"On a Saturday evening?"

"She won't admit it, but she's worried. He told her he's getting too old to work so hard. I think she's afraid he's not coming back." Roxanne fluttered her eyelashes. "Unrequited love."

"Maybe she changed her mind, and she's encouraging him."

"We can only hope."

Now Yiayia was back in the kitchen working on tonight's feast. She was at her best when food leaped out of the refrigerator, ready to be eaten. By the time she assembled, combined, reworked and heated, there was usually so much to choose from that the staff had leftovers to take home.

Amber would miss the feasts and everyone at the Kouzina. Leaving Cassie and Savannah would be harder than it had been to abandon her own family. And Travis? She'd known there was no hope for a long-term relationship, and she'd made certain to remind herself every time they were together. Unfortunately the reminder had been as hollow as an echo. She was well on the way to falling in love with him.

None of it mattered, because she and Will had to move on. As she'd recounted her story, she had realized she couldn't stay any longer without putting the lives of her friends in jeopardy.

Roxanne cocked her head. "You hear something?"

The front door was locked, but when they turned to look

Travis was at the plate glass window overlooking Dodecanese Boulevard. He tapped again to get their attention.

"Well, looky who's come calling," Roxanne said. "I think I'll let you get that. I'll just need you to verify when I'm done at the register stand. Then we'll lock the cash away until Nick gets here."

They had already cleared the cash register at the bar, and Roxanne would leave the smallest bills in the one by the office for Tuesday, when they reopened. The two women had already counted and added up the credit card receipts, but Roxanne would do a recount, just to be sure.

She went to let Travis inside. He had told her he was coming, but she'd assumed he would enter through the kitchen, where Will was helping Yiayia.

"No parking left in the alley and there's a car blocking the back entrance. I parked down the street." He kissed her quickly before he stepped inside.

"Nothing stands between you and a good dinner."

"Dinner was the other reason I came. You were the first."

Amber made sure Roxanne couldn't hear. "You mean you haven't already eaten your way through Tarpon Springs tonight?"

"No, but tomorrow night you and I celebrate. You're looking at the *Sentry*'s new full-time food critic."

"Hey!" They kissed again and Amber stepped back. "That's wonderful. You're glad?"

"I'll be doing a fair amount of traveling, but this will be home base. I can't imagine a job I would love more."

Amber was delighted. She'd expected him to get the job, but it was nice to have it confirmed. "Just don't mention it to Yiayia."

"It won't be that long before people figure out I'm Dallas Johnson."

"You'd better give her a good review before they do."

"She'd better give me a reason to."

They moved away from the door, and Amber locked it behind them. "I have to help Roxanne. You can make yourself comfortable out here or go lend a hand in the kitchen."

"I'll see what Yiayia's up to."

"Will's there with her now. Buck's probably coming later, maybe Cassie and Savannah. Nick Andino shows up sometimes before he takes our receipts to the bank. Other staff wander in."

"Maybe we can sneak out when it gets packed?"

"We'll see, but I have to go home tonight."

"Eventually."

Just for a moment she wondered what would happen if she told him what she had told Cassie. But Travis would be certain he could help, and Amber knew better. She remembered stories Billy had told about his brother. Darryl had routinely tormented, even tortured anything or anyone smaller or younger than he was, and his father and uncle had never discouraged him. She'd seen him at his worst. He had learned his lessons well.

Travis pushed through the swinging traffic doors to the kitchen, and Amber joined Roxanne to finish the receipts. They were just about to gather and lock everything in the safe in Yiayia's tiny office when Amber heard more tapping on the window. Darkness had fallen, but under the front lights she saw that this time the visitor was Cassie.

"What's with everybody tonight?" Roxanne said. "Nobody's using the back door?"

"Travis said the lot's full and a car's blocking the walkway."

"I'm not real fond of opening the front door when we've got the cash drawer open, too. Let her in quick. She tries to steal anything, I'll slam it shut."

Amber opened the door just wide enough so Cassie could enter. "Travis just got here. Savannah's not with you?"

Cassie grabbed her arm and held it, bumping the door closed with her hip. "Lock it fast."

Amber frowned but did, since that's what she'd intended anyway. "Are you okay?"

From across the room Roxanne looked up. "Something going on I should know?"

Cassie looked torn. "We need to talk privately," she told Amber as quietly as she could. "Right now." She crossed the room to her aunt. "Rox, I have to talk to Amber. Can you spare her a minute?"

"Sure, I have to mail a letter anyway. Let me lock up the night's receipts first."

Amber waited anxiously until finally the front door closed behind Roxanne. "You're scaring me," she told Cassie.

Cassie didn't waste time. "Listen, Savannah told me something you have to know about right now. Will has been in touch with Darryl Hawken."

Amber just stared at her, trying to take in the words. "That's impossible."

"Savannah gave him a DNA test kit for his birthday. When he got a list of people he's related to, Darryl was at the top, because he's Will's closest relative to be tested, his uncle. Darryl got his information and contacted him through the service. Will was smart enough to use a fake name, and he told him he was a foster kid in Georgia. But Darryl wants Will to meet him somewhere. And he's told Will that he's his father's brother."

Amber heard it all, every word, but for a moment she was unable to speak or breathe. Finally she repeated one word. "Uncle?"

"Yes, his uncle! Amber, this has to be the man who killed

Will's father. Billy's brother, who you've been running from all these years. The one you told me about!"

All the words that had jumbled in Amber's head were sorting themselves out now. "A DNA test?"

"He was anxious to find out who he really was, Amber."

"But I told him. I told him his father's name and—"

"He knows you were lying. The weekend of the field trip Savannah and Will went to the town in Georgia where Roger Hart was buried, even though she was the only one we caught. They figured out Hart couldn't really be Will's father."

"But he didn't tell me. Why wouldn't he confront me if that's true?"

"Because he loves you. He must have figured out that if you were lying it was important."

"He went behind my back and did this?"

Cassie touched her arm. "He couldn't do it any other way. And he tried to be careful. He's smart and he knew you had to have a reason to keep the past a secret. But from everything you've told me, lies may not be good enough with this man. He may find you anyway."

"We have to go somewhere else, start over again. We have to do it immediately."

Cassie looked as if she wanted to cry, but she didn't argue. "I'll give you every cent I can spare, Amber. What else can I do? I can talk to Savannah's mother, ask her to help. You can drive across country, and Gen will give you a place to stay until you find a job."

"You've done enough." Amber knew if she stayed connected with Cassie in any way now, even through Savannah's mother, Darryl would find them. She had to slip out silently, find a town large enough to hide in but not so large that she and Will would simply be empty crime statistics. She had to secure false papers, change their names, and she had to do it without help.

"I hate this!" Cassie said.

"I'm so sorry I've put you in danger. And you are, Cassie, because you and Savannah will be in his sights now, too. You have to come up with a story about why we left and spread it around. You have to stick to it. Tell people you were betrayed, that after everything you did for me, I just disappeared like an ungrateful con artist."

"Will is doing so well here. Are you going to tell him?"

"I should have told him before! This is my fault. But how do you tell a kid something like that? I thought I had time, that I could wait until he'd at least gotten out of high school."

"He's going to be in danger for the rest of his life, isn't he? How can you register him anywhere? Records are probably public for somebody like Darryl. You can't change Will's name and erase all the extraordinary classwork he's done. Please, go to Nick and tell him what's going on. He'll find a way to help you. If nothing else maybe he can put you in witness protection—"

"Don't you see? There has to be a crime to witness! And I can't prove there was. Especially not after all this time. People in Chaslan think Billy and I snuck off together to see the world. If I tell a different story, Darryl will brand me a liar and then a murderer. If he doesn't kill both of us first."

Amber squeezed Cassie's arm, and then dropped her hand. "I'll get Will and tell him there's an emergency. Then we're going home to pack. We'll be gone before morning. Please don't try to find us. If someday we're no longer in danger, I'll get in touch. But until that happens, if it ever does, you just have to let go."

"There has to be a way to help."

Amber started toward the swinging doors into the kitchen. "You have helped already. I'll always love you for it."

She didn't wait for a response, although she knew Cassie was right behind her. She pushed the doors and stopped so suddenly she could feel Cassie's warm breath against her neck.

"Run," she said softly.

"I wouldn't run," said the man with a bandanna covering most of his face and a stocking cap pulled low over his ears. He pointed a gun at both women, and then he swung it to one side where Will and Yiayia were plastered against a counter. "You run, either of you, and I'll take out these two so fast you'll never get to say goodbye."

46

FOR THE FOURTH TIME SINCE HER MOTHER HAD
bolted out of the house, Savannah tried Will's cell phone, but
he still wasn't answering. He'd probably left it in the pocket
of his jacket and it was hanging in the Kouzina's coatroom.

Or maybe he couldn't answer.

Will needed to know that very soon—and possibly
already—all their lies were going to blow back on them big-
time.

She banged her forehead against a great room wall until
she realized nothing could jump-start good sense. Will had
trusted her, and now she'd screwed that up, too. But Cassie
had acted as if Darryl Hawken was some sort of psychopath.
And after everything that had happened, Savannah wasn't sure
she could trust her own instincts. She'd been wrong so often,
she was no longer sure what right felt like.

She thought about calling Helia for a ride to the Kouzina.
Her friend didn't drive or have a car, but her brother did. Of
course, what if Will really was in danger? Wouldn't showing
up there put them in danger, too?

By now she was pacing, which was marginally better than banging her head. In the last days of his life, her father had paced the hallway of their apartment. Sometimes she had heard his footsteps as she was going to sleep. Why hadn't she stationed herself at one end of the hall and demanded he tell her what was wrong?

Why didn't she ever know what to do until it was too late?

She wished she could drive. The Mustang was parked in their garage, waiting patiently for her to take possession once she had her learner's license. Her father had taught her a little and Will had showed her a few things on their trip, but she'd never driven more than a hundred yards.

Tonight was a Saturday during tourist season. The streets would probably be crowded. If she made it unscathed to the Sponge Docks, she would have to park. She wasn't sure she could put the car in reverse.

She grabbed the key off the peg by the garage door anyway. The Mustang belonged to her, and so did the problem. There was only one way to find out if she could use one to solve the other.

By the time she backed out of the garage and onto their street, Savannah had learned a lot the hard way. The worst part was the clutch. The car jumped, the car stalled. On the street, she ran up on the curb and across the center line because she overcorrected. But somehow, she managed to stay in her lane once she was in a higher gear. The guard at their gate was surprised to see her behind the wheel.

"Just got your license?" he asked.

She pasted a big smile on her face. "Isn't it great?"

He looked skeptical, but he didn't ask to see proof. Proof probably wasn't in his job description.

A trip that should have taken less than ten minutes took

thirty, largely because she stalled every time she stopped. She figured Cassie was twenty minutes ahead of her, and by now it was probably too late to warn Will. But at least she could stand with him and take the heat.

By the time she took the final turn onto Dodecanese, she was sweating, despite temperatures in the low sixties. The good news was that she was still alive and the car relatively undamaged if she didn't count the front bumper, which she'd banged into a metal cabinet in the garage more than once trying to put the car in reverse. She was in no hurry to survey the damage.

As she slowed to a halt across from the Kouzina, she saw an empty spot at the curb. She thought she could nose into it, but she was pretty sure the rear half of the car was going to stick out. That didn't matter. She had to do what she could. If Will was still speaking to her, he could come out and park for her. Or somebody less angry.

When she opened her door, she realized just how far from the curb she was, but she slid out anyway and slammed her door, locking it with the key fob before she shoved it in the pocket of her jeans. When she turned toward the Kouzina, a uniformed police officer was standing about six feet away watching her.

For a moment, she was terrified this might be Will's uncle. Then she realized that a West Virginia sheriff wouldn't be wearing his state's uniform here, and this man was wearing the same one she'd seen on local police officers during the Epiphany celebration.

The cop looked to be about Cassie's age, tall but not thin, strong, like somebody who worked out. He had olive skin with penetrating brown eyes. He might be Greek. That gave her something to work with.

She forced a smile. "I'm sorry, Officer. The car stalled. I

was just going in there." She pointed to the Kouzina. "Yiayia is my mom's grandma. Somebody in there will help me."

He tilted his head an inch, as if he didn't believe her but wasn't quite ready to write a ticket. "Who's your mother?"

"Cassie Costas. Well, she's actually my stepmom, but in my life she's the real deal." She hoped that Cassie's notoriously combative father hadn't beaten up anyone in this man's family.

"You have a reason to be in there after hours?"

"I'm invited to the Saturday-night feast. It's a tradition. My mom's there now. Do you know her?"

"Why don't you show me your license." He held out his hand.

She put her own hands behind her back. "The thing is…"

"You left it at home."

"Not exactly."

"Explain *exactly*."

"I don't have a license." She could feel tears filling her eyes. "Look, it's an emergency, okay? I had to come. I had to see somebody who's in there. It couldn't wait. The car belongs to me, it's just that, well, I don't know how to drive it."

"And yet, here you are."

"Yes, but you can see I don't know how to park!"

He seemed to debate, then he shook his head. "Give me the keys and stay right where you are, Savannah. Exactly."

"You know my name?"

"I know your mother." He held out his hand. Savannah fished for the keys and put them in his palm.

"Stay right there."

She nodded. "I won't move."

"I bet you told your mother that earlier today."

"It's an emergency!" She watched as he expertly moved the car into the parking spot and turned off the engine. She wanted to dislike him. Cops and teenagers weren't exactly sworn enemies, but she'd heard enough to worry. Still, even though she clearly wasn't going to get away with anything, he was relaxed, almost as if he was struggling not to smile.

Back on the curb he pocketed the keys. "These go to Cassie. Let's find her."

"You don't have to come with me. I'll tell her."

"Save it. And besides, I was on my way in."

"You're going to the party?"

"Maybe." He didn't say more.

"Savannah!"

Savannah turned and saw Roxanne heading their way. "That's Roxanne," she said. "She's sort of my great-aunt."

"Nick." Roxanne came up. "What on earth is going on?"

"This young lady drove here without a license, and then left the car in the middle of the street where it would have caused an accident."

"I parked it." Savannah realized that arguing with a cop probably wasn't good strategy. "I tried to," she amended. "I don't drive in reverse very well. Roxanne, I have to get inside and talk to Will. Right away."

"What's with all the secrets tonight? Your mom and Amber practically kicked me out of the dining room. What's going on?"

Savannah didn't know what she could say, but Nick didn't hesitate. "When was that?"

"A while ago," Roxanne said. "Ten, fifteen minutes? I went to mail something and ran into a friend. I figured they needed privacy, so I took my time coming back."

Without moving closer, Nick peered inside. The lights were still on, but nobody was visible. "Where were they when you left?"

"In the front. Amber locked up after me. Now they're probably in the kitchen with everybody else."

"Who else is there?"

Roxanne ticked off names on her fingers. "Mama, Will, Amber—she's Will's mother—oh, and Travis. It's possible other people showed up while I was gone. Travis and Cassie had to park out here. He said the lot was full and some fool blocked the back entrance, right up to the door. So anyone else will be parking out here."

He turned to Savannah. "Is there any chance that whatever you came to tell Will might have to do with a dangerous situation?"

Savannah figured that from this point on, Will would never speak to her again. Now a cop was asking questions that would blow the whole identity thing wide-open, if it hadn't exploded already.

Roxanne stepped forward and clamped her hands on Savannah's shoulders. "The Andinos and the Costases go way back, and he takes the Kouzina's profits to the bank every week to help Yiayia. That's why you're here, right?" she asked Nick. After he nodded, she went on. "If something's going on in there that he needs to know, tell him right now."

"I should have stayed home."

"Too late for that," he said. "I'm going inside in a minute, and I need to know if I'm walking into a dangerous situation."

Roxanne dropped her hands, and Savannah blew out a long breath. "Will's been looking for his father. I helped him find an uncle who wants to meet him. His mom doesn't know, but I told my mom tonight. She said the uncle is really dangerous. So she left in a hurry to come here and tell Amber."

"What else about the uncle?"

"He's a sheriff somewhere or other. But Will didn't tell him anything that would lead him here, honest. He was careful. He used a fake name, a fake bio, a fake hometown."

"A fake town?"

She squirmed. "Well, it's a real town. Will and I were there a little while ago, looking for his father's family. But we didn't tell anybody where we were from or anything."

"You didn't show ID?"

She started to say no, then she remembered. "Only at the library, so we could look at microfilm. And…well, at the motor court where we spent the night. Will showed them his driver's license. I wasn't supposed to tell anybody this!"

He nodded. "You did the right thing."

"This is crazy," Roxanne said. "They're all probably in the back having a high old time. I happen to know Yiayia's planning to fry calamari. Can't you get Amber and Will off to one side and see if anybody's really in danger? Nothing good's happening out here, and I'm hungry."

"Nobody goes in until I check. I'm going around the back and in through the kitchen. You get in Savannah's car and roll up the windows. Or better yet, head away from here."

"Don't you, like, have to call for backup or something?" Savannah asked.

"Not unless I think there's a reason." He swept his hand toward the car. Then he took off down the block, walking fast. There was a narrow passage that cut between two businesses leading to the alley behind the restaurant. In a moment he disappeared.

"Get in the car," Roxanne said. "I'm going to see what I can find out. I can peek in the kitchen through the swinging door windows."

"I can't get in the car. He locked it and took the keys. Besides, I'm not going to let you risk your life."

"If I thought it was risky, I wouldn't go. But that's my mama in there and I'm not taking chances. Everybody can sort this out later on full stomachs." Roxanne waved down the block. "Stay in sight and don't go far. Just far enough."

Pulling keys from her purse, Roxanne opened the door. Savannah noticed she didn't lock it behind her. She probably wasn't taking a chance on being locked inside, just in case. Savannah didn't debate for long. She eased over to the porch that ran along the sidewalk and hid behind a column where she was least likely to be seen from inside. Then she peered into the room. The glass was lightly tinted and the glare from inside made it hard to make out much. Still, she didn't notice movement. Roxanne had already disappeared and was most likely in the kitchen.

She didn't hear anything, although she expected Roxanne to come out any moment and beckon her inside. Nothing happened.

Her choices were all bad. She could follow Roxanne's lead and try to peek through the doors into the kitchen, but that might not have turned out well. She could call the police and tell them there might be a robbery in progress, but what if they showed up with sirens blaring and started a terrible chain of events inside? Or what if they showed up and found nothing more sinister than bottles of cheap ouzo and empty plates of calamari?

She went with her final choice, slipping away from the windows to follow the path Nick had taken. Once in the back she could shelter behind the dumpster and see what was going on.

The space between buildings was dark, and she stumbled over a mound of cardboard boxes. Finally in the alley, she started toward the Kouzina, listening carefully as she crept closer. The lot behind the restaurant was crowded, and there was a car parked on the walkway blocking the back door. The driver had backed in, like someone who wanted to make a quick exit. As she edged around it, she recognized the Georgia license plate, like so many she'd seen on her trip with Will, complete with peach. That was suspicious enough. More suspicious was the man on the back steps with his gun drawn.

Nick.

He glanced at her, glared and motioned for her to get down. If everything was all right, he would have motioned her inside instead.

She knew better than to move closer. Nick might waste time trying to protect her. She couldn't go inside. She couldn't rescue her mother or anyone else. There was one thing she could do, though. She could make sure the suspicious car that Will's uncle had driven here was stuck right where it was for the foreseeable future.

She said a brief prayer of gratitude to a God who had sent Helia into her life, pulled one of the pins out of her hair and silently set to work.

47

TRAVIS STILL APPEARED TO BE BREATHING, EVEN though he was unconscious at Darryl's feet. Amber didn't know what had happened before she and Cassie were beckoned at gunpoint into the kitchen. She didn't see blood, and she hadn't heard shots—even though Darryl was holding a gun massive enough to easily kill everyone in the room. When she had tried to kneel and find a pulse, Darryl had kicked her away.

The bandanna and the stocking cap didn't fool her. Darryl had probably planned to pass off his presence at the Kouzina as a burglary. Only Amber would guess his identity, and he could quickly dispense with her. Most likely he already had an alibi. There would be cohorts in West Virginia schooled to say that he had been with them all night.

The kitchen smelled like smoke and hot grease. Cassie had steadied her after Darryl kicked her, and now Roxanne stood by the swinging doors, like a guard afraid someone else might try to enter.

"You," he said, pointing the gun in Amber's direction.

"I'm getting out of here, and I'm taking you and the boy." He swung the barrel of his gun toward Will. "As hostages."

"You don't need hostages," Cassie said. "Just leave. You—"

"Shut up!"

Roxanne finished Cassie's thought. "Get out while you can, mister. You haven't done anything yet, and nobody's going to catch you."

"I'm going to shoot everybody here if you open your mouth again!"

"Leave my mother," Will said. "I'll go with you. This is my fault."

"You shut up, too!"

Amber knew Darryl didn't want to kill anybody right there in the kitchen. He wanted to get rid of his two problems outside of town, where no one would find them.

"This is between you and me," she said. "Leave them out of it."

"You come over here."

She didn't move. "Nobody here knows you. We can settle things, but just us. You can tie up the others. It will be a long time before anybody finds them. We'll be gone."

She couldn't see his expression behind the bandit bandanna, but his eyes were shining, as if the whole scene was feeding something inside him, the same dark, twisted impulses that had made it easy for him to kill his brother.

He swung the gun toward Will. "Want me to shoot the boy? You think I won't? You don't think I'll kill this little bastard if you don't get over here, Heather? I killed his father for less."

There was a loud screech near the stove. Yiayia put her hands over her mouth.

"I'm not in the habit of killing old ladies." Darryl swung

the gun toward her. "But I will just the same if you make another sound."

Hands raised, Yiayia backed closer to the stove, and Amber realized that Darryl intended to kill all of them anyway. She doubted that multiple deaths had been his intention, but now everyone in the kitchen knew this was something far more personal than a robbery. Even fake alibi witnesses wouldn't save Darryl if anyone in the kitchen tonight lived to tell the tale.

Cassie had obviously reached the same conclusion. "More people are on their way here."

"Then we'll need to act fast, won't we?" He motioned with his gun toward Will. "Get your ass over here, boy, or I'll shoot your mother to hurry you along."

"You go, Willy," Yiayia said, giving him a little push. "Hold on tight to your mother."

Amber shook her head at Will, but he came anyway. "Just take me," he told Darryl.

Darryl moved closer to the stove to shove the boy toward Amber with the barrel of his gun. "Now you two put your arms around each other's waists, nice and cozy like. That's how I want you to go out the door together. Don't either of you try to run. I'll be right behind you, and even if I miss one of you, I'll shoot the one that's left behind."

Will fell against Amber, and she slipped her arm around his waist. "We're doing—"

Darryl took a step toward her. "Shut up!"

There was a loud clang from the stove, pan against metal. Yiayia, brandishing the industrial-size frying pan that had been heating on the front burner for the calamari, threw the contents at Darryl's head. He screeched and fell backward, directly on top of Travis, who had risen to a crouch. Travis grabbed for his legs to bring him down, but Darryl fired wildly as he tried to wipe the smoking grease from his eyes.

The back door flew open. Nick was silhouetted against the outside lights with his service weapon aimed straight at Darryl. "Drop the gun! Now."

Darryl, still pawing at his eyes, fired wildly again, and Nick flattened himself to the side of the doorway. Darryl stumbled past him, firing blindly as he went. Nick followed, but didn't shoot.

"Lock the door!" Yiayia shouted.

"Savannah!" Roxanne yelled. "Savannah's probably out there somewhere."

Amber grabbed Cassie, who leaped forward to go after Darryl. Travis stumbled to his feet, and Amber saw blood soaking through the side of his shirt.

She launched herself at him to catch him if he fell. "He shot you."

"Sure tried." He sounded shaky.

Outside they heard a man screaming obscenities, and another shot.

Then there was silence.

Everything had happened so quickly no one had managed to lock the door. Roxanne threw herself across the room to do it now, but it opened before she could get there.

Savannah stepped into the kitchen and closed it behind her. They heard sirens coming down the alley and saw the flash of lights.

"Nick's okay. The…" She paused as if she couldn't think of the right word. "The *other* guy's in handcuffs now. He was trying to leave." She turned her palms up.

"Travis…" Amber had to let go of her son, knowing he was all right, and lifted Travis's shirt. The bullet had grazed his side, and it was bleeding, but she thought maybe the bullet had kept going. She grabbed dish towels from the counter and wadded one against the wound.

The door opened, and Nick came in, along with a second cop, a woman who took in the scene, shaking her head.

"He needs to get to the hospital," Amber said, motioning toward Travis. "He was hit."

Travis looked embarrassed. "I'm going to be fine. It's already stopped bleeding."

Nick pointed to the chairs around the table. "EMTs are on the way. You sit, and we'll get someone to check you out. Anybody else hurt?"

"Mama threw hot grease at his head." Roxanne circled the crowd and went to Yiayia, making her show her hands. "With or without the calamari, Mama?"

"You think I'd waste fresh calamari?"

Roxanne gave a shaky laugh. "Nick, the EMT needs to look at her, too."

Yiayia scoffed. "I get worse burns every day I cook. All these years my hands are like leather."

Cassie grabbed Savannah and the two were hugging each other tight.

"Helia's a good friend to have in a situation like this one," Savannah said.

Cassie held her away, frowning. "Helia's out there? She brought you here?"

"Not exactly." Savannah paused, but then she sighed. "Nick will explain."

"*You* explain."

"I kind of drove myself. Then…well, when I realized what was happening in here, I kind of let the air out of that guy's tires."

"You did what?"

"Helia showed me how, but she doesn't do it anymore."

She looked over to Will, who was being hugged hard by his mother. "That guy? He's who I think he is?"

Amber answered instead. "That guy's name is Darryl Hawken. His brother, Billy, was Will's *father*." She thought of everything she would have to explain, all the years of running, of hiding, of giving up a normal life to keep herself and her son safe. She wondered how their lives would unfold now. If the law did its job, they would never have to hide from Darryl again, but she wondered if she would know how to live a normal life. In one place. With real friends. With Travis. With Cassie.

Most of all, she wondered if Billy could finally be put to rest.

"There's so much to tell you." She embraced Will again, and then she let him go. "But this is most important. Your father was nothing like his brother. He was a wonderful young man, and you are every bit Billy's son. He would be so proud of you."

"This is all my fault."

"No, it's mine," Savannah said, slipping her arm around Will's waist. "I'm the one who couldn't leave well enough alone."

Amber spoke for everyone else in the room. "There's only one person at fault. The one who is out there in police custody. And if there's any justice in the world, he'll never interfere in our lives again."

Finally back at home for the night, Cassie handed Amber a mug of herbal tea, since that was all the liquid comfort she had in the house. Savannah and Will were in Savannah's room, probably conferring about everything that had taken place.

"Travis is sleeping?" Cassie asked. They had given Travis painkillers at the emergency room, and afterward Will, who felt responsible for his injury, wouldn't let him go home. He had given Travis his bed and intended to sleep on the sofa in the sitting room tonight where Will could hear him if he woke and needed anything.

"The pills knocked him out. I'm going to sleep in the den."

"No, you sleep in my suite. My futon is great." Cassie flopped down on the sofa beside Amber. "Heather? Your real name?"

"Heather Parsons. I had to change it after Billy was killed."

"Amber suits you."

Amber sipped the tea, although her stomach was still tied in knots. "I've told Will enough to satisfy him, at least for tonight. I don't have photos or mementos to pass on, just memories. There's probably nothing left of Billy's back in Chaslan, except maybe school yearbook photos. We can call the library and high school to see if we can find those when things settle."

"His parents?"

"His mother died a few years after Billy did. His father's been gone awhile, too. I'm sure they thought Billy left town with me. According to Betsy, that was the story that went around. I'm sure his mother was so disappointed he didn't get in touch, just to tell her he was okay. His father may have suspected the truth or worse, he might have known. But he wouldn't have done anything about it."

"Everyone heard Darryl say he killed him."

Amber was silent a moment, remembering the full horror of the night it had happened.

"You okay?" Cassie asked.

"Nick says he's going to work with the authorities in West Virginia, hopefully get cadaver dogs out to the Hawken property to see what they can find. Maybe now that Darryl's safely in jail, somebody will come forward. His uncle's still alive, so maybe if the law goes after him, he'll save himself and tell them what they want to know. Loyalty's never been much of a prize in the Hawken family."

"I'm glad Travis is going to be fine. Yiayia told me that when he saw Darryl holding a gun on Will, he jumped him. They fought, and Darryl managed to hit him with the gun and knock him out," Cassie said.

"My hero."

"Everybody's."

Amber still couldn't find the strength to smile. "Do you know why Nick didn't fire at Darryl when he pushed past him?"

"Because Savannah was out there, where she wasn't supposed to be, of course. He was afraid he might hit her. Otherwise, I'm guessing Darryl would be dead. As it is, he wounded him once he tried to get in his car. Not that getting in would have done much good."

"With everything that was going on, Savannah still managed to let the air out of his tires."

"She's a natural for a life of crime. She told me how. Twist the cap off the valve stem, put something sharp into the hole, push. She used her hairpins."

"She gets all kinds of points for quick thinking under pressure."

"Do you know what happened before we got there?"

"Will told me. He was taking garbage out to the dumpster for Yiayia. Darryl was waiting in the dark beyond the lights at the back. He came out of nowhere and told Will he was his uncle, but Will had the good sense to realize he must have tracked him down for some other reason. He told Darryl he was going to go inside and get me—I think Darryl asked him to. But when he got close to the back door he took off. Darryl got inside before Will could lock the door. Apparently Darryl had hoped to grab us both and disappear."

"How did he trace Will to Tarpon Springs?"

"When the kids were in Georgia looking for Roger Hart's grave, Will had to hand over his license a couple of times. Nick thinks Darryl flew to Atlanta and rented a car because Will said he lived in the town of Blayney. Will had sent him a photo of himself in front of the Blayney library. So he probably showed it around and ended up with Will's address from his license."

"Both Will and Savannah were so sure they'd covered their tracks."

Amber couldn't stop thinking about the past. "And now you know why I had to run. He wanted to silence me in the worst way, and once he knew I had a son, he thought he was in twice as much danger. I'm not sure how I managed to stay ahead of him. Luck, some. A desire to live, more. And I had to do it without explaining the truth to Will."

Cassie covered her hand. "Will's been through a lot. He's going to feel guilty and angry at everybody for a while. He could probably use some help working through this."

"Spoken like the psychiatrist's wife. Help me find somebody good, okay? You'll know what to look for."

"You may need help, too, so you can put the whole story to rest."

"Nobody knows the whole story."

"Have you told enough of it to start healing?"

Amber wasn't sure. She felt her way, ready to stop if Cassie resisted. "There was something else. Something even Betsy doesn't know." She turned to see Cassie better and measure her expression. "How much do we have to tell, do you think, to find peace?"

"As much as feels right." Cassie squeezed her hand. "Are you asking if I want to hear the rest?"

"You may not want to."

"I do if you want to tell me."

"I never…" Amber drew a deep, shaky breath and her eyes filled with tears. "The night Darryl killed Billy…" She tried again. "You remember what I told you?"

Cassie nodded, as if she didn't want to interrupt.

"I told you I got away. And it's true. But…" She covered her mouth with her fist until she could speak again. "Not soon enough, Cassie. Darryl saw me when I tried to run, and then he grabbed me. It was clear he was going to kill me. But before he did…" She shuddered. "He was high on adrenaline, or maybe something worse. He had just killed his brother, but…"

"Oh, God," Cassie said, as if she knew what was coming.

Amber nodded. "He raped me." The words felt like acid in her throat. "Darryl left his gun by Billy's body, and afterward he couldn't reach it without letting go of me, so he tried to strangle me…" She paused until she could breathe again. "My hand closed on a rock on the ground, and when he moved enough, I brought it up and smashed the rock against his skull. He fell back and I managed to get up and run. I knew those woods. Billy and I used to meet there after dark. I still don't know how I did it, but I ran far enough before he was able to come after me, and I managed to escape."

"Oh, Amber." Cassie wiped tears from her cheeks.

"If Savannah hadn't gotten the 23andMe test kit for Will?" Amber shuddered again, and suddenly, she was crying, too. "If it weren't for that, Cassie, I would never know for sure whose son Will really is. When I discovered I was pregnant, I knew if the baby was Billy's, it was the only part of that sweet young man that was left. So I told myself Billy was Will's father. But there was always that question, deep down. Now finally it's been laid to rest."

The two women held each other and rocked silently back and forth.

Finally, Amber pulled away, wiping her eyes and cheeks. "I want Darryl to spend the rest of his life in prison without parole. A former sheriff won't be popular. Some of the other inmates might even be men he put there. If my word carries any weight, that's what I'll ask for."

"I hope the judge listens."

"I'll have to ask forgiveness every day of my life for the joy that would give me."

"Something tells me God will understand."

Amber managed a smile. "Maybe she will."

48

THREE WEEKS LATER CASSIE PARKED HER RENTAL
car in front of a small shingled cottage in Westfield, New
York, and peered at the numbers by the front door to be sure
she had the right address. The house was painted a soft cream,
the door a bright red. Brass numbers beside it were large
enough to show she had arrived at her destination.

Westfield was a historic small town with lovely old houses
along its main road and sweeping yards dotted with centuries-
old maples and oaks. At one time the town had been the head-
quarters of Welch's grape juice, and she'd glimpsed vineyards
and a processing plant on the trip from the airport.

A part of her wished the flight to Buffalo, and the long drive
here, complete with early April snow flurries, had just been
a wild-goose chase. But the cottage was real, exactly where
it was supposed to be, and now all Cassie had to do was walk
up the long sidewalk and find out why the woman who lived
here had shared a savings account with her husband.

As she locked the car door, she wasn't sure whether she
was grateful or sorry that Amber had discovered a record of

the joint account in Mark's files. Information was sketchy, a few notes jotted along the side of another statement, a letter from an unfamiliar bank that had refused to help when she and Amber dug deeper.

Mark's tax form from the previous year, plus some assistance from Cassie's New York attorney, had confirmed their suspicions. The money that was missing from Mark's other accounts had found a home in one he'd held with a stranger named Elana Lindquist, and because Lindquist was the joint account holder, the contents were not subject to probate.

Everyone who knew about this trip had warned Cassie not to come alone. Amber had wanted to accompany her. Travis had advised she hire a local investigator to meet her at the house. Nick had uncovered Lindquist's conviction for the criminal sale of a controlled substance and advised her to consult the local police. Cassie had listened, but she hadn't wanted to wait. She needed to know why her husband had ripped open their financial safety net and poured it into the arms of another woman.

She needed to put Mark and the chaos his death had caused behind her once and for all.

The steps up to the stoop were slippery, but she was wearing low boots with a thick tread. After months of flip-flops and sandals, the boots felt alien, a memento from another life. At the door she buttoned her wool jacket to ward off gusts of wind whipping down the narrow street. She didn't intend to stay long enough to take off the jacket inside.

If she made it inside.

She lifted her hand to the doorbell before she noticed the sign above it. A handwritten Post-it note taped in place asked visitors not to ring. She took a deep breath and knocked instead.

Nobody answered, but she thought she heard the television

or perhaps music playing inside. She knocked again, louder this time, and stepped back to wait.

Finally, a young woman opened the door. Cassie made a quick inventory. She was young, late twenties or early thirties, pretty but disheveled. Sandy blond hair held back by a knotted headband fell to her chin. She wore no makeup, but her flawless, rosy skin didn't need enhancing although her gray eyes sported dark circles. A shapeless sweatshirt fell over jeans that looked uncomfortably tight.

On the plane Cassie had silently auditioned ways to introduce herself to Elana Lindquist. In the end she chose the simplest. "I'm Cassie Costas. Mark Westmore was my husband."

The young woman looked stunned, but not as if she was surprised Mark's wife was standing on her doorstep, more as if Cassie's arrival had been anticipated for some day in the future. That and all her impressions were so fleeting Cassie didn't know if any of them were real.

"I guess you know who I am."

"I've come a long way, so I hope you're Elana Lindquist." Cassie pulled her coat tighter as another gust of wind tried to send her skidding across the porch.

"I am. I'm sorry, come in. I'm just… My manners are usually better." Elana moved to one side to let her in. "How did you find me?"

"From financial records more or less hidden in Mark's files. Nobody's invisible anymore. Were you trying to be?"

"I didn't know if you'd look."

"Surprise."

Elana led her into a tiny living room with just enough space for a blue sofa and dark coffee table, a chair and a modest television on a bookcase. Cassie got a glimpse of a galley kitchen and a den beyond that with a brick fireplace. Elana lifted a remote from the table, and the television went dark.

She motioned Cassie to the sofa. An old-fashioned granny square afghan was thrown carelessly over the back, and two cushions of the sofa fabric were piled at one end. She had been napping.

After Cassie sat, Elana stood over her. "Would you like hot tea? It doesn't feel like April."

"I don't think either of us wants to talk about the weather, do we?"

Without answering, Elana took a seat across from Cassie and silently folded her hands in her lap.

"Was Mark's death a shock for you?" Cassie asked.

"Yes. But I hadn't seen him for—" she shrugged "—months. Word got to me well after the fact."

"Then the bank didn't notify you? But I suppose why would they? Maybe they don't even know."

Elana shrugged again.

Cassie wanted to reach over and slap her shoulder. "I'm told the bank can't interfere with you keeping all the money that should have gone to Mark's daughter and me, although my attorney tells me I can take you to court." She didn't add he had also advised against it. A lawsuit was unlikely to yield anything except more bills, unless Elana was convicted of extortion.

"How much do you know?" Elana asked.

"Why? Do you want to embroider a pretty story to go with my facts?"

"I understand why you're angry."

"I really doubt you understand the full weight of it."

Elana looked away. "I don't want to embroider anything. I guess I was asking how much you knew or wanted to know."

"Hit me with your best shot."

Elana picked at a thread on the arm of the chair. "Mark was really good at hiding things."

"You, for instance."

Elana tried to find a way into the conversation. She started once, and then stopped. After another try, she managed a sentence. "Do you remember when he injured his back?"

Now Cassie realized where the hesitation had come from, and she was surprised Elana hadn't just paraded Mark's addiction in front of her. "I know he became addicted to painkillers, although I didn't know it at the time."

Elana let out a long breath. "Okay."

"Next are you going to tell me you were supplying him? Out of the goodness of your heart?"

"No!" Elana jumped up and began to pace. "It was nothing like that."

"Or nothing you'd want to admit to. You've sold drugs in the past."

Elana whirled. "I didn't even know Mark until we both landed at the Grandy Rayburn Center. The court sent me there after two years of using and selling to feed my habit. My last shot at redemption."

Cassie knew enough about drug rehabilitation to also know that treatment centers could still be a hotbed of drug abuse. "You used your time there to *help* other addicts?"

"Never, at least not the way you mean. Mark wasn't sent by the courts, the way I was. He told me somebody he worked with made him come or his addiction would be exposed to the world."

"As it should have been! The administration at Grandy Rayburn should have done it themselves."

"You're right. I'm sure they knew Mark's history and background, but Grandy is very loose, more or less experimental in their approach. They stress community, meditation, facing the worst parts of ourselves. They pride themselves on anonymity so we can start new lives. We were even encouraged to find nicknames that represented the person we wanted to be."

Cassie was trying to imagine Mark in a facility that sounded like a rehash of sixties encounter groups. "He was serving a sentence imposed by a colleague. I doubt he went to seek enlightenment."

Elana began to pace again, but slower. "Sometimes we get things we don't expect. None of the patients knew he was a psychiatrist. I'm not even sure the therapists did. He was never addressed that way. He was just Mark, and we had no idea if that was his real name or his new name. He was quieter than anyone else, and when he did speak, he tried to help other people gain insight. I could tell either he'd had a lot of therapy or was in one of the helping professions. Of course the group leaders always turned his comments back on him. Eventually he started talking about himself a little."

"Can we get to the part when he turned over our savings to you because you were enabling him?"

Elana sat, grabbing the pillow on the chair behind her and holding it in front like a shield. "Without drugs and with so much stored up denial, Mark finally fell apart. Unfortunately, it happened in the middle of the community, with everyone watching. Falling apart was common enough, but not for somebody like him. When he shattered, he didn't know how to pick up the pieces, something the rest of us had done a dozen times. I helped him back to his room that night. The staff should have, but I don't think they understood how profoundly devastated he was."

Cassie leaned forward. "They left other patients to pick up the pieces?"

"It's a place like any other. Some staff were outstanding, some mediocre, some well trained, some winging it. Mark and I had become friends. I didn't know anything about him except that he needed somebody to stay with him that night.

So I did. And…" She held the pillow tighter. "I held him, and then he held me and things got out of hand."

Cassie closed her eyes. She'd known that sex had to be part of the equation. Mark had fallen prey to Elana in a moment of weakness or maybe Elana had been the one to fall prey. Apparently Cassie herself was no judge where her husband was concerned.

And maybe it wasn't just a moment. Maybe there had been more. What she hoped was that Elana had instigated this, maybe waited until he was at his most vulnerable. And now?

She opened her eyes and focused on Elana's face. "So you blackmailed him with the affair. You knew a lot more about him than you've said. Maybe you even knew we had a daughter who would be horrified and ashamed. More money."

Tears were trailing down Elana's cheeks. "Of course that's what you would think. Anyone would. But that wasn't it. I never threatened him. I never tried to get anything from Mark. I really didn't know—"

A wail sounded from the other room, the unmistakable cry of a child, a young one, waking up. Cassie looked from Elana to the hallway beyond. She tried to find words, but they lodged in her throat.

"I'm so sorry." Elana was struggling to control her tears. "I'm so, so sorry."

And then Cassie knew.

Elana rose. "He's sick. I have to go to him. I think you should leave."

She hurried down the hall, and Cassie sat stunned. If she left now, could she forget what she'd heard? Move on and pretend this day had never happened? She knew the answer. After a moment she got up and followed.

The first bedroom off the short hallway was a nursery. A

child of about a year was standing in a crib, his arms outstretched, vocalizing. "Ma—ma—ma."

Elana felt the little boy's forehead and didn't like what she found. He was chubby cheeked, like his mother, but he had a mop of hair the same cocoa brown as Mark's and Savannah's. Even so young, his features were as asymmetrical as his father's.

He was the child she and Mark had never had together.

"Come here, pumpkin." Elana lifted the little boy in her arms and turned, but she pressed his head against her shoulder, as if to hide him from Cassie. "He has an ear infection, and the antibiotics haven't kicked in yet. You really should leave."

Cassie watched her rock the little boy in her arms. Then she turned and retreated into the living room.

Half an hour passed before Elana returned. Cassie had listened to wails, to crooned lullabies, to periods of quiet when the baby was being rocked and probably fed. But now, he seemed to be asleep again.

Elana took her chair again. "He's been up for two nights. He only sleeps in spurts."

"Mark's?"

She didn't nod, but the truth was written on her features. "About two months after I left Grandy, I had to face the fact I was pregnant. Mark was well and truly gone by then, of course. Neither of us had expected or anticipated I might get pregnant. After…that night he told me not to worry, that he was unable to father a child. Then he avoided me during the weeks before he left, even changed therapy groups, claiming he needed a different kind of leader. From that point on I'm guessing he probably faked his recovery. The drugs were out of his system. Grandy had nothing to hold over him, so they discharged him."

"Was that when you came after him for money?"

Elana's face was drained of color, and she spoke without

inflection, clearly exhausted. "A staff member let his name slip. When I found his bio online, I saw he was married and had a daughter. In the meantime I was fighting hard not to fall back in the gutter. My family was practicing tough love. My friends were tired of my struggles. Before addiction, I'd almost earned an associate degree in dental hygiene, so when they discharged me Grandy helped me find a job as a dental assistant. But I was hardly making enough to support myself, much less a baby."

"So you went to Mark."

"He was devastated."

Devastated herself, Cassie could still imagine how her husband had felt. In that final year of his life, mistakes had piled up, one on top of another. Suddenly his whole image of himself had shattered. Mark had discovered that he was, after all, only human.

"And then?" she asked after a long pause that neither of them wanted to fill.

"I didn't think I'd ever hear from him, and I wasn't up for a legal battle. I didn't know what to do. I considered not having the baby, but even then, I wanted to. I believed if I tried hard enough, I could get my act together and be the kind of mother a baby needs. Then a few days later Mark asked me to meet him."

Cassie had run out of questions. She waited.

"He told me…" Elana grabbed the same pillow. "He told me he could never be a father to our baby. He said you and his daughter meant everything to him. He begged me not to tell you. As if that was ever my intention." For the first time she sounded bitter.

"It wasn't?"

"I never, never would have gone to you. What happened the night our son was conceived was one friend comforting another. But when he said that, when I realized he actually believed I might tell you about the baby just to extort money? I realized we didn't know each other, except as victims of the same terrible disease. That one night and our illness were all we ever had in common."

"The money?" Cassie asked at last.

"He said he would give me a sum large enough to support his son if I promised never to contact him again. It was more than I'd expected, but I was crushed he wanted to buy me off. A part of me wanted to walk away, but pregnancy and pride are mutually exclusive. He opened an account in both our names. I was astounded at how much he put into it."

"Did he tell you where the money came from?"

"He said it was money he could earn back before he retired. The amount was more than enough to allow me to finish my training as a hygienist, and then take a job here and buy this little house. The rest is in savings for…my son. My job is part-time now, but I can go full-time in a few years when child care won't be so much of a problem."

Cassie wasn't sure what she was feeling, but in the jumble, truth was emerging. "Mark lost his job. He started using drugs again sometime after he left rehab, at least for a while."

Elana looked stricken. "Maybe knowing he fathered another child sent him back over the edge."

Cassie's own words surprised her. "We can't take responsibility that was his, neither of us should, or it'll sink us. I hope rehab worked better for you than it did for Mark?"

Elana looked surprised that Cassie had asked. She gestured toward the baby's room. "I have Jeremy. Falling apart isn't an option. Every day gets a little easier, and I've made friends here. I go to meetings regularly. My parents live in a suburb of Buffalo, and they're back in my life. They adore their grandson."

Cassie got to her feet. "I'm going to leave now."

Elana rose, blocking Cassie's path. "I don't know how to ask this."

"Go ahead and spit it out."

"Mark didn't live long enough to earn back what he gave me, did he? And the money he gave me was yours before he put it in my account."

Cassie had imagined every possible scenario for the visit, but never this one. "Why are you asking?"

"Sometimes reciting the twelve steps is the only thing that gets me through a day." Obviously, they were ingrained in her memory because she began to recite. "We made a list of all persons we had harmed and became willing to make amends to them all. We made direct amends to such people wherever possible, except when to do so would injure them or others." She paused. "I also have my son to consider."

Cassie felt something welling deep inside her. Not tears. Not admiration, but the ragged beginnings of understanding. For one brief moment in his life, Mark had allowed himself to face the flawed, imperfect man who had always lived inside him. That night, this woman had helped him survive the terror.

She didn't know what Elana had meant, and she wasn't sure Elana knew, either. But she met her gaze and didn't ask for an explanation. "There were no drugs in his system when they found his body, but I can't help wondering if he died by his own hand."

She had surprised Elana again. "Never. He would never have done that to you or your daughter. When he walked away from his son, he made it clear how much he loved you both. No matter what he was going through, how guilty and torn he felt, he would never have resolved anything with suicide."

They stood staring at each other, then finally Cassie moved

past her. She opened the door and turned for one more look. "Take care of that little boy."

"He's my life."

Cassie stepped outside and closed the door behind her.

Epilogue

CASSIE BECKONED TO ROXANNE, WHO WAS READY to haul one of the lighter loads to their new house. Her aunt had arrived with the sun, but the movers had arrived even earlier to take advantage of slightly cooler temperatures. Unfortunately, August in Tarpon Springs wasn't even cool at midnight, and Cassie hoped they could get the worst of the move finished by noon.

"Maybe Savannah's party wasn't such a bad thing after all," Cassie said as Roxanne came to stand beside her. "At least I don't have as much furniture to move."

The *new* house wasn't new to Roxanne. She had sold Cassie her cheerful little bungalow, and in turn, Cassie had sold this house in Sunset Vista to a young family who was moving in next week. Two weeks ago, at the end of July, Roxanne had moved into the newly renovated apartment above the Kouzina, the first of several planned renovations for the old building. She was now literally on top of things, exactly where she wanted to be. In May Yiayia had officially turned over the restaurant to Roxanne, right before leaving to visit family in Greece with Buck. The two senior citizens had chosen to travel on a cruise ship, and the last Cassie had heard, Yiayia was making a killing in the ship's casino.

In the months since Darryl Hawken's arrest, so many things had changed Cassie found it hard to keep up.

"Right," Roxanne said. "And if Savannah hadn't found that money and spent it, you wouldn't have met Amber. And if you hadn't met Amber—"

"Croville County, West Virginia, would still have its corrupt sheriff, and Amber and Will would still be running."

"Funny how things work out, isn't it? Mama, for one."

When the story of Yiayia flinging hot grease at a killer had hit the news, Yiayia had instantly become a local celebrity, leading kitchen tours and filling the Kouzina with customers for weeks afterward. Roxanne said her mother had just been waiting for the right finale, and since nothing like that would ever happen twice, once the excitement died down, she released her grip on the Kouzina and turned the business over to her daughter, giving Cassie part ownership, too.

Cassie signaled one of the movers, who was carrying a potted plant, and pointed toward her car. The young man nodded and changed course. "Are you looking forward to the rest of the Kouzina renovations?"

"It's going to be a mess, but I'll be right there to make sure my part's done right."

Next week the restaurant was closing until the end of October. Roxanne would get her open kitchen and enhanced storage, and Cassie her bright little shop and party room. Cassie's sale of the house in Sunset Vista had helped raise the cash for her portion of the renovations. She, Roxanne and Amber had worked with a local architect and builder, gotten necessary permits and were ready to begin.

"I'll be close enough to be there every day, too," Cassie said. "Savannah and Will can walk to school if needed."

"When the weather cools maybe. Be sure you take some time to settle in. The first week of renovation will be demolition."

"We're keeping most things the way they are at the house. Our furniture's not nearly as bright as yours, but we like the color on the walls. I emailed Savannah, and she and Will said to keep it the way it is."

Roxanne's house was going to work out well. All the bedrooms were tiny, but there were four. Everyone was looking forward to settling into their own space. Best of all, there was room off the back patio for a real garden and fruit trees. Cassie could hardly wait to get to the nursery.

"It's going to feel small," Roxanne warned.

"Not for long. Will's off to college in a year, and between us, I'm guessing Amber will move in with Travis once Will goes."

"You mean Dallas Johnson?"

As far as the Kouzina was concerned, the *Sun Sentry*'s new food critic had been redeemed, giving Roxanne's updated, innovative menu a happy shout-out in the paper two weeks ago. Afterward Travis had confided his real identity and promised that once the restaurant reopened in October, he planned an in-depth review. Travis had to be fair, but no one was worried, because so far Roxanne's innovations had only drawn raves.

Savannah and Will weren't yet back from their month in Africa, although they would be home tomorrow or the next day, depending on the first leg of their flight from Nairobi to Geneva, which had been rescheduled twice. Cassie had hoped they would be home in time to help turn the empty little bungalow into a home, but it didn't matter. Furniture could always be rearranged. She and Amber planned to wait before putting pictures on the walls and decorating. They still wanted the teenagers to feel they'd had a part in the move.

"I've got a full carload, so I'm heading out. See you over at your house." Roxanne raised a hand and headed for the curb where her Miata was parked.

A minute later Amber drove up and parked where Roxanne had been. She wasn't alone. Will jumped out of the passenger seat and Savannah emerged from the rear. In a moment Savannah was in Cassie's arms.

"We got an earlier flight! They just squeezed us on. We wanted to surprise you. We cleared customs and took a shuttle to Roxanne's, and Amber was there."

Cassie hugged her tight. "Wow, the best surprise ever!" She held her away a moment. Savannah was wearing a white cotton skirt that swirled at her calves, a pretty striped blouse and bright beaded bracelets on both arms.

Savannah held up her arms and the bracelets slid to her elbows. "I brought some home for you, Roxanne and my friends. Aren't they gorgeous?"

"And so are you! I love your hair."

Savannah's hair just touched her shoulders now and she lifted it in both hands. "It took too much time and water to wash it when it was long. We were so busy. But the whole thing was great. I'm going to be a doctor."

"Well, it's in the genes."

"But I'm going into public health. I want to work with communities to stop problems before they begin."

Cassie and Amber were keeping a mental list of all the things their children planned to be someday. Savannah's enthusiasm was a joy to watch. "Your dad would be proud," she said. "Does it feel strange to see everything being carried out?"

Savannah surveyed the house. "This never felt like home, did it? I hope it does for the new people. But we need a new start, and Roxanne's house has character. We're going to be happy there."

A month in Africa had been exactly what Savannah needed. Getting out of the country into a completely new environment might not cure the heartache she was working through, but it had given her a different perspective that could only help.

Will had needed a different perspective, too. From his emails, Amber thought he was coming to terms with his father's death and his uncle's betrayals.

Billy's body had been discovered where an old chicken coop had stood on the Hawken farm. The gun that had killed both him and the store clerk was buried beside him. Apparently in all the intervening years, Darryl Hawken had been so sure of himself, he hadn't bothered to move either. It was unlikely he would ever see freedom again.

Billy's remains were now in a local cemetery beside his mother's, but Will didn't know. Amber wanted to tell him in person. Eventually, when they were both ready, they would visit Betsy Garland in Chaslan and pay their respects at Billy's grave.

Will came over now to give her a hug. He seemed taller, and his shoulders broader. The gawky adolescent was disappearing, and the man was emerging.

Amber joined them. "Will looks more like his dad every minute, and I have proof. Betsy rounded up some photos from the high school archives and made copies. Of both of us. He can admire his dad and laugh at me."

"You two must be exhausted," Cassie told the teens. "And no beds yet for naps."

"We slept a lot on the planes and in airports," Savannah said. "But I'm starving."

"Will, why don't you take the Mustang, and you two grab something to eat. Then you can park it at the new house." Before Savannah could complain, Cassie gave her another swift hug. "We'll get your learner's permit next week, I promise. I already hired an instructor. You'll be driving yourself before too long." She paused. "Legally."

"I might start with the Corolla. I probably need to learn to steer and stop before I focus on the clutch."

"Wise."

The teenagers headed for the garage, arguing about where they wanted to eat and who would call Helia and Minh to tell the girls they were home. Cassie knew Helia had news to share. Her adoption was going to be finalized next month, and all of them had been invited to attend the proceedings at the courthouse and the party afterward.

"Will seems more sure of himself," Amber said. "He wants to go back to Africa next summer. For the first time he doesn't have to worry about me."

Amber was now the new manager of Yiayia's Kouzina. Roxanne and Cassie were determined to pay her every cent she was worth. Even in the short time since she'd taken on her new role, everything was running more smoothly. She was helping plan the renovations, too. The three women were working together on decor, configuration and business systems to bring the restaurant up to date. Amber was delighted to finally be settling into the role she deserved.

Cassie slipped her arm around her friend's shoulders. "Somehow they both survived the past year. They're making their way through all the lies to the other side."

"Have you decided whether to tell Savannah about the baby?"

Cassie had spent weeks looking for the right answer until she'd realized that she didn't have to decide alone. Savannah had two parents.

"I managed to get through to Gen late last night, and I told her everything. She's coming here at Christmas. We decided that when the three of us are together, we'll tell her. Savannah needs to know she has a brother. Then she can decide if she wants contact. But no more secrets."

Amber squeezed her closer for a moment. "That's a good solution."

"When I said I told Gen everything, I mean it. I told her about the missing money. And I told her that Elana's lawyer and mine are working together to come up with a strategy to divide it."

Gen had been surprised, but not as surprised as Cassie when, weeks after her trip to Western New York, Elana's attorney asked to be put in touch with hers. Discussions about funds that remained in Mark's joint account with Elana were in progress.

"A fair resolution's going to take time," Amber said.

"We both want to find the right one. In the end I'm betting she'll get most of what's left, but I'll get enough to make everyone feel it was fair."

"You're doing okay, aren't you?"

Cassie thought she was. Knowing the truth meant she could now see Mark for the man he'd been, and she could finally begin to let go. She was meeting regularly with Lawrence Steele, Mark's former psychotherapy supervisor, who was helping her come to terms with everything that had happened. Savannah had agreed to see him, too, and Will was thinking it over. Amber had joined a group for survivors of sexual assault. They were all determined to move on.

Then there was Nick.

A year had passed since Mark's death. More time had passed since the death of Nick's wife. Neither of them were ready for another serious relationship. In the meantime, they were spending more time together every week. Nick listened, and he didn't evaluate every thought she expressed, the way Mark had. She liked his commitment to justice, his sense of humor, and his friends. As odd as it seemed, after all her years in Manhattan, Tarpon Springs was home again, and she was sinking roots into the sandy soil. She was even learning to scuba dive.

"I am doing okay," she said. "Even better. Do you feel like a door closed behind us after everything happened? The rest is just cleanup. Even moving out of this house feels like a beginning."

"My daddy always said you can't keep a bird from flying over your head, but you can keep it from building a nest in your hair. That's what we did."

Cassie burst into laughter.

"I feel like I got my life back." Amber's smile was genuine and relaxed, a pleasure to see. "After all those years, it's my own again."

"Here's to new lives. We need champagne."

"Or ouzo."

Cassie raised an imaginary glass. "Here's what *my* daddy always said. Opa!"

Amber raised her imaginary glass, too, and pretended to clink it against Cassie's. Overhead a pair of sandhill cranes gave their signature shrill cry as they flew toward the rising sun. Maybe they were flying back to their nest, or maybe they were looking for a place to build a new one. Wherever they landed, Cassie wished them peace and a safe homecoming.

★ ★ ★ ★ ★

Acknowledgments

I haven't taken the opportunity in many years to thank all those who have supported me and my career, so please indulge me now.

So many people have helped throughout my writing career, but first I want to acknowledge my family, who were at my side through all the years. My husband, Michael, has been unfailingly supportive, most recently on this book. This time around he managed everything possible to give me time to wrestle with this story at what turned out to be a difficult time in our history. He joined me in Tarpon Springs for research and scouted the best places to watch their annual Epiphany ceremony unfold and then took photos as it did. We ate fabulous Greek food together and later cooked it at home. We took a sponge boat tour, hung out on the docks, visited the Tarpon Springs Train Depot—home of the city's historical society—where we had the pleasure of talking about the city with the depot's helpful coordinator, Renee Sousa. Nothing we learned there led to my changing a few vital facts, most notably adding a high school that doesn't exist to improve my story.

We planned to return several more times, but the need to quarantine made that impossible. Through it all, Michael remained upbeat and cheered me on. I couldn't have done it without him.

My four children thought my writing career wasn't such a bad thing. Having Mom around during the day was handy, especially when she was so immersed in her books she didn't notice everything they were doing. As happily launched adults, they have thoughtfully ended up in cities we wanted to visit or revisit. My four delightful grandchildren put up with my propensity to give them books as gifts and read to them whether they want me to or not. They've all enriched my life and my writing immeasurably. For the record, when I had teenagers I was never as patient as Cassie is with Savannah in this story, but they love me anyway.

While my mother didn't live to see even the beginning of my writing career, I thank her for her deep love of books and of me. She is the original Emilie Richards, and I love seeing her name on my covers. She would love it, too. Thanks, too, to my wonderful aunt, Laura Coleman, who did live to read my work and was absolutely delighted, and to my brother and sister-in-law who always ask what's coming out next.

I've had wonderful writer friends from the beginning of my career. The incomparable Jennifer Greene has been my pen pal for decades, and we've lived through multiple changes in the publishing industry together. Karen Young was a tried-and-true buddy right from the beginning. Casey Daniels/ Kylie Logan and I start each weekday with catch-up emails. She's my friend and consultant and I can't start the day without her. Casey's a treasured part of my brainstorming group along with Serena B. Miller and Shelley Costas (Stephanie Cole), two talented, delightful writers I'm glad to call friends and colleagues. Diane Chamberlain has been my confidante and advisor for years, and Patricia McLinn, Judith Arnold and Kathy Shay have all given me more wonderful advice. Through the years and many lunches, Jasmine Cresswell reminded me that writing wasn't the be-all and end-all of life—even if sometimes it felt like it.

While many ministers' partners are expected to be unpaid and unheralded assistants, I am thankful that the churches my husband served understood that I had a career of my own and made few demands on me. I am grateful for their friendship and loyalty, and grateful for being an intimate part of the lives of so many wonderful role models.

Our neighbors at Chautauqua Institution, far too many who passed away this year, have taught me so much about friendship and grace. They will truly live on in my memory.

I've been blessed with wonderful editors from the beginning. Leslie Wainger, editor extraordinaire, edited most of my romances and later my women's fiction until she retired. Leslie valued imagination, creativity and the individual author's voice. When she edited, she left all of them intact. My present editor, Emily Ohanjanians, is a delight to work with, a worrier in all the best of ways, and meticulous about details. I feel so fortunate to have worked with both of them, and in other houses with the talented Ellen Edwards and Cindy Hwang.

Dianne Moggy who brought me on board at MIRA Books, knew what to say and how to say it when I was worried or determined to have my way. I'll always be grateful to Dianne for her tact and enthusiasm.

Copy editors often go unnamed, but I've had many that found and corrected mistakes and improved my manuscript enormously. I am so glad they were there when needed, along with the proofreaders who caught mistakes everyone else missed, no matter how carefully we had combed through my paragraphs.

Covers have sometimes been a thorn in my side, but I'm so glad that Gigi Lau, art director, understands so well what my books are about and the art that best represents them.

Thank you to everyone else at MIRA who champions my books and brings them to readers: Loriana Sacilotto, Rachel Bressler, Margaret Marbury, Nicole Brebner, Heather Foy, Amy Jones, Randy Chan, Ashley MacDonald, Justine Sha, and the rest of the sales, marketing, publicity, art and production teams.

I've had two excellent agents, first Donald MacCampbell with Maureen Moran, and then and now, Steve Axelrod. They've been responsive, smart about when to give advice and when to keep silent. All are honest to the core. I know how lucky I've been and I'm thankful.

I'm thankful to the good folks at Authorbytes who created and maintain my website.

Finally I'm thankful for my readers, the ones who write me letters or emails, and the ones who simply read. The ones who give suggestions and the ones who give praise. The ones who wish I'd write this or that but keep reading me anyway. I've gotten to know some of you through Facebook, my newsletter and my website. I am so glad I have because you're the reason—at least one of the biggest—I write.

I've been so lucky, and best of all, I know it. I'm glad I can thank each and every one of you.

THE
HOUSE
GUESTS

EMILIE RICHARDS

Reader's Guide

mira

1. Cassie goes home to Tarpon Springs, Florida, after her husband's sudden death to restart her life with her stepdaughter, Savannah. Returning to a childhood home is a popular thread in today's fiction. What does the place we grew up represent for us? Why do you think it's a focus of so many stories?

2. Savannah, Cassie's stepdaughter, is in turmoil and she acts out in ways that would infuriate and disturb most parents. Were you angry at her, as well, or could you see the child in pain under her behavior? Were you rooting for Savannah to make needed changes? Did you believe they were possible?

3. When Cassie learns what Savannah has done, she invites Amber and Will to become her house guests until they can straighten out their financial situation. Why do you think she did this? To punish Savannah? To teach her a lesson? Because it was the right thing to do, even if it would make her life and Savannah's more difficult?

4. Trying to recover from her husband's sudden death, Cassie finds it difficult at first to summon the needed energy to

delve into the large sums of money missing from Mark's estate. Eventually she begins the search with Amber's help. What do you think galvanized her to move forward?

5. Amber and Will have moved from place to place, never staying anywhere for long. Amber has been silent about the identity of Will's father. Why do you think Will finally decided to find out the truth, even though it meant telling the mother he loved lies? Was this change inevitable?

6. The best-laid plans often go astray. Amber has done everything she can to save money so she can help Will attend college when the time comes. Then she contracts Hepatitis A at her restaurant job. Can you remember a time in your own life when you did everything right, and events that were out of your control occurred to change everything? Do you know someone who lost a job or a home, even though they worked hard and paid their bills as long as they could?

7. This novel is set the year before the Covid-19 pandemic began. How do you think the story would have changed if it had been set a year later?

8. How important were Yiayia and Roxanne in Cassie's life? How important was her Greek heritage? Do you think she was at least partly the woman she was because of family and roots?

9. Was Amber incredibly brave or incredibly foolish in the way she handled her life after the death of Will's father, Billy? Could you live with the stress that she did?

10. Traditional Greek dishes were often mentioned in the novel since the restaurant Yiayia's Kouzina (Grandmother's Kitchen) was important in the story. Do you have favorite Greek dishes you make or order at restaurants whenever you can? (The author makes pastitsio, moussaka, and horiatiki salad at home as often as possible!)